POWER PLAY

POWER PLAY

TONY KENT

Elliott&Thompson

First published 2020 by
Elliott and Thompson Limited
2 John Street
London WC1N 2ES
www.eandtbooks.com

Paperback original ISBN: 978-1-78396-491-8
Ebook ISBN: 978-1-78396-492-5
Library hardback ISBN: 978-1-78396-502-1
Special edition ISBN: 978-1-78396-490-1

9 8 7 6 5 4 3 2 1

A catalogue record for this book is available from the British Library.

Typesetting: Marie Doherty
Printed by CPI Group (UK) Ltd, Croydon, CR0 4YY

For my niece, Ellie.
For you, anything is possible.

'Nearly all men can stand adversity, but if you want to test a man's character, give him power'

— ABRAHAM LINCOLN

ONE

Three minutes . . .

David Webb and Jim Nelson turned their heads at the sound of four knocks. Webb instinctively glanced towards the cockpit door. Nelson did not, his eyes instead flitting to the small monitor to his left.

The screen showed two stewardesses. One was facing the door, while the other faced out onto the First Class section of the Pan-Atlantic Airlines Flight PA16. Standard security protocol for the few seconds that the plane's control centre would be vulnerable.

'It's Jade,' Nelson said.

He unclipped his safety harness as he spoke. Climbing to his feet, he took the few steps to the rear of the cockpit and released the one-way lock.

Jade Cox's smile greeted Nelson as he opened the door. It came as no surprise. She was always happy, or at least it seemed that way to him. He had to concede, though, that he was perhaps not the best witness. In Nelson's eyes, Jade could do no wrong.

He stepped aside, giving the young flight attendant enough room to enter. It was no easy task in the already cramped space, and was made more difficult by the fact she was carrying a large tray. But Jade had a practised routine and she manoeuvred her way around Nelson as he closed the cockpit door and returned to his seat.

'I hope you're hungry, Jim,' she said with a smile.

Two minutes . . .

Nelson glanced down at the foil-covered dishes on the tray Jade had placed on his temporary table.

'Looks great,' he said, looking back up at Jade. 'Whatever it is.'

'You got one for me?'

David Webb's voice was gruffer than Nelson's. The sound of an older man.

'Of course, Captain Webb.' Jade's tone was less familiar with the senior officer, but just as pleasant as she placed a second tray in front of him. 'Here you go.'

'What's that?' Webb was examining the dessert doubtfully.

'Treacle pudding, Captain.'

'Treacle pudding? Is that another English thing?'

'Yes, sir.'

'And here was me thinking we were on an American airline.'

'We flew out of London, David.' Nelson interrupted. He knew that Webb's abrupt manner could make the younger crew uncomfortable. Whether the captain intended it or not. 'We've got to cater for the Brits we've got aboard.'

'I doubt our guest back there would agree with you.'

Webb motioned towards the cockpit door as he spoke. It was unnecessary; Nelson knew exactly who his captain was referring to.

Dale Victor. A candidate for the Republican nomination for the next President of the United States of America. And already the runaway favourite to win that race.

Nelson chose to ignore Webb's political bait and turned his attention back to Jade.

'Have you spoken to him yet?' he asked.

'I have, yeah,' Jade replied.

'And what did you think?'

One minute . . .

'I thought he was bloody gorgeous!'

Nelson laughed. It was not quite the answer he had been expecting.

'Gorgeous? Jade, the guy's nearly sixty.'

'Yeah, but still. It's the charisma, isn't it? It's like you're the only person up here with him when he looks at you. It's . . . it's . . . well, it's a bit hypnotic.'

Nelson laughed again. He had flown with celebrities occupying the First Class cabin many times, often with Jade on the crew, but he had never seen her react so enthusiastically.

'Have I got some competition back there?' he asked, only half joking.

'Course not,' Jade replied. She waited a beat before adding: 'I mean, he's got his wife with him, hasn't he?'

This time it was Webb who laughed. Loud and hard.

'She's got you there, buddy,' he bellowed.

One second . . .

It is impossible to be sure what is faster: the speed of a human thought, warning that something is very wrong. Or the speed with which an explosion can spread throughout a fully fuelled commercial jumbo jet. And so it is impossible to know if any of them – David Webb, Jim Nelson, Jade Cox, or anyone else on Flight PA16 – was aware of the moment their lives were ripped away.

The explosion began in the luggage hold. A single case, filled to capacity with military grade C4 and a crude, home-made timer.

The C4 itself would have been enough to tear the plane in two. Enough to guarantee no survivors. But someone was taking no risks. The case had been carefully placed at the closest possible point to the base of the left wing, ensuring that the explosion ignited the fuel store within it.

The combination of the explosives and the fuel was devastating. The smooth, uneventful journey of the Boeing 747 was brought to an abrupt end, with white-hot, jet-fuel flames engulfing every inch of the massive flying machine.

No time for a brace warning. No time for oxygen masks. No time for crash positions. Just the sudden, fatal introduction of hellfire.

Flight PA16 from London's Heathrow to New York's JFK ended its journey in a violent storm of blazing debris, raining its charred remains across a five-mile stretch of the Atlantic Ocean.

TWO

Joe Dempsey sat in silence at the wheel of an aged Ford Galaxy people carrier.

The European-made MPV would stick out as unusually old in some parts of Manhattan – those neighbourhoods where a closet seemed to cost as much as a Midwest mansion – but it was entirely at home alongside the hard-worked cars and vans found in the island's Chinatown district.

Lost in plain sight. Exactly as Dempsey intended.

'How much longer?'

The question came from Dempsey's right.

'We'll go as soon as SWAT's ready,' Dempsey replied, turning to face the speaker. 'Not before.'

'Then they need to move faster. Longer we're here, more chance we get spotted.'

Dempsey did not reply immediately. Instead he just nodded his head in agreement, a smile threatening the corners of his mouth.

He forced that smile away. With the endless cultural differences between China and the West, Shui Dai might not understand it as an expression of admiration. And Dempsey would not risk an inadvertent insult. Not with Dai.

'Agreed,' he said to her. 'I'll see what I can do.'

He put his hand to his ear and activated his wrist-mic.

'How long until the safety net? Over.'

'Three minutes at the outside. Last birds moving up high now. Over.'

The reply said what was needed and nothing more, exactly as Dempsey had learned to expect from the NYPD's SWAT unit.

'OK, confirm when ready. Over.'

He changed the mic's frequency with a flick of his finger before speaking again.

'Alpha Two, you get that? Over.'

'Confirmed.' The response was immediate. Another American voice. 'Ready to move in three. Over.'

'Beta? Over.'

'In place and waiting. Over.' German this time. It was a clear, crisp response and would be worthy of a joke about Teutonic efficiency, if only the entire team were not equally well-drilled.

'Hold to my mark,' Dempsey instructed. 'Out.'

He lowered his wrist and turned back to Dai.

'Happy now?'

'I'll be happy when we get in there,' she replied.

'Then you won't have long to wait.'

Dempsey did not speak again. There was little point. He had seen Shui Dai like this before. 'In the Dai Zone', he had come to call it. The expression didn't translate well to Dai's native Mandarin, and he'd given up trying to explain.

Dempsey, though, knew exactly what he meant.

It had been over two years since he'd joined the International Security Bureau, a multi-national intelligence agency formed by the United Nations Security Council. In that time he had worked with agents from all over the world. Some were good: well-trained, intelligent and resourceful. Others were not. But a few – a very few – were exceptional.

And none were better than Shui Dai.

Dai had been recruited from China's Secret Service, an agency so effective that it had no official name, or at least no name known to the West. And while it had taken her time to settle in to New York City, where the ISB was based, Dai had taken to the Bureau itself like a fish to water.

Dempsey had rarely seen a more effective operative. Maybe never.

That Dai was smarter than most – certainly smarter than him – had come as no great surprise. But what *had* been eye-opening was her ability in the field.

Standing five foot one and weighing 115 pounds, Dai was over a foot shorter than Dempsey's six two and barely half his 225 pounds, yet she had proved to be every bit as fearsome as her team's English leader. Highly skilled and utterly ruthless, Dai's diminutive appearance gave no hint whatsoever of her physical capabilities.

Capabilities she would soon get to display, as the receiver in Dempsey's right ear whistled into life.

'All birds are perched. Over.'

Dempsey glanced towards Dai. He had no need to ask if *she* was ready. He lifted his hand back to his ear.

'On my mark.' Dempsey opened the driver's door as he spoke. Dai did the same on the passenger's side. 'Let's move.'

The entrance to the run-down tenement block was a green door that led directly onto the Chinatown section of Lafayette Street.

A busy New York thoroughfare, Lafayette was usually packed with streams of both locals and tourists. Today was no exception.

Too many potential obstacles here, and no way to remove them, Dempsey had concluded. *An operational nightmare.*

Luckily for Dempsey, those inside the building faced problems of their own. The tenement's blueprints revealed a bottleneck in the corridor that led towards Lafayette.

The slightest panic and that exit becomes a death trap, Dempsey had observed. *No way they'd risk that. They must have another route out.*

With Lafayette ruled out, there was only one viable way in *and* out of the building: the adjacent, much quieter Walker Street, by way of the tenement's fire escape.

Sharpshooters from the NYPD's SWAT unit were already in place, dotted high on both sides of Lafayette and Walker. All carefully chosen locations that offered clear, downward lines of sight into the target block. They provided a lethal blanket of firepower, ready to extinguish anything that emerged.

The ultimate insurance policy, should anything go wrong.

But still not quite enough for Dempsey. Although a SWAT team would probably be sufficient, he was taking no chances. He had placed two of his own ISB agents – both male, both Chinese – close to the green door. Inconspicuous and ready to react in an instant.

They'd be crazy to come that way, he had thought again, *but there's no accounting for bad decisions.*

Dempsey and Dai passed the two covert agents at the Lafayette entrance, turned the corner into Walker Street and headed for a break in the first block of buildings. The entrance to the alleyway that contained the tenement's fire escape.

As they approached the alley, Dempsey slowed his pace, his eyes fixed straight ahead.

Coming towards them, from the opposite direction of Walker Street, were two men.

One was larger than Dempsey; several inches taller and

significantly broader across the shoulders. A naturally huge frame that had been amplified by a lifetime of physical effort. And perhaps a few chemical enhancements.

The other man was much smaller than his companion. Barely five nine. Wiry build, with a hardness that cannot be honed in any gym.

The big guy was clearly armed. He was holding a rigid three-foot-long shape, poorly concealed by a sports coat he had draped across it.

'What part of "covert" don't you get, Sal?' Dempsey spoke quietly as the four came together and turned into the alley.

Without waiting for an answer, Dempsey turned his attention to two ISB agents who were already there, waiting. The final third of his Alpha team, they had reached the alleyway first and brought the unit's number to six.

In addition to Dempsey and Dai, the team was made up of Adama Jabari, a slim, quiet Ethiopian of Dempsey's height who looked like he could have been aged anywhere from thirty to fifty. Dylan Wrixon, the hard, wiry Appalachian Dempsey had spotted on the street. And Kate Silver, a fierce-looking blonde in her early thirties who, at almost six feet tall and with the build of an Olympian, looked like a physical match for any man there.

Except, perhaps, for the big one. Salvatore Gallo, the team's near giant.

Gallo had thrown the sports coat aside, revealing the M90 CAWS shotgun that had been so obviously beneath. Like every member of Dempsey's hand-picked ISB team, Gallo was ready.

All six were dressed in casual, baggy sportswear. The clothing served as street camouflage, as well as concealing the firearms, ammunition and kevlar that were strapped across their bodies.

Those firearms were now in each agent's hands. Small close-quarters assault rifles for everyone but Gallo.

Dempsey indicated to the lowered fire escape. He spoke quickly.

'As you were briefed: entry via the empty sixth floor apartment, then up one floor. All three seventh-floor apartments are supposed to be unoccupied. One of them won't be. That's where the hostage will be but we won't know which apartment it is until we breach. Or how many hostiles there'll be. Understood?'

All five agents nodded as one.

'We breach from the inside. Beta will be covering the rear via the roof. We go in hard. Anyone we don't hit, we herd towards Beta. Clear?'

Another five head movements.

'Silent all the way up,' Dempsey continued, 'then every apartment cleared in sixty seconds. I want you fast and fatal. Other than us, only one person is leaving that seventh floor alive. Understood?'

Four nods. Dempsey looked up towards Gallo, who had remained motionless.

'Think you can manage that, Sal?'

'*Guardami e basta.*'

Dempsey had picked up enough of Gallo's native Italian to know the meaning.

Just watch me.

It was all he needed to hear.

THREE

The six ISB agents had climbed the tenement's fire escape slowly and – in spite of the age and underuse of its metal frame – without a sound. Their movement once inside the building, as they made their way from the sixth floor to the seventh, had been just as silent.

Dempsey stepped up to the last of three closed apartments in the corridor. He looked to his left. Dai and Jabari were perhaps ten yards away, in front of the second apartment. Wrixon and Silver another ten, poised by the first.

Gallo was with Dempsey. Each apartment would be a two-man job.

Their intelligence could only take them this far. The building was old, its windows small and shrouded in years of grime. Its interior was all but invisible from the outside

Probably why the building was chosen in the first place, Dempsey surmised.

Even SWAT and Dempsey's Beta Unit – both positioned on adjacent buildings – had no clear view inside. It left them blind as to which apartment was holding the hostage; all they could be sure of was that two would be empty and one would offer resistance.

Just as well, then, that the Alpha Unit carried no weak link. Each apartment would be hit as hard and as fast as the others. No matter which one contained their targets – no matter which two-agent team breached – it would not end well for those inside.

Dempsey raised his open left hand, as if preparing a vertical salute. With one last glance to his left, he lowered his thumb.

It had the desired effect. His first four agents all visibly tensed for what was about to occur. His fifth – Gallo – adjusted his stance and placed the muzzle of his M90 inches from the third door's secure lock.

A second later and Dempsey lowered his little finger. One more and his ring finger was down. Another and only his index finger was left up.

Time.

Dempsey's remaining digit had barely touched the skin of his palm as the gunfire began. Three doors. Three weapons. One result. Two simultaneous semi-automatic three-round bursts saw to the locks on apartments one and two. A single round from Gallo's shotgun devastated the third.

The agents moved like clockwork. Countless hours of close-quarters assault drills had seen to that.

Dai and Wrixon moved in sync through their two doorways, rifles raised to their shoulders as they both swept to the right. Jabari and Silver followed their respective leads, each taking the left.

Perfect execution of the manoeuvres they had been taught by Dempsey.

He and Gallo were equally well rehearsed. So was their reaction when they instantly saw that theirs was the occupied apartment.

The door had been shattered by Gallo's single shot; the wood from a football-sized hole in its frame had peppered the back wall, sending the targets inside diving for cover.

Having spotted them, Gallo stepped to his right and made

space, allowing Dempsey to flick a flash-bang grenade through the doorway.

'COVER!' Dempsey stepped back into the corridor as he shouted.

The warning was unnecessary. Gallo had already shielded his ears and turned his back to the door. The corridor wall provided both men with a barrier to the blinding light that would follow.

But still, old habits die hard. And good ones never should.

Even with eyes averted and ears covered, neither man could miss the detonation of the flash-bangs. And so both were moving again in an instant.

Gallo breached the doorway first. He covered the entire right half of the apartment's reception room with one sweep of his shotgun.

Dempsey was a heartbeat behind, sweeping the room's left side with his own Heckler & Koch G36C assault rifle.

The first thing Dempsey noticed were two long tables, each running the length of the right and left walls of the apartment's main room. Both were covered with steel bowls, scales and – most telling – brick-shaped packages of solid white and brown powder.

Dempsey made the observation in an instant, and in the same moment he noticed something else: there was no hostage in this room.

Or in the apartment, he instinctively knew. *The intelligence is wrong.*

Dempsey's experience allowed him to register every detail at once, and to see the picture those details painted. It was a skill learned over countless days in the Killing House in Hereford.

Staged assault after staged assault. Every possible scenario covered. Every possible threat anticipated and enacted.

He'd been thankful for that training in the years that had followed. Time and again it had been the difference between life and death.

But today it told him that they were engaging the wrong targets. This was clearly a drug factory. Nothing to do with their hostage. And there was not a single thing he could do to change that.

The sound from Gallo's M90 was like a physical blow as the Italian discharged it to Dempsey's right. Once. Twice. The violence of the vibration could have disorientated even the most experienced soldier.

To Dempsey, it signified nothing more than an increased body count.

Two down.

The number was still passing through his mind as he noted the movement to his left. Four figures, dressed in sterile clothing. At first glance they looked like medics or forensic examiners – an impression ruined by the weapons each was now clumsily raising in Dempsey's direction.

He aimed his own G36C, already at shoulder height, and applied four kisses of pressure to its trigger. Each touch discharged a three-round burst. Each burst found a target. Still disorientated from the flash-bangs, none of the four had a chance against a weapon far more lethal.

Six down.

Dempsey glanced towards Gallo. The Italian was already facing him. Like Dempsey's side of the room, Gallo's was now clear.

Dempsey lifted his right index finger and drew a horizontal

circle in the air: the signal that they were now moving to the next stage of their choreographed assault.

This was not why they had come. These people were not who they were here to kill. But with the shooting started, they had no choice now but to see it through.

Gallo acknowledged the instruction with a nod and turned his back towards Dempsey's own, his shotgun now covering the only entrance to the apartment. They slowly progressed towards the sole interior door that led off the main room.

Dempsey stepped forward slowly. Carefully. The ringing in his ears from the gunfire had temporarily robbed him of a key sense. Hardly ideal, but he would manage without it. It was far from the first time, and he would not be the only one suffering.

Another step. And another.

Dempsey's eyes kept a laser-focus on the empty opening that led to the rest of the small apartment. He had no way to know if there were targets beyond it, but he had to assume there were. In his experience, drugs factories were always heavily defended.

And even if this one was not, it was diligence that kept professionals alive.

One more step and he would be through the inner doorway.

Gripping his weapon with his right hand, Dempsey took his left away from the rifle's magazine, slowly moved it past his own back and tapped Gallo's hip. The Italian – his own eyes still fixed on the apartment's main door – responded by placing a single flash-bang into Dempsey's outstretched hand.

It was their only cover for the breach that was to come. Or at least for the breach they *expected* to come.

There is a difference between being deafened and being unable to 'hear'. The key is to recognise the vibrations elsewhere. To detect that feeling that would ordinarily be called 'sound'.

It was this vibration that Dempsey absorbed, just as he lifted the flash-bang towards his right hand. The sensation of movement, emanating up through his boots. Too light to be a footstep. Almost too light, even, to be noticed.

Almost.

The small, brown object that rolled into the doorway was as rudimentary a hand grenade as Dempsey had ever seen. Barely larger than a squash ball and almost featureless, the antiquated fragmentation grenade's blast zone would be small, but it was still perfectly capable of tearing Dempsey and Gallo to pieces.

Dempsey stopped the deadly ball with his left boot, scooped it up from the floor and sent it arching back from where it had come. In the next instant he unpinned Gallo's flash-band and threw it in the same direction.

'COVER!'

Dempsey grabbed Gallo hard by the shoulder as he shouted, using his full strength to pull the Italian to the floor and behind whatever protection the interior wall could provide.

It was not a moment too soon.

The sound of the first bang would have been deafening if either man could still hear, while its flash – fifty per cent of its disorientating arsenal – was harmless on this side of the partition. Even alone, the weapon would have been effective.

But it was *not* alone.

The fragmentation grenade exploded almost simultaneously. As soon as it hit the floor, Dempsey assumed. Its devastating effect made the first device seem like a child's toy.

Large fragments of the grenade pierced the drywall that divided the main room from the rest of the apartment. None struck Dempsey or Gallo, thanks to their position on the floor. Had either man been standing, the result would have been very different.

'LET'S GO!' Dempsey yelled. If anyone was still alive through the doorway, they could not be given time to recover.

Both men were on their feet in an instant, with Dempsey first through the doorway and Gallo a step behind him.

The sight that met them was like a snapshot of hell. Whatever damage the grenade had done through the wall was multiplied ten times over on the partition's other side.

It took a literal headcount for Dempsey to determine that a further four targets had been eliminated in the explosion. Two in the tight corridor off the main room – presumably the original source of the grenade – and two on the threshold of the first bedroom.

None of the four bodies were fully intact.

Ten down.

Dempsey was not distracted by the carnage. He continued along the corridor without missing a step.

He swept the first bedroom at speed. The two dead bodies in the doorway told him that the room had taken the brunt of the blast. The odds of a survivor were slim, but still the area had to be cleared.

'NEXT ROOM!'

This time it was Gallo who shouted. He had passed Dempsey as the British agent took the first door, and it seemed that his search had borne fruit.

Dempsey covered the few feet between rooms at speed. He

entered to find Gallo with his shotgun raised to his shoulder and aimed towards the room's large open window. A thick black curtain billowed in the breeze, obstructing both agents' view.

Dempsey stepped forward, placed his palm on the barrel of Gallo's M90 and guided it down. Gallo glanced towards him and Dempsey simply shook his head. He knew what was to come: the sound of three rounds, discharged just outside.

Eleven.

Dempsey lowered his own weapon and stepped towards the window. He moved the curtain aside and stepped through, onto the metal fire escape outside. Ahead of him was the body of a white man, his bloody eyes staring lifelessly into the sky.

'Empty apartment, Kate?'

Dempsey looked across to the furthest end of the fire escape. Kate Silver was standing with her rifle raised to her shoulder.

'Yeah,' Silver replied. 'Unlike yours.'

Dempsey pointed towards the first apartment.

'No sign of a hostage in there, I take it?'

'No.'

'What about Dai and Jabari?'

'I don't know.'

Dempsey put his hand to his ear and reactivated his wrist-mic. He switched the frequency to the ISB band.

'Dai, you there? Over.'

The mic crackled to life.

'I'm here. Over.'

'What have you got? Over.'

'Nothing. Apartment empty. Over.'

Dempsey looked down at the body close to his feet. The

man had been armed. He had worked in a drug den. There was no doubt that he was a criminal, and maybe he deserved his fate. But he was not the man the ISB were here to find. None of them were.

'Dammit.'

FOUR

Michael Devlin held a champagne-laden ice bucket under his left arm, a glass of sixteen-year-old Lagavulin in his left hand and a cold Pinot Grigio in his right as he manoeuvred his way through the packed room.

The temperature outside was only a degree or two north of zero. Still, the wood and glass main doors of the busy wine bar were wide open. With so many warm bodies rammed inside its two rooms, the colder fresh air was badly needed.

With the bar filled past capacity, the sheer size of the crowd made Michael's journey from bar to table difficult. His recognition of what seemed like every second face slowed him further: a succession of colleagues and opponents from almost two decades in London's criminal courts, all wanting to say 'hi' – in some case much more – and transforming Michael's few necessary steps into a nightmare of forced smiles and inane pockets of conversation.

Daly's Wine Bar had been an icon of the British legal system for as long as Michael could remember, and probably much longer still. Well positioned just outside of Temple and a stone's throw from the Royal Courts of Justice, the place seemed to possess a homing beacon to which the majority of working barristers responded. Michael was not in that majority.

He had never understood the appeal. A bar filled to the brim with drunken lawyers, many of them lying to the others about their recent successes? Michael could think of many places he would rather be.

But tonight's venue had not been his to choose. Tonight was a celebration. One he would not miss.

Finally through the tightly packed first room and into the much clearer second, Michael was able to speed up over the final few feet. Just as well, as he could feel the ice bucket under his left arm beginning to slip. He reached the table just in time, placed his own glass down and used his now free left hand to grip the wet metal container.

'Here you go.' He handed the glass of wine to the only man at the table. 'White wine for Will, champagne for everyone else.'

'Thanks,' replied one of the four women. A slim blonde in her early thirties, she had taken the natural lead. 'But are you sure neither of you will join us in some bubbles? It *is* a celebration.'

'Not for me. I can't stand the bloody stuff.'

Michael had not met Will Duffy before tonight, but he knew the man's reputation. Duffy was maybe ten years older than Michael, a busy criminal solicitor with a loyal following among the capital's organised crime families. He was known as a rough, bluff Glaswegian who rarely sugar-coated his words.

Michael, on the other hand, was a natural diplomat.

'Doesn't agree with me, Jenny,' he said, giving Duffy's answer no time to land. 'Besides, the only fizzy stuff an Irishman should drink is Club Orange.'

'Suit yourselves. More for us.'

Jenny Draper reached out, picked up the open bottle of Krug and filled the four champagne glasses that were already on the table. Once done, she turned back to face Michael with an expectant smile.

Michael took the hint and raised his glass. He then waited for Duffy and for Draper's three younger friends to do the same.

'I think a toast is in order,' Michael began, having fully understood Draper's unspoken message. 'To Jenny. A terrific lawyer. A wonderful friend. And, as of today, the youngest Recorder *I've* ever heard of. Be respectful and be nice, all of you, because the way she's going she'll be running this profession in no time.'

Draper beamed at the compliment but, tellingly for Michael, she did not blush. It proved what he already knew: the young lawyer was every bit as ambitious as his few words had suggested.

'To Jenny,' he concluded.

'To Jenny,' the rest of table echoed. Four voices as one, each keen to toast Draper's professional success. It brought a smile to Michael's face.

The two barristers had met less than a year ago, when Michael had been appointed in his first case as Queen's Counsel to represent a young man charged with murder. Draper had come with the case, already attached as junior counsel, and she had brought her reputation with her. But Michael had seen through the smokescreen, behind the single-minded ambition, and he had found a brilliantly talented woman. The events surrounding that case had been horrifying for them both, but there had been at least one positive outcome: Michael and Draper had formed a bond. A genuine friendship.

And now here they were celebrating her success. A Recordership is the first step towards life on the bench, serving a few weeks a year as a judge and the rest as an ordinary barrister. It was a much sought-after honour and hard to obtain, and yet, at the age of just thirty-one, Draper had secured one of the most important positions a lawyer could achieve.

Michael had no doubt in his mind that she was up to the task.

'So, Michael. I've heard a lot about you.'

Will Duffy had the voice of a man raised rough and proud of it. It pulled Michael out of his own thoughts.

'How come we've not done a case together?' Duffy asked in his thick Glaswegian accent.

'We have, Will,' Michael replied. 'Just not for the same clients.'

'Well, I've not seen you in court. I reckon we need to change that. I mean, seems we've got a bit in common, eh?'

Michael hesitated for an instant as he considered Duffy's words. They could be referring to a number of things: some good; some bad. Michael could do nothing about the rumours that surrounded him. Not least because most were less sensational than the truth. But references to his past – real or imagined – still made him uncomfortable.

'I thought most of your firm's good stuff went to Jenny's place,' Michael said, moving the focus of the conversation to the rival set of barristers' chambers where Draper was based. 'They wouldn't be happy to see you using me or Eight Essex Court.'

'Her place is not what it was,' Duffy replied. 'Jenny aside, last ten years they've recruited a bunch of public school boys. It's weakened 'em. Left 'em with no one who connects with the people *I* represent. No real experience of that world. Not like you and me, eh?'

The final sentences removed any doubt: Duffy – as blunt as his reputation – was referring to Michael's background.

Michael did not respond immediately. Instead he focused on

Duffy, trying to read his intentions. Michael was a private man. Most knew that, and so any mention of his past was usually deliberate. An attempt to put him on edge.

But Duffy didn't know him well enough for that.

As Michael studied the man he observed for the first time the small, almost imperceptible facial scars and the damaged knuckles, both of which suggested a tougher start to life than most. He also seemed unusually fit for his age; a hangover from a life where the ability to handle himself was essential, perhaps?

The observations caused Michael to doubt his own reaction. Perhaps Duffy *did* just see him as a kindred spirit?

Whatever the reality, it did not make the subject any more welcome.

'The past's the past, Will,' Michael finally offered. 'You can't judge people on where they've come from. Any more than they should judge you. And besides, there's plenty of people in Jenny's place we'd love to poach to Eight Essex. They're a strong bunch.'

Duffy nodded. He took a deep drink of his wine before speaking again.

'You're probably right,' he replied with a smile. 'Usually are, I hear. But don't think I won't be sending you a case anyway.'

'Well, if I can't talk you out of it . . .' Michael laughed, happy that the conversation was moving in a more comfortable direction. 'Now listen—'

He didn't finish his sentence.

Interrupted by a chime from his iPhone, he instinctively glanced down and read the breaking news headline displayed. An annoying habit caused by his inability to switch off the news notifications, it was usually no more than a flicker of the eye.

But not this time. This time the words on screen brought the conversation to an end.

'Jesus.'

Michael was speaking to no one in particular.

'What is it?' Draper asked, an instant before her own iPhone's screen came to life. Its message was identical to the one Michael had received.

Michael did not answer the question. Instead they both turned their eyes towards the silent television screen that took up much of the room's left wall. It was displaying live footage beamed directly from London's Heathrow Airport, obviously the subject of the muted commentary from a young reporter, familiar to them both, who was positioned front and centre.

But neither Michael nor Draper needed to hear Sarah Truman's report. The news alert had said it all: 'Death at Thirty-Five Thousand Feet: Pan-Atlantic Airlines Flight PA16 from London Heathrow to New York JFK crashes into the Atlantic Ocean two hours into flight. All 534 lives lost.'

FIVE

Nizar Mansour picked up his heavy, outdated Nokia handset and activated its darkened screen.

He had no idea how many times he had done this in the last hour. Ten? No. Twenty at least. Maybe more. And each time the result had been the same.

The screen showed no alerts.

No missed calls. No messages. Nothing.

Mansour placed the phone on the table ahead of him and watched its screen fade back to black. An appropriate colour. For five days, his mood – his life – had been darker than he could remember. Only one thing could change that. One call.

As every minute passed, that call became more and more unlikely.

Mansour forced his eyes from the handset and the thought from his mind. Obsessively counting the seconds only made things worse, he realised. He needed a distraction, and that was exactly what the long bar at the far side of the room offered.

His unsteady legs at first struggled to support him as he climbed to his feet. It was by now a familiar sensation; the anxiety that had eaten away at his gut for almost a week made his usual calm demeanour a distant memory. If he had expected the almost two pints of imported Belgian lager he had sunk in the past hour to counter that effect, he had been *very* mistaken.

Not that Mansour was in any place to learn that lesson. The alcohol had failed to bring him the hoped for calm, but anything that took his mind elsewhere remained welcome.

He drained the final third of his glass in one swallow, reached deep into his pocket and pulled out the few remaining coins inside.

Four pounds sixty-five pence. Enough for one more.

The price differences between London and Aleppo had long since lost their shock value and Mansour gave no thought to the cost of his single pint order. But the contrast in strength between Syrian beer and the imported lagers popular in the UK? That was harder to ignore. Mansour was no drinker, not back home and not in London. On the rare occasions he went beyond a single order, the alcohol hit him hard.

And his next would be his third.

The Rose and Crown pub on Stoke Newington Church Street was unusually quiet for a Wednesday evening, even for early January. If Mansour had wondered why then he would have blamed the weather. Who wanted to leave a warm home for a cold beer when the conditions outside were near arctic? But the question did not cross his mind. Tonight, only a single thought concerned him.

The walk to the bar. The order. The pour. The payment. With less than ten customers in the cavernous barroom, the whole process took barely a minute. And yet not for an instant did Mansour's mind stray from his phone.

Barely a minute more and he was back at his table in the corner of the room, Nokia in hand, its illuminated screen still blank.

'*Ibn il sharmoota!*'

Mansour slammed the handset onto the table as he spoke, his frustration irresistible. The few sober eyes in the barroom turned at the sound, forcing him to regain his composure.

'Idiot,' he hissed under his breath, irritated by his own

outburst. He pushed his fingertips deep into the skin around his eyes, as if to push the pain of his stress – the pressure – back down.

What was he thinking, calling attention to himself?

They could be in here, he thought. *They could be anyone.*

He couldn't take the risk. Not after everything he had done. He had to see this through to the end.

But why have they not called?

He forced his gaze away from his phone. The obvious alternative was the large projection screen at the rear of barroom. No doubt installed to fill the bar with drinking customers, keen to see whatever sports event would attract the biggest crowd. Tonight there was no football, no rugby, no boxing. And so the screen was silent.

But it was not blank.

What Mansour had experienced in his thirty years of life had, he thought, prepared him for much. Loss. Violence. Fear. They had been commonplace in Syria and, at least for Mansour, non-existent in the UK. That had all changed five days ago. The fear had returned. A terror beyond anything he had felt before. Since then it had gripped him for every waking moment.

As his eyes settled on the headline displayed on the screen, he felt that grip tighten.

SIX

Sarah Truman spat a lug of mouthwash into the sink and wiped its residue from her lips. The taste was harsh – antiseptic – but much preferable to what it had replaced.

'Shit,' she said aloud, placing the mouthwash bottle down and reviewing her reflection in the ladies' room mirror.

The face that looked back at her gave no indication of the nausea she felt. Her stomach was still turning, threatening to send her rushing back to the vacant toilet cubicle. But thankfully her discomfort was invisible. Her hair was still in place; her make-up the very definition of professional.

She could not explain how, but it was a win. She would take it.

Maybe we can pull this off. If I can just keep the rest of my damn dinner down . . .

One more breath – deep and long. The nausea was going nowhere. That much was clear. But she would not let it affect her work. Not here. And especially not now.

She took one last look in the mirror as she steeled herself to leave, physically shaking her head, shoulders and arms in an exaggerated, prolonged shudder.

She spotted a few last drops of mouthwash at the bottom of its plastic bottle.

Can't hurt, she thought.

Sarah took a slug, swirled it around her mouth and spat it into the last of the row of sinks as she strode towards the restroom door.

'Are you OK?' Nathan Benson sounded concerned as Sarah rejoined him. 'You ran off a bit quick.'

'I'm fine.'

The impatience in Sarah's tone was unmissable, even to her. Harsh enough that Benson instinctively straightened his back in response. Like a military brat brought to attention.

He doesn't deserve that, Sarah thought, noticing his reaction. *Cut him some slack.*

'Look, just, er, just ignore that. Ignore me. I felt a little queasy, that's all.'

Benson visibly relaxed, the tense moment over.

He had been Sarah's regular cameraman for almost a year and she knew that he counted himself lucky. Because Sarah's was a career in a million. Just twenty-nine years of age, she was the Senior Home News correspondent for the UK's Independent Television News – second to only the BBC in size and coverage – and already far ahead of any other reporter of their generation. Benson's career could only benefit from their connection but, like anyone, he deserved respect. And that was exactly what Sarah gave him.

She looked around the large, plain room. Row after row of makeshift seating was occupied, each and every chair taken by reporters she recognised. But Benson had ignored the seating, as every other camera operator had done. Instead they had all positioned their recording equipment in front of it, for a clear, unobstructed view of the long table now set up at the front of the room.

'Sorry I couldn't save you a chair,' he whispered as he made final adjustments to his camera. He looked behind them. 'I think there are still a few at the back.'

'I don't need a chair,' Sarah replied. The answer was a lie, but she was not going to let her nausea slow her down. 'It's more important you have the shot.'

'But how will you get a question in?' Benson asked. The concern had returned to his voice. 'If you're not seated with the rest? They won't see your hand.'

'They won't be answering anything that's worth asking. Not today. We'll get a statement about the crash, a few safety passes with answers straight from that same statement, then they'll disappear. These things always go the same way. All that matters is that *you* catch that first statement.'

Benson nodded his head but he didn't seem convinced. Not that it mattered. The decision was Sarah's to take.

And he'll learn, she thought.

'I'm heading outside,' Sarah said. 'I need some fresh air.'

'You said you were quitting those,' Benson observed.

'What are you, my mother?'

'Someone has to look out for you.'

'Lucky I have you then, I guess. But no need for you to worry. I really do mean fresh air this time. I just need to clear my head.'

Benson's expression moved from amusement to its previous concern. He seemed to want to say something more. Instead he reached for a pile of what had looked like thick rags at the base of his camera stand. Out of it, he picked a grey tracksuit hoodie.

'At least put this on,' he said. An instruction rather than a request. 'You're already sick and it's bloody freezing out there.'

Sarah smiled. She was as bad at taking orders as she was at apologising. Both were weaknesses in a world of alpha personalities vying for advancement. But Benson's concern was genuine, and on this occasion his instruction was harmless.

And besides, Sarah thought, *it* is *bloody cold out there*.

The British Airways branding that dominated the exterior of the Waterside Building was impossible to miss. The UK carrier's insignia seemed to be emblazoned on every spare part of the wall. A branding campaign that left no hint of the complex's other occupant: Pan-Atlantic Airlines.

People sure as hell know it's here now.

Sarah stood for a moment and stared out across the Waterside car park, at the mass of outside broadcast vans occupying it.

The sheer number of them was not unusual. These days Sarah rarely covered a story that didn't attract the full attention of the rival news networks. But for that story to take them somewhere big enough that they could actually park?

That *was* new.

She looked away from the vehicles and down at her hands. They were shaking in the cold of the night.

Benson's hoodie was doing its job well. Every covered inch of Sarah's body remained warm, despite the rapidly falling temperature. But her hands were exposed. Sarah needed them out so she could watch the press conference on the increasingly shaky screen of her phone. It was a sacrifice she was fast coming to regret.

She used her left hand to hold her right steady as she watched the opening remarks, the sound relayed crisply through the handset's wireless earphones.

The voice speaking was American; East Coast, like Sarah, but maybe two hundred miles further south. 'Ladies and Gentlemen, I can sadly confirm that at four p.m. Greenwich Mean Time, the one fifty-five p.m. Flight PA16 from London

Heathrow to New York JFK lost contact with control over the Atlantic Ocean.'

Why's David Edleson chairing this? Sarah wondered.

She hadn't known that the Pan-Atlantic Airlines CEO was even in the UK.

Her thought was interrupted by the feeling of a physical presence beside her. It made her look up, away from the screen and towards a uniformed British Airways pilot standing a few feet away.

He glanced at Sarah as he lit a cigarette, careful to make eye contact. Sarah's own eyes must have flitted towards the lit smoke, encouraging him to hold the packet out towards her.

'Thanks.' Sarah reached out and took a Marlboro from the open pack. 'One way to warm up, huh?'

The man smiled back and held up a silver lighter, its flame ready.

Well, that's been tried and tested.

Sarah could spot a well-honed flirting technique when she saw one. She would let him down lightly in a moment. But first things first. She put the cigarette to her lips, leaned towards the flame and inhaled.

It did not have the effect she was expecting. The taste of the smoke hit first. The same taste she was used to, and yet somehow completely different. It caused a wave of her earlier nausea to flow over her. An urge to throw up that she barely suppressed.

Pull yourself together, Sarah. You're all out of mouthwash!

It was an easy demand to make. A harder one to obey. She hadn't reacted that way to a cigarette before. She threw it away and took a deep breath. Her suspicions about the source of her nausea were looking increasingly likely.

'Are you OK?'

The pilot's voice sounded confused. He looked it, too, when Sarah glanced towards him. Flustered and still feeling unwell, she did not think before she answered.

'Yeah. Yeah, sorry. I just shouldn't be smoking. I . . . I'm pretty sure I'm pregnant.'

She felt herself freeze as she heard her own words, the first time she had said them aloud. And who was she sharing it with? Some guy who, moments before, thought he was on track to pick her up.

The final thought amused her, and, for the first time in days, Sarah felt herself smile.

'Which I guess is the last thing *you* wanted to hear, right?'

Sarah opened the door to the conference room and placed herself against the back wall.

David Edleson's statement was coming to an end. She had missed almost all of it, but that did not matter. The content was always the same. Sarah could have written it for him, from memory.

'. . . speculate at the cause of the loss of Flight PA16 at this time. Our entire focus is instead dedicated to the five hundred and thirty-four passengers and crew who lost their lives in the tragic events of this afternoon. Within those parameters, I will now take questions.'

Perfect timing.

Sarah had been at more press conferences than she could remember. Back in the day – before Trafalgar Square, before Belfast – they had been almost daily. So she knew what to expect, as she had told Benson.

An empty statement, followed by questions that just echoed

that emptiness. The story would not reveal itself here. Not tonight. It would come in the days to come.

That was the way these things worked.

Or at least it was how they were *supposed* to work.

At first Sarah couldn't hear any individual questions. The press conference had descended into the usual shouting throng, with fifty reporters speaking at once. But then her sharp hearing picked one out against the background noise.

And she felt her entire body go cold.

'Mr Edleson, Mr Edleson, can you please confirm that potential presidential nominee Dale Victor and his wife were aboard Flight PA16?'

Sarah did not move a muscle. She could not quite believe what she had just heard. Or that others still seemed to have missed it.

The question was asked four more times as the noise gradually died away, the surrounding media shocked into silence.

Finally there was quiet enough that the question could be heard clearly by all.

The entire room went still. Waiting for the answer. But Sarah did not need to hear it. She had watched David Edleson at the moment he had first heard the question, while it was still mostly lost in the surrounding noise, and she had noted his reaction.

The shocked look. The ashen face. The whispered consultation. All of them could mean only one thing.

Finally Edleson removed any doubt:

'Yes. I can sadly confirm that candidate Dale Victor, his wife and a small number of Mr Victor's corporate and campaign staff were on Flight PA16. Tragically they were all among the lives that have been lost today.'

SEVEN

Apartment 35D of The Stratford building on Manhattan's Upper East Side had little that marked it out as 'special'.

Its front door was one of an identikit number that lined both sides of the thirty-fifth-floor corridor. It opened directly into a living area that was longer than it was wide, but not by much.

Inside and to its immediate left was a doorway that led to a poorly equipped, narrow galley kitchen. A few feet further on, along the same wall, was a second door. Behind it was a strong contender for New York's smallest hallway and the entrances to a bathroom and a single bedroom, both barely furnished.

At the apartment's far end – a term that stank of exaggeration when describing a distance that could be covered in five good strides – was a steel-framed window and door that matched the width and the height of the living room.

Even in high-rise heavy New York, buildings as tall as The Stratford were rarely built in clusters. With no other residence close enough to view into the apartment, there was no need for curtains or blinds; 35D's position on the top floor of the block was privacy enough. And so even a single step inside revealed a clear view over the neighbourhoods of the Upper East Side from a height of thirty-five storeys.

It was this view that drew the eye of any visitor; it made every other of the apartment's deficiencies irrelevant.

Joe Dempsey picked the antiquated kettle from the electric stove at the first hint of its ear-shattering whistle. The sound of bubbling water had already told him that the liquid inside had boiled. The kettle's in-built 'alarm' was an unnecessary and annoying addition to the exercise.

He turned 180 degrees, to the cracked wooden worktop opposite the bulky cooker. Two mugs were waiting. Both were hospital clean and hospital basic: a description that could be well applied to almost everything in Dempsey's apartment.

Two minutes later and Dempsey was done. He exited the kitchen, a steaming mug of hot English tea in each hand. He headed for the far end of the room. Towards the large, picture-frame window and the concrete balcony that sat on its other side.

The door on the left-hand side of the window was ajar, letting the cold air from the late New York afternoon into the apartment. Even a relatively warm January in Manhattan would be thought cold in Dempsey's native London, but the loss of the apartment's heat did not concern him. Extremes of weather had been an occupational hazard during his military career. Four degrees Celsius – or thirty-nine degrees Fahrenheit, as his American thermometer insisted – was nothing.

The small, basic balcony that sat beyond the metal framed door would win no awards for aesthetic design: a concrete rectangle that nudged out into the sky, 350 feet clear of the streets below. And yet the moment Dempsey stepped out and felt the cold waterproof resin beneath his socked feet – as soon as he saw the top of The Carlyle Hotel in the distance – the tension between his shoulders begin to lessen.

The little that was special about Apartment 35D was all out here. On its balcony. It was the reason Dempsey called the place 'home', and he was reminded of that every time he looked out across the city.

'Come on, man. You just gonna let that tea go cold?'

Dempsey had not noticed that he was standing in place until the deep, accented voice broke through his distracted thoughts.

He turned with a shake of his head and held out one of the two mugs to Father Sam Cooke.

'It's a hell of a view,' Dempsey said, explaining his pause with a hint of a smile.

'Get used to it. It's not going anywhere,' Cooke reached out and took the mug Dempsey had offered. 'And neither are you, at least for a while.'

Dressed head to toe in black, Cooke had removed the clerical collar that otherwise explained his clothing choice. Dempsey knew why. Constantly identifying as a priest prevented Cooke from also being himself: a tall, thin miner's son from County Durham in Northern England. And a man who enjoyed a dirty joke, the sight of a beautiful girl and even the occasional foul-mouthed blasphemy.

Cooke did not get to be that guy around many people. Dempsey was one of the few exceptions.

The tea was still steaming as Cooke took one of the two seats that sat beside a tall metal table at the far right of the balcony.

'Still warm enough for you?' Dempsey asked. The same small smile had returned. He already knew how Cooke would respond.

'It's alright,' Cooke replied, with the tone of someone who thought otherwise. 'Not like I can send it back anyway, is it?'

Dempsey laughed to himself as he took the second seat. The table formed a buttress between the two chairs, with both facing outwards across the darkening sky.

Neither man spoke as they slowly drank their tea, enjoying

the warmth of the drink as the cold began to bite. They were surrounded by the sounds of the streets far below – horns, shouts and sirens – and the whipping wind that crashed between the high-rises and skyscrapers.

It was comfortable. Two men who knew each other well, and who did not need to fill silence with meaningless chatter. For Dempsey, at least, it was the ideal version of a friendship, and only when he noticed Cooke drain his cup did he finally speak again.

'Need a refill?' he asked.

'Could you be any more English?'

'What does that mean?'

'It means I've known you for two years and in that time I've been in your place, what? Ten times? And every one of those has been after someone died.'

'That can't be right,' Dempsey replied, not even convincing himself. 'And what does that have to do with me being English?'

'I'm telling you it's right. And what do you do whenever I first get here? You avoid the real subject and you talk about tea. Like I said, you couldn't be more English if you tried.'

Dempsey had no argument. He knew that Cooke was right. But then, when was he not? It was the reason Dempsey turned to him in times like this. Not because of Cooke's faith; Dempsey was far from convinced that the priest was a full-on believer. And Dempsey's own Catholicism was as confused as it came.

No. It was Cooke's mind that Dempsey needed. His sense of right and wrong. And his habit of telling the absolute, unvarnished truth.

Dempsey had met Cooke on his first day with the United Nations' newly formed International Security Bureau, less than twenty-four hours after arriving in New York.

As an officer in the British Army and later as an agent of the UK's Department of Domestic Security, Dempsey had seen the world. He had operated for months at a time in little-known locations in Asia, Africa, even South America. And yet somehow his experience of New York – the closest thing on Earth to a world capital city – totalled a single three-day holiday, too many years before.

And so Dempsey had arrived a stranger, living out of a suitcase in a downtown hotel room. It was an existence that had suited him. One he was used to. But his superiors at the ISB had seemed less happy. Less secure in their Primary Agent's isolation. It was for this reason, Dempsey was sure, that he'd found himself introduced to the only other Englishman on staff.

Not that Sam Cooke considered himself a part of *anyone's* staff.

Cooke had been in the United States for fifteen years by the time Dempsey joined the ISB. Most of his working life. In that time he had moved from parish to parish, never finding a permanent home until appointed as Catholic chaplain to the staff of the Secretariat Building. This was four years before Dempsey's arrival and it technically made Cooke an employee of the United Nations, which owned the entire UN Complex in Manhattan's Midtown on an extraterritorial basis.

If Cooke accepted that status, he certainly didn't show it.

'So it's a no to the extra tea?' Dempsey asked.

'Of course it's not a "no" to the tea.' Cooke, as always, seemed oblivious to the amusement his friend found in his own short outburst. 'It's never a "no" to another cup of tea. Especially when it's cold as bollocks out here like today. But then we talk about Chinatown, yeah?'

'Yeah,' Dempsey replied, rising to his feet. 'Then we talk about Chinatown.'

'Eleven of them?'

'Yeah.'

'All dead?'

'Yeah.'

'And you accounted for eight of them?'

'Depends how you look at it. Four directly. Eight if you include the redirected grenade.'

'Ah come on, man. Don't piss about. Eight is eight. At this point what's the difference anyway, eh?'

Dempsey said nothing. With all Cooke already knew about his past, the priest's comment was to be expected. Because it was the same thought that kept Dempsey awake at night.

At this point, what was *the difference?*

Dempsey had spent the first two-thirds of his working life as a killer. Nothing more. Nothing less.

From the moment he had joined the British Army he had been conditioned. Institutionalised. His natural patriotism and his sense of right and wrong had been corrupted, just as his body and his skills had been perfected. By the time he had passed through the elite SAS and had been seconded to the clandestine Chameleon Unit, he was little more than a machine.

What had followed was an entire decade of blind dedication to 'duty'. For Dempsey – like the other nine members of the Chameleon Unit – that duty was to infiltrate and to kill. Whenever and wherever he was ordered.

He had done so without question. Without hesitation. Without doubt. Always safe in the belief that any decision to end a life was a decision well made by his superiors. A decision deserved.

If the stakes had been lower, his naivety would be laughable. But they were not. Dempsey's blind obedience had resulted in the deaths of hundreds. Some, maybe even most, were deaths they thoroughly deserved.

But not all of them. Not everyone.

Dempsey had sent innocent men to hell. And with them, he had sent himself.

'So eleven dead. Plenty by you, let's just say that. Did they deserve it?'

The final question broke into Dempsey's thoughts.

'What's that mean?'

'It means did they deserve it?'

Cooke's blunt way of speaking cut through the niceties. Dempsey worked in the world's biggest hotbed of diplomacy and tact. To him, it was a breath of fresh air.

'Something brought you and your team to their door,' Cooke continued. 'What was it? And did they deserve to die for it?'

'It was . . . it was complicated.' Dempsey hesitated. What Cooke was asking was classified, and the ISB was not in the habit of handing out high-level security clearance to priests.

'Is this now confession?' Dempsey asked, settling on the one rule that bypassed questions of confidentiality.

'Like you believe in that,' Cooke muttered, taking the cue.

'It's not a question of what I believe, Sam. It's a question of how much God can forgive. Even he has his limits.'

Cooke didn't answer, and Dempsey knew why; Dempsey rarely gave a glimpse into his own soul – even in confession – but he suspected he had just done so.

It was not a subject on which Dempsey intended to dwell.

'Are we doing this?'

'Yeah. Yes. Sorry. OK.' Cooke seemed to regain the composure that had faltered. He indicated towards the ever darkening view from the balcony. 'Face out that way.'

Dempsey did as instructed; Cooke did the same.

'In the Name of the Father, and of the Son, and of the Holy Spirit. Amen.'

Dempsey followed Cooke in the blessing.

'May the Lord help you to confess your sins.'

'Amen,' Dempsey responded. Autopilot was now kicking in. Lessons learned since early childhood. 'Forgive me, Father, for I have sinned. It has been three months since my last confession.'

'I remember. It was warmer out here then.'

'It was.' Dempsey smiled, grateful for any delay in what he had to say.

'Now come on, man. Get on with it.'

Dempsey took a final breath and began.

'The raid was a rescue mission. A Russian operative. We were told he had been looking to defect, which had been discovered by an Iranian cell. They were trying to use him as leverage, play the US off against Russia. Far from ideal from the point of view of the Security Council. We were given some intelligence; we acted on it.'

'And?'

'And the intelligence was wrong. Meaning a lot of the wrong people died.'

'What does that mean? I know you, Joe. There's no way your team shot up a room full of innocent people.'

'I didn't say that,' Dempsey replied. 'They weren't innocent. But that doesn't mean they deserved to die.'

'Who were they?'

'Drug dealers. Producers, even. Turns out the intelligence sent us to a serious drugs factory. Cocaine. Heroin. Tonnes of the stuff. We were expecting professional resistance. Trained Iranian agents. So we went in hard. Trouble is, that made them fight back. And once they were fighting back, there was only one way to end it.'

'What way?'

'What do you think? We couldn't just back out apologetically. Once the shooting started, all bets were off.'

'Who fired first?'

'We did. Gallo.'

'Gallo. There's a surprise. But look, he's your team. He's drilled by you. Would he have fired without any threat?'

'No. Absolutely not. They must have gone for their weapons. My target did and that was a moment later at most.'

'Then I'm not getting it.'

'What?'

'The guilt, Joe. You raided a drugs factory and the criminals inside tried to kill you and your man. You killed them first. That's the job, surely?'

'No. No, that's not the job,' Dempsey explained. 'I do what I do for a reason. I do it because almost no one else can. I stop threats. Real threats, things that matter on a global scale. I don't kill petty criminals.'

'Isn't that a bit of a bullshit distinction?'

'How is it?'

'Take someone whose son or daughter has moved to New York. To college or to work or whatever. They come from a sheltered life; suddenly they're beneath the big lights. Temptation everywhere. They fall into drugs. Pretty soon they're on heroin. A year later, dead. To that parent, Joe, do you think the slime that got them hooked matters less than some Russian defector? Than some Iranian terrorist? Is that what you think?'

Dempsey said nothing.

'You think you're the only one who suffers for their work?' Cooke continued. 'Then let me tell you something. It's a shit life, being a priest. Shit. I had to give up all the things I loved best. Women. Getting drunk. Even having a bit of a scrap now and again. I don't get to do *any* of that. Probably a bit long in the tooth for the first and the last anyway, but still, the closest I get to fun is smoking a joint, and even that stuff's too strong now.

'And what's it all for, eh? For a God who seems to do everything he can, at every opportunity, to make me doubt that he even exists. I gave up all the things I loved and married myself to this concept – this Church – which most of the time I'm not even sure I agree with. So yeah, it's a shit life. But it's also the life I chose, isn't it? I mean, love it or hate it – and I usually fucking hate it – the Catholic Church is the team I'm on.

'And you've done the same thing, Joe. You've chosen a life that's every bit as shit as mine. And like me, you made that choice because of what you believe is right. Because that's what you *always* do. At least in all the time I've known you. You do the right thing. That's good enough for me. And it should be good enough for you, too.'

Dempsey said nothing.

'And one more thing, Joe. If some piece of shit in a drugs den starts firing bullets at you and your team, I reckon you can safely say that they deserve whatever they get back. So stop with this shit.'

Cooke's harshly worded sentiments were basically correct – Dempsey knew that – but he also knew a whole lot more. Other factors that he could not ignore. Things he had done. Things he had to make up for.

What was the saying? he thought. *Having red in the ledger?*

Dempsey had so much red in *his* ledger that he would never erase it all. He had accepted that long ago. But the last thing he wanted was to add any more.

'I don't think it's as simple—' he began.

The sound of Dempsey's landline telephone interrupted his words.

'I need to answer that,' he explained as he rose to his feet. 'Only the Director's office has that number.'

'I take it I won't be giving you any Hail Mary's today, then,' Cooke called out as Dempsey slipped through the metal framed door and back into the apartment's main room.

Cooke was right. For now, confession was over.

EIGHT

*PAN-ATLANTIC AIRLINES FLIGHT PA16 FROM
LONDON HEATHROW TO NEW YORK JFK
CRASHES OVER THE ATLANTIC OCEAN.*

The abrupt headline was all that filled Nizar Mansour's mind as he rushed along the streets of Stoke Newington. The news – and what it meant for *him* – was seared onto his brain.

He could focus on nothing else.

The short walk from the Rose and Crown to his small bedsit usually took five minutes, but tonight Mansour had been walking for at least ten. He needed time to rationalise what he had learned – to understand it – and so he had taken a longer route.

He lit a cigarette, his third of the walk. Benson and Hedges brand. They were the closest he could find to the harsher, stronger cigarettes of home, and yet they were pathetically weak in comparison. Usually Mansour could ignore the difference, but right now he craved the rougher hit of an Alhamraa.

It was a momentary distraction. How could it be anything else? A thought banished almost immediately and replaced by the jumbled barrage of questions that had fuelled him this far.

What if it was not a bomb?
What if it was just coincidence?
Did they lie to me?
If they had, why?
And why had they still not called?

They were questions that answered themselves. Mansour knew that, even as his mind whirled, desperate to find a more palatable version. Knowing and accepting are very different things but ultimately, when all alternatives have been rejected, the truth is all that remains.

A truth that Mansour could finally see.

It has to be bomb, he told himself. *It has to be.*

Like many of his countrymen, Mansour's unskilled job in the UK did not reflect his profession in Syria. Before the war he had been a mechanical engineer and so he knew the difference between impact and explosion. And from what little he had been able to see on screen, there could be no doubt that Flight PA16 had exploded while still at altitude.

It was rare that anything but an incendiary device could cause such a catastrophic event in a state-of-the-art aircraft. But in this case? With everything else Mansour knew?

It has *to be a bomb. Because it cannot be coincidence.*

His head was beginning to clear. The cold night air was starting to hit, slowing his heart rate and his blood pressure. Soon that drop would begin to be a problem. But for now it had halted his anxiety, lessening the adrenaline that was running through his system.

They lie to me, his thoughts continued. *They lie to me because they know I would not do what they asked if I know the truth. If they told me what was in that case.*

It was the only logical conclusion. And it made the answer to his final question inevitable.

That is why they didn't call. Because they were never going to call. They were never going to let her go.

Mansour felt himself stagger at this final realisation. It had been at the back of his mind from the beginning, he was sure.

But now it had fought its way to the front, and he could no longer lie to himself.

They were never going to let her go.

Within seconds of seeing the headline on the pub's video screen, Mansour had joined the dots and realised his own connection to the story. The shock had sent his already unsteady world into a tailspin and resulted in him rushing out onto Church Street, where he had promptly thrown up both pints of the Stella Artois he had been drinking inside.

The third pint remained untouched on the table he had left behind. Next to a now-abandoned Nokia.

Even with his stomach emptied, he had not considered going back into the pub. His lager, his phone, his overcoat. None of them had crossed his mind. Instead he had staggered into the night, into a cold he was too distracted to feel.

It was only now, after the fear, the confusion and the last remaining effects of the alcohol had subsided, that he even noticed the temperature. Even so, it barely registered in his thoughts.

His mind remained elsewhere. Except now it was focused.

Now Mansour could see the threats that lay ahead.

If they were never going to give her back, they must be sure I stay silent. And only way they can be sure of that . . .

He was running before the thought was fully formed.

NINE

Mansour had fled conflict in the past. A flight that took him from his home city of Aleppo to his new home in London. All to be free of the war that was tearing his country apart.

But that flight did not make him a coward. Mansour had stood and fought for Syria for as long as there had still been hope. Longer, if he was honest with himself. For years before that hope was gone, he had been a soldier. A freedom fighter. A man willing to run towards danger in order to protect what he loved.

Exactly as he was doing now.

They have to be coming, he thought. The knowledge drove him on. His lungs were burning in a perfect storm of tobacco, cold air and rare exertion. On any other day – in any other circumstances – Mansour would have stopped to catch his breath. But not today.

I have to reach Rifat before they do.

Rifat was Mansour's brother. His youngest, twelve years his junior. He was also his roommate, sharing a cramped bedsit that was already too small for a single occupant. Like his brother, Rifat was a refugee. And like Mansour, Rifat was also employed as a baggage handler in Heathrow Airport.

But unlike Mansour, Rifat knew nothing about Flight PA16. Mansour had tried to protect his brother from that, and so Rifat had no way to know the danger that was coming.

Don't be home, Mansour thought to himself as he continued to run. A desperate hope. *Please don't be home.*

It was all he could think. The mantra that drove him on.

Don't be home.

Mansour would never remember how long he ran. It could not have been more than three, perhaps four minutes. But it was flat out, as fast as he had ever moved, and so it felt like so much more. Even with adrenaline flooding his system he could only fight the exhaustion for so long. His legs could only be pushed so far.

As he turned the corner into his own street, they reached their limit.

Unable to take the strain of the hard turn, Mansour's right knee buckled, sending him heavily to the ground. He fell forward and, too tired to react quickly, his forehead hit the pavement hard.

The impact cut deep into the skin above Mansour's right eye and left him crumpled in a heap, dazed and hidden in shadow.

It also saved his life.

If Mansour had not fallen he would have been ten, maybe twenty seconds quicker. He would also have been upright, and so much more visible. But he was neither of these. He *had* fallen, and so he remained unseen as he watched his deepest fears unfold.

Three men were climbing the steps of the dilapidated townhouse where Mansour and Rifat had their bedsit. Mansour recognised only one of them, but that one was enough. It was a face he had sworn he would never forget.

The man's name was Romeo. Or at least that was what he had called himself on the two occasions they had met. On those occasions Romeo had seemed to be the boss, and that fact now made him the devil in Mansour's own personal hell.

Romeo reached the top of the stairs. His two companions stayed one step lower, further exaggerating the height difference that already existed between them and their six-foot-six superior. One of them read something from a scrap of paper, before Romeo pressed one of the building's intercom buttons.

My buzzer, Mansour thought. *Rifat's buzzer.*

He suppressed the urge to climb to his feet. To reveal himself. There was still a chance Rifat was not home. And even if he was, Mansour could not be sure what Romeo would do. Whether seeing Mansour would put Rifat at even greater risk.

For a moment there was no response to the buzzer and Mansour felt his hopes grow.

Allah willing, Rifat is not there. Please, Rifat. Don't be home.

The light of the interior hallway – cast outwards and onto Romeo as the house door was opened – told Mansour that his prayers had not been answered.

From where Mansour still lay, he could see Rifat's profile as his younger brother stepped out of the door towards Romeo. Mansour climbed to his feet, keeping his body low and still in shadow. The pain that had wracked his lungs and chest, even the damage he had done to his knee, faded into nothing. His focus was now absolute.

Attack them, he thought. The worst possible plan, but the only option he could see. *And give Rifat a chance to run.*

He steadied himself, preparing to use whatever he had left to protect his brother.

His heart was beginning to race. He was ready.

And then he saw Rifat smile.

Just a small movement, but it made Mansour pause. Whatever was being said, it could not be the threats or the intimidation that Mansour had expected. Rifat was a small man, much shorter and thinner than his elder brother, and without Mansour's experience of war. He was not difficult to intimidate, especially by a man as physically imposing as Romeo. And yet he was smiling.

The exchange, it seemed, was friendly.

Mansour's racing heart began to slow. His adrenaline replaced by hope.

Maybe they do not hurt him, he thought. *Maybe they leave him.*

The innocent Mansour – the baggage handler who lived a peaceful life – began to believe. But deep down, there was another Mansour. The old Mansour. The man who had fought his way out of war and torment.

And *that* Mansour knew better how the world worked.

Romeo and Rifat's conversation was coming to an end. It still seemed friendly, enough even for a polite handshake. As Mansour held his breath, he watched Romeo turn and begin to walk back down the steps.

For an instant, it seemed that Rifat would be OK.

And then that instant was over.

Rifat stayed put as Romeo and one of his companions walked down the steps, towards the street. He raised his hand in a friendly goodbye, and at the same time turned to look towards the man who had stayed.

Mansour saw confusion creep into his brother's expression and in that moment he knew that he was too late – too far away – to stop what was about to happen. In one swift movement, Romeo's man swept a hand across Rifat's throat.

It was almost casual. But it was enough. Whatever the man was holding had done its job, and even from a distance Mansour could see the arterial spray fire into the air.

'NO!'

The adrenaline came flooding back in an instant, expelled in a roar from the very pit of Mansour's stomach.

'*AYREH FEEK!*'

Shock. Rage. Grief. A combination of every primal reaction poured out as he stood up, clearly visible in the light of the nearest street lamp.

'*AYREH FEEK . . . YA IBN IL SHARMOOTA!*'

The screams kept coming. The sheer violent despair. But another instinct overrode all others and prevented him from moving forward.

Survival.

Rifat was dead. Had that not been so clear then Mansour would have risked his life for his brother's. But that was no longer possible. There was no reason for him to die as well. And one look at Romeo and his men, as they slowly registered who the bloodied and raging figure in the street actually was, told Mansour that death would be the inevitable outcome of all but one decision.

He stopped screaming.

For a moment no one moved. Not Romeo. Not his two companions. And not Mansour. All four, somehow frozen by shock and indecision. A moment that was ended by the aggressive ignition of a car parked one hundred yards away.

The explosion of noise kick-started Mansour's adrenaline. He had been so focused on the men ahead of him that he had not considered the possibility of more. This changed the instant he heard the car.

Like a sprinter at the sound of a starter's pistol, he reacted without a further thought.

'CATCH THAT SON OF A BITCH!'

Mansour could hear Romeo's shout behind him. He easily recognised the distinctive and intimidating voice. And he understood what the shouted instruction meant. If they caught him, Mansour was a dead man.

The sound of footsteps beat behind him. He could not tell how many sets – certainly two, maybe three – nor did he have a moment to turn and see. Instead he pushed himself onwards, as fast as he could run, towards the only place where he knew he would be safe.

Four hundred yards.

The adrenaline was still in full flow. Nature's jet fuel.

Mansour had no idea how he was keeping his pace, even as he heard the footsteps racing ever closer. He pushed himself even harder.

Three hundred yards.

The sound of a car engine was coming closer, drowning out the sound of his pursuers on foot.

The car drew level. Between them was a line of empty vehicles, parked for the night along Stoke Newington High Street. They formed an accidental barrier of metal, preventing the car from mounting the kerb and swatting Mansour like a fly.

Two hundred yards.

Mansour risked a glance. In the front passenger seat was Romeo, a pistol in his hand.

Somehow Mansour managed to duck without breaking stride as he heard the first gunshot. He doubted he could do it twice, but then perhaps he did not need to; the bullet had missed even where Mansour would have been by maybe ten feet.

It suggested that Romeo was struggling to aim from the moving car.

When the second bullet missed by even more, Mansour was sure.

One hundred yards.

The gunfire stopped as the car suddenly accelerated, driving off ahead.

Fifty yards.

The car came to a screeching halt up ahead. Romeo stepped out. And now Mansour understood. Romeo had ordered the driver to pull ahead, so he could take a static shot. A shot that could not miss, not with Mansour running towards him.

But there was one flaw with that plan: Mansour would not *be* running towards him.

Romeo had no time to even raise his weapon as Mansour took a sudden turn to his left and ran inside a building he was sure Romeo had not noticed among the long line of outlets on the High Street.

Stoke Newington Police Station.

There were two officers, one civilian police worker and one member of the public in the desk area of the station. All turned as Mansour burst through the door, struggling for breath.

'Sir, do you need help?'

The speaker was the senior of the two officers. The desk sergeant. As he spoke, he indicated for the other officer – a constable – to assist the bleeding man.

'What happened to you?'

'I . . . I need confess . . .' Mansour was struggling to spit out the words as his heart rate and blood pressure spiked. 'I need confess.'

'To what?' The desk sergeant's mood had changed. He seemed to take in Mansour's injuries with concern. 'What have you done?'

'Flight . . . Flight PA16,' Mansour gasped. 'It was me. I planted the bomb.'

TEN

D ale Victor was one of four people occupying the sofa on screen, but he might as well have been on there alone. The news show's three-person hosting team was huddled together on the right side of the couch, while Victor held the left and with it the room.

Dempsey had not watched the original broadcast but even now, as he watched the recording, he could not help but be impressed. He had had no time for Dale Victor's politics and even less for what he had seen as the man's bullying tactics. But he had to admit, Victor had commanded attention.

From every camera angle, attention was somehow drawn to him. Every pair of eyes fixed.

The show itself was one of the cable news network's biggest hitters. And so its three hosts were well used to important guests. Hell, President John Knowles himself had appeared six times since taking office. The journalists' reputations were fearsome, but even they seemed to shrink – to fawn – next to Victor.

For the last fifteen minutes it had been very much Victor's show. An endless opportunity for the man to criticise not only the current American government but every alternative there was to it, other than himself, including the other potential Republican candidates.

Not that any of them were presenting much of a challenge to Victor. At the time of the recording, he was polling at fifty-eight per cent. New York State Governor David Smart and

Texas Senator Chris White were a distant second and third respectively, their combined votes less than half Victor's total. Even the riskiest Vegas casinos had become hesitant to take bets on his nomination, giving odds that made a gamble pointless. It had seemed inevitable.

And yet now it was impossible.

Following the Pan-Atlantic Airlines press conference in the UK less than an hour ago, the world now knew of the death of Dale Victor. The result of that news was blanket coverage across all major networks and a succession of hastily thrown together tributes to a life that had been too large for them to do it justice.

Of them all, Fox News had been lucky. They had an entire recently recorded show to fall back on, less than a week after its first broadcast. Which was why, unusually, the network was Dempsey's choice today.

It would soon become an iconic interview, Dempsey could see that already. With Victor holding court – the very definition of confidence – and with his blistering debate performances adding colour, it would, Dempsey realised, become the ultimate example of 'what could have been'.

It is not often that the world sees a myth in the making. But that was exactly what Dempsey was now witnessing. And he knew it.

Victor *was* incredibly charismatic. Or, more accurately, *had* been. Classically handsome even as he approached sixty, the man's practised charm eclipsed every other person around him. Place Dale Victor in any room and no one else mattered.

Victor had been one of America's most famous men for almost forty years. Born wealthy, he had been the main investor in a fledgling software company which, in just two years, had revolutionised home computing. That one investment had made Victor a billionaire many times over. From there he seemed to have moved from one success to another. Always the consummate front man; a public relations master.

Even more impressive had been his skill as an orator. The way he could deliver a speech. The changes in tempo. In inflection. Even the placement of his pauses. It was a once-in-a-lifetime talent that could sweep up a crowd and take them to places they would never have thought to go.

And that was exactly what had concerned Dempsey.

Dempsey's career had shown him more of the world than most people had seen. In that time he had seen democracies rise and fall. And he had seen autocracies do the same. He had watched entire populations manipulated, cajoled and ultimately abused, all to serve the interests of the few.

And he had no doubt that manipulation was exactly what Dale Victor had been doing. He had just never seen anyone else do it so well.

'Thank God we won't be dealing with *that* next year.'

Dempsey had not heard the room's glass door open and so ISB Director Elizabeth Kirk was already halfway into her own office before she spoke.

He rose to his feet at the sound of her perfect Upper New York State diction.

'Ma'am.'

Dempsey was rarely taken unawares. It was a testament to the magnetism of Dale Victor's performance that Kirk had managed it now.

'Sit down, Joe.' Kirk reached up and touched Dempsey's shoulder as she passed, applying the gentlest of downward pressure.

'Ma'am.'

Dempsey retook his seat, switched the TV off with the remote and turned to face Kirk's desk as she sat down behind it.

Just five foot two with a waif-like build, Elizabeth Kirk was tiny in comparison to most of the agents in the building. Others might have felt daunted by this, but Dempsey doubted that such a thought had ever occurred to Kirk. She was as confident in herself and in her own abilities as anyone Dempsey had ever met. After two years as her Primary Agent, he had no doubt that confidence was well-earned.

'No need to ask if you've heard the news, then?' Kirk indicated the television screen with a nod as she spoke.

'Hard to miss,' Dempsey replied. 'Looks like a future problem avoided, the way things were going.'

'Silver linings.' Kirk did not smile as she spoke. 'We'll come back to that. What's your first take on what you've seen?'

'It's a bomb. It'll take an investigation to know more details, but with debris scatter like that? No doubt.'

'My thoughts exactly.'

'Has anyone claimed it?'

'Not yet. But it's only been half a day, and just an hour since Victor was confirmed on board by the airline. I wouldn't expect anything for another twenty-four hours. Maybe thirty-six, even.'

Kirk was not looking for Dempsey's agreement. He moved on to the next question.

'Any word from the White House on this?'

'None.' Kirk's voice was flat as she answered.

'They'd have known about Victor as soon as they knew the flight was down, surely?'

'Certainly before it was reported, yes,' Kirk replied.

'They'll have been monitoring his movements. And that means the White House has known Victor was dead since this morning.'

'Have they reached out to us? To you?'

'When do they ever, Joe?'

There was a hint of bitterness in Kirk's tone as she asked the question. Dempsey recognised it well and he knew its source.

The White House and President John Knowles.

President Knowles had been sworn in three years earlier, and before that he had been elected on a wave of public and political support that rivalled Dale Victor's following. But unlike Victor, Knowles had achieved it without controversy. Without manipulation. Instead he had pursued an agenda of justice and old-fashioned morality. A campaign of right versus wrong that had ultimately gained the support of even the most cynical political operators.

None more cynical than Elizabeth Kirk.

A lifetime with the CIA could make a disbeliever of anyone; access to information only a few would ever see tends to wash away naivety and dispel myths. In her thirty-two years with the agency, Kirk had seen man after man rise to power on a campaign of promises, and time and again she had seen those promises broken. Any hope she may have had that *any* candidate would be different had died long ago.

Then she met Senator John Knowles.

As a senior intelligence officer, Kirk had long been aware of Knowles' military service. Uniquely for a politician, the current President was even more of a hero than his political campaigns claimed. As a former Lieutenant-Commander of Red Squadron, US Naval Special Warfare Development Group – or SEAL Team Six, as it was more commonly known – his role and the details of his service were highly classified and so not generally known to the public.

But they were known to Kirk.

It was this, Kirk had once told Dempsey, that set Knowles apart from every other politician she had ever known. But more than that had brought her to his side. The causes he pursued as a two-term senator had shown her a man of both kindness and steely determination. His refusal to claim credit for his successes and his dedication to his young family had shown her a man of integrity. And his dedication to the military – both to the men under his command and beyond – had shown her a man who had not forgotten his origins.

All of this, Kirk had explained, was why she had thrown her support behind Knowles as he campaigned for the nomination, and then for the presidency. Support which was repaid with a promotion to the Deputy Directorship of the CIA when Knowles took office.

But that was then. Three years later and the friendship between Kirk and Knowles was a distant memory. Dempsey had never known what had happened between them, but he knew that Kirk considered her appointment as Director of the ISB less than a year into the president's first term to be an exile.

Not that this had hindered her performance. Kirk was as dedicated to duty as she had ever been. Still, Dempsey could detect a difference in her demeanour whenever Knowles or his administration were discussed. It was a difference he saw now.

'Whatever the White House knows about this, I think we have to assume they won't be helping us with our investigation.'

'Helping us?' Dempsey was confused. 'You want us to take this on?'

'I want you to make some enquiries, yes.'

'But what about Chinatown? What about—'

'I'm keeping Dai on that, with your team in support. I want you on this one. And only you.'

Dempsey took a moment to consider what Kirk was saying. It was unusual. The ISB was the special intelligence division of the United Nations Security Council. If there was one thing it had, it was immense resources. So why a one-man job?

'Why just me?'

'Because it's delicate and I could have this very wrong,' Kirk replied. 'In fact, I probably *do* have it wrong. So the last thing I need is a whole team of agents blowing it out of proportion.'

'What's the theory?'

'It's not a theory.'

'What is it anyway?'

This time it was Kirk who paused. Dempsey could see that she was struggling. That she did not want to say the words.

'It's . . . it's something we need looked into. That's all.' The confidence had disappeared from Kirk's voice. 'Something Victor hinted at a week before he died.'

'Which was what?'

'I'll show you.'

Kirk reached out for the TV remote and the screen came back to life. It was now showing a frozen image of Dale Victor. He was back behind a podium but this time there was no one else around him.

'One of his press events?' Dempsey asked.

'Yes. Given in London seven days ago.'

'Why was he in London with the primaries coming up?' Dempsey asked. The thought had not occurred to him until now.

'Business interests,' Kirk replied. 'He claimed to be over there closing them all off before the official race begins next month. To prevent conflicts of interest. He was getting a little ahead of himself. He thought he had as good as won the nomination already.'

'Hadn't he?'

'Probably. But who knows. Anyway, listen to what he says here.'

Dempsey turned back to face the screen as Kirk pressed play, with Victor in mid-answer.

'. . . confident that by the time I am officially announced as the Republican Nominee at the National Convention in July of this year, every business interest I have outside of the United States of America will have been divested into trusts and subsidiary companies, preventing any possibility of any conflict between me and my position as US president.'

'We can agree on one thing,' Dempsey said, turning to Kirk as he spoke, 'he was definitely getting ahead of himself.'

'And then some,' Kirk replied. 'But listen to the next part.'

'Mr Victor, you're obviously very confident when it comes to winning your party nomination, and perhaps understandably so, given the current polls.'

Dempsey recognised the American voice. Sarah Truman. It was no surprise to him that his friend would be taking the lead at a Dale Victor press conference in the UK.

'But surely you can't justify such a level of confidence when it comes to winning the presidency itself? After all, in John Knowles you're up against an incumbent with a sixty-six per cent approval rating just months ahead of the presidential campaign, leading one of the most vibrant economies in US history.'

The question was a good one. Dempsey would have expected nothing less. What he did *not* expect was the answer.

'Miss Truman, isn't it? Well, thank you, Miss Truman, for that question. I'm sure John Knowles' chief of staff will consider it money well spent.'

Dempsey glanced sharply at Kirk as he watched Sarah Truman begin to protest the false, scandalous allegation.

Kirk simply shook her head.

'Wait for the rest.'

'Ordinarily, Miss Truman, I'd give you the full facts and figures about the deficiencies of your wonderful John Knowles. But since the likes of you people don't listen to the truth about him and his administration, I don't see that there's much point in me wasting my breath, is there?'

The answer was an attempt to belittle and to bully. An attempt which, Dempsey knew, would not work with Sarah Truman.

Without missing a beat, Sarah proved him right.

'Then surely this is your chance to have your say direct to camera, Mr Victor? Instead of going through "the likes of me". Surely this is your chance to explain to us how you are going to succeed in an election against someone as well supported as President Knowles.'

Dempsey smiled at her quick response. For the first time Victor looked uncomfortable – uncertain, even – as he considered his answer. A glance off-stage suggested that he was looking for some assistance. He did not seem to get it. The answer that followed was uncharacteristically vague.

'Perhaps, Miss Truman, you don't know everything there is to know about John Knowles. Maybe he isn't what you think. Maybe there are things that you'll learn about your heroic president that'll make you change your mind.'

Victor's confidence was visibly returning as he spoke.

'Things happen in war. Bad things. We'll see what the president has to say about those things when the time comes.'

And with that final cryptic comment, Dale left the stage.

The screen turned black and Dempsey looked towards Kirk.

'You think he was threatening to expose something about Knowles?'

'He certainly seemed to be. It was all very vague, of course. But then, days later, he's dead? Killed with over five hundred others.'

'And you think . . . you think Knowles . . .'

'I don't think *anything*, Joe. Not yet. But if there *is* something to this, what are the chances that the White House will have it properly investigated?'

'If Knowles *is* involved in some way, you mean? Well then there's none, obviously. But that's a leap, Elizabeth. It means believing that Dale Victor had something so serious on the president that Knowles would kill him for it. Him and five hundred innocent people. If there was anything like that – anything at all – we'd have heard of it, surely?'

Kirk said nothing. Instead she looked away, staring into space. Finally she exhaled deeply, and sat forward in her chair.

'I never did tell you what happened between me and John Knowles, did I?'

'I never asked.'

'Well, now you're going to know anyway,' Kirk replied, her voice sounded tired. And sad. 'And once you do, Joe, I'm gonna need you to go see an old friend of mine.'

ELEVEN

It was almost 11 p.m. as Sarah Truman climbed the steps to her front door; the end of what had become a sixteen-hour shift. Long, unpredictable days were an occupational hazard in Sarah's career. She was well used to them and had experienced far longer than today, and yet rarely had she ever felt so tired.

But then Sarah had never been pregnant before. And as much as she kept telling herself that she could not be sure, well, she *was* sure. And, having made a short detour to her local all-night chemist, she would soon have the proof.

As Sarah reached her front door, the lights through the windows told her that Michael was already home. One turn of a key and Sarah could join him inside, ready to put the day behind her.

The smell of smoky paprika mingling with garlic, tomatoes and onions greeted her, along with the classic tones of Frank Sinatra.

As she heard Michael's random, tuneless singing drowning out the Chairman of the Board, there was nowhere else Sarah would rather be. She slipped off her suit jacket and headed for the kitchen door.

'What's all this?' she asked.

Michael turned at the sound of her voice, his surprise quickly replaced by a broad, happy smile. The handsome Irishman was exactly who Sarah needed to see.

'You're home,' he bellowed over the sound of the music. 'I thought you'd be later.'

'So what, you decided to put on a concert for the neighbours while you waited?'

Sarah knew that Michael could not mistake her words as serious. Not with the grin she could feel on her own face.

'What, me and Frank? They should be so bloody lucky!'

Michael walked towards Sarah as he spoke, grabbing her hand as Sinatra kicked the song up a gear and into the chorus.

'I've been a puppet . . .' he sang as he pulled her close, his soft Belfast accent more pronounced than when he spoke '. . . a pauper, a pirate, a poet . . .'

'Where do you get the energy?' Sarah asked as Michael spun her away, until their hands were barely touching. 'How are you not exhausted?'

'. . . I've been up and down and over and out . . .' he continued as he pulled her back in, stopping only to kiss her as she spun back into his arms.

For a moment she allowed herself to get carried away, to forget the worries that had been preoccupying her all day. But a lurch in her stomach brought her back to reality. The knowledge of what might be forced its way back to the front of her mind.

Sarah stepped back, pushing Michael off.

'What's wrong?' he asked, his expression concerned.

'I'm just not feeling too great,' Sarah explained. 'I'm really sorry.'

'Don't be.' Michael stepped back as he spoke, but stayed close enough to place the back of his hand on Sarah's forehead. 'What is it? You're not hot.'

'Not hot?' Sarah laughed. Michael's instinctive kindness had calmed her. 'You didn't think that a second ago.'

'Very funny. And a damn sight too quick for a sick person.

I'm starting to think you're not ill at all. That you're just not that into me.'

'You're safe on that front and you know it,' Sarah replied. She looked past Michael, towards the large kitchen island and the eight-ring range cooker beyond it. 'What are you making?'

Michael glanced behind, as if to remind himself.

'Hungarian goulash,' Michael replied. 'But it won't be ready for another half hour. Like I said, I thought you'd be later than this, what with the plane crash and Dale Victor and all that.'

'Nothing to keep me busy now the big news is out there.'

Sarah climbed into a tall chair that sat against the kitchen island and rested her elbows on the unit's marble top.

'Besides, I'll be lucky if I even get to keep the story after missing the Dale Victor element.'

'What? Why? How were you to know about Victor?'

'Chris Parker knew,' Sarah replied. Parker was the Sky News journalist who had asked the key question. 'I should have had a source, too.'

'Oh, come on. That's a bit much. You can't have a source for *every* occasion. And it's not like anyone else did. From what I saw on the TV, Parker was the only one there with even a hint about Victor being on that plane.'

'Maybe.' Sarah was not convinced. And it was not the point. She knew she was off her game. But she couldn't tell Michael why. Not until she knew for sure. 'But even so, I should have been ready for a follow-up question. Instead of trying not to throw up all over Heathrow.'

'Really? Look, are you sure you don't need a doctor or something? You know the guy five doors up has a place in Harley Street. We could ask him to take a look at you?'

'No, honestly, it's only a bug,' Sarah lied. 'It's no biggie.'

Michael did not reply. He just nodded and held Sarah's gaze, until the sound of the cooker's alarm broke the silence. It spurred him into action. Removing a large, orange Le Creuset pot from the right-hand oven, he threw in some chopped bell peppers, stirred the contents and placed it back in.

Once done, he turned back to Sarah.

'So, you think having no clue about Victor is going to come back and bite you in the arse?'

'It could. But it won't if I can get ahead of the story.'

'And how are you going to do that?'

'I have absolutely no idea. But next time there's a development in this, I need to be the one breaking it. And I can't let . . . a stomach bug get in my way.'

TWELVE

Detective Chief Inspector Bruce Bull switched off the car's ignition and glanced at his watch.

2.35 a.m.

Far too late for a day to end. Far too early for the next to begin. Not that shift times applied to Bull right now. The moment Flight PA16 went down, his usual working hours became meaningless.

Bull had been with Counter Terrorism Command – a specialist police unit designated SO15 – since its formation in 2006. He had joined as an already experienced investigator, having spent the previous eighteen years with Special Branch. Now fifty-eight and with any notable contemporary long since retired, no officer in the Metropolitan Police had witnessed even half of the horrors Bull had endured.

His career focus on terrorism had begun over thirty years before, with the bombing of Pan Am Flight 103 over Lockerbie in 1988 that had killed 270 people. Britain's single biggest terrorist atrocity, just months after his appointment to Special Branch.

In the thirty-two years since then, Bull had witnessed the very worst of humanity. Every terrorist attack on British soil – or against British citizens or British interests abroad – fell within the jurisdiction of Counter Terrorism Command. But that made up only a fraction of the unit's work. The majority of its time was focused upon prevention. The countless planned attacks which, thanks to 1,500 specialist operatives like Bull, never happened.

It had been an entire career dedicated to a single end: to never again allow devastation on the scale of Lockerbie.

For thirty years, Bull had achieved exactly that.

Until today.

Now there were almost twice as many dead as '88.

As the only member of Counter Terrorism Command with experience of the Lockerbie investigation, and as one of the unit's senior officers, there was never any doubt that Bull would take the lead on this bombing. And so it was Bull who took the call that turned a tragedy into a political nightmare.

Within an hour of the plane going down, the Command had been contacted by the US Secret Service to confirm what already appeared on the passenger manifest: that potential US presidential candidate Dale Victor, his wife Susan and several members of his campaign staff were on board when the plane went down.

The mere fact of Victor's death meant little to Bull. Sure, he had heard of the man, but to SO15 he was another victim among hundreds. The same could not be said of the Secret Service. The death of a man almost certain to have become a presidential candidate? On what they would no doubt regard as *their* watch? They would want direct involvement in the investigation. Every step of the way.

And when it was the White House asking, nothing was really a request.

It was this thought that returned to Bull as he climbed out of the warmth of his car, into the sub-zero cold of Stoke Newington Police Station's secure parking area. The fact that – whatever his superiors might claim – the involvement of the US Secret Service meant he had already lost control of his case.

Or at least I had, he thought. *Up till an hour ago.*

'Who else knows about this?'

Bull had been inside Stoke Newington Police Station for less than five minutes. In that time he had already dispensed with the police constable who had escorted him in, satisfied the young man lacked any useful knowledge.

Now he was speaking to two more senior officers.

'By now? The whole station, probably.'

At almost 3 a.m., Sergeant Richard Langley was the de facto officer in charge. And he was not about to lie to a DCI from Scotland Yard.

He continued.

'There's no way we were keeping this quiet, guv. Not among ourselves, anyway.'

Bull nodded. The answer was as expected.

'What about anyone from outside the station?'

'There was one member of the public present when the suspect surrendered himself.'

This time it was the desk sergeant, Andy Nelham, who spoke. Unlike Langley, he had been present when Mansour had burst through the station's front doors almost five hours ago.

Bull nodded again as Nelham spoke. The man seemed oddly uncomfortable, even considering the unique situation they were in. It was nothing Bull hadn't encountered before. It was becoming rarer, but some of the older officers could still be thrown by the sight of a black DCI.

Bull chose to ignore it. It hardly mattered tonight.

'Anyone else?' he asked.

'A civilian worker, but she won't say a word outside of this building.' Nelham seemed to be warming up. 'She's as discreet as any copper.'

And that's supposed to be reassuring, is it?

Bull kept the thought to himself and continued.

'What about the member of the public?'

'Whatever he was in here for got lost in the mix, guv.' Nelham again. 'By the time we had the suspect sorted and taken in, he'd long gone.'

'But I presume he heard everything?'

'Hard to miss what Mansour was shouting.'

'That's what I thought. Give me a sec.'

Bull took out his mobile phone and placed a call. It was answered on the first ring.

'Kim, we need to cast a social media net. Everything from Flight PA16 to Stoke Newington Police Station and all terms in between. Err on the side of caution on this one, OK? Blanket coverage.'

Bull disconnected the call and turned back to Nelham.

'Check your records, see if there's any way to identify the civilian. If there is we can be more focused on any leaks that might come from that end. Keep me up to date.'

Bull turned back to face Sergeant Langley as Nelham moved away. He did not miss a beat.

'What about other channels of enquiry? Who else has been officially spoken to about this? Which other agencies?'

'Officially, guv? Just your boys. As soon as we confirmed that Mansour wasn't a crank or some drunk, we followed normal protocol. I took the lead and I contacted SO15.'

'So no one beyond my unit?'

'Not by me.'

'What about the US Secret Service?'

Langley's brow furrowed in confusion at the question.

'Yanks? I wouldn't even know where to start.'

Bull experienced a moment of relief at his response. If the Secret Service was unaware of Mansour's arrest – of his very existence – then Bull had the time he had hoped for. He could question Mansour without them breathing down his neck.

It would make his life a whole lot simpler, but there was still a difficult job to be done. And who knew how long the Americans could be kept in the dark.

'So what do we know about Mansour?' Bull asked.

'Very little beyond the initial confession. He was a mess when he came in. Physically wiped out. He could hardly breathe and his blood pressure was through the roof. We had him checked out with the ME in case of a heart attack. But after that, once he was calm again? Nothing.'

'What do you mean, "nothing"?'

'I mean he hasn't said a word. He won't even confirm the name he gave us.'

'Then how do you know he isn't a crank? Do you know how many lunatics we have claiming credit for this sort of thing?'

'I know. But we acted on what he *had* told us, and it gave us enough to take him seriously. Enough to bring you in.'

Bull was intrigued; all of this was news to him.

'Tell me.'

'We got his name and his address while he was still frantic, and so once he stopped cooperating we sent a couple of boys to the home – it's minutes from here – and they found a body there. Young Arab guy, throat slit.'

'Really?' The information was not what Bull had been expecting. 'Any idea who it is?'

'Best evidence suggests the guy's name was Bilal Essa. There were payslips in the place, from Pan-Atlantic Airlines. Suggests he was a baggage handler there.'

'Pan-Atlantic Airlines?'

'That's right, guv. But we're not convinced about the ID. We looked into Bilal Essa. Checked the guy's National Insurance and tax status. All of which has him older than the dead kid by maybe twenty years, and resident in Hounslow. CID have got men heading to the address now.'

'Still a bugger of a coincidence.'

'Course it is. I'm not saying there's *not* something here. I'm just not sure what it is.'

'And if this dead kid isn't Bilal Essa? Do we know anything else about him?'

'Not too much. The other residents at the address, they weren't too talkative. Obviously not the most legal of immigrants is why. But we at least found that the dead guy shared a bedsit with Mansour.'

'*Shared* a bedsit? Were they some sort of couple, you think?'

'Not sure. Whatever they are to one another, they're close. No doubt about that.' Langley paused for just a moment. 'Well, they *were* close.'

'Anything else?'

'Yeah. We've had reports of what could have been gunfire. Or it could be fireworks, in fairness. But it corresponds in time with Mansour handing himself in.'

'Where?'

'Close. On this street, in fact. But none of my guys heard it, and we've found no trace outside.'

Bull nodded his head in silence, assessing the information, trying to make sense of it.

'OK. Get your guys to search outside again,' he finally said. 'Do it now. Before the street comes alive for the day. And have them do the full distance between here and Mansour's bedsit. Understood?'

'Yes, guv.'

Langley took off as efficiently as Nelham had done. It left Bull alone and so he took a seat in the station's custody area.

He exhaled heavily as he began to think through all he had learned.

The obvious conclusion was low hanging fruit, there to be grasped. An Islamic terrorist attack on America's national airline, targeting a high-profile political figure. The story wrote itself.

Nizar Mansour was an immigrant from an Islamic nation. Exactly the person that one side of the tabloid media warned the public to fear. Exactly the person that the other side encouraged the public to embrace.

Nothing is that simple, Bull told himself. *People are people. Some are saints. Some are bastards. Most, they're somewhere in between. And someone being from that part of the world – from that religion – it doesn't make them guilty.*

But it sure as hell doesn't make them innocent, either.

Still, the obvious conclusion was there. Tantalisingly close. And so perfect that it seemed inevitable.

But something didn't feel right.

'The team are heading back out now.' Langley had returned. 'And CID are about ten minutes outside of Hounslow. So we'll know more about Bilal Essa soon, too.'

Bull said nothing for a moment, as he added the sergeant's update to the mess already in his mind. Finally he looked at Langley.

'Do you think Mansour's good for this?'

The question was clearly unexpected. It caused Langley to flounder.

'I . . . I . . . erm . . . well, he confessed, didn't he? Surely . . .'

'Does it seem like a terrorist attack?' Bull interrupted.

'What else could it be?'

'Something about this doesn't add up. Why would he give himself up like this?'

'Sorry, guv. I don't . . .'

'Two and two isn't always four. That's all I'm saying.'

'Again, guv, I . . .'

'Never mind.' Bull had overestimated the only other copper in the room. 'It's time we asked him for ourselves.'

THIRTEEN

Dempsey switched off the ignition of his Triumph Daytona 675, kicked down the bike's side stand and climbed off.

The cold air hit his face as he removed his motorcycle helmet. Great Neck Village was only twenty-three miles out of Manhattan, but with one being a heavily populated island of densely packed high-rise buildings and the other a sparsely populated district with wide roads, where even a third storey was a rarity, those few miles were marked by a two- to three-degree difference in temperature.

Dempsey tapped the upper left torso of his black motorcycle leathers, searching for its concealed pocket. The feeling of a small, hardback notebook hit his fingertips.

He pulled it out and turned directly to the only tagged page.

There was a single entry.

Thomas Quilty, Two Town House Place, Apartment 2J.

Dempsey looked up at the white columned porch that served as the entrance to the apartment block.

It was the right place. Dempsey knew that immediately. But he kept the notebook open, as if reading something else in its empty pages. And as he did that, he placed his helmet onto the bike's seat and pressed the fingertips of his free right hand to his brow.

To an onlooker, he would give the impression of a man unsure and deep in thought. Which was exactly as Dempsey intended.

It was a distraction from his real purpose: the use of the reflective visor of his helmet as a mirror, carefully placed to take in as much of the street as it could. Dempsey was in Great Neck because Elizabeth Kirk was afraid for the safety of an old friend. If she was right – if Thomas Quilty was in danger – then that danger could already be here.

And it could be watching.

Dempsey twisted right and then left, as if unsure of his location. Combined with the uncertain look he kept on his face, it disguised his effort to get a clearer view of the area outside Two Town House Place. A view which, like the helmet's visor, revealed nothing. If anyone *was* watching, they were doing so with care.

There was no one to be seen, Dempsey concluded. That did not mean that there was no one there, of course. But if there was, they were good. He picked up his helmet and walked towards the building's entrance.

The pathway from the pavement to the porch was perhaps thirty yards long, leading towards a wide wood and glass doorway that doubled as a near-mirror. It provided Dempsey with one last chance to survey the area behind him. Still nothing.

He reached the doorway and the intercom system. It carried no names. Only numbers. He pressed the buzzer marked '2J'.

Dempsey looked down at his watch. An unnecessary habit; his internal clock was as precise in Eastern Standard Time as it was in Greenwich Mean Time, but he still liked to double-check. The black Bremont confirmed it was 10 p.m. Late enough that a visit should be a surprise, but still early enough for an answer.

He reached out to press the buzzer again. The sound of static stopped him.

'Who is it?'

A man's voice. It sounded out of breath.

'Sir, my name is Agent Joe Dempsey, from the International Security Bureau at the United Nations. I'm looking for a Mr Quilty. Thomas Quilty.'

'It's Tom, son.' The strain in the speaker's voice was impossible to ignore. Even this short conversation sounded like a physical effort. 'Only two people ever . . . ever called me Thomas. Both sounded a lot more . . . a lot more . . . ladylike than you.'

Dempsey waited for a moment, expecting Quilty to say more. When he heard nothing but laboured breathing, he spoke again.

'Sir . . . Tom . . . I would really appreciate it if I could step inside and speak to you. It's important.'

'I don't doubt . . . that it is, when you're buzzing . . . buzzing my door this . . . this late.' Quilty paused, audibly regaining some breath. 'But it's . . . it's ten p.m., and with all due . . . all due respect, son, I . . . I don't know you from . . . from Adam. So maybe we meet somewhere tomorrow. Somewhere . . . somewhere public.'

'All due respect right back to you, Tom, but are you sure you'll still be with us tomorrow?'

'What?'

'It's a fair question. No offence, but it sounds like your own lungs are trying to kill you. And I'm afraid they might not be the worst of your worries.'

'You think I'm . . . I'm worried about the . . . the spooks I saw . . . out there?'

'The what?' Dempsey was surprised by Quilty's question. He spun on his heel in response, looking behind him with no pretence that he was doing anything else. Still he saw nothing.

'Where'd you . . . say you were from again?'

'The UN, sir. The International Security Bureau.'

'And who sent you?'

'With everything that happened today, I think you know who sent me.'

'Still need to hear you say it, son.'

'Elizabeth Kirk.'

'Of course . . . of course it was.' There was resignation in the voice, drowned out as the buzzer release sounded. 'Come on up.'

FOURTEEN

Bruce Bull took a deep breath as Nizar Mansour was brought into the small, bare interview room.

He had not known what to expect. How could he? He knew nothing of the man beyond the name he'd given, the fact he had admitted to placing the bomb on Flight PA16 and that at some point in the last few hours the man with whom Mansour lived had been murdered.

Still, it was natural to make assumptions. And so somewhere in the back of Bull's mind he had been expecting . . . what?

Something more, he admitted to himself. *Something more.*

The single most significant terrorist attack in British history. Five hundred and thirty-four deaths. Carried out – if Mansour's confession was accurate – by a man whose most significant feature was how very ordinary he looked.

Bull knew all the clichés about books and covers. But he also knew other clichés, too. Ones about going with his gut. And right now his gut was not quite buying this.

Mansour had been escorted into the room by a stocky police constable. A rugby player, by the look of him. There were a few in every station, Bull knew. A hard sport, it helped with the more physical aspects of the job.

And shoulders that wide helped keep suspects in check.

You run, you run through me, he thought. *That's the idea.*

It was an unnecessary message to sell to Mansour. He would not be running anywhere. After a lifetime as an investigator, Bull could tell a broken man at a glance.

Which only fuelled his uncertainty.

He gestured to the constable to remove Mansour's cuffs. The man did as instructed, then positioned himself between Mansour and the door.

'Outside, please,' Bull instructed.

The constable looked confused.

'Sir? Are you . . .'

'I'm sure,' Bull interrupted. 'Mr Mansour and I are going to chat alone.'

Bull's eyes remained on Mansour as the officer did as ordered. They stayed there, too, as Bull reached out and pressed the record button on the sleek audio device that sat on the small table between them. A discreet replacement for the analogue tape decks Bull had been using for decades. Progress of sorts, he figured.

The fixed, unbroken stare was a practised technique. Designed to show the suspect who was in charge. That he could not be intimidated. It was wasted on Mansour. He hadn't lifted his head once to meet Bull's eyes.

It was, like so much else, confusing.

Why the hell confess? Bull found himself thinking, and not for the first time. *Why confess and then pull this shit?*

Bull reached out to a more discreet switch, activating yet more modern equipment: the interview room's video recording system. From that moment, everything that occurred within the room would be recorded both visually and audibly.

Still Bull had not blinked.

'Nizar, you understand that I am about to ask you some questions about what happened today. From what I've been told about your conduct earlier I have no doubt that you speak and understand the English language. Is that correct?'

There was no response.

Bull continued.

'Because before we begin I need you to confirm for me that you know you're entitled to have a lawyer to advise you during this interview? You *have* been told that, haven't you?'

Bull looked carefully at Mansour as he spoke. It was essential to show that the suspect understood, because what Mansour said in reply could be all important. The last thing Bull wanted was for some smart-arse lawyer in a horsehair wig to suppress that evidence within a maze of technicalities.

Mansour looked up for just a moment, meeting Bull's eyes. It was a little more than an instant, but it was enough.

This guy understands everything.

'If you could please reply to my request verbally that would be a great help. So that the tape can record your answer.'

Mansour looked up again.

'I understand.' His voice was low and dry. His accent was heavy, but his use of English seemed effortless. 'And I want no lawyer, because I will answer no questions.'

Bull nodded in response. It was more than he had expected. The words used could seem arrogant – belligerent, even – but Mansour's empty tone said otherwise.

There's no fight left in him, Bull thought.

'In that case, I need to give you the following warning before we begin. It's called a caution and it's something that we have to say – legally – before every interview. And I have to make sure you have understood it. OK?'

Mansour indicated his assent. Clear enough that the camera would have seen it. It allowed Bull to continue.

Mansour looked utterly disinterested as Bull recited the legal requirements. Was it arrogance? Acceptance of his fate? Or the reaction of a man who had already lost everything? Bull paused when he had finished to await Mansour's acknowledgement.

'I understand. And I will say nothing more.'

Bull ignored the final statement.

'OK, well, let's just make sure that we're all clear about why we're here. As you know, at four p.m. this afternoon, Flight PA16 – Pan-Atlantic Airlines from London Heathrow to New York JFK – was destroyed as the result of a bomb being planted upon the plane. What do you know about that?'

Bull didn't expect a response. His question had been intentionally broad. Designed for the record. Those that followed would be more specific. Harder for Mansour to ignore.

He moved on to his first real question.

'A little before eleven p.m. this evening, you entered this building – for the purposes of the tape, we are in Stoke Newington Police Station – and you informed the officers at the front desk that you had planted the bomb that destroyed Flight PA16. What did you mean by that?'

Mansour did not move a muscle.

'Is what you said true, Nizar? Did you plant a bomb on that plane?'

Nothing. Not even a flicker.

'Why did you say that you did, Nizar? If you're not saying that now?'

Bull waited a beat before continuing. He took a few moments to observe Mansour's breathing. It was short and shallow. The man was keeping himself under control; the sign of someone who had made a decision to which he intended to stick.

A resolve Bull was determined to test.

'OK. Then let's assume for a moment that you were telling

the truth. Let's assume you put the bomb on the plane. Where did you get the bomb?'

Nothing.

'It's not like you can pop down to Tesco and pick up military-grade Semtex, is it? So where'd you get it?'

No answer. No change.

'Did you make it yourself?'

Nothing.

'Did someone make it for you?'

It was as if Mansour was not even hearing the words.

'Was it your roommate then? The dead guy? Did he make the bomb?'

Mansour did not let out a sound, but his body betrayed him. He visibly winced at the mention of the other man.

Bull filed the reaction mentally. They would be circling back to that one . . .

He continued.

'So either you made that bomb, or your dead pal did.' The repeated mention did not get the same response; this time Mansour held himself together. 'Or someone else?'

Mansour's eyes stayed down. His body still.

'And you're not telling me where you got the Semtex?'

Bull didn't even wait for an answer.

'OK. Let's move on a little, then. You've got the bomb. But how did you get it on the plane?'

The questions were coming thick and fast. Designed both to irritate and to leave Mansour with little opportunity to think. And the last one had caused an almost imperceptible shake of Mansour's head.

Bull was getting somewhere.

I might not break you. But I'll sure as hell get under your skin.

'What was it, Nizar?' he continued. 'Did you send someone on with the bag? Did some other poor sod have to sacrifice himself for the cause?'

Mansour took a deep breath, seeming to realise that his head had been shaking. The movement stopped.

'That's it, isn't it? You've got a bunch of young believers involved in all this, to do your dying for you. Someone on the plane with a bomb. So what does that make you, Nizar? The holy leader? The mini-Ayatollah? Sending these kids out to die while you're safe at home, ready to walk in here and take the credit? Is that what this is? Is this you making yourself a hero to your people? Off the backs of gullible idiots willing to die for you? Like that poor sod at your house with his throat slit.'

His reaction was more obvious this time. Almost a physical recoil. Bull could see the effort it was taking for Mansour to keep himself in check. It was causing his hands to shake.

Bull suspected what had caused the changed reaction. The dead man at Mansour's address. He was on the right track.

Bull opened his mouth to continue. He was interrupted by a knock on the interview room door.

The stocky officer opened the door before Bull could respond to the knock.

'Guv? A word?'

Bull hesitated. He did not welcome the interruption, but the look on the man's face said that he should listen.

'One second, Nizar.'

He climbed to his feet and took the two short steps to the door.

'What is it?' Bull spoke as quietly as he could, his face uncomfortably close to the other man's wide features.

'It's the Americans, guv.' The voice was even quieter than Bull's. 'They're here.'

'Bollocks.' Bull looked towards Mansour, then back to the constable. 'How long?'

'They've just been let through into the car park.'

'How long does that give me?'

'Depends how long the sarge can slow them down on the way in. Few minutes at least.'

'Tell Sergeant Langley to stretch that as much as he can.' Bull slapped the officer's upper arm as he spoke, a friendly indication to get to it. 'And thanks.'

Bull retook his seat, his mind now racing.

He had known that the US Secret Service would find out about Mansour sooner or later. Sooner, he had expected; they seemed to know everything else. And so he had known that he would not get the man to himself for very long.

But what he had *not* expected was for Mansour to raise so many doubts in his mind. So many questions. Doubts that the Secret Service were unlikely to share.

It left Bull very little time. He had to change tactics.

'You heard what was said just then, Nizar. The US Secret Service are here. You know what that means?'

Mansour did not answer, but his breathing became faster.

'It means that we're about to be joined by highly trained, highly motivated special agents who think you killed a huge number of their fellow citizens.'

The breathing speed increased again.

'Agents who outrank me, Nizar. From a country that can pretty much do whatever the hell it wants, anywhere in the world. Do you understand what I'm saying?'

Mansour said nothing. Instead he took a long, slow breath.

After a moment of panic, he seemed to be regaining control. Bull could not understand why.

'Do you not follow what I'm telling you, Nizar? If you don't cooperate with me, I can't protect you from them.'

'It sounds that you can't protect me whatever I do.'

Bull opened his mouth to respond, but stopped himself. Mansour had called the situation in one. There really *was* nothing Bull could do to protect him. Not from the Secret Service.

'Where are you from, Nizar?' Bull changed the subject again. With the clock against him, he was scrambling for the connection. 'Originally?'

No answer.

'It's a Syrian name, isn't it? Nizar Mansour?'

No response at all.

'So you're from Syria?'

Nothing. Bull could feel his anxiety increasing. They had no more than minutes.

'When did you arrive in this country?'

Nothing.

'*Why* did you come to the UK? Were you fleeing the war? Or did you come here intending to commit offences of terrorism?'

Again, nothing.

Bull paused. He was trying to give no indication of his growing frustration, but his constant glances at his watch were unmistakable. He knew that, and yet he could not stop himself.

He needed a result, and he needed it fast. And there was only one thing Mansour had reacted to so far.

'Who was the man we found dead at your home, Nizar?'

Mansour looked up. Only for a moment, but quickly enough and for long enough that Bull saw the pain flit across in his eyes.

Got you.

'His name was Bilal Essa, right?'

The shake of Mansour's head was almost imperceptible. Almost.

'OK. Then what *was* his name, Nizar?'

This time the shake was more obvious. Tears were beginning to fill Mansour's eyes, tracing down the premature wrinkles that marked his sun-damaged face.

'Was he a part of this, Nizar? Did he plant the bomb with you?'

'He did . . .'

Mansour's voice broke as he tried to answer. When he could not finish his own words, he just shook his head, peppering the table with his tears.

'Did he use his access as a baggage handler in Heathrow Airport to plant the bomb for you? Because that's what he was, wasn't it? He was a baggage handler at Heathrow, for Pan-Atlantic Airlines.'

'He did . . . he did nothing.' This time Mansour found the words, his voice stronger but strained with emotion. 'He was nothing to do with any of this. NOTHING!'

'Then who was he?' Bull demanded, his own voice rising. 'Did you kill him?'

'HE WAS MY BROTHER!'

The roar was primal, screamed towards Bull as Mansour half-rose to his feet. As if he was physically discharging any remaining denial of his brother's fate, he remained on his feet afterwards, doubled over in pain.

Bull sat back into his seat in silence and watched as Mansour began to sob.

For Bull the new information had been unexpected, but not as unexpected as Mansour's change of demeanour.

None of this is how it should be, he thought. *None of this fits the template. This is . . . it's just not what terrorists do.*

The door to the interview room opened, a response to Mansour's shout. The wide-shouldered officer was there, ready to come to Bull's aid in case of violence.

There would be none.

Bull dismissed the interruption with a discreet shake of his head and his hand. With the door closed, he turned his eyes back to Mansour, now back in his seat and still crying. Bull moved forward again, placing his fingertips gently on the table.

'Is there something you need to tell me?' Bull kept his voice gentle. Quiet. 'Because this is all looking wrong to me. Your brother's death. The way you came to be here. Even your confession. There's more to this, Nizar. Tell me what it is.'

Mansour didn't answer, but this time his silence was neither obstinate nor absolute.

It's only a matter of time. I just need to ask the right questions.

'I know you didn't kill your brother.' Bull believed what he was saying. He might not know very much, but he was confident of at least that. 'Tell me who *did* kill him and maybe I can help you.'

Mansour looked up, as if seeing Bull for the first time.

'Tell me,' Bull continued. 'If you tell me, I can help you.'

'No one can help me now,' Mansour growled. His voice was lower. Guttural, almost. And it sounded certain. 'No one.'

'*I* can, Nizar.' Bull was determined to push his breakthrough. 'Whatever happened with your brother – and whatever happened with the plane – I *can* help you. All you have to do is tell me. Tell me who killed your brother and why.'

Perhaps if he had been given more time then Bull would have gained Mansour's trust. Just a few more minutes. Seconds even. Because he felt in that instant that they were close. That Mansour was about to tell him what he needed to know. That Mansour would take his offer of protection.

But Bull would never have those extra seconds.

The door to the interview room was opened by the constable, who then stepped back without a word. The figure that replaced him was taller than the doorway itself. The newcomer was forced to duck as he stepped inside.

Bull looked up from his seat.

'Who the hell are you?' he demanded as he rose to his feet. He needed the man to think the interruption was unexpected.

'United States Secret Service, sir.'

Bull hated to admit it but he was impressed by the sheer size and presence of the newcomer. A matinee idol in the body of a WWE wrestler. All in a sharp, perfectly fitted black suit.

'I can tell *what* you are.' Bull gave no hint that he was now in the subordinate role. 'I asked *who* you are?'

'Apologies, Mr Bull. I should have introduced myself.'

The agent stepped forward, close to Mansour.

'I'm Special Agent Romeo Meyer.'

FIFTEEN

Tom Quilty was sixty-four years old and had been for a week. Both these facts came from Quilty's official file. Had Dempsey been guessing, he would have added around fifteen years to that number.

The apartment was spaciously decorated. A minimalist approach that was either a clever way to hide a lack of funds for furnishing, or a foolish way to spend far too much on far too little.

Dempsey had seen enough in Quilty's file to know which one it was. A lifetime in intelligence was no path to riches, and whatever savings Quilty had managed to build up had long since been eaten away on medical bills.

At Quilty's indication, Dempsey took a seat on the living room's steel-framed leather sofa. It immediately threatened to buckle under his weight; a sure sign it had not come from an expensive SoHo showroom. He moved slowly and positioned himself carefully to ensure that the two-seater survived its ordeal. Only then did he turn his attention back to his host, as Quilty was lowering himself into a much older, more worn but no doubt sturdier armchair.

It took a few moments for Quilty to complete his descent, then a few more as he struggled to regain his breath from the effort. Finally he reached out to the oxygen tank that was positioned at the chair's right-hand side. Placing the attached soft plastic mask so that it covered his mouth and nose, he spent the next minute or two breathing noisily.

'So are you gonna tell me why you're here, son?' Quilty finally asked, briefly pulling the mask away from his face and beating Dempsey to the first question. He was taking the lead, Dempsey realised. A show of seniority. The younger man respected it with a smile.

It's not like he hasn't earned it.

'Sir, I'm—'

'Tom, son. Like I told you.'

'I'm sorry. Tom. I'm here because of what happened earlier today. The bombing of Flight PA16 and the death of Dale Victor.'

Quilty said nothing as he took another hit of oxygen.

'Elizabeth Kirk's worried about you. She thinks that after what happened to Victor, that you might have made yourself a target.'

'She does, does she?'

'She does, yeah. And judging from what you said on the intercom – about spooks – it doesn't look like she's alone in that, does it?'

'You know the worst thing about getting old, son?' The mention of a threat seemed to briefly energise Quilty. 'About getting sick? It's the underestimation. Sure, I'm . . . I'm no use to anyone in the field any more. And they . . . they want analysts who can . . . who can breathe for themselves. I get that. But putting those . . . those . . . those amateurs out there . . . and . . . and expecting me not . . . not . . . not to make them? Assholes who wouldn't know covert . . . surveillance from a kick in . . . in the balls? Do that to a man with *my* history? That's just . . . just . . . it's a goddamned insult.'

Quilty's anger was evident. It was also destructive. The short rant was too much for him; his words were increasingly pained as he spat them out, desperate to finish before his need for breath defeated him. Only sheer force of will saw him to the end.

He slumped backwards into his seat when he was done, exhausted and fumbling for the oxygen mask that had dropped from his hands as he spoke.

Dempsey rose from his seat, picked up the mask from where it had fallen and moved to place it over Quilty's mouth and nose. Halfway there Dempsey rethought the instinctive action; from what Elizabeth Kirk had told him, Quilty might see it as an insult.

Instead he placed the mask in Quilty's hand and turned his attention to the gas bottle, increasing the airflow by twenty per cent. Then, while Quilty recovered, he moved to the open-plan kitchen area behind Quilty's seat, filled a chipped highball glass with water from the oversized but under-stocked refrigerator and brought it back to the older man's lips.

Quilty drank painfully as Dempsey retook his seat. He barely managed two fingers of the cold liquid, but it seemed to do the trick.

Dempsey waited a few more seconds, but the time had come for him to take back control.

'I need you to keep calm about all this,' he said. 'Getting worked up and your lungs giving out isn't going to help either us, OK?'

Quilty nodded.

'Now tell me about the spooks. What have you seen?'

'Just what I said. Couple . . . of them. Grey Sedan, parked in . . . in different spots up and down . . . the road. Arrogant shits didn't . . . didn't even have the . . . the respect to change cars.'

'How long?'

'Four days.'

Dempsey nodded. After reading Quilty's file, he had no doubt in the man's ability to spot a tail. Even one Dempsey had missed himself. It looked like Kirk's worst fears had come true; Quilty had put himself on someone's radar.

But who? And did they have a connection to President John Knowles?

Quilty took another hit of oxygen. The increased flow seemed to be helping.

'Sorry . . . about this,' Quilty gasped out. 'Emphysema. That's what you get . . . from a forty-a-day habit.'

Another intake of oxygen.

'But I blame . . . the job . . . for that. Never touched the things . . . before . . . Afghan . . . Afghanistan.'

'Your file says you were an analyst first, then you moved into the field during the Russian–Afghan war.'

'On and off. I did my time as a . . . as a field . . . operative. But mainly I was an analyst. Specialised in . . . in . . . following the money.'

'So Elizabeth Kirk said. She said you knew more about what went on in Afghanistan than any man born west of Zaranj.'

'For a time, yeah. That was true.'

'And now?'

'Some contacts, son . . . some contacts you keep . . . you keep for life. People trust me. Men I've . . . fought with. Suffered with. Not much I can do for them any more, but . . . but sometimes . . .'

Quilty's voice was growing weaker with every word, but Dempsey already understood. He placed a hand on Quilty's knee, passed him his water glass and smiled. He needed no more explanation.

Dempsey waited for him to recover, but he wasn't sure how much Quilty had left in him; it was time to get to the point.

'Tell me about the president, Tom. Dale Victor thought he had something damaging on Knowles. Tell me what it was.'

Quilty did not answer immediately. He held Dempsey's gaze, his breathing growing deeper through the mask. Dempsey could see his guard was back up. A dangerous subject had been raised, and Quilty was ready to defend himself.

'You said . . . you said Elizabeth had sent you.'

'She did.'

'Then she wouldn't have sent you blind, son. You want what I . . . what I know, you tell me what you know first.'

Dempsey nodded. It was a fair request.

'OK. Elizabeth told me that you contacted her shortly before John Knowles' inauguration. That you'd heard rumours about his time in Afghanistan, when he was leading SEAL Team Six.'

'What . . . what type of rumours? I told her a lot more . . . a lot more . . . than that.'

'She said it related to his Medal of Honor. Well, to the operation where he earned it.'

'And what do you . . . know about that?'

'Everyone knows the story, Tom. Knowles' unit was heading back to base outside of Jalalabad after a mission in a border village. Knowles, half his team and two rescued hostages were in the front Black Hawk, the rest of his team and two more hostages in the second. Halfway back, the rear chopper was shot down. Knowles ordered his pilot to turn and go back, to look for survivors.

'When they did, they found the burning wreckage and could see that at least some of the men inside it were alive. But the fighters who'd shot it down were already heading straight for it. So Knowles' pilot lay down fire and took out a whole bunch, but then their chopper was hit, too, and was forced to land, with a small army still heading their way.

'Knowles led a thirty-minute rear-guard against wave after wave of Afghan fighters, all while he herded his injured team across to the other chopper, where three of the guys were too badly injured to move themselves. And so Knowles and his chief petty officer went for them. They ran into heavy fire to rescue them and physically carried each one of them over a hundred yards to cover. The chief died saving those men. And Knowles came close, taking three hits in the process.

'But he survives. Support arrives and the team is extracted. Knowles is invalided out of the service but wins the Medal of Honor. He becomes the poster boy hero of the whole War on Terror and begins a meteoric political career. Hence now it's President Knowles to the likes of us.'

'And that's all Elizabeth told you, is it?' Quilty's tone dripped with cynicism when he finally spoke. 'Because that sounds a lot . . . a lot . . . like a Google search, son.'

Dempsey smiled. The man was a veteran of the CIA, the most active, effective covert intelligence service on the planet. He was giving nothing away for free.

Which meant that *Dempsey* had to.

'You know she told me more, Tom. The stuff that hasn't found its way to Wikipedia.'

'Tell me what it is.'

'She told me that every word of what I just said is true. That everything we know about Knowles the hero is true. But she also told me that not everyone is a good guy the whole time.'

Quilty smiled, to Dempsey's relief. What the older man was hearing was finally easing his caution.

Dempsey continued.

'Elizabeth told me that a man had contacted you, shortly before Knowles' inauguration. And that he told you the true nature of the mission Knowles' unit had been on. The official line was they'd gone to the village – Tootkai, right? – to rescue four American hostages, military advisors, being held by a residual faction of the Taliban.'

'That's what we . . . what we were told, yes.'

'But your informant said there was more. He said that Knowles and his team had also been ordered to find a mujahideen leader who was supposed to be there. And that when they didn't find him, and the villagers wouldn't give up any information, Knowles ordered his men to torture and rape and kill indiscriminately, to force their cooperation. Scores of men, women and children, maimed, raped, killed. In other words, the mission that made Knowles a hero – the very basis of his presidency – was a war crime. And instead of sitting in the White House, he and his unit should be rotting in a cell. Maybe even on death row.'

Dempsey stopped speaking. He had said enough; if this much information did not convince Quilty that he had Elizabeth Kirk's trust, nothing would.

For a few moments there was nothing but the sound of pained breathing.

'That's right,' Quilty finally replied. He pulled as hard as he could manage on his oxygen supply before continuing. 'My contact said that the rescue . . . the . . . rescue was a cover. So they could find . . . the Taliban chieftain.'

Quilty paused for breath and a sip of water.

'When he wasn't found . . . as you say, things took a . . . a bad turn. Twenty-three dead. Over . . . over a hundred more . . . injured. And . . . and . . . two of the American . . . hostages killed, too. When they . . . they ob- . . . jected.'

'What?' The final claim was new to Dempsey; Kirk had not mentioned the murder of Americans. 'Are you sure?'

'No. I'm not . . . not sure of any . . . any of this. But it's . . . it's what my . . . source told me. There were . . . six . . . hostages, not . . . not four. Two of them . . . two . . . stood up to . . . to Knowles. They were . . . were killed for it.'

Dempsey said nothing. He thought that Kirk had told him everything. Perhaps she had. At least everything she knew.

'My source . . . my source said that . . . it was this . . . what happened in Tootkai . . . that brought the full . . . the full Afghan force out. Why they . . . why they shot down the Hawks.'

Dempsey sat in silence as Quilty's strained account came to an end. A thousand thoughts ran through his mind. But only one question.

'Tom, do you actually believe any of this?'

Quilty did not hesitate.

'Back then? No. No, I didn't. My source . . . my source wasn't an eye- . . . witness. He was telling . . . telling me what he'd heard. Enough for me . . . for someone . . . to have to investigate. But when I did . . . when I did more . . . digging . . . none of my other contacts . . . were telling this . . . this story. So I doubted it.'

'But you still took it to Elizabeth?'

'Elizabeth was my . . . my superior. I thought she . . . she needed to know . . . no matter . . . no matter how unlikely.'

Quilty's voice was weakening again. Dempsey gave him a few moments to regain his breath.

'Elizabeth didn't believe . . . didn't believe it either. Not for a . . . moment. She went to Knowles with it. She didn't go into . . . into any . . . any detail with . . . with Knowles, she told me. Just very . . . bare bones. And she didn't name me as . . . as her source.

'Elizabeth told me that Knowles . . . Knowles laughed it off. Exactly . . . like we both . . . both thought he would. Didn't even . . . even want to know any more . . . detail. Which put an end . . . to it . . . for us. But then . . . a short . . . short time later . . . Elizabeth was . . . was removed from her . . . position and moved to . . . to . . . to the ISB. Without . . . any . . . explanation.'

Quilty was visibly tiring now. Dempsey could see he wouldn't get much more from him today.

'Elizabeth told me that since that day she has never had another conversation with President Knowles,' Dempsey said.

'She would know that . . . better than me. All I can say is . . . Elizabeth was moved out of Knowles' . . . Knowles' circle very . . . very quickly. No more . . . no more direct access. That's what made me . . . wonder if there was some truth to it.'

Dempsey nodded. It was exactly as Elizabeth Kirk had described. But that had been where her story had stopped. She had sent Dempsey here to find out if Tom knew anything more.

'Did you ever investigate any further?'

'Investigate?' Quilty laughed. A horrible, hacking expression of humour. 'Son, I'm in no state to be . . . to be investigating . . . anything. I was already getting . . . getting sick when it all happened. But I made a few more . . . a few more . . . enquiries, yes.'

'And?'

'And nothing. Still . . . only that one . . . only that one

contact had heard about any of this. But then . . . then . . . Dale Victor.'

The mention of Victor brought Dempsey to his next question.

'What about Victor? What does he have to do with any of this?'

'I . . . I . . . spoke . . . I spoke to . . .'

Quilty was trailing off. Dempsey had to speed this up.

'You spoke to Victor?'

'I spoke to someone who . . . who worked for him. They . . . they contacted me. Maybe . . . one month . . . ago. Asking questions about that . . . mission.'

'How did they know to contact you?'

'I . . . I don't know. But Victor was . . . a rich man. Mega bucks. That kind of money . . . buys anything. Including . . . intelligence. Who knows how . . . they would have got wind . . . of anything. But once they knew . . . the story was from Afghanistan . . . they could have found out . . . there were only five . . . five agents operating there. One of them . . . was me.'

Dempsey nodded. That made sense.

It was a bloody fishing expedition.

'So what did you tell them?'

'Nothing they didn't . . . already know.'

'So it's possible Victor didn't know any details,' Dempsey concluded. 'Unless they found the information elsewhere?'

'I . . . doubt it. My source is the only one . . . only one I know of,' Quilty wheezed. 'And he wouldn't say . . . anything without talking . . . to me first.'

'Which would mean that Victor was killed for it anyway, just in case.'

'It . . . it looks that way. And now . . . they're watching me.'

'Yes,' Dempsey agreed, speaking almost to himself. 'Which I guess brings me back to why I'm here.'

Quilty looked Dempsey in the eye and gave a weak, weary smile.

'To tell me I'm . . . I'm in danger? I think we've . . . covered that . . . son.'

'Whoever it is out there watching you, Tom. Whoever it is they work for—'

'John Knowles,' Quilty interrupted. 'Let's not . . . let's not be . . . delicate about it now.'

'OK, for now let's say that,' Dempsey agreed. 'Knowles was willing to kill over five hundred innocent people to get to Victor. To keep what he knew hidden. If he'll do that, he'll sure as hell come for you.'

'And yet four . . . days . . . later and I'm . . . I'm still alive. What does . . . what does that . . . tell you?'

Dempsey paused. Thought for a moment.

'They're not sure you're the source.'

'Exactly. They . . . they must have . . . the same suspects . . . the other four agents . . . I'm . . . I'm just one of . . . them.'

'And you think that makes you safe? There was enough to point them towards you, Tom. What if they find the proof it *was* you?'

'If they . . . get to that . . . to that point, let . . . them . . . come.'

'Tom, I—'

'Do I look . . . look like . . . a man with lots . . . to . . . lose, son? They come for me . . . at least I . . . at least I get to go . . . to go down with a . . . fight. I'm looking . . . looking forward to seeing the amateurs . . . try. They'll be in for a few . . . for a few surprises . . . trust me.'

'But . . .'

'But nothing. Now listen to . . . to me. All that matters now is my . . . my contact. The one who knows . . . the truth . . . about this. If they confirm my . . . my involvement . . . they'll start looking for him. That's . . . that's who you need . . . to protect. And that's . . . that's who can help . . . you find the truth.'

'You'd be willing to share your source?'

Dempsey was relieved the information was being offered up. It was one of the other reasons Kirk had sent him here. To find a way back to the original story.

'Jangi Shah. And his . . . adopted last name is . . . Karzai.'

'From the Karz in Kandahar?' Dempsey suggested

'You know Afghanistan?'

'I've spent some time there,' Dempsey replied. Enough to know that Afghans did not use surnames in the way the West would understand, and instead relied upon tribal affiliation. It made identification difficult.

'Then you'll know that . . . Jangi . . . Jangi has plenty of places . . . places to hide. At least for . . . for now. And if he . . . if he wants to stay hidden then . . . then they will never . . . find him.'

'Then how will *I* find him?' Dempsey asked.

Quilty smiled.

'That's where I come in.'

SIXTEEN

Dempsey had his phone to his ear before he had left the building. Even at the late hour, his call was answered on only the second ring.

'Agent Dempsey.' Henry Garrett's voice came through clearly. 'How can I help?'

Henry was the logistical assistant to the Director of the ISB, Elizabeth Kirk. Or at least that was his job title. In reality, his responsibilities went far beyond that. So far, Dempsey had found that there was nothing Henry could not arrange. And almost nothing he did not know.

It was almost a cliché. If you want something done, you call Henry.

'I need a protection detail placed on a potential witness.'

'You mean Thomas Quilty, sir?'

Dempsey was not surprised by the question.

'I do. You have the address, I imagine.'

'I do, sir. Is the detail to be inside or out, sir?'

'Outside,' Dempsey replied. 'And discreet. If Quilty knows I've put a team on him he's going to be pissed.'

'Understood. I'll have men there within the hour.'

'Thanks, Henry. I'll stay outside until they get here.'

'As you wish, Agent Dempsey.'

The line went dead, and Dempsey took a look at his watch. An hour. He could live with that.

*

The apartment across the street from Quilty's had turned out to be empty. It was dark and it was unfurnished, but it was ideal for observing their target unseen. And it beat the hell out of a cramped Sedan.

'Who do you think he is?'

The question came from the man standing away from the window. Short and overweight, he wheezed as he spoke. The sedentary nature of his job did his health no favours.

'No clue,' his companion replied, holding a pair of non-glare digital binoculars. They gave him a clear view of the biker who had taken up sentry duty outside of Quilty's building. 'But if he's here looking out for Quilty then maybe we've got the right guy.'

'Maybe. Should we call it in?'

'Homework first. Take a few close-ups and send them over. They can get an ID on this guy, work out why he's here.'

'OK.' The shorter man moved closer to the window, a high-powered surveillance camera in hand. 'If Quilty *is* the one they're looking for, what do you think's gonna happen?'

'Who knows,' the second man replied. 'But whatever it is, I doubt it ends well for the old guy.'

His accomplice nodded. There was nothing more to say. He raised the camera to his eye and zoomed in on the biker's face.

SEVENTEEN

Nizar Mansour had not needed to look up. The voice had been familiar enough, but he was sure he would be able to recognise the sheer physical presence. It was as if the man had some sort of gravitational pull.

It had left no room for doubt. Even before the agent had used his name.

Romeo.

In the hours since he had entered the police station Mansour had thought repeatedly of coming face to face with the man who had ordered his brother's murder. In his grief, he had envisaged violence. He had envisaged blood. He had envisaged death.

What he had *not* envisaged was the sheer terror that had overtaken him. Or the effect it had upon his exhausted body and his battered soul.

It had paralysed him. Unable to move. Unable to speak. And, at first, unable even to think.

As the fear gripped him – as the hopelessness of his position sank in – Mansour's mind spun in every direction. He thought about DCI Bruce Bull, who had stepped outside the interview room with Romeo.

He'd been so close to trusting Bull. Now he didn't know what to think. Bull had *seemed* genuine. He had *seemed* like he wanted to help. That perhaps he could see there was more to this than met the eye. But now he was outside with Romeo. Mansour had no idea what they were discussing. Fuelled by fear and paranoia, he imagined their conversation. Saw them collaborating against him.

Panic was beginning to take hold, making the room spin. It was accompanied by the sound of static, pitched at an ear-piercing level. It was all-pervading, distracting Mansour as he struggled to regain control.

He could feel his breath coming shallow and fast, his heart racing wildly. There was no way out of this. And soon he would be trapped in this room with the man responsible for all of this. With his brother's killer.

*

'It's been agreed with your superiors that I should join this interview, Bull. By all means check.'

Bull had taken an instant dislike to Special Agent Romeo Meyer. He realised that. And he did not have to wonder why. It was Meyer's tone. An unbearable combination of smug and condescending authority.

But it was not his dislike that was now driving Bull; he would not be so unprofessional for that alone. No. There was something else. Something he just could not quite place. And while there was little he could ultimately do – he knew he would have to allow Meyer into the room in the end – he was determined to be as difficult as hell for as long as he could.

'I don't doubt they've agreed,' he answered. '*My* lot will do whatever *your* lot tell them. But right now, having you in that room is going to hinder the progress of this interview.'

Bull indicated towards the closed door of the interview room as they spoke.

'I've managed to build a rapport with this guy and I think he's close to trusting me. You insist on sitting in there with us, we're gonna have to start that from scratch. And there's no guarantee he'll take to you as he has to me.'

'Are you listening to yourself, Bull?' Meyer's tone was now a mix of mockery and anger. 'You've built a rapport? With a Muslim terrorist who has murdered more than five hundred people? Including a prospective presidential candidate who was weeks from being under the protection of my agency?'

'You don't know any of that,' Bull replied, his own temper beginning to show. 'You don't know he's an Islamic terrorist. And you sure as hell can't say that he murdered anyone.'

'Can't I? The piece of shit confessed. What the hell other conclusion do you want me to reach?'

'He confessed to the physical act of putting that bomb on the plane. That's all we know at the moment. That doesn't automatically make him a terrorist. It doesn't automatically make him a murderer. I don't know about you but my job is to investigate. *Not* to jump to the most obvious conclusion because it suits me. And it's Detective Chief Inspector Bull, by the way.'

'Here we go.' There was no longer any genuine anger in Meyer's voice. It had been replaced by the same condescending, arrogant tone he had begun with. 'This pathetic country. No wonder you've declined so far in the world that you're no more than a punchline. Even your law enforcement, filled with liberal ass-kissers who won't say it like it is 'cos the truth might upset someone.'

'Who the hell do you think you are?' Bull demanded. 'What gives you the right—'

'You've got a fucking Muslim who surrenders himself,' Meyer continued, ignoring Bull's interruption, 'who confesses to the single worst terrorist attack in this sad little island's long,

long history of being a victim. And what do your police do? They send one of *you* to deal with it. Is *that* a coincidence? Or is it so no one can cry "unfair" or "racism"? It's fucking pathetic, that's what it is.'

'"One of you"?' Bull could feel his heart rate spike. 'You mean "black", right? You're suggesting I've been put on this case because I'm a black man?'

'Hey, if the jazz hands fit.'

For an instant Bull almost forgot where he was. He almost forgot *who* he was. And he almost forgot that the man insulting him was at least twenty-five years younger and a whole lot larger.

Bull almost forgot all of this as he imagined himself swinging for Meyer. One good hit with everything he had, to wipe the self-satisfied, racist grin from that obnoxious face.

Almost.

Fortunately for Bull, his professionalism beat his anger. He took a deep breath, his eyes remaining fixed on Meyer's.

'I'm gonna ignore what you said there, Agent Meyer,' he finally said, breaking the few seconds of charged silence that had passed between them. 'For now, anyway. I'm warning you, though, any more of—'

'Save your warnings for someone who gives a fuck,' Meyer interrupted. 'I'm stepping inside that room and I'm speaking to this piece of shit. And I'll show you how the US Secret Service deals with terrorist scum. You got that?'

Meyer did not wait for a response. He was moving before he had finished speaking, pushing his way past the DCI and striding through the door of the interview room.

It took Bull a few seconds to react as Meyer disappeared through the door. He was a senior officer in one of his country's most important police units. He was not used to being disregarded. To being ignored.

As the momentary shock passed, Bull rushed after him. He was taking no chances. Meyer had made no explicit threat of injury to Mansour, but the man's very being bristled with violent possibilities.

Bull reached the doorway and was met by the sight of Meyer looming over the prisoner. For a moment, he thought the worst.

'GET AWAY FROM THAT MAN!'

Meyer slowly turned his head at the shout, but his body remained fixed. Close – too close – to Mansour's seat. His massive frame entirely obscuring the prisoner from Bull's view.

'Every word and every action in this room is being recorded.' Bull announced. 'You lay a hand on my prisoner and there *will* be an international incident.'

Meyer's smile disappeared as he instinctively glanced at the corners of the room. He could not miss the video lens looking right back at him from high on the wall, Bull knew. Or the steady light that indicated it was still recording.

Meyer stepped back, away from Mansour and closer to Bull.

'What kind of a fucking game do you think you're playing here, Bull?' he hissed, low enough to avoid the tape.

'I'm protecting an unconvicted man from mistreatment and God knows what else at *your* hands, Special Agent Meyer.' Bull's voice was raised. This was no longer a conversation. He wanted the mic to hear everything. 'And having made your intentions here clear, I want you out of this room.'

'Or what, old man? An "international incident"? You really think your shitty little island is up to that?'

'Is that what this is, now?' Bull asked. 'My dad's bigger than your dad?'

'My dad's always bigger,' Meyer smirked. 'Not that he needs to be this time. Because we both know how this ends. You ask this garbage your questions, he'll say nothing, and when you're done you'll have to bail him. And when you do, I pick him up outside. Whatever happens, he ends up with me. You're only delaying the inevitable.'

'Nothing's ever inevitable. Live a little longer and you'll realise that. And until you do, piss off out of this room, 'cos you're in my way.'

'I'm going nowhere.' Meyer raised his voice for the tape. 'Like I said, your superiors have authorised the involvement of the US Secret Service. I *will* be in this interview.'

'Over my dead body.'

Cold, hard anger flashed across Meyer's face. He raised himself to his full, imposing height. His shoulders now ramrod straight, his sheer width was as impossible to ignore.

When he spoke, Meyer's voice was calm, low and cold. He no longer seemed concerned about being recorded.

'Over your dead body? Do I really need to go *that* far?'

The words should have been chilling, but they were lost on Bull. Instead his full attention was now on Nizar Mansour.

For the first time he had a clear view of the effect Special Agent Romeo Meyer was having on his prisoner: Mansour had pulled himself as far from Meyer as his restraints would allow, the metal tearing at his skin through the strain. His eyes were fixed on the towering agent, wide with fear.

Minutes earlier, before Bull had left the room, the man had seemed ready to cooperate. Ready to talk. Now he looked terrified. Bull could even see urine puddled beneath his seat.

But why? Granted Romeo was an intimidating figure, but that wasn't enough to explain such a powerful reaction.

'Why is he so afraid of you?' Bull's words were soft and slow. As much to himself as to Meyer.

'The Secret Service has that effect on terrorists,' Meyer replied. The arrogance was back. Dripping from every word. 'Shame the same can't be said of you SO15 inadequates.'

'Bullshit.'

The smell of urine was beginning to fill the room. Bull was in no mood for diplomacy.

'There's something more going on here. This man knows you. Not the Secret Service. *You*. I want you the hell out of this room until your identity is verified.'

'My identity has been verified already.' Meyer smiled as he spoke. 'You know that. And I'm authorised to be in this interview. So let's get to it, Detective.'

Bull had no doubt in his mind that there was a history between these men. And not a good one. Romeo Meyer was a danger to Mansour. Bull didn't know why. But he didn't need to. He had a responsibility to his prisoner.

But how do I protect him? By reporting Meyer? A Special Agent of the US Secret Service? And on the basis of what? A gut feeling? Yeah, that'll work out well.

There was only one solution Bull could think of.

At least for now.

'OK.' As before, Bull spoke loudly for the tape. 'You can stay.'

'Thank you.' The sarcasm was clear in Meyer's voice as he began to make his way around the table. To the chair next to Bull's.

'And if Mr Mansour continues to say nothing, then we

will have to bail him,' Bull continued, his voice loud and slow.

'What?' Meyer seemed surprised by the suggestion. 'That's not—'

'On the other hand,' Bull continued, his voice still slow, his words pointed, 'if Mr Mansour *does* answer – if he *does* tell us what we need in order to charge him – well, then it ends differently, doesn't it.'

'What?' Meyer stopped, confusion clear on his face. But Bull was no longer talking to him. He was looking directly at Mansour. He just hoped the message was clear enough.

'Because we're in your hands here, Nizar. If you confess now, on tape? If you say that you planted the bomb and that you *intentionally* blew up Flight PA16? If you say those words, then neither one of us – not me and not Special Agent Meyer – gets to speak to you again. You'll be taken to your cell and neither one of us will be allowed near you.'

'What?'

Bull could tell from Meyer's tone that *he* had now understood the message that the DCI was trying to convey. But had Mansour?

'You heard me,' Bull repeated. Just as slowly. Just as firm. 'If Nizar confesses now, on tape, that he intentionally blew up the flight, then we *have* to charge him. And once we've charged him, neither one of us gets to speak to him alone again. Not me. And certainly not *you*.'

'And what if he *does* confess?' Meyer countered. 'What good does that do him? He'll be found guilty in ten seconds by any jury.'

'Not if he gets himself a good lawyer.' Bull was ready for the point. 'Confessing after some Secret Service giant has burst into the room and scared the shit out of him? A good lawyer gets that thrown out in five seconds, before a jury even hears it. And this shitty little country of mine, it's got some damned good lawyers, believe me.'

'You can't—'

'I confess,' Mansour interrupted, speaking fast. 'I planted the bomb on Flight PA16. I did so . . . intentionally. I wanted to blow up those people.'

Bull wanted to smile. To punch the air. He suppressed both. Instead he reached out and took a grip of Mansour's right wrist.

'In that case, Nizar Mansour, I am charging you on your own confession with the murder of five hundred and thirty-four named victims on the eighth of January twenty-twenty. You will be remanded in custody until your first court appearance on the ninth of January twenty-twenty – that's in a few hours from now – where you will be represented by a lawyer of your choosing or one who is recommended to you by someone you trust.

'In the meantime, Mr Mansour, this interview is over. And now *no one* is entitled to question you further. Understand?'

Mansour nodded enthusiastically, his eyes flitting between Bull and Meyer.

Bull turned his attention to the still standing agent, enjoying the look of shock on Meyer's face.

'And that, Special Agent Meyer, means that you can go fuck yourself.'

EIGHTEEN

'But it's got to be a relief, right?'

James Links sat at the far end of the table.

He was one of six guests at a late-night dinner party in a classic but discreet colonial townhouse in Georgetown, Washington DC.

Each of the guests were men. One in his early forties and the other five well past middle age, with two of *them* well into what should be their retirement years.

These six men were rich and powerful enough that, in any other company, any one of them would be the focus of all attention.

In any *other* company.

Around *this* table, only one man mattered.

'Why?'

Kelvin Cunningham's voice was slow. His soft Atlanta accent drew out the single syllable of the word.

As a response it was both a message and a challenge. A clear indication that the topic was as unwelcome now as it had been earlier in the evening.

Back when his guests had been sober enough to avoid it.

He was daring Links to take it further.

At 11 p.m., and with the group's sixth bottle of Burgundy now as empty as the first five, Links was less cautious than usual.

'Well, come on, let's, let's be honest,' Links unwisely continued. 'If Victor had lived . . . if he had, you know, if he had run for president, your man would have been toast, surely?'

'You think so?'

Another clipped response from Cunningham. Another hint.

'What I think, it's . . . it's not relevant.' Links was still missing the message. 'The polls, though? *They* matter. And they had Victor beating Knowles in every swing state if the election was called tomorrow.'

'President Knowles.'

'What?'

'John Knowles is the president of the United States,' Cunningham explained, a hint of malice in his voice, 'our current commander-in-chief and not only is he a close, personal friend, he also happens to be my employer. So when you refer to him while you are in my home, I would prefer that you do so with the due respect. Is that clear?'

Links looked confused. And suddenly a little nervous.

The reaction made Cunningham smile.

Few people could so easily dominate a man like James Links, the CEO of three companies listed in the Fortune 500 and a dollar billionaire. Cunningham – a poor black boy from Georgia, as he always styled himself – was one of them. And it pleased him immensely.

Cunningham controlled this room. And it was important to him that they all knew that. They were men from generations of privilege. Ruthless men. Powerful men. Yet every one of them sat in thrall to Kelvin Cunningham, deputy assistant to the president of the United States. And so much more besides . . .

He fixed his small, unblinking eyes on Links and continued.

'As for Victor winning if an election were called tomorrow? Do you have any idea how this world works, James?'

'I . . . I can assure you . . .'

'You can assure me of nothing,' Cunningham interrupted,

his voice firm and calm. It gave away no emotion. 'The White House had no concern for Dale Victor. He was an ill wind that would have blown itself out long before this thing reached the ballot box.'

'But what about what Victor knew?'

Cunningham shifted his gaze to Harry Moore, also at the far end of the table. Like Links, he was a white man in his fifties. Unlike Links, he was carrying too much fat for even his expensively tailored suit to hide.

A sure sign of indiscipline, Cunningham thought to himself as he focused on Moore.

'What did he know?' Cunningham asked, prompting the inevitable.

'Victor said he knew something about the president. Something he'd done during the war.'

'Have you been waiting to ask me about this all night, Harry?'

Cunningham's voice was as calm as it had been all evening. And yet he knew how to coat it in menace.

Moore faltered. Cunningham did not.

'It certainly seems like you have,' he continued. 'And that you were just waiting for someone braver – or less sober – to knock on the door. So tell me, what is it you want to know?'

Moore did not answer immediately. Not with Cunningham's unblinking eyes burning into him from the head of the table. A glint of sweat appeared on his left temple as the silence continued; none of the other guests – not even Links – were looking to take Moore's metaphorical bullet.

'It's . . .' Moore trailed off as soon as he began.

'It's what?'

The venom in Cunningham's voice was now unmistakable.

He leaned closer to his prey. It should have had no effect. Rail thin and barely five foot eight, Cunningham should have lacked the physical presence to impose upon the much larger Harry Moore.

And yet Moore seemed to shrink.

'It's what?'

No longer a question. Now a demand.

'It's . . . it's . . . I don't know, it's just convenient, isn't it? That's all. Damned convenient.'

'Tell me what you mean by that.' The low purr of a predator. More spine chilling than any shout or scream could ever be.

'I just mean . . . you know . . .'

'Clearly I don't. And clearly . . .'

The appearance of a figure at the end of the room made Cunningham pause. His instructions had been clear. No calls, unless . . .

. . . *unless it was* this *one. This one* had *to be taken.*

'. . . and clearly we've all had far too much to drink.'

Cunningham climbed to his feet and flashed the closest thing he could to a smile. Every face at the table returned it, all grateful for the change in mood. No matter how forced that change might be.

'And so, gentlemen, you all have homes to go to, businesses to run and an early meeting tomorrow morning. So I suggest we call this night to a close.'

The guests rose as one. Six of the richest men in the United States. The one per cent of the one per cent. Visibly relieved to end the evening as wealthy and as influential as they had begun it.

'Special Agent Hodge will see you out. I have something to which I need to attend.'

Six billionaires. Dismissed as casually as the undocumented Mexican immigrant who tended Cunningham's manicured Washington lawn.

Dismissed by the poor black boy from Georgia.

That's what real power is.

'Who's this?'

'Jack, sir.'

The voice at the end of the line was deep and familiar. It conjured images of the man Cunningham trusted beyond any other.

'News?'

'Sir. The baggage handler. He's not dead.'

Cunningham felt the urge to shout. He pushed it down. Panic helped no one.

'Explain how that's possible.'

'I'm not clear on the exact details as yet.'

'So Romeo's screwed this up.' Cunningham took a deep breath. 'I warned you not to ask too much of him.'

'I didn't. And I can assure you, this was *not* Romeo's fault. In any case, it is not as bad as it sounds.'

The response irritated Cunningham. How could Jack Meyer — the assistant director of the US Secret Service — possibly know if his son were to blame for this failure if they didn't have all the details yet? Such a knee-jerk response was unacceptable. It betrayed Meyer's blind spot.

But for now, Cunningham would put that aside. Jack Meyer's second statement took priority.

'What do you mean, "not as bad as it sounds"?' Cunningham asked.

'I mean that the baggage handler confessed. Romeo was

present in the room when he was being questioned by the Brits, and he reports that the handler confessed to intentionally planting the bomb on the plane.'

'Your son was in the police interview?'

'Yes, sir. I—'

'And you don't see the problem there, Jack?' Cunningham could no longer suppress his irritation.

'Sir, I—'

'Jack, Romeo met with the baggage handler. Personally. He didn't use a middleman.'

'Sir, yes he did.'

'Against your direct instructions.'

'Sir—'

'We chose to overlook that, Jack. Because he's your son. But now you're telling me that he was in the damn police interview with the man?'

'Sir, he—'

'He *nothing*, Jack. There is nothing you can say that makes this right. You're gonna tell me the baggage handler didn't name him, right? That's what you're gonna say? Is it?'

'Yes, sir. Yes, it is.'

'And you think that makes it OK? What the hell kind of an idiot takes a risk like that? What kind of an over-entitled, braindead moron risks the guy saying "there's the bastard that made me do it, sitting right there"? Who the hell does that, Jack?'

'I . . . I can see that. What can I say, sir? He made a mistake. He—'

'No, Jack. He made another mistake. Yet another mistake. And that's gonna have to be dealt with when this is all done, you understand that?'

Cunningham heard no reply. Just the sound of Meyer breathing. His point had been made.

'OK. The baggage handler. What has he said exactly?'

'He just confessed to placing the bag on the plane.'

'Nothing else?'

'Nothing.'

Cunningham paused for a few seconds to consider the information.

'OK, this could be good for us. Very good. But things have to move fast.'

'Agreed, sir.'

'I want eyes on literally anyone who has contact with Mansour from this point onwards,' he said. 'We need to restrict any opportunity he has to retract his confession, or to go into greater detail. I want a net on that, understood?'

'Sir.'

'And I want Mansour dead tomorrow. Today, in fact, if we use British time.'

'Sir, he's confessed to the single biggest terrorist attack in British history. He'll be held in a maximum security prison. The chances that one of my guys can get to him there at that sort of notice . . .'

'It won't be one of your guys,' Cunningham interrupted. 'We have *other* friends who can help with that.'

'Sir.'

A single word, but it was enough to tell Cunningham that Meyer had now followed his meaning. The assistant director would make the necessary arrangements.

'This could turn out perfectly,' Cunningham said, almost thinking aloud. 'We have a Muslim refugee confessing to the bomb. Provided he stays silent until he dies, it could be the end of this.'

'Understood, sir.'

'Provided what, Jack?' Cunningham needed to be sure. 'Provided what?'

'Provided he stays silent until he dies, sir.'

'Exactly. Make sure that's what happens.'

Cunningham disconnected the line. As he did so, his eyes flitted to a second, thick-looking handset on the table. He almost reached out for it. Then he stopped himself.

No. The boss doesn't need to know. Not yet. Not until this is done.

He walked away.

NINETEEN

Sarah Truman stared at her reflection in her illuminated bathroom mirror. She took a deep breath to calm her nerves. Readying herself to find out if her suspicions were correct.

She moved away from the mirror and towards the bath. Or, more accurately, towards the narrow, white and blue plastic stick sitting on the bath's edge.

She stared at the small digital screen that occupied the centre of the device.

Two blue lines.

Pregnant.

The next few minutes were a blur of a hundred jumbled thoughts. But one overrode all the others.

How do I tell Michael?

They had spoken about this. Of course they had. They were an adult couple, engaged and living together. It was something they wanted, but not quite yet. Sarah was younger than Michael by a decade, and she had wanted to concentrate on her career. To push the incredible strides she had made in the last few years for just a little longer.

Michael had respected that. And for his part he had always wanted them to be married before starting a family. A throwback to his Irish Catholic upbringing. Sarah's outlook was less traditional, but she understood his feelings.

All planned. All settled. And now all out the window.

Sarah opened the bathroom door and stepped into the master bedroom.

So how the hell do I tell him?

She had left Michael sleeping in their king-size bed when she had rushed into their en suite, racing against her need to vomit. Twenty minutes later and he was wide awake. But unlike the previous three mornings, he had not come to check on her. Instead he was sat at the end of their bed wearing only his boxer shorts, with his mobile telephone pressed against his ear.

As they always were, Sarah eyes were drawn to the heavy scarring around Michael's right bicep. It was impossible to miss. The same was true of the older, equally severe damage to his left shoulder that became visible as Sarah moved closer and around the bed.

The remnants of two gunshot wounds. Reminders of the dangers that Michael and Sarah seemed to attract.

The dangers that could one day threaten . . .

Sarah forced the thought from her mind and looked at her watch. 6.10 a.m. Even for Michael, this was an early call.

'. . . but how did it come to you?' Michael was asking. 'It's not the work you usually do.'

Michael's question said that the call was professional, not personal. A relief. In Sarah's experience, no 6 a.m. personal call was ever good news.

'OK. OK. Well, look, yeah, I'm interested. Who wouldn't be? But it's a first appearance at a magistrates' court. Don't you think me turning up could look a bit like overkill?'

The sound of a voice speaking in reply was just about discernible to Sarah. She could tell it was a man, but nothing else.

'If you think it's the way to go then yeah, of course, I'll make sure I'm there. Where do you want to meet? At the court or before?'

Sarah had to stop herself moving even closer. Her inquisitive nature had made her career choice inevitable. Hell, it was what had brought her to Michael's door that first time years before.

But Michael's profession often required secrecy, and Sarah had always respected that.

She turned what would have been an instinctive step forward into a purposeful stride back.

'OK. That's the one right next to Edgware Road Station, yeah? I'll see you there. Thanks for thinking of me.'

Michael put the phone down and looked up at Sarah for the first time. A smile slowly spread across his face.

'So, sweetheart, you still want to get ahead of that story?'

Sarah smiled back. Michael's question had made the decision for her: their news would have to wait.

TWENTY

Will Duffy walked through the door of the Minos Café and scanned the room. One of the few old-fashioned English 'greasy spoons' in a heavily Middle Eastern part of London, its now rare offerings of traditional breakfast and strong, over-brewed builder's tea attracted a mixed crowd.

It was the kind of establishment that reminded Duffy of his native Glasgow, where the Scottish version of this type of café was much more common.

Every table was taken, the café filled to capacity by a mix of construction workers, traffic wardens, van drivers, doctors, lawyers and who knows what else.

The man Duffy was looking for was at a small table in the furthest corner, separated from the next seat by a seemingly randomly placed coat stack. It provided the closest thing in here to privacy, Duffy realised.

He moved carefully through the room, a zig-zagging path that passed almost every over-crowded table. Some customers looked up. Some stared resolutely into their crossword puzzles.

On any normal day Duffy would be studying every person here. Trying to spot the undercover officers who so often 'sat in' on his meetings with clients, noting information they were not supposed to hear.

But today was no normal day. Today – uniquely – Duffy would be sitting with the cop.

Bruce Bull did not get to his feet as the solicitor approached.

Instead he lifted a rucksack from the chair that sat across from him and indicated for Duffy to sit.

'Good to see you, Will,' Bull offered as Duffy took the seat. 'It's been a long time.'

'You too, eh.' Duffy reached out a hand as he spoke. Bull shook it. 'I'll be honest, I didn't expect your call.'

'You and me both,' Bull replied.

Before either could say more a small, middle-aged man with a Mediterranean appearance and an accent to match approached. He carried a large white steaming mug in each hand.

'One coffee, one tea.'

'Tea's mine,' Bull replied. He looked towards Duffy. 'I took a risk on yours. Black coffee it was, wasn't it?'

'Good one.' Duffy was genuinely impressed. 'How'd you remember?'

'Just stuck in my mind.'

'From fifteen years ago, eh?'

'You're a memorable man, Will. Not many like you in your game.'

Duffy smiled. Everyone likes to be flattered. He was no different. Not that he allowed it to distract him. They were here for a reason.

'Tell me about Mansour. What the hell is the lead investigator doing recommending a non-tame solicitor? And why me?'

Bull looked around before replying. Duffy could recognise the body language; Bull was ensuring he could not be overheard. It was rare that anyone spoke to Duffy professionally without doing the exact same thing, but none of *them* were police officers.

When he finally spoke, Bull's voice was quiet. Duffy had to strain to hear it over the noise of the café's other customers.

'There's something up with the case, Will. I don't know everything and it may well be that Mansour planted that bomb, like he said. But there's a whole lot more to it. Plus there's some sort of shit going on with the American Secret Service. Particularly some nasty giant piece of shit called Romeo Meyer. The whole thing's a mess and Mansour needs someone who'll look out for him properly. Someone who'll put his interests first.'

'And when you thought that, you thought "Will Duffy", eh?'

'First and only name that came to me.'

'Why? You know my reputation. I represent villains. I'm not a terrorist's brief.'

'You also represent the innocent, Will. At least you used to. And from the one time I saw you doing that, you do it fearlessly. Fearless is what Nizar Mansour needs.'

Duffy felt the smile returning to the corner of his mouth. He pushed it away, but he would not deny that he enjoyed hearing what Bull had just said.

Duffy's reputation was built on his status as lawyer to London's leading crime families. It was a reputation well earned, and was itself a side effect of two things.

First was Duffy's personal background: a street fighter from the east side of Glasgow who had dragged himself out through a combination of intellect and ambition, he understood the criminal underworld more intimately than any other solicitor.

Second was his willingness to take on the establishment; it was his gut instinct to fight, wherever that fight might take him.

Still, Duffy had set out to be more than a 'villain's brief'. He had seen men dragged into a life of crime, just to feed their children. And he had sworn that when he could, he would protect those men from the system that had created them in the first place.

In the years since he had enjoyed only a few chances to live up to that promise. Including the case on which he had first met Bruce Bull.

And so this opportunity was difficult to pass up.

'Tell me about the Secret Service,' he finally said, indicating his interest.

'There's not much I can tell you. Except I have no doubt that Meyer knows Mansour. And Mansour knows him. Nizar was absolutely terrified at the sight of the man.'

'Terrified?'

'Literally pissed himself with fear.'

'Jesus.'

'Jesus is right,' Bull continued. 'All Agent Meyer wanted was time alone with him, until I pointed out the cameras. Whatever he intended to do – however he intended to do it – I'm far from sure that Mansour would have left that room alive.'

'You're not serious?' Duffy couldn't quite believe what he was hearing. A murder in custody? If the suggestion were coming from just any man he would have dismissed it. But this was Bruce Bull. 'You reckon he'd have killed him? Inside a police station?'

'You think it can't happen?' Bull replied. 'And you think the Americans wouldn't try it, if they had good cause? They basically own us, Will. What they say goes. So who knows what we'd let them do. Maybe they don't even know themselves.'

Duffy took a moment to consider what Bull had said. All of

this – the question of international relations – was far outside of his experience. Or it had been, at least.

'What about the confession?' he finally asked. 'You said he admitted the whole bloody thing. That's a problem, eh?'

'The only part of that confession worth a damn is what he said when he handed himself in. That he put the bomb on the plane. I believe he did that. But my instinct tells me there's more going on here. That this man doesn't seem capable of killing hundreds of people.'

'And the rest? Why don't you buy it?'

'The rest he said because it was his way out of that room. You'll hear the tape. You'll hear me tell him that if he confessed to the whole thing – to knowingly setting the bomb – then he'd get away from Romeo Meyer. Like I said, you'll hear the tape. Your barrister will get that confession excluded no problem.'

'The fella I've got in mind for this? He'll do that with his eyes closed. But so we're clear, you're saying he confessed just to get out of the same room as this Romeo Meyer character?'

'Exactly right.'

'Then you're not kidding, are you? He really *was* terrified.'

'He was. And I don't mind telling you, that massive Yank worried me too.'

'You thought he was a threat to you?'

'Thought has nothing to do with it. He *was* a threat. And I believe he will be to you, too, Will. That's why I needed a lawyer who can take care of himself.'

'You think he'll come for me, eh?'

'I think if you're an obstacle to what he wants then you could be in danger, yes. Does that change things?'

Duffy waited a beat to consider his response before replying.

'Well, the whole Secret Service thing's a new one on me, Bruce. But it'll not be the first time I've made enemies. Screw it. They can have a fight if they want one. Any kind of fight they want, eh.'

It was Bull's turn to smile.

'That's what I thought. Looks like I came to the right man.'

'Looks that way.' Duffy nodded as he spoke, suddenly grateful for the call he'd made two hours earlier. 'And looks like I did, too.'

TWENTY-ONE

Michael Devlin's watch read 9.15 a.m. as he and Will Duffy turned the corner that led from the Old Marylebone Road to the A40.

They had met at the Minos Café, and Duffy filled him in on his meeting with Bruce Bull as they walked towards Westminster Magistrates' Court.

The court was a sprawling building, an imposing concrete design. Not particularly tall but unusually deep, stretching far into the surrounding streets.

Its entrance was a much showier effort. A multi-storey glass fronted edifice, dominated by a coat of arms carved from an unnecessarily massive slab of stone. It was a design that left no one in doubt of the building's importance.

'Press are here,' Will Duffy observed. 'And if I'm not mistaken, Michael . . .'

'No harm in telling her, was there?' Michael asked, taking Duffy's meaning. 'Word would have gone out as soon as the case was announced. It's just an hour's head start.'

'Doesnae bother me,' Duffy replied with a smile. 'I almost suggested it when I phoned you.'

Both men stood a little taller – a little straighter – as they approached Sarah Truman and her cameraman Nathan Benson. Their strides slipped into sync. Both Michael and Duffy were old hands at this. They knew the footage would make the evening news. Not least because – thanks to Michael – Benson's was the only lens there to catch them.

Neither looked towards the camera or to Sarah as they passed. Tip-offs aside, they were professionals. And professionals remain detached. It was the price required when Sarah reported on any story that involved her increasingly high-profile fiancé.

The tall, automated glass doors were already open as they approached the building's entrance.

Michael and Duffy joined the back of the line that had formed inside the building but which, thanks to the court's high-security safeguards, now snaked out front. It left them on the wrong side of the glass doors and just feet from the warmth of reception. And on a zero-degree January morning, those few feet could feel endless.

Not that Michael was willing to acknowledge the effect of the cold. Not with Sarah so close by. Dressed as smartly as either Michael or Duffy – and therefore just as unsuitably for the weather – she was looking at a much longer wait in the icy London wind.

He would grin and bear it.

'I thought those letters after your name would at least mean a bit of special treatment, big man.'

Duffy rubbed his cold hands together as he spoke, making no effort to hide his discomfort. The letters he referred to were Michael's professional honorific of QC, a rank Michael had achieved the previous year, which was supposed to set him apart as a senior barrister, superior to the rank and file.

Michael held little stock in his elevation. It was a promotion he felt he had hardly earned and which others he knew deserved more. That self-doubt had driven him to prove himself worthy of the title, which had in turn seen his professional profile soar to new heights.

'They make no difference at all,' he replied, pretending to ignore the cold. 'We get the same treatment as everyone else. Trust me, if any random member of the public has to take their shoes off here then so do I.'

'Maybe they know how we both got here, eh?' Duffy said with a chuckle. 'And where we both started.'

Michael didn't reply. It was another reference to his past and he had no doubt it was intentional. He was not offended; Michael was sure that Duffy regarded their mutual unconventional upbringings as both a badge of honour and a personal connection. But still, Michael's past was filled with memories he didn't want to discuss. Especially with a man he still hardly knew.

The line moved quickly, with neither man saying another word. Soon they were through the door and had passed security.

'What courtroom are we in?' Michael asked.

'Court One,' Duffy replied. 'They've given us a district judge. George Bell. You know him?'

'No. You?'

'I've come across him a few times, aye. Pompous old bugger with a big case of judge-itus.'

'Then I'll bet he's going to love today,' Michael replied as he walked straight ahead, towards the glass-walled staircase that was positioned next to a dual elevator bank. 'Case like this, he's not trusted to do anything but send it to a big boy court.'

'He'll find a way to make himself feel important,' Duffy replied, following close behind as Michael began to walk down the staircase. 'He always does.'

'I'll be impressed if he manages that. He has literally no power at all today. And I'll make sure I remind him of exactly that, if he really is that much of a tosser.'

'Now that I'd pay to see.'

The lawyers chuckled as they descended the two short staircases that led to the entrance of the building's custody area. They were early, Michael knew. Most prisoners did not arrive until after 9.30 a.m., when the prison vans usually reached the court. But Nizar Mansour had been held in Stoke Newington Police Station overnight, and Bruce Bull had already confirmed that he had been delivered to the building.

'Tell me about your connection to Bull,' Michael said, intrigued by Duffy's role in all this. 'He seems to be sticking his neck way out on this. No matter how well he hides it, he's taking on the Secret Service and backing a man who seems to have killed hundreds of people. If he's wrong, his career's over.'

'Without question, aye.'

'Then why you? This couldn't be more serious. Why does he trust you?'

'We were in a case together fifteen years ago,' Duffy explained. 'Only terrorism trial I ever did. Bull was the officer in charge. I was defending a kid from South London who they said had been radicalised.

'It was one of those where everyone went through the motions. Bull was Special Branch back then and he had done a great job. Everyone thought their clients were guilty, Bull thought he knew they were, and so none of the lawyers had any fight left in them. No one was pleading, so they treated the trial as a formality.

'My boy, though. He was different. They'd tried to radicalise him, aye. And they'd done a decent enough job to convert him to Islam and all that. But they hadn't made him a terrorist. No as far as I could see. So I made my silk fight every step. I had him fight them on publicity. On experts. On covert surveillance. And all the while, I spent months digging through the unused material.

'By the time the trial was halfway through, I'd found stuff that the normal police had even kept from Special Branch. Emails and web searches that showed my boy wasnae what they said. Bull saw it, pulled rank and made the prosecution drop the case. Even had a couple of coppers kicked off the force for sitting on evidence. Everyone else was convicted. And I think Bull appreciated that, because what I'd done had kept the rest of the convictions safe.

'Anyway, we came to kind of trust each other in that case. More so than either of us trusted our own sides, eh? I haven't seen hide nor hair of the man in the meantime, but I guess he's got a long memory.'

Michael nodded his head and realised that he was now looking at Duffy in a different light. The fact was, Michael had also encountered Bruce Bull before. And he knew that the SO15 DCI was as straight as they came; he was what a copper *should* be, at least in Michael's opinion. And if Bull trusted Duffy, then that said something about Duffy.

'Nice to be well thought of, eh?' Michael said with a smile, bringing the subject to an end as he gestured towards the thick security door that led to the court's custody area.

'Shall we?'

TWENTY-TWO

Ten minutes.

For ten minutes Michael had sat in near silence, in a cramped interview room in the magistrates' court's secure custody area. Thanks to the screwed down position of his undersized chair, he was half-crushed against the bare right-hand wall. Some rooms are not designed for comfort. Michael realised that. But this room seemed specifically designed to avoid it.

Seated next to him was Duffy. The chairs were fixed awkwardly close together. But Duffy at least enjoyed a two-foot-wide space between his free shoulder and the room's white-washed left-hand wall.

Across from them was Nizar Mansour.

It is unusual for a barrister to be present when a solicitor first meets a defendant. In ordinary circumstances Duffy would have met with his client in Stoke Newington Police Station, before Michael was even aware of Mansour's existence. But the circumstances of this case were anything but ordinary, and so here Michael sat, quietly observing as Will Duffy fought to gain Mansour's trust.

A fight that was not proving to be easy. Duffy had achieved little more than grunts by way of response.

'Nizar, I can understand why you'd not want to speak to us. But I promise you, we're the good guys here. We're here to keep you safe.'

As he had from the beginning, Mansour gave no reply. He

just continued to sit back into his chair, his eyes fixed on Duffy. He seemed to be studying the man.

Duffy continued.

'But if we're to do that, son – if we're gonna keep you safe – then you got to help us to help you. It won't do anyone any good if you don't speak to us.'

Mansour remained motionless.

This is no good, Michael thought to himself. *I can't tell if he's even listening to what Will says. Or, if he is, whether he understands it.*

It was at that moment that Mansour's eyes moved. They drifted downwards and rested on the documents that sat on the table, obscured by Duffy's large, gnarly hands.

Michael would not let the brief moment of curiosity pass.

'Those are legal aid forms, Nizar.'

Michael's voice – softer than Duffy's, and coloured by a Belfast accent that was less pronounced than the solicitor's Glaswegian – seemed to surprise Mansour. He looked up, meeting Michael's eyes for the first time.

'They're nothing to worry about,' Michael explained. 'They're nothing to do with the judge or with the court or with the prosecution. All they do is make sure that Mr Duffy and I get paid to represent you. And that's only if you decide that you want us. If that's what you decide today, then we can fill these in at the end.'

Mansour glanced at the papers again, then back towards Michael. For a moment he looked as if he was about to speak. Then he seemed to change his mind.

It's still progress, Michael thought. *I'll take that over nothing.*

'Everything Mr Duffy has told you so far is right,' Michael said. 'It *is* our job to defend you. *If* you'll have us. But we both know that you've no reason to trust us yet. Why the hell would you? You don't know either of us from Adam. But that'll change, Nizar.

'That'll change because this is only day one. It's one short appearance before the district judge in the court upstairs. All he'll do is order that your case goes to Woolwich Crown Court, which is where you'll be taken tomorrow morning. We'll be there with you again then. Both of us. And that's when you'll plead – when you say whether you're guilty or not guilty. Assuming you say you're not guilty, the judge in Woolwich will fix a trial date. What that means, very simply, is that he'll pick the date when your trial will begin. A date which will be in a few months time.

'And in those months, Nizar, you'll see Mr Duffy and me regularly. One of us will come and visit you in prison at least once every week. Maybe more than that, depending on how the case is looking. So you see, it's OK that you don't trust us yet. We understand that because we know we have to earn your trust. And we will. We will earn it over the course of the next few months.'

Michael stopped speaking. This time he knew that Mansour had listened to and understood every word. He could see it in his eyes; a sign of life that had not been there until now. Michael could practically see the gears turning as Mansour considered what had just been explained.

It was almost a minute before Mansour spoke, with neither Michael nor Duffy breaking the silence.

'The months?' he finally asked, his voice unexpectedly deep, his words understandably slow. 'Between now and my trial? Where would I be?'

'Where would you be?'

'Would I be free? Or would I be prisoner?'

Duffy beat Michael to the answer.

'In a case like this? You won't get bail in a case like this, son. You'll spend that time in prison.'

Mansour's eyes flitted from Duffy to Michael, in search of confirmation. Michael provided it with a nod of his head, and as he did so he saw something that confused him.

He saw relief. He saw a man to whom imprisonment was good news.

In all of Michael's years as a criminal barrister, the one consistent desire of every client had been for freedom, no matter how unrealistic their chances of achieving it.

So to see someone *pleased* with the prospect of months in a high security jail?

What the hell is going on in this guy's head?

'What do you say, son?' Either Duffy had missed what Michael had seen, or he had chosen to ignore it. 'Do you *want* our help? Because I can assure you, you damn well need it.'

Mansour turned his full attention on Duffy as the question hung in the air. To Michael he somehow seemed more certain. More confident.

At the very least, he's a hell of a lot more engaged.

'Why do you help me?'

The question was unexpected, but Duffy's reply was instant.

'Because it's our job.'

'No one has the job to help *everyone*.' Mansour's response was just as fast. 'Why do you help *me*?'

'Because a man I trust asked me to,' Duffy replied. It was the more honest explanation. 'A man who thinks I can do this better than anyone else.'

'Which man?'

'The same man *you* trusted last night, Nizar.' The answer came from Michael. 'DCI Bruce Bull. The man who protected you from Special Agent Meyer.'

A flicker of anger crossed Mansour's eyes at the mention of the name.

'Romeo.'

'What?'

'His name is Romeo.'

'Romeo Meyer,' Duffy confirmed. 'That's right.'

Mansour's eyes moved from Duffy to Michael, then back again.

He's considering his next step, Michael could tell. *Judging whether or not he can trust two strangers. No matter who sent them.*

'How do I know you tell the truth?' he finally asked. 'That you are sent from Mr Bull? And not from Romeo?'

'You think we're from the US Secret Service?' Duffy asked. He sounded bemused at the suggestion.

'No. I think Romeo lie about being agent. So I think maybe you lie about being lawyers and knowing Mr Bull.'

'What do you mean, he lied about being an agent?' Duffy asked.

Mansour went silent again. Michael had wondered the same thing, but he could see that they were losing Mansour. Interrogating him would only accelerate that.

'Let's forget Romeo for now,' Michael said.

He hoped Duffy would realise why he wanted to change the subject.

'For now let's focus on today. No names. No accusations against anyone else. Just the simple facts. Will you be happy with that?'

Mansour's eyes stayed down. He seemed to be bristling with distrust. With paranoia.

Who can blame the poor sod, Michael thought.

'Nizar, please. You don't have to tell us anything you don't want to. But please. Help us look after you. If only for today. Then if you want someone else, you'll never have to see us again.'

Mansour looked up and fixed his gaze on Michael.

'Just for today,' Michael repeated.

This time Mansour did not glance towards Duffy. Instead he focused on Michael as he considered his decision.

'If I speak,' he finally asked, 'who else will hear my answer?'

'Not a soul, if that's what you want,' Michael replied. 'Neither Mr Duffy nor I can repeat a word of what you say if you tell us not to. Those are the rules.'

Mansour took a moment. Longer this time. Michael understood why: an assurance of confidentiality was not worth much if there was no trust between them.

He would need to keep the questions uncontroversial if they were to make progress.

'What do you want to ask?' Mansour's deep voice faltered. It was filled with uncertainty; he was unsure of the step he was taking.

'You confessed to bombing the plane. Let's start with that.'

'I confess to be free from Romeo. Mr Bull said I be protected from Romeo if I am charged, and that I would be charged if I confess.'

'You're saying you confessed for your own protection?'

'Yes.'

'So you *didn't* put the bomb on the plane?'

Mansour paused. Just for a moment.

'What I say now? You won't say it? You won't tell?'

'Not unless you instruct me that I should. Otherwise whatever you say, it does not leave this room.'

'Then yes. I did it. I place the bomb on the plane.'

Michael sat back in his chair, confused. He glanced towards Duffy, who seemed less surprised by the answer. Michael realised then the solicitor had not told him everything.

Duffy did not miss a beat.

'But did you know *what* you were putting on there?'

'It was a bag,' Mansour answered. 'Luggage. And I knew it should not be on there. But I did not know it was dangerous. I did not know it was bomb.'

'What did you think it was?' Michael asked.

'I thought drugs. I was told my job as baggage handler allow me to place bag in hold. I was told where in hold. I was not to open. I was not to ask question. I had to do just this one thing.'

'And you were paid for this?' Michael asked.

'No,' Mansour answered. His tone was suddenly outraged. 'I would not do this for money. I am not a criminal. I came to this country to escape what happening in *my* country. I came to work. I do not break the law.'

'But if you weren't being paid . . .' Michael began, '. . . if you weren't doing this for money . . .'

Michael's thoughts ran back to Mansour's words.

'I had to do just this one thing.'

They were not the words of a paid accomplice. No. They suggested something else.

'Nizar, was someone threatening you?'

Mansour said nothing. He did not have to. The colour drained from his face at the question, telling Michael all he needed to know.

'Was this about your brother?' Duffy asked. 'Did you do this to protect your brother, Nizar?'

Mansour did not reply. Tears began to fill his eyes.

'It was your brother who died, though, Nizar.' Michael had abandoned his promise to keep the questions uncontroversial. 'That's right, isn't it?'

Mansour gave a small nod in response.

'Then I'm sorry I have to ask, but how was he involved in all this?'

'He was not involved,' Mansour managed, his voice breaking. 'He knew ... he knew nothing. He ... he was my brother. I keep him out. I keep him ... safe.'

Emotion broke Mansour's voice as he spoke. It made his heavy Syrian accent difficult to understand. But to Michael, the underlying message was clear.

'Then who was being threatened, Nizar? If it wasn't your brother, who did they threaten to make you do this?'

Mansour looked up, directly into Michael's face. Tears now stained his cheeks, his hold on his emotions broken.

For once, there was no sign of conflict in his eyes. No distrust. Only pain.

'My sister,' he replied, his voice breaking as he forced out the words. '*Our* sister. They have her. What I did? This was price for her delivery.'

Michael could see the genuine despair on his face. And he knew then that Duffy had been right: this man needed their help.

'OK, Nizar. I think you'd better start at the beginning.'

TWENTY-THREE

'Well, no one can say we lied to the lad, eh? We said it'd be quick.'

Will Duffy stepped forward as Michael watched Mansour disappear behind the dock door and head back towards the cells. The hearing was over. It had taken all of five minutes.

'Stupid quirk of the system that it even comes here at all,' Michael replied with a sigh. 'But at least we can start the real fun and games in Woolwich tomorrow.'

'You reckon?' Duffy did not sound convinced.

'Nah,' Michael admitted, a smile spreading across his face. 'But I have to lie to myself to face that train journey to Plumstead.'

The two men walked towards the back of the court as they spoke, to the heavy double doors that sat to the right of the public gallery. As they passed through, Michael spotted two reporters he recognised.

'Word's out,' he said, indicating towards them with his head.

'And then some,' Duffy replied, pointing towards the window as they stepped through a second set of heavy doors and onto the concourse.

Every waiting area on every floor of the building looked out onto the glass frontage of Westminster Magistrates' Court. It allowed for a clear view of the entrance from every level. And from here on the first floor, they could see that Sarah and Benson were no longer alone.

'Damn.' Michael counted seven cameras already, each accompanied by their on-screen reporter. 'That's quicker than I thought it'd be. Has to be a tip-off from court staff.'

'You say that like it's a bad thing,' Duffy said with a smile.

'Pots and kettles, eh?' Michael replied. 'Anyway, it's not *me* who'll be running the press gauntlet by the time we're out of here. You might want to check your make-up before we leave.'

'A natural beauty like me?' Duffy laughed. 'I—'

Michael raised his hand before Duffy could say any more. Duffy turned to see what Michael was looking at. A man in a black suit had followed them from the courtroom and was now striding towards them.

The man was around Michael's height but younger. Perhaps by as much as a decade. As he came closer the strength that was hidden by his tailored suit became more evident. Michael could not miss the tell-tale bulges of honed muscle, pressing out against the fabric.

The confident stride was almost admirable.

'Michael Devlin.'

The man spoke with the self-assured American accent that suited his every physical detail. So much so that Michael had almost expected it.

'May I ask, sir, if you'll be Nizar Mansour's lawyer through this case?'

'I'm sorry but who are you?' Michael asked.

'That's not important, sir.'

The man in black thrust out a hand as he spoke. Thick fingers. Battered knuckles. The strong, rough hand of someone who used it as a tool. Now offered in greeting.

He seemed entirely unconcerned when Michael did not take it.

'So the answer, Mr Devlin? Will this be your case?'

'I don't know who you are, sir,' Michael replied. He kept his voice firm, but it was an effort. There was something about this man. Michael was not easily intimidated, but right now that was exactly how he was feeling. 'And even if I did, I would not discuss any aspect of Mr Mansour's defence.'

'It's just a simple question, counsellor.'

'So was mine. And I suspect we've both had our final answer.'

Michael straightened his back and shoulders to show his full height as he spoke. An unconscious display of strength. A survival instinct.

It didn't work. The man in black took a half step forward. When he spoke again, his tone was flat.

'Your attitude, counsellor. It's a mistake.'

'I'm sorry, is that a threat?'

'Take it how you want. All I'm saying is that it would be better for you to cooperate with us.'

'With us?' Duffy stepped between them. If he was intimidated, he was hiding it well. He just sounded angry. 'And who's "us", eh? You and Romeo Meyer, is it? You're in this with that Romeo guy, eh?'

Michael felt himself wince at Duffy's mention of Romeo Meyer. By the look and sound of this man, Michael had assumed a Secret Service connection. But there was value in keeping those details to themselves. Still, he couldn't dwell on it. What's done is done. And he had to admire the solicitor's complete lack of fear.

The man in black seemed less impressed. Michael watched a smirk evolve as he slowly turned towards Duffy.

It was a mistake. The arrogant response only seemed to rile Duffy further. The Scotsman took his own half-step closer.

'What, you think we're as easy to push around as Nizar Mansour? You think youse can frighten us like you frightened him? Well, don't make that mistake. We know what you're at, son.'

The man in black did not move an inch. His smirk broadened into a smile. It was no more attractive.

'And who might you be?' he asked.

'I'm Nizar Mansour's solicitor,' Duffy replied. He reached into his jacket pocket and retrieved a business card as he spoke. 'So if you have any questions about this case, you ask *me*. And you stay the hell away from Mr Devlin. Now if you'll excuse us, we've got another appointment.'

Duffy slotted his business card into the breast pocket of the man's black jacket, patted it hard with his open hand and walked away, their shoulders colliding as he passed. Intentional by Duffy, Michael was sure. And hard. But the impact did not seem to have bothered the man in black. The unattractive smile remained fixed as he turned his head to watch Duffy go.

Despite what Duffy had said, Michael did not follow. Not yet. There was something he wanted to know.

'You weren't surprised,' he said slowly, his mind only a step ahead of his voice. 'Or confused.'

The man turned his head back towards Michael.

'What?'

'Will Duffy just accused Romeo Meyer of being involved in all this. You, too. Yet you didn't bat an eyelid at the suggestion, or at the mention of his name.'

Michael saw the flash of uncertainty and anger in the man's face; he didn't like what he was hearing.

Michael continued.

'And if none of it surprised you, and if none of it confused you, what's the logical conclusion?'

Michael was now doing what he did best. He was cross-examining. But unlike a trial, this witness could not be compelled to answer. Or to stay.

The smile returned.

'We'll see you very soon, counsellor.'

He turned and walked away, leaving Michael with his moment of bravado ebbing away, replaced with a leaden feeling in the pit of his stomach.

It was an instinct that had never failed him before.

This just got dangerous.

TWENTY-FOUR

'The problem, surely, is the groundswell of public opinion on this?'

It was 8 a.m. in Washington DC, and Kelvin Cunningham was attending a presidential meeting. His second of the day. The first had been just Cunningham and President John Knowles himself, but the follow-up was much more heavily attended. Cunningham, Knowles and seven others. Six of whom had left Cunningham's Georgetown home barely nine hours earlier.

It was the seventh man – Nicolas Dupart – who now held the floor.

Cunningham watched Dupart from his usual seat next to the Resolute desk, an ornate wooden unit gifted to the United States by Britain's Queen Victoria in 1880 and first appointed to the Oval Office by President John F. Kennedy in 1961. Now a mainstay of the world's most famous workspace, the desk had become an iconic symbol of the position Knowles held.

Like most presidents since JFK, the current commander-in-chief conducted his day-to-day business from its far side, looking outwards onto those who had secured their time in the presidential presence.

From the perspective of the seven men facing him, Knowles was framed by three floor-to-ceiling windows and the two flags that flanked them.

Cunningham was sat by the president's side. It was an auspicious position. Exactly where one would expect to find a second-in-command. And that was, as far as Cunningham was concerned, no less than his role deserved.

The office of deputy assistant to the president did not carry the kudos of a secretary of state or a vice-president. Or the public attention of the senior sounding assistant to the president. But where were any of them right now? Where were they while Cunningham was in the room and beside the man? Unlike politicians with more impressive titles and media profiles, Cunningham's position placed him at the ultimate seat of power. Trappings of office be damned; for him, nothing mattered more than the unseen influence he enjoyed.

An unelected political mandarin in a role loosely defined, the deputy assistant was the unofficial head of the White House Office. An office that was, in turn, the beating heart of the presidential staff system. That position alone gave Cunningham a level of influence that could be described as world shaping.

And yet that did not begin to describe Cunningham's power.

Frequent visitors to the Oval Office had grown used to Cunningham. To his omnipresence, always at Knowles' right hand. After three years of Knowles' presidency, it was no longer even questioned. These days, if Cunningham missed a meeting it was a sure sign that the meeting was not important.

Knowles' reliance on Cunningham was hardly new, although it had definitely increased since he had taken office. In fact, it went back to the very beginning of Knowles' political career, shortly after his receipt of the Medal of Honor and his honourable discharge from the US Marine Corp.

Back then, Cunningham was already well known as the CEO of the discrete but powerful political lobbyist company

Hotspur Futures. Washington DC legend now told how he had seen something in Knowles before anyone else. Something special.

And so, the story went, Cunningham gave up his own ambitions, stepped down from a company that was paying him millions of dollars a year, all to join with a man who he truly believed would make a difference.

That was the legend. And, like most legends, it was not worth the paper on which it was written.

Sure, Cunningham *had* seen something in Knowles. And that something was electability. The classic handsome war hero, Knowles had the making of a Hollywood president. One who would be swept into the White House on the crest of an effortless wave. A wave which, thanks to Cunningham, had taken the now-deputy assistant and the organisation he *really* worked for along with it.

It had been a long-term project. One which had required Cunningham to leave Hotspur behind just as he had finally taken the reins at the company.

But then everything the organisation did was long term. And success with them? Success *for* them? That far outweighed anything he could ever achieve at Hotspur. Or at any of the countless other companies the organisation owned.

Media. Tech. Military. Oil. Aviation. Law. The organisation had interests in them all. Financial stakes that ran into the hundreds of billions. Maybe more. And the best way to protect those investments and ensure that they flourished?

Washington DC. Or, to be more specific, 1600 Pennsylvania Avenue.

What was it the boss used to say? Cunningham thought to himself. *You take the White House, you take the world.*

With Knowles at his side, that was exactly what Cunningham had done.

'And just what do you believe the public opinion to be, Nick?'

Knowles' voice broke through Cunningham's thoughts, bringing his attention back to the subject of the meeting.

Climate change.

Everyone's attention was on Nicolas Dupart, a recent addition to the White House staff. Dupart's skin was deeply tanned, complimenting his sharp, angular features and some premature greying of his black hair. At five foot ten and boasting a body fat ratio in the single figures, he was not dissimilar in size to Cunningham. He was also the heir to one of the world's great fortunes and easily the richest man in the room, yet somehow he was also the least known; the anonymous billionaire.

Dupart had recently been appointed senior advisor to the president on climate change. Officially this tasked him with the presentation of the real-life, scientific, practical and political impact of global warning and the so-called 'climate emergency'. But as with almost all of Cunningham's personnel appointments, Dupart's remit went much further than that.

The president had not even heard of Dupart before Christmas. And now, a month later, he was an essential part of the team. One of the long list of men and women who had come and gone from the White House Office in the three years of Knowles' administration. All of them there to play a small, isolated part in Cunningham's bigger picture.

'The tide has turned over the last decade or so, Mr President,' Dupart explained, in answer to Knowles' question. 'Of course, we still have die-hards and hold-outs on the question of climate change, but the vast majority have now bought the science. And of that majority, a good chunk are getting pretty damn militant about it, sir. How are we planning to address that?'

'That's a good question,' Knowles replied. He turned to Cunningham. 'Any thoughts on that one, Kelvin?'

'What was it Lincoln said, Mr President? You can't please all of the people all of the time?'

'I'm fairly sure Lincoln was talking about fooling the people, Kelvin. Not pleasing them.'

'With all due respect, Mr President, what's the difference? Every one of us in this room knows the science. Every one of us in this room knows that the arguments against fossil fuels – against oil, against coal, against fracking, even – are indisputable. If we stick to the science, we lose. And we can't afford to do that. None of us can. So if we're to keep the majority happy – if we're going to change our political direction without causing an outcry – we're going to have to fool them.'

Cunningham looked around the room as he spoke, at its eight other occupants. All now primed to follow the script he had given them over dinner.

A charade, Cunningham thought to himself. *But a necessary one.*

'But that doesn't answer Nick's question, does it?' Knowles observed, bringing Cunningham's attention back to him. '*How* are we going to do that? How do we overturn the majority feeling on the subject and get the public's support?'

'I have some arrangements in place for that, Mr President.'

The comment came from Mark Luthor. The youngest of the six guests, the thirty-four-year-old was both the COO of the world's largest social media provider and the de facto majority shareholder of its only real rival. It was a monopoly hidden from the Bureau of Competition thanks to the patronage of the organisation, which in turn owned most of what was left of both companies.

A patronage that Cunningham would never allow Luthor to forget.

'And with the release of sufficient funds,' Luthor continued, 'I think we can go much further still.'

'What do you have in mind?' Knowles asked.

'An extension of what we already have underway, Mr President.

'We have over three hundred clickbait news sites running already. Between them these sites carry hundreds of thousands of news articles of every type. Celebrity stories. Conspiracy theories. History. Sports. Whatever we need. I have a team already working on the necessary algorithms. Using data mining, we can use those algorithms to send the best-suited headlines to each and every social media account on every provider we control. So, for example, let's say we have a Knicks fan. Well, he'll get bombarded with news headlines about anything and everything associated to the Knicks. No matter how tangential.

'But the data-mining is the easy part. Where the algorithms really kick in is the next step. You see, every one of these sites – once they've been clicked on – will begin to offer further headlines. To articles that address climate change, but tweaked to the interests of the particular user. So that people who wouldn't usually be interested in the subject still find some reason to read. Click on these and that user will be taken to whatever article best suits them. Whatever will hold their attention long enough to get the message across. To get our message.'

Cunningham nodded in agreement. He had heard this speech before. Hell, he had written most of it.

'So what do you need?'

'I estimate six hundred and fifty million dollars to push us across the line, Mr President. That will make the difference between impact and saturation. With the right investment, I can guarantee that every social media user in the United States is never more than three irresistible clicks away from climate change denial.'

Cunningham turned to Knowles, again nodding his head. A clear indication of his own thoughts on the plan. The cost to the taxpayer? A mere drop in the ocean compared to what the organisation could earn from even a small U-turn on environmental regulation.

'What's the estimated timescale of the turnaround?' Nicolas Dupart asked the question before Cunningham could return to the script. The interruption did not matter. It was exactly what Cunningham would have asked. Dupart knew the brief.

'We can have this moving full scale within two months,' Luthor replied. 'After that, the time it will take to change people's perception? Based upon saturation levels, we estimate six months to a year.'

'So that puts us ahead of Rio by four months,' Dupart said. He turned to Knowles and Cunningham. 'Mr President, if that timescale is realistic then this can be done. We can have public opinion behind us in time to derail the 2021 United Nations Climate Change Conference.'

'Amazing.' Knowles sounded genuinely impressed. 'No denying it. You boys are good at what you do.'

Cunningham looked from face to face. Dupart's showed no reaction. But the others? Their satisfaction with the president's compliment was unmistakable.

Pathetic, Cunningham thought. *One word from him and they're on top of the world. As if any of this was down to them.*

'We'll see if that's still true by 2021, sir,' Dupart replied, with a glance towards the president's guests. He seemed to share Cunningham's view of their reaction. 'There's a lot to be done.'

'Not least finding the money, I expect?' Knowles' question was directed at his deputy assistant.

'That's already in hand, Mr President. I've authorised an additional one point two billion over inflation in administrative costs across seven departments, to be put before Congress over the course of the month. It's everything Mr Luthor needs and more, just in case. Over that number of offices, the increase will effectively go unnoticed.'

'You've thought of everything.'

'I'll take that as a compliment, Mr President. Does that mean we have a go on this?' Cunningham looked at the expectant faces of the other men in the room, all waiting to hear the final verdict. Only he had no doubt what the answer would be.

'Yes,' Knowles finally replied, proving Cunningham correct. 'We have a go.'

TWENTY-FIVE

With the meeting over and their next steps authorised, Kelvin Cunningham had dismissed everyone. As they had the previous night, most had seemed relieved to go.

The president was on to his next meeting, in his usual seat and with Cunningham at his side. The seven men had been replaced by just one: Jack Meyer, assistant director of the United States Secret Service. The agent in direct operational charge of all aspect of Presidential Protection, Meyer was the immediate superior of every Special Agent in the building.

A naturally massive individual, Meyer was as tall as his son – somewhere near six and a half feet – and looked capable of breaking both Knowles and Cunningham in two with nothing but his bare hands.

Like both the president and the deputy assistant, his attention was firmly focused on a news report playing on a discreet TV screen mounted on the wall to Knowles' left.

The network was British, Cunningham knew, but the reporter was an American woman. Her commentary was delivered over footage of two men – defence lawyers, Cunningham concluded from the context – as they pushed their way out through a crowd of reporters outside of the court building.

'. . . by all accounts handed himself in last night at Stoke Newington Police Station. There has been no explanation as to why he would have done this, although circumstances are complicated by rumours of the death of Mansour's brother, with whom he is said to have lived. There is no more detail at this time.

'Appearing before District Judge George Bell in Court Number One of Westminster Magistrates' Court this morning, Mansour was represented by prominent criminal barrister Michael Devlin QC and solicitor Mr William Duffy of Duffy Associates. No plea was indicated and the matter was set down for a hearing before the Woolwich Crown Court tomorrow morning.

'We will have more on this story as it breaks, but for now, Nizar Mansour, a Syrian baggage handler working for Pan-Atlantic Airlines, has been charged with five hundred and thirty-four counts of murder and has been remanded in custody ahead of an appearance before the Crown Court tomorrow morning.

'This is Sarah Truman, reporting for ITN outside Westminster Magistrates' Court in London.'

Knowles switched off the screen as the footage cut back to the studio. He looked towards Cunningham, an expression of fury on his face.

'This is a mess. This is a monumental mess.'

'It hasn't worked out exactly as we'd planned it, no,' Cunningham conceded. He glanced towards Meyer as he spoke. A look of blame. They both knew at whom that blame was directed. And that, when all this was done, there *would* be consequences. 'But it could be a whole lot worse.'

'It hasn't worked out exactly as you'd planned? And exactly what *was* the plan, if you don't mind me asking?'

'Do you really want to know?'

'*Yes*, I want to know!'

Knowles was angrier than Cunningham had ever seen him.

For a moment, and for the very first time, he saw the special forces killer instead of the politician.

It put Cunningham on the back foot.

'The plan was to kill Mansour at his home yesterday,' Cunningham explained, taking care to give no sign of being ruffled. 'All the evidence was already in place to point to him as a lone bomber. The British police will be finding it over the course of the next few days. So when it was discovered he had been tracked and killed by a US Secret Service deployment, it would have been justifiable homicide. A minor blip with the Brits over an operation on their soil, yes, but it's the Brits. What's the worst that would have happened? A sternly worded letter?'

Knowles looked unimpressed.

'So what *did* happen?'

'We're still getting to the bottom of that.' Another glance at Meyer. 'But it seems that somehow Nizar Mansour escaped and handed himself in at the nearest police station.'

'You're kidding me, right? A team of trained special agents couldn't take out a baggage handler?'

'Like I said, we're still getting to the bottom of it. What matters is where we are now. Nizar Mansour is in custody. He'll be taken to a prison called Belmarsh. The place where the Brits keep all their terrorism suspects.'

'And?'

'And the wheels are already in motion.' Cunningham's moment of uncertainty had passed. His confidence was back.

'And what exactly does that mean?' Knowles demanded.

'Why so many questions, Mr President?' Cunningham spat out the final two words. An intentional show of disrespect. He was beginning to feel irritated by the stream of questions.

'You're usually happiest when you're blind to the steps I have to take.'

'That's because the things you do don't usually come directly back to *my* door,' Knowles replied. 'But this time? This shit can't go anywhere else.'

'Self-preservation. How noble of you, sir.'

'Don't take that tone, Kelvin.' Knowles' temper was returning. 'I didn't ask for this. I didn't ask for *any* of this.'

Cunningham opened his mouth to respond. To remind Knowles of their arrangement. But as he did he realised the truth of the president's words.

Everything they had done so far – from Knowles' inauguration onwards – had been risky. That was the nature of the beast. But the decision to dispense with Dale Victor in such an extreme way? This one *was* on him, Cunningham had to admit that. And Knowles was right. While the president had played no part, what Cunningham had done could do more damage to Knowles than any other part of their agenda.

The realisation forced Cunningham to hold his tongue. At least for now. He turned to Jack Meyer.

'Tell the president what he wants to know.'

Meyer shifted in his seat. Cunningham knew why. They were in this situation because of poor decisions, most of which had been made by Meyer's own son. He did not want to expose his own boy to the wrath of the US president.

He took a moment before he spoke. When he did, Cunningham saw that Meyer had taken care about where he chose to start.

'Well, Mr President, we have ... we have certain relationships with certain ... organisations in Europe, as well as at home.'

'You mean criminal organisations?'

'Yes, Mr President.'

'Mafia?'

'Something like that, Mr President. And these . . . friends of ours . . . they have access we don't have. People inside European prisons.'

'So what you're telling me is that we have people in this Belmarsh place.'

'Yes, Mr President. And we've been promised that Nizar Mansour won't make it to the end of the day.'

Knowles nodded.

'Which means,' Cunningham interjected, 'by the time you're tucked up in bed, there will be a dead Muslim baggage handler who has confessed responsibility for the bomb and to whom all incidental evidence will point. Which, from your point of view, is problem solved.'

'What about the loose ends?'

'What loose ends?'

'There are *always* loose ends, Kelvin. What about the two lawyers we saw leaving the court on TV? By the looks of it, those men just spent a whole morning speaking with this Mansour guy. You think he didn't tell them something?'

Cunningham glanced from Knowles to Meyer, then back to Knowles. He had already considered this problem. And he had wanted to avoid the discussion. It was Cunningham's preference to present solutions found, not solutions planned.

This time he had no choice.

'Unless they sat in silence for those hours, yes, we have to assume he told them something.'

'I can confirm that, sir.'

Knowles and Cunningham turned as one, towards Meyer.

'What do you know?'

'One of my agents, sir. Frank Hart. He made an approach, outside the courtroom.'

'Why?' Cunningham interrupted.

'Why what, sir?'

'Why did he make an approach? Why draw attention to himself? What the hell is wrong with your team over there?'

'They thought you'd want to know who had spoken to Mansour ASAP, sir. And Hart didn't identify himself. They don't have any reason to connect him to the White House.'

Cunningham nodded, though his anger remained obvious. He was still concerned at the recklessness of Romeo Meyer's team, but at least no names had been given this time. He pushed his irritation aside.

'What was the outcome?'

'When Frank made the approach, sir, it became clear that Romeo's name had been mentioned by Mansour.'

The flash of anger that hit Cunningham was difficult to suppress. This was *exactly* what he had feared.

'Raised in what context?' he asked, his tone low. He could not fully hide the anger, nor could he disguise the threat now in his voice.

'They suggested that Mansour was already familiar with Romeo before his arrest.' Meyer sounded dejected as he explained. 'And that the only explanation for that would be some sort of criminality on Romeo's part.'

'And Romeo's status? Do they know he's Secret Service?'

'That wasn't said expressly, no. But with everything else, sir, we probably need to assume that they do.'

Cunningham sat back in his chair. Placing his hand on his chin, he shook his head in disgust.

Knowles said nothing.

Meyer, too, remained silent, his head down.

There was no hiding it: this was bad news.

The silence lingered. Finally Cunningham climbed to his feet and walked to the windows behind the presidential desk.

He stood there in silence, staring out towards the manicured lawns and expertly crafted topiary that surrounded the world's most famous residence. None of it caught his attention for even a moment. Cunningham's mind was elsewhere. He was working through the problem. Searching for an answer.

Finally he turned.

'I was in two minds about this. It's only two men, I thought. Two deaths. The Brits won't like it, but if we spin them the right BS they'll go along with what we choose. They always do in the end.

'Not that it's that simple. Not when there's the likelihood of the media getting involved. As pliable as their government is, the British tabloids are out of control. So I thought it might be best to silence them another way. Bribery. Threats. I hadn't decided.

'But with what you just told us, Jack? Can we really trust that they'll stay silent, if we leave them capable of speaking? I mean, with Mansour dead their client confidentiality goes out the window.'

Cunningham was now just speaking his thoughts aloud. Thoughts too fast for Meyer.

'What are you saying, sir?' Meyer asked.

'I'm saying I need more time to think about this one,' Cunningham admitted. 'It's not easy but there's one thing I *do* know. If Mansour dies and then *both* his lawyers go too? With

TV footage of their faces outside his first court hearing? That's a damn guarantee of press attention. So for now – until I've got this worked out – I want you to put a team on them both. Pull out all the stops. Closest possible observation.'

'Sir.'

'And move forward with Mansour. *That* sonofabitch has to happen today, exactly as arranged.'

'Sir.'

'Get it done.'

Cunningham walked back around to his seat, then looked at Meyer expectantly. Despite having his orders, Meyer had not moved.

'Is there something else, Jack?'

'I'm afraid there is, sir.'

Cunningham did not like what he detected in Meyer's tone. Anxiety. He was not used to hearing that from the assistant director of the Secret Service.

'It's Tom Quilty, sir.'

The name was familiar, but Cunningham could not place it. That bothered him. It made his reply seem impatient.

'Who?'

'Tom Quilty, sir. The CIA analyst.'

Still nothing.

'I need a little more than that, Jack.'

'Sorry. Yeah. He was one of the five possible sources. For what Dale Victor said about the president.'

Knowles sat more upright at the reference to himself. This was not something that Cunningham had discussed in his presence. That was about to change.

'OK. OK.' Cunningham finally had the name. With his uncertainly gone, he was back in control. 'What about him?'

'We . . . we think we've confirmed him as the source. As the *original* source.'

Knowles sat forward in his chair.

'You mean this Quilty guy, he's the one who briefed Elizabeth Kirk three years ago?'

Both Cunningham and Meyer turned at the president's question.

'That's what we believe, Mr President,' Meyer replied.

'And why do you think you suddenly know this?' Cunningham asked, bringing Meyer's attention back to him. The deputy assistant was impressed at Knowles' quick uptake. But this was *his* ballgame.

'Seems he had a visitor. Last night.'

'Who?'

'An agent Joe Dempsey. One of Elizabeth Kirk's team over at the ISB.'

'Do you have any idea what the meeting was about?'

Cunningham was sure that he already knew the answer. He just needed to hear someone else say it.

'No way of knowing for sure, sir. But I think it's safe to take an educated guess on this one.'

'But Elizabeth Kirk never believed that information was true,' Cunningham said.

'She didn't, no,' Meyer replied. 'At least not back then. But with Dale Victor dead only days after hinting at it? Maybe she's had a . . . re-evaluation.'

'Enough to revisit her source.' Cunningham nodded as he spoke. He was quickly coming to the same conclusion Meyer had reached. And it was a problem. 'Why am I only hearing about this now? If the agent was there last night?'

'It took us this long to identify him,' Meyer replied. 'He

could have been anyone, sir. Until my guys ran the facial recognition. Now we know who this guy is. And he's definitely one of Kirk's.'

'He's a whole lot more than that.'

Once again, the president's interruption made both Meyer and Cunningham turn towards him. But this time there was something different in his voice. Cunningham could not place what it was. He was in no mood to wait and find out.

'What? What does that mean?'

'It means that Joe Dempsey is not just "one of Elizabeth Kirk's agents".'

Knowles' voice was flat. Whatever emotion Cunningham had detected moments before, it was gone.

'Joe Dempsey is Kirk's *first* agent. And her best. If Kirk sent Dempsey to Quilty, she did so because she thought Quilty was in some sort of danger. Which means Jack's right. She's re-evaluated what he told her three years ago. She thinks it might be true.'

Cunningham looked beyond Knowles as the president spoke. A vague memory was beginning to coalesce.

'That's a hell of a problem. You know what has to happen if she's taking this seriously. We need to be sure.'

'I'm sure.' Knowles' voice carried no room for doubt. 'She sent Joe Dempsey. That's all I need to know.'

Still Cunningham could not place the name. The man. The answer was just out of reach.

Knowles seemed to see the deputy assistant's struggle.

'The English agent, Kelvin. The guy from Trafalgar Square. Remember?'

Cunningham remembered.

'The guy who took down Anthony Haversume?'

'The same,' Knowles confirmed.

'Shit.' Cunningham could not quite believe his bad luck. 'Shit. What the . . . how is he working for Kirk? How is he even in the US?'

'They disbanded his agency after what happened.' Knowles' tone was still flat. 'When they did, I suggested him for the ISB.'

'You? Why?'

'Why not?' Knowles did not react well to the veiled criticism in Cunningham's voice. 'She needed an agent, I knew he was available. And more than capable. How was I to know back then that you'd blow up a goddamn seven-four-seven over international waters?'

Cunningham said nothing. He wanted to, but it was a losing argument. Knowles was right.

And besides, he now had a much more important concern. He remained silent as he thought through their predicament.

'Maybe this isn't the problem it seems,' he finally said, his mind working at speed. 'All Dempsey will know is whatever Kirk told him. Sure, Quilty might have repeated it last night. And maybe right now it seems compelling. But once the Brits start finding the evidence we've laid for them. Combined with the baggage handler's confession, and with him out of the way? It all starts to look a lot shakier. Just another conspiracy theory.'

Cunningham could hear a note of desperation in his own voice. He was speaking to convince himself as much as he was the other men in the room.

It was working. His own logic was beginning to sound compelling. And from his positive reaction, Meyer seemed to be in agreement.

Knowles, however, seemed far less sure. He powered up his tablet and the screen came to life. Moments later, a familiar female voice filled the room. The same TV report they'd seen earlier.

As it ended Knowles turned to face Cunningham.

'You recognise that lawyer's name?'

'Which name?' Cunningham was confused

'Michael Devlin. It didn't hit me at first. Not until Jack mentioned Joe Dempsey.'

'It still hasn't hit me. Who the hell is Michael Devlin?'

'Devlin was the lawyer who exposed Anthony Haversume. And he was there when Dempsey killed him. They know each other.'

For a moment Cunningham had found himself impressed at Knowles' recall.

It was not a reaction that had time to last. Not with the words that had followed.

They know each other.

The connection changed everything. It meant that there was a risk Dempsey would find out what Mansour had told Devlin. He would hear the name Romeo Meyer. And that name would lead to only one conclusion.

Cunningham shot Meyer another disgusted glance.

That fucking idiot kid.

His voice was curt when he spoke again. Efficient. There was now only one way this could end.

'Change of plan, Jack.'

'Sir.' Meyer sat up straighter.

'Keep the surveillance on the Scottish lawyer for now. But Devlin? He has to go.'

'How long, sir?'

'Twenty-four hours at the outside. But make it look like an accident so we don't have to start playing nice with the Brits.'

'And Dempsey, sir?'

'Dempsey?' Cunningham paused for a beat. His mind was made up. 'Dempsey dies today.'

TWENTY-SIX

The industrial buzz of Tom Quilty's apartment intercom tore the former analyst from his sleep. His eyes open wide, for a moment he forgot not just where he was, but when. In that instant between sleep and consciousness he was a young man again. Fit. Healthy. Formidable.

The illusion did not last; his wrecked body had dispelled it even before his mind had cleared. The feeling of age in his limbs was evidence enough, but it was nothing next to the pain of his lungs and throat. Within moments he was already struggling for breath.

The buzzer sounded again as he slowly lifted himself from his bed. He was weak for his age. But it was not physical weakness that drained him as he climbed to his feet. It was the desperate need for oxygen.

He glanced towards the tank that sat beside his bed. His nasal cannula was in place, an outlet into both nostrils. Quilty flicked it, to dislodge whatever was now blocking its flow. It made no difference; its air supply seems non-existent. He turned his attention to the tank's valve. Moving close, he listened for the sound that would tell him that the oxygen was flowing. He could hear it, but still he felt no benefit.

A quick inspection of the gauge told him why. The container was practically empty, reducing the airflow to a trickle.

The buzzer again.

'For Christ's sake, I'm . . . coming.' It was intended as a shout. It was a croak at best.

Sonsofbitches would wake the dead, he thought to himself as he pulled the cannula from his nose and headed towards his apartment's main room.

The second of Quilty's oxygen tanks was in the living room. It was the same tank he had used the previous evening, when Dempsey had been with him. Quilty reached it, placed the mask over his mouth and turned the output valve.

This time he felt the hit. The cold, concentrated oxygen filled what little capacity his lungs had left. He allowed himself to sit for a moment, as he took breath after breath. He sucked in mouthfuls of air, as if each might be his last.

The buzzer sounded again, longer than before. He placed the mask on the side of his armchair, climbed to his feet and walked to the intercom. It had no handset or camera. Just an open mic and speaker.

'Hello?'

'Mr Quilty?'

'Who's this?'

'AirGen delivery, sir. I'm here to change over your oxygen tanks.'

Quilty looked over his shoulder. With his bedroom tank empty the timing was about right. And he could see the AirGen logo on his other tank from here.

'How many of . . . how many of you are . . . there?'

'Just me, boss.'

'I'm . . . two floors up and no . . . no lift. You'll need to make . . . to make two trips.'

'Not a problem. If you buzz me in, I'll be straight up with the first tank.'

'OK. I'll leave the . . . the door on the latch.'

Quilty pressed the key icon on his intercom, releasing the

main building door downstairs. Then he opened his own locked door and left it ajar.

He turned to the key table that sat next to the wall beside the door. Opening the middle of three drawers, he reached in and took out an old, battered pack of cigarettes. A remnant from a less painful time in his life. They had sat there untouched for maybe two years. Beside them was a cheap plastic lighter.

The exertion was beginning to take its toll. Quilty could hear it in his breathing even before he could feel it.

He shuffled back to his armchair and lowered himself in. Once down he placed his mask back on his face and took five long hits of air. The deepest he had managed in months.

On the fifth breath he reached out and moved the oxygen tank closer, positioning it just ahead of himself but still within easy reach. He made an adjustment to the valve and then sat back into his chair, facing the door and awaiting his guest.

Once down he didn't have to wait long. Three minutes at most.

The first thing Quilty noticed was the AirGen logo on the right-hand chest of the newcomer's grey boiler suit. He had come in uniform. For a fleeting moment, Quilty felt a doubt. Maybe this guy *was* from the air company.

The second thing he noticed dispelled that doubt. His eyes scanned the full length of the boiler suit, taking in the distinctive bulge at its waist. Left side. Easier for the right hand to reach.

SIG Sauer P229 probably, he thought. *Standard issue Secret Service*.

The man stepped closer. Even in the uniform, Quilty recognised him as one of the men he'd seen over the last few days. The men who had parked outside in the grey sedan.

His colleague was nowhere to be seen. This guy was on his own.

Shame, Quilty thought to himself, as the man stepped through the door and into the apartment.

'You . . . forgot the . . . air.'

Quilty showed no trace of fear. Today was his day. It had been a long time coming.

'You don't seem too surprised by that,' the man replied. He closed the apartment door behind him, never taking his eyes away from Quilty. 'How'd you know?'

'AirGen.'

'We've seen them come here. We know they're your supplier.'

'They are. But . . . they don't . . . they don't deliver to a Mr Quilty.'

Boiler Suit smiled.

'Fake name, eh? You really are a paranoid old bastard, aren't you? I guess we should have caught that.'

He drew his pistol and aimed it towards Quilty.

'But then it hasn't made much difference, has it?'

'Still . . . still worth . . . a try.'

Quilty could feel his breathing become more laboured. He did not have long.

'Is it worth me asking what you told your visitor last night? If I promise to make this quick?'

'You've read . . . my file. What . . . what do you . . . think?'

'I think you're a determined old sonofabitch and I shouldn't waste my time.'

'Then you . . . you *have* read my . . . file.'

Quilty managed a laugh. It quickly became a hacking

cough, causing him to wheeze as he fought for air. It was time.

Quilty reached up and fumbled with his mask. His hands were now shaking wildly from lack of air.

'What are you doing?'

'I need . . . I need . . . a . . . cigarette.'

'Are you serious?'

'What . . . harm . . . can it do . . . now?'

The man stood still for a moment, considering the answer. An answer that was unarguable. Whether it was compassion for Quilty's suffering or just guilt from what was to come, he made a decision.

With his gun still aimed at Quilty's chest, he stepped forward, pushed the old man's shaking hands aside and took the oxygen mask from his face. With his free hand he took a cigarette from Quilty's pack, placed it between his lips and picked up the cigarette lighter.

Quilty moved his head forward, bringing the cigarette nearer to the lighter.

And nearer to the oxygen tank.

And watched as the man flicked the aged, long unused lighter into life. Once. Twice. Three times.

The explosion was both instant and devastating. It sent fiery gas and the deadly shrapnel from the oxygen tank in every direction around the apartment. An instant inferno that no one could survive.

Exactly as Quilty had intended.

For five full minutes he had gone without air. Starting from the moment he had taken his seat, moved the tank and disconnected his mask's supply hose from the output valve.

It was the longest he had breathed unaided in almost two

years. But as damaged as Quilty's lungs were, he still had his determination. Determination to fill the air around him with highly flammable, concentrated oxygen from the tank's open valve.

It was a last act of defiance. Quilty would leave this life on his own terms. And he would take one of them with him.

TWENTY-SEVEN

J ack Meyer scanned the small secure meeting room, located within the White House Office. The door was closed and the space was filled to its capacity of six. Meyer himself and five of the Secret Service agents under his immediate command.

Four of those agents were intimates. Men that Meyer had known for years. Men he trusted with his life, and with much more besides. Each of them skilled and experienced in the kind of work with which he was about to task them.

The fifth? She was an outsider. Here at the insistence of John Knowles. Meyer had tried to resist the introduction of an unknown element to his team, but an executive order from the president was not something he could ignore. Especially when that order was a response to the mistakes of Meyer's own son.

Knowles wanted someone on the team who had *his* confidence. And so Special Agent Eden Grace was now a part of this, whether Meyer liked it or not. But she would face a harsh introduction to reality.

Meyer took his seat at the head of the table. Eden Grace was at the table's far end. In Meyer's direct line of sight, and – for now – entirely oblivious to what she was about to learn.

'Gentlemen . . .'

Meyer stopped himself. He looked to the end of the table, towards Grace. She was looking back, and Meyer held her gaze as he continued. He needed to read her reaction to everything he had to say.

'And ladies, of course. Today will not be your typical day in the office. Another little project has come up. One which needs to be dealt with in the next twelve hours. In other words, the president has need of your . . . extra-curricular expertise.'

Meyer's eyes swept the room. His core team was engaged. Listening. Grace, however, seemed confused.

That was to be expected.

'As always this is not something I can order any of you to do. It's on a strict volunteer basis, but as ever your involvement will be well compensated.'

'Where is it?'

The question came from Meyer's right. From an agent who, in any other company, would be described as 'the big guy'. Far less imposing when next to Meyer, the man's physical capabilities were still obvious.

'Manhattan,' Meyer replied. 'The jet is already waiting at Reagan. For those of you who *are* in, it's wheels up in an hour.'

'And the target?' The question came from the same man.

Meyer picked up the remote control that sat on the table ahead of him, and with a single click he brought the room's seventy-inch, paper-thin display screen to life.

Every pair of eyes in the room focused on the image that appeared. It was a close up of a man, aged in either his late thirties or early forties. He appeared fit and strong; a physical specimen not unlike the agent who had so far led the questioning. Unlike the agent, the target carried facial damage: a heavily broken nose and a ragged six-inch scar down his left cheek.

Meyer was silent as he studied the image. Like his team, this was his first sight of Joe Dempsey. And what he saw concerned him. Meyer did not know what it was, but there was something about the man . . .

'Sir,' Eden Grace's voice broke through Meyer's thoughts. 'Do you mind if I ask—'

'Who is he?' The same speaker as before interrupted her abruptly.

'His name's Joe Dempsey,' Meyer replied, choosing to ignore Grace for now. 'He's the primary agent with the International Security Bureau of the United Nations.'

'And the mission is?'

'What do you think the mission is?' It was not an attempt at sarcasm. They were against the clock and Meyer had no time for stupid questions. 'Look around the room, Braddock. If it's you four on the team then it's your speciality, isn't it?'

Special Agent Braddock smirked in reply, as a murmur of understanding ran around the rest of the room occupants.

Except for one.

'Sir.' Grace's look of confusion was rapidly turning to a look of concern. 'I really need to know—'

'Within twelve hours, sir?' Once again Braddock interrupted. And once again Meyer allowed it. 'You know that's not long enough to do this the right way? Not if you want it to look like an accident?'

'Sir, I—'

'What it looks like is not as important as time on this one,' Meyer replied, still ignoring Grace. 'The president has his reasons. This absolutely has to happen today.'

The murmur rolled again. Fuelled by the few words each man needed to consider the offer. It was efficient, and it was over almost as soon as it had begun.

Meyer was unsurprised. This particular group – or *his* four agents, at least – were well used to these briefings. For years and for successive presidencies, they had been doing what their superiors deemed to be both necessary and necessarily discreet.

To them it was a patriotic duty that just happened to include a significant source of extra income into the bargain.

'How much?' Braddock asked. He seemed to have appointed himself spokesman.

'The usual bonus,' Meyer replied. 'Paid in the usual way.'

'Sir, I really need to know what's going on.'

For the first time there was no interruption. Which meant that Meyer's team were satisfied that they knew enough.

That left only Special Agent Eden Grace.

Time for her education.

The room fell silent as Meyer focused on Grace. Flanked by large, physical men, it was inevitable that she would seem small in comparison. But equating that size difference with weakness would be a mistake, Meyer knew. Grace was as well-trained in the field as any of her colleagues.

None of which made her any more suitable for the task Knowles' had appointed her today. What they were here to do was not about physical ability. It was not about strength or speed. It was about *willing*. It was about *trust*. It was about obeying orders without question.

And Meyer sensed that this description did not fit Eden Grace.

'Agent Grace, you've been included in this briefing at the direct instruction of President Knowles. He wanted you brought up to speed on a threat that has arisen against the security of this presidency, and he wanted you involved in the . . . unorthodox steps we will be taking today to neutralise that threat.'

'I don't understand what this is, sir.' Grace's voice was firm. 'You seem to be discussing killing a man. Unless I've misread this?'

'You've misread nothing, missy.'

The last statement came from Special Agent Cobb. His first contribution to the meeting. Meyer watched with interest as Grace ignored it entirely.

'Sir, what you're discussing. It's a crime. It's murder.'

Meyer nodded his head. He had no intention of denying it.

'You can call it that if you like, Agent Grace. Others would call it democide. I prefer to look at it as an executive action. I suggest you do the same.'

'Sir. You can't be—'

'There's a lot more to the Secret Service than our official role. Sometimes the president has problems. Things that need to be dealt with discreetly. With no questions being asked and with no trail coming back to the White House.'

Grace did not respond. Meyer could not tell if she was shocked by what she was hearing, or just letting it sink in.

He continued.

'That's what *we're* for. That's what *we* do. And it's what we've done for decades. For president after president. Our little unit, it's a team within a team. A family. We do what needs to be done and no one else ever has to know. And if President Knowles hadn't insisted I bring you in, you wouldn't have had to know about it either.'

The uncertainty on Grace's face was undisguised. Meyer could understand why. What he was telling her, he knew it made sense. It did not take any kind of keen analytical mind to realise that yes, of course the Secret Service were the obvious foot soldiers of a ruthless president.

Her confusion, then, was that such a description could be applied to President Knowles.

'How do I know President Knowles is involved in what you are doing here?' The question Meyer had expected. 'How do I know he has ordered any of this?'

Meyer smiled. It was the perfect reaction. No criticism of their proposed action. No disgust. Just a need for certainty. It showed her loyalty to the president. Maybe Knowles was justified in placing his trust in her after all.

'What, you think I've gone rogue?' Meyer's words suggested impatience with the young agent's question, but his tone didn't match.

'I'm the assistant director of the Secret Service, Agent Grace. You don't trust me when I say this order comes straight from the president?'

Grace said nothing more. She just held Meyer's gaze. As if his words had made no impression on her. It left him no other option.

Meyer picked up the handset of the telephone that sat in the middle of the table and pressed 'zero'.

'Get me the president.'

For a few seconds no one spoke. A silence broken by Meyer.

'Jack Meyer, Mr President.'

Meyer paused.

'Yes, Mr President. The unit is engaged. They'll be in New York today. But we have a problem.'

Meyer looked at Grace as he spoke.

'Special Agent Eden Grace, Mr President. She seems . . . hesitant to accept that her orders have come from you . . . Yes, Mr President.'

Meyer placed the receiver down and pressed the loudspeaker

icon on the cradle. The voice that immediately filled the room was unmistakable.

'Agent Grace?'

'Mr President.'

'Agent Grace, I'm sorry to involve you in what will happen in New York today. Truly sorry. But I have no other choice.'

'Mr President, are you saying . . .'

'Yes, Agent Grace. Assistant Director Meyer is telling you the truth. What has to happen today has to happen. For the good of this administration.'

'But sir . . .'

'There are no "buts". This must be done. And I need someone there in whom I can have complete confidence. Your record is immaculate.'

'Sir? What . . . what are you expecting me . . .'

'I'm expecting you to be you. Mistakes have been made in the last twenty-four hours, Agent Grace. Mistakes that have weakened this office. Made it vulnerable. I can't have any more of those. I know *you* won't make them and that you won't allow them to be made. I know you'll do your duty. I know you'll do what's right.'

'I'm sure Agent Grace understands now, Mr President.' It was Meyer who spoke, finality in his voice. The repeated mention of 'mistakes' was hitting too close to home. He was bringing this to an end. 'This will be dealt with. You have *my* guarantee of that.'

'I hope so, Assistant Director. And Agent Grace?'

'Mr President?'

'My apologies again that I have had to involve you in this. But I know I can count on you. Do your duty. Do what's right.'

'Mr President.'

The speaker disconnected. Knowles was gone.

Meyer turned his head to face Eden Grace. She looked blank, as if the blood had left her face.

'Happy now?'

Grace looked up in response. She gave no hint of emotion. Not until she spoke, her voice firm and her words for the first time informal.

'Happy? No, I'm not happy. But don't you worry, Jack. I'll do my job.'

TWENTY-EIGHT

Belmarsh.

Mansour had heard the word before today. Not often. In news reports, mainly.

It had meant nothing to him. Why would it? He'd had no reason to think that he would ever go there. Not as a visitor and certainly not as a prisoner. Hell, he'd had no need to even know where it was.

That was then. Now? *Now* it meant something. Devlin and Duffy had told Mansour what he needed to know.

Belmarsh was not just any jail. It was a state-of-the-art, high-security facility on the outskirts of London, fifteen miles or so from the Marylebone Court.

Like most closed prisons, Belmarsh housed ordinary inmates from the local area. Which in this case meant men from across London and Essex, either serving sentences or waiting trial.

But that was not the Belmarsh Mansour was about to experience. That, for want of a better term, was the 'outer Belmarsh'. Mansour was heading somewhere very different. He was going to the Category A facility that existed behind the walls within it.

A prison within a prison.

Regarded by many as Britain's version of Guantanamo Bay, the 'inner Belmarsh' had been built to hold the very worst of the worst. Serial killers. Hitmen. Feared underworld figures. And terrorists.

Especially terrorists . . .

And that was where he was headed now.

Mansour could discern very little from his secure cell in the back of the prison van. Its window had been blacked out from the inside. Mansour doubted this was usual — why have windows in the first place if it was? — and the effect was disconcerting.

With no way to see out, he could not use exterior details to help guess at the van's location in London. And without a watch or a clock for reference, he could not even be sure how long he'd been in there.

But what did time matter now anyway? As for the cell's cold temperature and seemingly intentional discomfort, he had experienced far worse during his time fighting in Syria; this was near luxury compared to what he had suffered at home.

No. None of these things had concerned Mansour. But something else had. Something he had not expected. Because despite being the only prisoner occupying one of the six individual cells in the van, he was not making the journey alone.

His cell door had been left unlocked and open, and in the opposite cell was a guard.

Dressed in a standard uniform of black trousers, white shirt and black jumper with the company logo on the breast, the guard was older than Mansour by perhaps five years. Overweight and with short, receding brown hair, Mansour had noticed the guard's stubby fingers and fat wrists as he sat in the open cell across the van's gangway, steadying himself against every slow turn by placing a free hand against the wall.

Mansour had no such luxury. With less than twelve inches between either shoulder and its corresponding wall the cell was claustrophobic. And yet having a foot either way was enough for Mansour to be thrown hard against those walls with every sharp turn the van made.

It would have been helpful for Mansour's hands to be free to protect against this. But instead each wrist was bound by a stiff cuff – tough leather and steel – with the other end of each connected to secure, immovable loops situated either side of him, on the short cell bench.

If the restraints had been designed to minimise whatever movement was still possible, they were unsuccessful. All they did was make that movement a lot more painful.

Probably the real reason for them, Mansour had concluded.

A cynical conclusion, based very much on the behaviour of the guard, who had been openly hostile from the very beginning of the journey.

Referring to Mansour as 'Abdul' was just the start. A crude attempt to insult him, it had been followed by a consistent campaign of verbal abuse against his religion, his country, his people. Every cruel word was an insult. Every sneer a challenge.

Mansour had ignored it all. They meant nothing, he reasoned. Just the words of a man who believed his prisoner was responsible for the deaths of hundreds of innocent people. If anything, Mansour understood both the guard's hatred and his need to voice it.

And so they had spent the entire journey facing each other across the gangway, with the guard baiting and Mansour refusing to bite. A battle of wills that Mansour was determined to win.

The vehicle picked up speed, which meant the traffic must have eased off.

Mansour's first reaction was relief. It suggested that they were finally out of London. Which in turn meant they could not be far from their destination. His ordeal was almost over; soon he would be in Belmarsh, away from the abusive guard.

But that relief was misplaced.

Almost immediately the prison van took a corner at speed. Fast enough that Mansour was thrown repeatedly sideways in his seat with much more force than before. The uncontrolled movement caused his restraints to bite deeper into his skin. It felt like they were rubbing against his bones.

If the first turn could be dismissed as accidental, by the third Mansour had no doubt that the driving style was intentional. That the unseen driver was doing it to show their disgust with the 'criminal' the van was carrying. Exactly as the guard had been doing throughout the journey. Only now the torment was more than words. The memory of the last hours of cold, impatient discomfort were dismissed, replaced by pain and anger as his wrists burned.

And all the while the guard watched, his free hands steadying him against the worst of the van's movement and his smirk growing with every painful turn.

'FUCKING ... FUCKING ... FUCKS!'

It was all Mansour could think to shout as the van turned again and caused his left wrist to buckle. Like any joint, it could only go so far in the wrong direction.

'YOU ... YOU WILL BREAK MY FUCKING WRIST!'

He shouted the words through gritted teeth, fighting to keep his body rigid and still. For an instant he was sure that effort would fail. And then it was over. The corner was turned, and the speed of the van decreased.

Somehow, his wrist – bloody and bruised though it was – was unbroken.

A fact which did not make Mansour any less angry. After everything he had been through – his sister's kidnapping, finding himself under the control of Romeo and his friends, the bomb on the plane, his brother's death – the intentional physical pain being inflicted on him was more than he could tolerate.

Enough was finally enough.

'FUCKING ARSEHOLES!' he shouted. '*EMAK DLALE!*'

'HEY!' The shouted interruption came from the guard. His smile was wide but grim. He was enjoying Mansour's reaction. It was the satisfaction he had been seeking since the beginning. 'Watch your language, sunshine.'

'Fuck you.' He spat the words in anger. 'Your fucking friend driving, he try to break my fucking wrist.'

'I told you to watch your language, you murdering fuck.'

The words struck hard. It was not the first time the guard had used them, but it seemed to be the first time Mansour had heard them. They combined with the lightning bolts of pain still shooting through his wrist and arm to test whatever self-control he had left.

As he looked upon the other man's reddened, bloated face and listened to the torrent of abuse, Mansour felt something stir.

He felt his fire return.

'That's what's wrong with you lot, Abdul.' With the sound of the van's engine quietened, the guard resumed his barrage of abuse. 'You come to this country and do whatever the hell you want, don't ya? It starts with disrespect to us what let you in. And it ends with you blowing up women and kids on planes. Why? All because you ain't got the balls to fight a proper war.'

Mansour said nothing.

The guard's words tailed off as the sound of heavy machinery shook the van. He climbed to his feet.

'Home time, Abdul. We're here.'

Again, Mansour said nothing.

The first gate had opened. A mechanised steel barrier that slowly slid aside, to allow the few vehicles permitted inside the prison to come and go.

Only once the sound had stopped did Mansour feel the van pull forward. He could not tell how far, but when the same sound started again – this time to his rear – he assumed that they were now inside.

'Not long now, Abdul,' the guard said. 'Nearly time to meet up with all yer dirty Muhammad mates inside, eh?'

Mansour did not reply. Instead his gaze remained fixed on his battered wrists. Finally shaken out of the shock that had seemed to paralyse him, he could finally comprehend what lay ahead.

Inner Belmarsh.

It was the term Michael Devlin had used. When Mansour had first heard the words, they meant nothing. How could they? But now he knew more, and so now they sounded daunting.

The van moved to a final stop.

'Yer home, Abdul. Last place you'll ever be.'

The guard smiled and rubbed his eyes as the van's thick, steel back door opened and outside light filled the space.

Mansour stayed silent.

'Get him out, Bob.'

The order came from the now open back door. The gangway between the cells was not wide enough for two officers and a prisoner, making it a one-man job.

Mansour's guard moved immediately.

'You ready to meet your pals, Abdul?' he asked as he moved into the few available inches of Mansour's cell. His voice was low now, enough that only he and his prisoner could hear. 'They'll be waiting for ya, I'll bet. So you can all celebrate what a murdering little fuck you are.'

He leaned forward, roughly shoving his shoulder into Mansour's nose.

He unlocked the left-hand restraint from the bench and slowly put it onto his own right wrist. As he did so he twisted and turned the cuffs.

Mansour gritted his teeth through the pain and faced forward, determined to show no reaction. He would not give this man any further enjoyment.

'Stubborn fucker, ain't ya?' the guard whispered, applying yet more pressure to Mansour's cuff, tightening it at the site of his injury. 'That won't last. They'll break you in here, Abdul. In every possible way.'

He moved sideways and reached for the right-hand bench restraint. As he did so, he brought his mouth closer to Mansour's ear.

'And when they do, you'll wish it'd been you that had your throat slit, and not your piece of shit brother.'

The guard must have believed that Mansour was now a dog on a leash; that, with the left cuff in place, he could control his prisoner. But the final taunt – the reference to Rifat – was too much for Mansour. He snapped. Just as the right restraint clicked open.

Positioned between crouch and standing, the guard was off-balance. His only steadying support was his connection to Mansour; the cuff that linked him to the prisoner's damaged wrist.

Mansour moved without warning, exploding upwards. The movement pulled the guard even further off-balance; blind to the renewed damage to his wrist, Mansour pulled his left hand into the cell wall, dragging the guard with it and exposing his face and torso to what was coming.

'HELP!'

The guard managed just a single shout as the top of Mansour's head collided with his open mouth. The force would have been enough to damage a closed jaw. To an open one, it was devastating. The guard's upper four front teeth were shattered by the impact, digging deep into Mansour's skull as they were ripped from their roots.

Mansour ignored the new pain, too; it was nothing he had not felt before, and it was dwarfed by his burning need to damage something. To damage someone. To finally – truly – vent his grief and his anger.

The guard had goaded the wrong man on the wrong day.

Mansour drove him back into the opposite cell. The place from which he had chosen to torment his prisoner.

The guard stumbled backwards, falling against the cell bench. His cuff pulled Mansour with him, and Mansour used that momentum to bring his forehead crashing into the man's nose, his full falling weight crushing every last iota of cartilage that gave it its shape.

Mansour pushed himself upwards with his right arm, intending to use it to strike down as soon as he was stable. He didn't get the chance. In the few seconds it had taken him to deal with his guard, two prison officers had entered the van and grabbed him.

He took the moment he had left to look at his earlier

tormentor, bloodied, beaten and unmoving against the cell bench.

Mansour would pay for what he had just done. He knew that.

And he knew something else besides.

Whatever the price, it was worth it.

TWENTY-NINE

Joe Dempsey crossed First Avenue at a run, accelerating into a sprint as soon as his feet touched the pavement on its east side. He had one long block before he reached home, The Stratford on York Avenue.

The details of East 73rd Street passed in a blur as Dempsey pushed himself ever harder, holding nothing back for the final 250 yards.

Even aged thirty-eight, when most physical men were taking their feet off the gas, Dempsey knew no other way. Either he kept himself in the best possible shape, or people died.

Himself included.

He came to a stop at the corner of 73rd and York. He was breathing hard.

Dempsey glanced at his watch as he recovered his breath. Midday exactly. Later than he had intended. With no time to cook before heading to the office, he would need to get his protein hit from elsewhere.

One of his favourite things about living in New York were the bodegas. Small, cheap convenience stores that seemed to inhabit every street corner. Even on the Upper East and Upper West sides, where such places might be surrounded by the kind of gourmet restaurants and high-end clothes designers that were more suited to the richer locations.

He began to walk towards York Avenue itself, breaking into a jog when he saw a break in traffic. It was one of the habits which set him apart from 'other' New Yorkers; like almost everyone else from England, he struggled with the whole concept of jaywalking. He could not understand waiting for a 'walk' signal when he knew no cars were coming, particularly on an arrow-straight road like York Avenue where he could see for maybe half a mile in either direction.

And so he did what the English always do. He ignored the 'Don't Walk' signal and jogged across to the bodega that sat on the other side of York, directly across from The Stratford.

'Hello, Mr Joseph.' The greeting came from Ali, the bodega's manager. A serious, dedicated man, Ali had been in Manhattan for far longer than Dempsey. 'More exercise today?'

'No, that's it for today,' Dempsey replied. 'I've got work to do.'

'Like always,' Ali observed. 'Egg and sausage muffin, yes?'

'Please.'

Dempsey smiled. The idea that someone knew him well enough to know his habits? Sure, it was a small thing – the order was his go-to for the necessary post-workout mix of protein and carbs when he was pushed for time – but it was also a first. Outside of the military, remarkably few people had ever played any kind of part in Dempsey's life.

Now he had a shopkeeper who knew his diet. And who, he was sure, suspected a whole lot more besides.

'Two minutes.'

Dempsey watched as Ali moved away from the cash register. His interest in the man was as piqued as ever. The way he walked. His particular physicality. Dempsey could spot the imprint of elite military training anywhere. He had seen it in Ali the first time they'd met, and every time since.

He suspected that Ali saw the same thing in him. Not that either would ever raise the subject. Whatever Ali's past in

Pakistan – and whatever had brought him to the US – that was *his* business. And so they would go on as they always had. With the fiction of them as just a pair of civilians. Normal men. A shopkeeper and his customer.

Dempsey distracted himself with the bodega's television, while he waited. The story was in mid-report by the time he looked up, but the images were unmistakable.

The wreckage of Flight PA16.

'Ali, can I turn this up?'

'Of course.'

Dempsey reached across the counter for the remote. A second later and he could hear every word from CNN's international correspondent.

'. . . was arrested in the early hours of this morning, British time. It seems the British police held him overnight and brought him to Westminster Magistrates' Court this morning, where his case was processed and sent to a superior British court for trial.'

Dempsey turned towards Ali.

'You know what this is about?'

'Yes, Mr Joseph. They have arrested the man who bombed the plane yesterday.'

The news was a surprise. To have caught a suspect already. If this did all lead back to Knowles, Dempsey would have expected the person they'd used to plant the bomb to have vanished without a trace.

'Are you sure?'

'Yes, sir. Watch the screen. You will see.'

Dempsey turned back to the TV.

'The suspect has been identified as Nizar Mansour, a Syrian refugee who had found work as a baggage handler for

Pan-Atlantic Airlines. From what little we know at this time, it's been said that he confessed to the bombing.'

Dempsey's mind started racing.

A Syrian refugee. What the hell does that have to do with Knowles?

It was not the information that Dempsey had been expecting. Had Kirk and Quilty been wrong to connect Knowles to this?

From what Quilty had said the night before, Dempsey could see a clear path from President John Knowles to the bombing of Flight PA16. Sure, it was an extreme reaction to what Dale Victor had said on camera. Not least when Quilty had told Victor's people nothing of value. But still a plausible theory, if Knowles thought the threat was real. If he believed his administration – hell, his liberty, maybe even his life – was at risk.

But now this? How did the confession of a Syrian baggage handler play into that whole theory? Had he raced ahead of himself, too keen to believe what Quilty had told him? Could it have just been a terrorist attack? That would be a more straightforward scenario than a complex government conspiracy. And the simple explanation was usually the right one.

It's the logical conclusion, Dempsey thought. *And yet . . . and yet . . .*

And yet having met Quilty, and knowing Kirk's doubts and suspicions, Dempsey was finding it hard to accept it.

Confessed to planting the bomb. The thought derailed Dempsey's others. *Confessed? What kind of a terrorist kills hundreds of people, gets away with it and then turns himself in?*

The question answered itself.

Terrorists did not surrender themselves; Dempsey knew that better than anyone. They might proudly claim their actions once apprehended, especially when those actions had resulted in mass destruction. But they did not willingly give themselves up.

Accidental killers. *They* confessed, usually driven by guilt. Criminals too, when the evidence was against them. But a terrorist? Within hours of his greatest triumph? When he was free to plan another attack?

It's too convenient.

The screen changed again, just as Dempsey's thoughts were coalescing.

The correspondent disappeared. Replaced by footage of a press scrum outside of a building Dempsey instantly identified.

Westminster Magistrates' Court.

A moment more and the building was no longer the only thing he could name. On the screen, pushing through the crowd of cameramen and reporters, were two men.

One of them Dempsey had never seen before.

The other he would recognise anywhere.

THIRTY

Michael Devlin poured a double dash of sixteen-year-old Lagavulin into a Waterford Crystal tumbler, replaced the cork and set the bottle back among his whisky collection.

He raised the glass to his nose and breathed deeply. The smell of smoky peat was all-pervasive. Exactly as it should be. And exactly as it was on the tongue as he took his first sip.

The house was empty. Michael had no idea when Sarah would be home, but it was 5 p.m. and he'd had enough. It was early by his standards – by Sarah's, too – but it had been a long and stressful day. One that had left Michael with concerns he did not need.

Not again.

The whisky collection – the good stuff, at least – was kept in the living room, on top of a large, antique sideboard. It was a room that Michael and Sarah rarely used, and so the collection of framed photographs dotted near to the whisky was rarely seen.

Michael took another sip. Bigger this time, a full slug. And as he felt the burn in his throat, he reached out for the picture that always caught his eye first.

Liam Devlin had been older than Michael, but not by much. Just a year ahead of his brother at school, Liam's life had taken a drastically different route. Prison followed by a decade at the pinnacle of the Belfast underworld. And then death in the hills of Wicklow, the victim of a bullet meant for Michael.

The two boys were young in the photograph. Liam had

been the bigger of the two back then, with a shock of dark hair in contrast to his brother's blond. But there could be no doubt of their family connection. Almost identical faces – full of life and of mischief – saw to that.

Full of life, Michael thought again.

The words brought tears to his eyes. Tears of grief, and of guilt.

Michael rarely thought of Liam. He had taught himself not to, because that was the only way to get past his brother's death. A death for which he would always blame himself.

He smiled sadly and touched his fingertip to the image of his brother's face.

Another deep gulp of whisky left the glass in need of a refill. He placed the frame down carefully and dealt with his drink, before turning to another photograph.

Three men. One a full-grown Michael, exactly thirty years old on the day it was taken. To his right, Daniel Lawrence. The same age but four inches shorter, back when Daniel had been whippet-thin. And to his left, Derek Reid. Michael's former pupil-master. Almost twenty years older than Michael and Daniel, he was two inches taller than Michael's own six foot one and was half again as wide across his broad shoulders.

Michael's two closest friends and – after Liam – as close as anyone could come to being family.

Both dead. Both murdered.

Michael shook his head at the thought, glancing across again to the picture of Liam as he did so. His three brothers; one by nature, two by choice. All dead.

And yet somehow *he* was still here. Somehow *he* was living his best life, engaged to a beautiful, successful woman and at the top of his profession. Despite everything he had done – all of the wrongs that came back to his door – it was always others who had paid the price.

Always his brothers.

It should have been me, he thought, taking another mouthful of whisky as a tear slowly made its way down his right cheek. *It should have been me.*

But it had not been him, and Michael had learned to accept that. Moments of weakness aside, he had learned to live with the guilt. With the knowledge that the people he loved had paid for his misdeeds. He had done so because the alternative was unthinkable.

That they had died for nothing.

It was exactly that which concerned him now. The threats from the American as they had left the courtroom. Michael had seen enough of life to know instinctively how dangerous that man was, and to trust that he did not make threats lightly.

Which left him where? Back in danger? Back in the firing line?

And who'll die for me this time. Sarah?

The thought was almost too much to bear, and so Michael was happily distracted when the sound of his mobile broke through his downward spiral. He reached into his pocket and pulled out the handset, unsure if he intended to answer.

The name on the screen made the decision for him.

That cannot be a coincidence.

'Joe Dempsey. How the hell are you?'

THIRTY-ONE

Bruce Bull replaced the telephone handset into its cradle and sat back into his chair. The call had been from Belmarsh. And like everything else, it had only served to complicate Bull's investigation.

'Gonna share, boss?'

Sean McConnell was Bull's most experienced detective sergeant. Originally from Dublin in the Republic of Ireland, at fifty years old he had worked alongside Bull for exactly half his life. First at Special Branch, then at SO15.

He was one of the few people Bull trusted completely.

'Seems our boy attacked a prison guard,' Bull said. He made no attempt to hide the resignation in his voice. 'As they un-cuffed him on arrival at Belmarsh.'

'Shit. More fight in the little fella than you thought then.'

'Well, it sure as hell doesn't fit the guy who pissed himself at the sight of the Secret Service.'

'You think you've been played, boss?'

Bull took a moment; the thought had crossed his mind.

'I don't know,' he finally answered. 'The way it's being told to me, Mansour went berserk and beat the shit out of the guy. Doesn't seem likely, from what I saw of him.'

'Be careful you're not reaching now. To find excuses for the fella.'

'Don't worry about that. I'm not jumping to any

conclusions. If it all stacks up then that'll be a different story. Now, where are we?'

'Close to it all stacking up, if you want my take,' McConnell replied grimly. 'Everything points to him, boss.'

'Tell me.'

'Well, first off, Bilal Essa. That was a red herring.'

'How?'

'He was just a lazy fecker who sold his National Insurance number to Rifat Mansour. So Rifat could have worked for Pan-Atlantic Airlines with Nizar.'

'So we assume he didn't have one?'

'No. Nizar is here legally. Rifat wasn't.'

'So Essa exists, but he's nothing to do with this?'

'Doesn't seem to be.'

Bull nodded his head. The assessment made sense.

'What else do we have?'

'Footage from Heathrow. A lot of it.'

'What does it show?'

'Well, it's got Nizar Mansour paying a whole lot of attention to a particular bag. Marked up as 'Heavy'. The cameras show him taking hold of it from the point it comes through the front desk, right up until he places it in the hold. Doesn't let the thing out of his sight the entire time.'

'Which proves he put the thing on the plane. As he admitted.' Bull looked away. A thought occurred to him. 'How much footage is "a lot"?'

'What do you mean?'

'I mean how many cameras caught this little journey Mansour took?'

'All of them, far as I can see.'

'All of them?'

'Yeah. What I mean is, there doesn't seem to be any of the journey between check-in and the plane that's not covered. It's a complete set of footage.'

'Are the cameras manned?'

'No, pre-programmed. They move through the day, following a set pattern.'

Bull nodded his head. He had anticipated the answer.

'That's a hell of a stroke of luck, don't you think?'

'What is?'

'The fact that these pre-programmed cameras all happened to be facing in a direction that caught Mansour, all at exactly the right time.'

'Boss?' McConnell looked confused for a moment. A look soon replaced by understanding. 'Oh.'

'It's too convenient, surely?'

'It's . . . it's . . . not usual, is it?'

'No, it's bloody well not.'

Neither man spoke for a moment. Bull was considering the implications of what they had just discussed. He could see that McConnell was doing the same.

It was McConnell who broke the silence.

'OK, let's assume for a moment that someone's behind this. That Mansour's being set up somehow. Why would he confess?'

'I've been thinking about that,' Bull replied. 'What if Mansour handed himself in to save his own life?'

'What?'

'It's not so hard to believe, Sean. He confessed to the whole thing to get Romeo Meyer out of the room. What if the first confession was something similar?'

'I don't follow.'

'Someone killed Rifat Mansour. Within a timeframe

that could have been just minutes before Nizar got to Stoke Newington Police Station.'

'Could have been minutes, boss. But it could have been up to an hour either way, too.'

'I know that. But bear with me. What if Nizar was there when Rifat was killed? What if Nizar saw them do it and had to run? And headed straight for the station to save his own life?'

'It's a stretch.'

'Is it? What did the desk sergeant say? Nizar Mansour burst through the doors out of breath, hardly able to speak as he made his confession. At almost the exact same time as a local resident reported what could have been gunshots outside.'

'OK, let's say that's how it happened. You think whoever's pulling the strings meant to kill Nizar too?'

'Let's assume they did. Where would that have left us? We would have one dead Syrian baggage handler – the *right* one – and then our investigation would have led us to the footage of him planting the bomb. Footage I wouldn't have questioned if I hadn't seen Mansour and Romeo Meyer together last night. Because if Mansour had died, this case would have been open and shut.'

McConnell listened carefully, a small smile threatening the corner of his mouth. Bull could see that he was excited.

'This could really be something,' he said, his head nodding along to his own words. 'But what you're saying? Someone with the ability to mess with the camera programme at Heathrow. And the audacity to kill Nizar on British soil. You know where that's leading, boss.'

'I didn't say the theory didn't have some issues,' Bull admitted, sitting back into his chair once again. 'What we need to know is *why* Nizar placed that bag on the plane. I'm sure Romeo Meyer has to be involved in that part. In all of this, in fact. If you'd seen him, you'd understand. Only someone with that kind of influence or authority could pull this shit. And that's a whole world of trouble, given his position within the Secret Service. One way or another, though, we need to bring him in and find out who it is he's working for.'

'Seriously?'

'Seriously. I just have to work out how we get away with doing that.'

'Rather you than me, boss.'

'Thanks.'

The two men sat for a moment longer, considering the trouble ahead.

When McConnell finally spoke, his voice was filled with concern.

'Bruce, are you sure about this?'

Bull sat up slightly at McConnell's use of his name. Even after twenty-five years, it was rare that his DS spoke to him informally. It deserved his attention.

'What choice do I have?'

'You could step out. Take yourself out of the firing line. Blame your age; say you're not up to this one. You don't need this shit, Bruce.'

'And don't I know it. But someone has to do this, Sean. And who else is going to? Who else is even going to see what I've seen? Someone's committed mass murder, and if we're right, they've set Nizar Mansour up as a patsy. And anyone who steps in from here? Who hasn't seen what I've seen? They're almost guaranteed to fall for it. I can't walk away knowing that. I can't walk away knowing that an innocent man might be on the hook for this, and that whoever is really behind it is walking free. I just can't do that, Sean.'

McConnell nodded his head, took a deep breath and rose to his feet. Once up he held out his open hand.

'Well, when you put it like that, count me in. If you're going up against these feckers, you'll need a good man by your side.'

Bull took McConnell's hand in his own and shook it as his DS spoke again:

'And until you can find one, you'll have to make do with me.'

THIRTY-TWO

'Thank you for telling me. Have his family been informed?'
Elizabeth Kirk wiped away a tear as she listened to the answer.

'OK. Any problems with anything here – funeral arrangements, probate, anything – I want to be kept in the loop. Understood? Thank you. Again.'

Kirk hit the red disconnect icon and ended the call. She took a deep, calming breath. It was rare for her to lose her composure, and she would not do so now. Still, the news was upsetting, and even the director of the ISB was allowed her emotions.

She wiped away a second tear as her desk intercom buzzed.

'Yes?'

'Joe Dempsey here to see you, ma'am.'

Kirk coughed to clear her throat and took a moment to check her reflection.

'Send him in.'

Moments later and Dempsey was in the room.

'Take a seat,' Kirk offered. The instruction was necessary; Dempsey's military past was long behind him, but Kirk knew that he would stand unless told to do otherwise.

Old habits, she thought.

Dempsey took a chair and Kirk sat forward in her own, placing her hands on the desk between them. She thought about sharing her news with Dempsey, but first she wanted to hear what he had to say.

'How is the investigation going?' Kirk asked.

'You've heard they've made an arrest in London?' Dempsey asked.

'I have. And a confession, it seems.'

'That's right. And at first blush that doesn't really sit with the John Knowles/Dale Victor theory, and certainly with what Quilty told me.'

Kirk swallowed hard at the name. Dempsey gave no indication that he noticed, but Kirk had no doubt that he had. Joe Dempsey noticed *everything*.

'What did you think of him?'

'He's a professional. What he told you three years ago, he wouldn't have passed that on to you unless his source was to be trusted.'

'So you believe there's a connection?'

'I don't believe it and I don't disbelieve it. It's plausible. And with what happened to Dale Victor, it becomes much more so. It would need further investigation, but as a starting point it was solid intel.'

'I thought the same. But now? With the arrest in London? Do you think that takes this in another direction?'

'Like I said, at first it doesn't seem to fit. It seems to make a terrorist attack the more likely explanation. But what if that's the point?'

'What do you mean?'

'What if things were arranged to point right instead of left. Away from the White House, instead of towards it?'

'You mean a fall guy?'

'Exactly.'

'OK. That happens.' Kirk exhaled hard. 'Christ, in a previous life I'd have been the one *making* that happen. But the guy has confessed, Joe. Why would a fall guy confess?'

'What if it's not on the level? The confession, I mean?'

Kirk sat forward in her seat. Until now they had been discussing information they both knew. From Dempsey's expression, that state of affairs had come to an end.

'What do you know?' she asked.

'Mansour confessed to putting the bag on the plane, that's true. But he didn't know it was a bomb. He believed the bag was full of drugs.'

'How can you know that?'

'Trust me when I say it's come from a solid source.'

Kirk hesitated. She would usually want more. But this was Joe Dempsey. He had earned the right to be discreet.

'OK. But I'm not promising we won't come back to that question.'

'Understood, ma'am.' Dempsey's reply was immediate and formal. The instinctive response of a soldier.

'So if Mansour thought he was placing drugs on the plane, then who was he working for?'

'An Italian crime group. The same group who had helped his brother reach Britain from Syria a few years ago. They gave Mansour the bag, telling him it was filled with cocaine, and instructed him to place it in a very particular part of Flight PA16's baggage hold.'

'And he just did what he was told, did he?' Kirk was sceptical. 'I've got to tell you, Joe, this doesn't exactly sound compelling. The "I'm not a terrorist, I'm a drug trafficker" defence isn't the best one I've heard. And why would anyone take the word of a self-confessed criminal?'

'Mansour's no criminal,' Dempsey replied. 'He wasn't involved willingly. Not in what he did, and not in what he thought he was doing. Every action the man took, he took it for his sister.'

'His sister?'

'She was trying to get to England. To join her brothers. When Mansour had saved the money to get her there, he used it to engage the same Italians who'd brought his brother to Europe. He paid them and they brought her from Syria to Italy. To Naples. But once she was there they changed the terms. She became a captive, and they told Mansour they'd only release her if he placed a package on a plane for them. If he did that, they'd bring her the rest of the way. If he didn't, they'd kill her.'

Kirk took a moment to consider what she was being told. It sounded plausible.

'So where is she now?'

'There's no way to know for sure. But the group already killed Mansour's younger brother and tried to kill Mansour, too. That's why he handed himself in.'

'Which means the sister is probably dead, too,' she observed.

'Most likely. Why keep her alive?'

Kirk shook her head. None of this was making sense.

'So what do you think this is, Joe? If it's an organised crime group — and it sure as hell looks like it is — then we're wrong. The bomb wasn't Knowles silencing Dale Victor. But it also means it's not the terrorist attack the news is reporting either. Where does that leave us? Why would a bunch of people traffickers want to take down a commercial airliner?'

'This is where it gets interesting,' Dempsey replied. 'My source says that Mansour's contact with the group isn't Italian.'

Kirk went with her gut.

'Italian-American?'

'Maybe, but not in the way you're thinking, Elizabeth. According to my source, this guy is Secret Service.'

Kirk sat back, shocked.

'Are you telling me the man who orchestrated getting the bomb onto the plane – the man responsible for killing over five hundred people – are you telling me that man works for the president of the United States of America?'

Dempsey allowed himself a grim smile.

'Yes. Yes, he does.'

THIRTY-THREE

The prison guard looked upwards as he waited behind the red iron gate. It gave the camera a clear view of his face and the security credentials on his chest pocket. Both were needed to authorise his entry, via the control room inside.

The whole process took almost four minutes. No two gates within the block could be unlocked and open at one time, and so the guard patiently waited his turn.

Nizar Mansour stayed silent as the seconds passed.

The unlocking of the gate was heralded by a metal clang and an electronic buzz. As the guard pushed the gate open, the strain visible in his muscled arms was testament to the barrier's weight.

Once the gate was open, they stepped through. Mansour first. The guard behind him.

'Move on.'

The prison guard prodded Mansour in the back as the gate closed behind them. As if his verbal instruction had not been clear enough. It was unnecessary. Mansour was already walking as he felt the stiff, solid fingertips and the effortless forward pressure.

Strong man, Mansour thought to himself. *They're taking no chances after the van.*

The gate had been the entrance to Belmarsh's High Security Unit. And beyond it was the HSU nerve centre; a central hub built over two floors. Four more gates – positioned like four points of a star, with the red main gate as its fifth – led to four segregated wings, each built in a simple straight line, again across two floors.

All were visible from the central point of the hub, which sat as the centre of the star. But Mansour could see that the wings themselves were isolated. With their gates closed, each one only allowed a view of itself and the unit's heart.

'Over there.'

Another forceful prod in the back. The guard was directing Mansour towards the second gate to his right.

Wing Three.

Mansour complied without a word. Within seconds he was at the gate, watching the guard as he went through the same security routine. This time it was quicker. Ninety seconds at the most, before the same heavy clang and piercing buzz. Seconds more and they were inside, the gate closed and locked behind them.

For some reason Mansour had expected Wing Three to be full. A hive of activity, with inmates mixing in the common areas and moving in and out of each others' cells. He had no idea why. Perhaps something he had seen on TV.

The reality could not have been more different. The long, corridor-like common area through which Mansour and the guard were now walking was empty.

Empty, but not silent.

The noise coming from behind each of the closed cell doors was intense. Incessant banging of what sounded like steel on steel. Shouting voices, only some of which Mansour could understand. Loud, almost animal screams came from some of the rooms.

It was designed to unnerve him, Mansour realised. An intimidating welcome from the other HSU Wing Three inmates.

It sounded like hell on Earth.

'Up there.'

No prod this time. Mansour took the order and climbed the long, single flight of stairs that led to the upper floor of Wing Three.

The first floor was much the same as the ground, aside from the large, empty space in the centre that led directly down. Two rows of cells, three each on either side of the wing, each accessible by a metal walkway that passed every door.

Mansour focused on the metal barriers that ran alongside the walkways, there to prevent inmates from falling over the side, all the way back to the ground floor.

Falling. The thought was almost comical.

The noise did not lessen as Mansour turned left and then right at the top of the stairs. He still couldn't make out what was being said. Only the occasional swearword rose above the din. They added an extra hint of violence to the already aggressive atmosphere.

'Last one,' the guard instructed, unnecessarily pushing Mansour forward. Towards the final cell on the left-hand wall. 'Cell Twelve.'

The cell was open and unoccupied. Mansour was surprised. He had been warned at court that Belmarsh – like all prisons in Britain – was overcrowded, and that he would most likely have to share a cell with at least one other inmate. Possibly two. He was relieved, then, that he seemed to have a cell to himself.

He stepped inside and turned to face the guard.

'No one else?'

'No. Not in here,' the guard replied. 'You lot get your own luxury space.'

The guard smiled as he spoke, ironically indicating

Mansour's minuscule surroundings. Barely ten feet long and no more than six feet wide, the cell was furnished with a small, dank bed next to the door, a plastic desk in one far corner and a metal toilet in the other. A small, old-fashioned portable television was fixed to the wall, and a tiny, wire-meshed window offered the view of an exterior whitewashed wall.

Luxury.

'What now?'

Mansour had been given a full briefing on arrival of what to expect, but he had taken in very little of what he had been told. Few first-time prisoners do.

'Now you sit down and wait for court in the morning,' the guard replied irritably. 'And count yourself lucky because it's twenty-three-hour lock-up in here at the minute. And most don't have a trip to court to break that up.'

'And food? I can eat?'

'You'll be allowed out between seven p.m. and eight p.m. for dinner. Which is when you'll get to know that lovely lot you heard as we came in. So you've got that to look forward to.'

'And . . .'

'Enough questions. After what you did to that guard, you're lucky you're in here at all and not locked up in solitary already. So keep the questions to yourself, alright?'

Mansour said nothing as the guard turned, closed the cell door and locked it from outside.

Lucky?

He looked around at the bare walls surrounding him and listened to the screams from outside as he considered the guard's words.

And for the first time in weeks, Mansour laughed.

THIRTY-FOUR

Bruce Bull noticed a smattering of snowflakes on his windscreen as he pulled into the car park of The Spaniard's Inn.

The meeting had been Will Duffy's suggestion, as had the historic Hampstead pub. Bull had been hesitant at first. Even on the outskirts of the city, far from Scotland Yard, a second meeting with a defence solicitor was a risk. But as he took the parking space nearest the back entrance, he realised that he had worried for nothing.

The car park was practically empty, except for Duffy's red Maserati and a grey Audi.

The beauty of snow in London, Bull thought. *First hint of it and everyone stays home.*

Bull had passed The Spaniard many times. It was an impossible building to miss; its historic status as an original sixteenth-century pub made it untouchable, and so the road outside was forced to narrow to a single lane as it passed. But until now he'd never been inside.

The interior was as empty as its car park. It had been decorated with a very clear brief: highlight the history of the building, but make the wealthy locals feel at home. Gleaming oak panels vied with chandeliers for the patrons' attention, while open log fires and crooked wooden beams reminded them that they were glimpsing the past.

None of this mattered to Bull. He was here for a reason, and that reason was sitting in the far corner of an otherwise empty room.

Bull approached the table as Will Duffy looked up. The lawyer rose to his feet and put out his hand.

'Twice in twelve hours, Will,' Bull said as he shook Duffy's hand. 'You sure your reputation can take the hit?'

'Mine can if yours can,' Duffy replied. 'Drink?'

He indicated a bottle of white wine and two glasses sitting on the table. The bottle was open, and Duffy's glass had clearly been filled and emptied once already.

'Just the one,' Bull replied. 'We're both driving.'

'Always a cop, eh?'

'Always.'

Duffy poured a good measure into Bull's glass before refilling his own. He held it up, towards Bull.

'Cheers.'

'Cheers,' Bull replied, tipping his glass to Duffy's. 'So, what was so important?'

'Straight to business, eh?'

'No offence, Will, but the less time we're together the less risk we're both taking.'

Duffy made a point of looking around the empty room, then back to Bull. He raised an eyebrow.

'Whatever you say, big man.'

'So?'

'We've got some information from Mansour. Might be worth looking into.'

'Go ahead.'

'To start with, you were right about Romeo. They knew each other alright.'

'How?'

'In the worse possible way. Mansour says Romeo was involved in the bomb.'

Bull's eyes widened. His own analysis had been taking him in the same direction. Why else would Romeo – or whoever Romeo was working for – have sought to stack the evidence so heavily against Mansour? Still, such explicit confirmation was a surprise.

'Involved in what way?' he asked.

'In every way,' Duffy replied. 'He gave Mansour the bag that he planted in the hold.'

'Romeo supplied the bomb?'

'According to Mansour, aye.'

'Jesus.'

Bull sat back into his chair and took a swig of wine.

'Tell me everything.'

Bruce Bull had been inside The Spaniards Inn for almost forty minutes. Forty minutes in which the first few snowflakes had grown into a full January blizzard, heavy enough that an inch already sat on the front of his Mercedes.

Bull was steady on his feet as he reached his car. The second glass of wine did not seem to have affected him as he climbed into the driver's seat and turned on the engine. A few moments later the Mercedes was moving, exiting the car park.

Will Duffy soon followed. His departure from the car park was more dramatic in his Maserati, with a roar of the engine, a rear wheel-spin and full-tilt acceleration.

It was in every way a more attention-grabbing vehicle, something it didn't need to be. Because both Bruce Bull and Will Duffy had the full focus of the only person there to give it.

Special Agent Frank Hart had been careful to park his rental car away from Duffy's Maserati, and so he had been able to sit unobserved as Bruce Bull arrived. He had watched unnoticed as the two men spoke inside, in full view of the window that looked out onto the car park.

And by the time they had left he was sat under the protection of a windscreen full of snow.

With both gone, Hart started his engine. As Duffy had done, he turned right at the car park exit. From here he could immediately see the lawyer's rear lights on the road far ahead. He accelerated, just enough to close some distance but not enough to draw attention to himself.

As the rear of the car came closer, Hart held down the voice control button on the Audi's steering wheel.

'Call Romeo Meyer.'

The call connected almost immediately. It was answered just as quickly.

'Frank. You good?'

'Depends what you think of this.'

'What is it?'

'Bruce Bull, your friend from the police station.'

'What about him? You're on the lawyer, aren't you?'

'I am. Which is how I just watched the two of them drinking together in an empty pub near to Duffy's place.'

'What? You sure?'

'Positive.'

'You think Duffy's told the police what Mansour's told him?'

'What else could it be? Why else would they be meeting?'

There were a few moments of silence at the end of the line.

'This is a problem, Frank.'

'It sure looks that way.'

'A problem *we'll* deal with. I don't want the White House brought in on this.'

'Not even your fa . . . not even the assistant director?'

'*Especially* not the assistant director. This is *our* problem. And we'll deal with it *our* way.'

THIRTY-FIVE

'When, ma'am?' Dempsey couldn't believe what Kirk had just told him.

'This morning. The Great Neck Fire Department was called a few minutes after ten a.m.'

'Bastards.'

He stood up as his mind filled with an avalanche of thoughts.

The Protection Detail wasn't enough. Should I have known?

Should I have stayed? To protect Quilty?

Should I have made Quilty leave with me, to somewhere he could be protected?

The questions came thick and fast. But beneath them all was one overriding truth.

Quilty's dead because of me. They weren't sure it was him. And then I showed up last night . . .

Still on his feet, Dempsey turned to face Kirk.

'What exactly happened?'

Kirk indicated for Dempsey to retake his seat before she answered.

'An explosion. Fire Department theory is it was one of his oxygen bottles.'

'But the timing – it can't be a coincidence.'

'No. And Quilty had a visitor when he died. Another man caught up in the explosion.'

'Someone got past the detail we placed there? How?'

'They thought he was from the oxygen company. Seemed legitimate.'

'And we're sure it wasn't?' Dempsey asked, already sure of the answer.

'I don't know many delivery men who do their rounds armed with a now very charred SIG Sauer P229. Do you?'

'Secret Service issue,' Dempsey observed.

'Well, not *just* Secret Service issue. But in the circumstances I think we can reach some logical conclusions.'

Dempsey smiled as he processed the information.

'So he took one of them with him?'

'It seems that way.'

'Like he said, if they're going to send amateurs . . .'

'What?'

'Nothing, ma'am. It doesn't matter now.'

Kirk poured them both a glass of water from the crystal jug she kept on her desk.

'So where does this all leave us, Joe?' she asked, pushing a glass towards him. 'Do we have enough to justify a push on this?'

'Between what my source told me and Quilty's sudden death? Yeah, I'd say we do.'

Kirk nodded in agreement.

Dempsey knew the decision had already been made. He was providing moral support, nothing else. Just a second voice, confirming to his director that her instincts were right. That what they were about to do was justified.

It needed to be. Because the implications were almost unthinkable.

'So how do we deal with this?' Kirk finally asked. 'We're talking about investigating a sitting US president for mass murder and war crimes. How the hell do we do that, Joe?'

'The same way as we do everything else. It doesn't matter

who the suspect is; we go back to basics and do this from the ground up. We have to confirm the intelligence. Without that, this whole thing falls down.'

Agreed. So what are you going to do?' she asked.

'I need to go to Afghanistan. I need to speak to Quilty's source. And I need to see Tootkai for myself. To see if there is any truth in any of this. In what Knowles and his unit are said to have done.'

'And if there is?'

'If there is, well, we build a case for the International Criminal Court. Same as we would for anyone else.'

'But this is not anyone else, Joe. This is the president of the United States. Plus his entire SEAL unit and God knows how many members of his administration.'

'That can't matter, ma'am. No one can be above the law. No one can be allowed to just do what they want. To kill indiscriminately, in their own interests. Not even the president. If we allow that then we're no better than them.'

'If we allow it? You're assuming we can stop them.'

'Maybe we can't. Maybe we would be taking on too much. But we can't let that stop us, surely? We can't only pick the fights we know we can win. We have to pick the fights where we're right. No matter how big the other guy might be.'

Kirk took a moment. When she finally spoke her voice was softer. Uncertain.

'You know Knowles won't just let this happen, Joe? He'll do whatever he has to stop us. You know that, right?'

'Knowles is *already* trying to stop us, ma'am.' Dempsey had no such uncertainty. 'They're already cleaning house. Quilty was only the first. That makes you a target. And it sure as hell makes me one. They killed Quilty for what he knew. They'll have to assume he told me the story, so it's a dead cert they're coming after me next.'

'And that doesn't scare you?'

'I'm not a fool, ma'am. Of course it scares me. But it won't *stop* me. I'll get to the bottom of this. I'll find out what Knowles did and I'll prove it. And when I've proved it, I'll take the murdering bastard down.'

Kirk shook her head. She was reeling, and Dempsey could understand why. They had moved from a vague theory to a full investigation in the course of a single day. An investigation whose subject was the president of the United States. And an investigation that risked both of their lives.

And the lives of others.

They're cleaning house already.

The thought leapt again to the front of Dempsey's mind, but this time it had a different meaning. He climbed back to his feet.

'Ma'am, if you'll excuse me. I have to make a call.'

THIRTY-SIX

Sarah Truman stepped from the black cab and rushed to the steps that led up to her front door, shielding her face from the driving snow as she ran.

The weather had taken a dramatic turn. As cold as it had been that morning, the temperature had dropped throughout the day and in the last two hours London had been turned picture-postcard white with snow.

Sarah could hear the music before she had climbed the first step.

Johnny Cash. The slow stuff.

It was all the warning she needed. Michael had a mixed taste in music, most of which he played for enjoyment. But Johnny Cash, played loud while Michael was alone? Sarah knew exactly what that meant.

The hallway lights were on as Sarah closed the front door behind her. So were the lights in the living room, which was unusual. They rarely used that room.

Sarah looked inside. Michael was not there, but he had been. The photographs on the sideboard had been moved. The whisky, too. And next to both was Michael's phone, its battery dead.

Sarah left everything as she had found it and headed towards the kitchen. The source of the music. The door was just slightly ajar. She pushed it fully open, not expecting the sight that greeted her.

Michael was dressed in jeans and a blue T-shirt, and was

slumped in one of the tall chairs positioned beside the island unit. In front of him was an empty crystal glass, and next to that a whisky bottle that was equally drained.

'Michael?' Sarah was surprised to see her fiancé asleep. 'Michael? Are you OK?'

He didn't respond. Not even a flicker.

Sarah moved closer, concerned. She reached out a hand, placing it gently on his shoulder as she spoke again.

'Michael? Are you awake?'

Michael jumped from his seat at Sarah's touch. He seemed unaware of his surroundings – of Sarah, even – and he reacted on instinct. Sarah was pushed forcefully away, a near blow to her sternum with Michael's open palm.

For just a moment Sarah saw the madness in her fiancé's eyes. The hidden, violent streak that had, in the past, kept them both alive. It was gone in an instant, but that was long enough to remind Sarah of Michael's other side. Of his other nature.

As the dream state from which she had awoken him faded, the violence was replaced by horrified concern. Michael covered the distance between them in a single stride, his arms outstretched.

'Sarah. Jesus. I'm so sorry. I didn't know . . . I didn't know it was you.'

Sarah was shaken. Her first concern had been for the baby. But she couldn't say that. This was not how she had envisaged telling Michael that he was to be a father. Instead she stepped forward and found herself pulled into her fiancé's embrace.

'I must have been dreaming.' Michael voice was shaken. Emotional. 'God knows where I was, sweetheart. I'm so sorry.'

'It's OK, Michael.' Sarah returned the hug as she spoke.

'Stop apologising. I shouldn't have woken you like that. Not after you'd been drinking.'

She pulled her head back so that she could look in his eyes.

'And certainly not after Johnny Cash.'

Michael did not take the reassurance being offered. He looked ashamed as he stepped back, his hands placed gently on Sarah's upper arms.

'I should be more careful,' he said. 'I could have hurt you.'

'Forget it. It was nothing.'

Sarah stepped away and turned down the music. Michael's gaze followed her. His eyes were still unfocused, she noticed. As good as his alcohol tolerance usually was, tonight's intake had hit him.

'So am I gonna hear what's brought this on?' Sarah asked, placing his empty glass in the sink. She noticed her own Boston accent strengthen as the question came out. It was her default 'serious' voice.

'Just a . . . just a bad day,' Michael replied, his voice unsteady. 'Brought back some bad memories.'

'I saw that,' Sarah replied. 'I saw the photos in the living room.'

'I'm sorry.'

'For what?'

'I . . . I don't really know.'

'Sit back down,' she said, gesturing to his original seat.

At first he didn't move.

'It's not a request, Michael Devlin.'

Michael meekly retook his chair, while Sarah filled their kettle and began to prepare him a strong black coffee. For good measure, she placed a pint glass of water in front of him.

'Drink that.'

'But . . .'

'Drink it. You'll thank me in the morning.'

Again, Michael did as he was told.

'So what happened?' she asked. 'What started this?'

'Just . . . just work.'

'Work? You've been on the Mansour case. Same as me. What's that got to do with all of this?'

'I don't want to talk about it.'

'Tough. We're talking. What the hell happened? What's got you drinking this early?'

Michael looked up and met Sarah's gaze. At first he seemed ready to refuse. But then his eyes softened. He looked like a man lost.

'I think . . . I think . . .' Michael was struggling. His usual fluency robbed by a mixture of whisky and worry. 'I think that this case . . . it might be dangerous.'

'What? Why?'

'I think there's more to it than there . . . than there seems. It . . . it reminds me of Eamon McGale.'

It was the last name Sarah had expected to hear.

'McGale? In what way?'

'I think Mansour was set up. And I think the people behind it will do whatever they must to keep it quiet.'

Sarah did not know what to say. Or even what to think. Could Michael be right? Was there more to the Mansour case than met the eye? Or was it the drink talking? There was no way that Sarah could know, but if he *was* right then that was another problem. Because if he was, then Sarah shouldn't be hearing this at all. Michael did not discuss his cases. Not the confidential details, anyway. And what he was now saying was dangerously close to crossing that line.

'I can't . . . I can't lose anyone else.' Tears were beginning to form in Michael's eyes. 'I can't . . . I can't let this . . . this job . . . I can't let anyone else get hurt for me.'

'Michael, no one is going to—'

'I can't let *you* get hurt. Not for me. Not because . . . because of a case.'

'Michael, no one is going to hurt me.' Sarah's concern was growing.

'I won't let them, Sarah.' Michael began to mumble as the blinking of his eyes became more pronounced. 'The Secret Service, I won't let them. Joe won't let them . . .'

He trailed off as he went back to sleep. Within seconds he was snoring, as unconscious as he had been before she'd woken him.

Sarah tried to work out what he'd meant. Joe . . . Dempsey? The Secret Service? Was it all gibberish? But he'd seemed so clear on the stuff about Mansour. So determined.

Not only that. He'd seemed scared. Frightened for himself. And for Sarah.

It was *that* which concerned her. That one thing. In the years she had known Michael – through all the hell they had endured together – she had never seen him afraid.

Not until tonight.

THIRTY-SEVEN

S pecial Agent Braddock sat in the driver's seat of a black 2018 Lincoln Continental. In the seat to his right was Special Agent Cobb. Behind them was Special Agent Grace.

They were parked on the corner of East 44th Street and United Nations Plaza, facing the massive United Nations building. Perfectly placed to follow anyone leaving it and heading towards Yorkville.

Exactly as they expected Joe Dempsey to do. They just didn't know when that would be.

Braddock had made his thoughts clear on the subject of Grace's involvement. But like Assistant Director Meyer, he had been overruled. An executive order trumped everything, and Knowles had been unmistakably firm.

Braddock, though, had no intention of accepting Knowles' instincts regarding her loyalty or reliability. Not at the risk of his own life and future. And so he was determined to keep a close eye on her.

Braddock tilted the rear-view mirror, to give him a clearer view of Grace.

He had known her for three years. Since her first posting as a newcomer to the president's protection detail within the White House. In that time, he had paid her little attention. They rarely shared a shift. Even if they did, why would she attract his eye? Braddock liked tall blondes in short skirts. Grace met those 'qualifications' in exactly zero ways. Although even with her short, dark hair, right now Grace seemed more attractive than he usually found her.

Probably the pants suits she's always wearing, he thought to himself, looking more closely. *Makes her look like a guy.*

His eyes wandered lower.

Which she sure as hell ain't.

'You want a damn picture?'

The question came from the back seat.

'Why, you got one?' he asked, meeting sass with sass.

'Why don't you keep your damn eyes on the road. That's where you're gonna see Dempsey. Not back here.'

'Don't worry about me spotting Dempsey, sweetheart. Cobb's got my back for that, ain't you, Cobb?'

'We can take it in turns.' Cobb turned his head just enough to eye Grace as he said the words. His leer made it clear that the double-meaning was intentional. 'That be OK with you, little lady?'

'Go fuck yourself, Cobb.' Grace practically spat the insult at him. 'No one else will.'

Cobb looked unconcerned. Braddock, though, was a little taken aback. Grace's aggression surprised him. Maybe there was more to her than he had thought.

'You got a lot more spunk in you than you usually show, lady,' he said with a smile. 'Knowles might be right after all. Could be you're good for this thing.'

'I'm good for whatever it takes.'

'Didn't look that way back in the briefing.' The momentary friendliness in Braddock's voice was gone. 'Looked more like you were gonna break down and cry.'

'And you reacted better when you found out the world wasn't black and white, did you?'

'As a matter of fact, yeah, I did. More money and time off the leash? Best news I ever got.'

'Then that's where we differ. Don't worry. I've got my orders and I'll follow them.'

'That easy, is it?' Braddock wasn't sure he bought it. 'One minute you're telling the boss it's murder, the next you're on board?'

'What else can I do? I took an oath. Might mean nothing to you, but it means everything to me. My job is to do what's right for the president and for the country. And if it's this . . . well, then it's this. I don't have to like it. But I do have to do it.'

For the first time, Braddock found himself being persuaded.

'Missy, if you're acting then you're damn good at it. I'm starting to think you really believe in all of this "oath of office" bullshit.'

'I *do* believe in my oath. And I don't think it's bullshit.'

'You're young, gorgeous. You'll learn.'

'Don't call me that.'

'What?'

'You heard me. We have to work together. That doesn't mean I have to let you talk to me like a piece of meat.'

'Hell, Grace, I was complimenting you.'

'You *thought* you were complimenting me. That's not the same thing. Keep it to yourself.'

'Yes, ma'am.'

Braddock said nothing more. Their final exchange had sealed it. If Grace was pretending, why would she pick that fight? Braddock could see no good reason.

No, the girl believed what she was saying.

She believed in her oaths. To her country and to her president.

However she felt about what they were here to do, she would play her part.

THIRTY-EIGHT

In the High Security Unit at Belmarsh, the standard day is made up of twelve hours in the cell and twelve hours out. A mind-numbing routine of mealtimes, outdoor exercise, gym use and association time.

Unluckily for Mansour, his arrival had coincided with a punishment schedule. Twenty-three-hour lock-up. Prison at its very worst.

With the cell doors opened at 7 p.m. for a single hour, the rush to secure the wing's limited facilities was almost animalistic. Two payphones. Two showers. Far too few of each for Wing Three's twelve prisoners. It was a nightly battle to reach them first. A battle which could – and usually did – lead to more violence, perpetuating the cycle that had led to the regime being imposed in the first place.

A failed approach to punishment and rehabilitation, sustained by a system too stubborn to try another way and by a public too indoctrinated to care.

Mansour stayed clear of the scrum. He had been here for only a few hours, so he needed no shower. And who did he have left to call? All Mansour required was food, and so he waited a full ten minutes before he ventured outside of his cell.

He could feel himself being watched as he walked the short distance to the single staircase that led down from the first floor. The feeling only increased as he descended. Guards at first. Then other inmates. All of them eyeing the new arrival.

It was to be expected, Mansour realised. Human nature.

Any new face would be carefully considered. Their natural allegiances guessed at. Their place in the hierarchy determined.

Especially when that new face is a mass murderer, Mansour thought.

He kept his eyes down as he made his way along the ground floor, towards the food server that had been set up at the end of the wing.

The volume of Wing Three had noticeably lowered with Mansour's presence, and even with his eyes down he could see small groupings of inmates speaking among themselves as he passed. Whispering as they followed his every step. Each making the connection between the TV news reports they had been watching all day and the man now living among them.

Some seemed to recognise him more quickly than others, but, with his eyes firmly down, Mansour could read none of their reactions.

He was not ready for that. Not yet.

The momentarily dimmed volume of Wing Three had risen back to its former level by the time Mansour reached the food server. The conversation was still about him, he suspected, but he couldn't make out what was being said.

There were two men ahead of him at the server. Both queuing beside the ten-foot-long metal contraption from which Wing Three's meals were dished out. Each of them was holding a single metal tray, onto which food was being placed by the three rough-looking prisoners who stood behind the food line, tasked with 'kitchen duty'.

Mansour picked up his own metal tray, collected a light tin mug for the tall tea urn he could see at the end of the server, and prepared to wait his turn.

'Use a different spoon.'

It was a simple enough sentence. In most circumstances, one which would attract no attention. But there was something about the voice. Something intense.

The background noise died away. All eyes were now on the food line and on the man at its head.

'There's no different spoon. Same for everyone.'

The answer came from the last of the servers. The tallest of the three by a head, he was a large man with a face that could not be the result of a peaceful life. It carried subtle scars, hints of long years of violence. Hints that became a statement thanks to his flattened, broken nose.

He was the very stereotype of a fighting man. And yet he was not the most intimidating side in the exchange.

'That spoon was in the pork. Find a different one.'

The speaker was not as tall as the server. Nor was he as wide. He did not shout. He did not even put down his tray. But then he did not need to. Intensity sparked off him like so much electricity. His even, cold tone was clear: carry on down this route and there will be consequences.

Mansour took one step outwards, so he could peer around the second man in line. He wanted a clearer view.

'You know the rules,' the speaker continued. His voice was now lower. Flatter. Somehow worse. 'That spoon touched the pork. That makes it haram. Use a different spoon.'

Mansour's eyes were fixed on the speaker. A light-skinned black man, perhaps six feet tall. His long beard and the taqiyah he wore on his head were a statement of his religion, but otherwise he was dressed like everyone else. In a thick, grey, two-piece track suit, which made it difficult to gauge his build.

From what Mansour could see, the man was no powerhouse.

Sure, he looked fit. But there were far more imposing men within touching distance.

But his intimidating presence had nothing to do with his physicality. It was the forcefulness of his lowered voice that had brought silence to the wing. Coloured by a thick South London accent, it was the voice of a man who would not be denied.

'Change the fucking spoon.'

The stand-off lasted a few seconds more. Until, as Mansour had anticipated, the server gave way. As the noise of the wing increased back to its previous level, a second, non-haram spoon was found. The speaker's halal meal was dished onto his plate and, without another word, he stalked away. To join a group of three other bearded men, on a table by themselves.

'You'll be wanting that spoon too, yeah?'

The question came from close to Mansour's ear. From the man ahead of him in the queue. Mansour had not expected to be addressed and so it caught him off guard.

'I don't . . . sorry?'

'You're a Muslim, ain't you?'

Mansour looked at him for a moment, surprised by the man's friendly tone.

'Erm, yes. Yes, I am. But . . .'

Mansour stopped himself. He had been about to say something about his own looser adherence to Islamic Law. But he remembered some advice given to him by Michael Devlin that morning.

Tell no one anything in there, Nizar, Michael had said. *You never know who you're speaking to.*

Mansour had been a soldier. He knew how to follow orders.

'Yes,' he said again. 'I am.'

'Do you wanna eat or not?' The question came from the

first server: a small, wiry man who looked in need of a shower. His hands looked dirty, but at least the serving ladle he was holding did not.

'Yes,' Mansour replied. 'I want to eat.'

'What do you want?'

Mansour glanced at the other man in line.

'Whatever is halal,' he replied. He could hardly call himself a Muslim and then say otherwise.

The first server ladled a gloopy, lukewarm soup into one of the smaller sections. The second server added a dollop of some sort of pink custard to another. Finally the third server spooned something more identifiable into the main section: rice and curry.

'Thank you,' Mansour said without looking up.

As he turned to look for a place where he could sit, he found that the other man from the line had waited for him.

'Come on. Eat with me,' the man said, indicating to the nearest of the tables set out in the wing's dining area. The only one still free.

They both took a seat, one across from the other. Mansour prepared to eat, but his new friend seemed less interested in the food they had placed down. His attention was elsewhere.

'So you're big news today, ain't ya,' he said. His tone was jumpy. Excitable.

'I . . . I . . .' Mansour did not know what to say to the statement. 'I think I should not speak about that.'

'Don't worry. No one speaks about it at first. Shit, it's early enough you're probably still saying you didn't do it.'

Mansour did not reply. He was not sure what to think.

His silence did not seem to concern the other prisoner, who held out his hand.

'David Carter, by the way. And just so we start out honest, I *did* do what I'm in for.'

Mansour took Carter's hand and shook it.

'Nizar Mansour.'

Mansour said nothing more. Instead he took his spoon and began to eat his rapidly cooling soup.

Carter seemed bemused by the lack of conversation. He offered a wide smile and spoke again.

'Drugs, for me,' he explained. 'Biggest importation of cocaine ever prosecuted in the UK. Me and Terry over there.'

He indicated to an older man, about mid sixties, who was playing pool alone in the recreation area.

Mansour looked from one to the other. He was surprised. Terry was a tall, serious-looking man. At least twenty years older than Carter. Maybe more. But it was not just a generation or two that divided them. Terry carried with him an air of authority. Of a man to be followed. A man to be obeyed. Carter had no such aura. If anything, he seemed more like one of the servers than he did the other occupants of the unit.

'Life imprisonment, we got. Minimum thirty to serve. That was eight years ago.'

Mansour looked up from his food.

'You have twenty years more here?'

'Twenty-two. At least. But not here, I hope.'

'Why are you here? In this prison?'

'That's down to Terry. He's, erm, he's a player, you know what I mean?'

Mansour shook his head.

'He's a big name. Head of a big organisation, I mean. So when we were on trial, he had the jury nobbled. Twice. Third one was kept in protective custody for the whole case. Then when we were convicted they tried to break us out of prison. Put a target on our backs, that did. We were classified as a high escape risk, or whatever they called it. So we ended up in here. That was five years ago.'

Mansour ate as he listened.

'So what about you? Who you working for? Al Qaeda? Isis? Someone else?'

'I . . . I don't work with anyone.'

'You did that plane alone?'

Mansour hesitated. He reminded himself of Devlin's advice. 'I do not speak about it,' he finally said.

'I get it.' Carter smiled as he spoke. 'No pressure.'

Mansour ate a final spoonful of vegetable curry. He looked at the pink custard dessert, scooped some up and lifted it to his nose. It smelled of nothing.

He threw it back into its section of the tray and rose to his feet.

'I am going to go back. I need to sleep.'

'No problem, mate. Totally understand.' Carter rose to his feet at the same time as Mansour. His smiled widened as he continued. 'I mean, it's been a long few days for you, ain't it.'

Mansour ignored Carter's meaning. He turned to walk away, only to feel a hand grasp his right wrist.

Carter's hand.

Mansour spun around at the contact. Carter's left hand was raised, palm open, as he turned. An indication that he was no threat.

'Look, I'm just gonna say, you need mates in 'ere, Nizar. Friends. That's how the place works. I can be yer friend. Me and Terry. And we're the kind you need. Just bear it in mind, OK?'

Mansour fixed his gaze on Carter, unsure how to react to

the words. He did not want friends; he did not intend to be here long enough to need them. Not with the help of Duffy and Devlin.

But he also did not want enemies. Not in here. Not with everything else he was facing.

So why make one now?

'OK,' he finally said, gently retracting his wrist from Carter's grip. 'OK. Friends.'

Mansour forced a smile as he spoke. One he was sure Carter could see through. Carter, in turn, kept his own grin fixed.

'Good,' Carter said. 'That's good. Now, sleep well, OK?'

'OK.'

Mansour walked away without another word, his eyes once again facing the floor as he passed the three other occupied tables.

Carter had been enough interaction for one day. He would not risk another.

THIRTY-NINE

Joe Dempsey hung up his cell as he walked away from the United Nations building. He was halfway to zipping the handset back into the jacket pocket of his bike leathers when he remembered that he had one more call to make.

The phone's log showed six outgoing calls in the last thirty minutes. All but the most recent had been to the same number. And all of those had gone directly to voicemail.

There could be any number of innocent reasons for that. Perhaps Michael Devlin was out of range. Or had turned off his phone. Maybe it was just that the battery was dead.

All perfectly good explanations. But after what had happened with Tom Quilty, he was taking no chances. Especially when his watch told him that it was not yet 3 p.m., and so before 8 p.m. in London.

Too early for him to be asleep.

Dempsey kept the phone to his ear as Michael's recorded voice came through again. For once, Dempsey would take Michael up on the invitation to leave a message.

'Michael, it's Joe Dempsey. Look, this thing's taken a turn. They've started tying up loose ends. One of my sources was taken out this morning. You're on their radar too, Michael, so take precautions. None of your heroic shit this time, mate. These people, they're well out of your league. We need to get you and Sarah somewhere safe. OK? Call me when you get this.'

Dempsey tapped the disconnect icon and slipped the handset

back into his pocket, just as he reached his bike. Moments later he had his helmet on and the engine purring. A few more and he was turning left out onto United Nations Plaza, following the one-way system round to the right and then onwards in the direction of First Avenue and Manhattan's Yorkville.

*

'It's him.' Cobb took the slim digital spyglass away from his eye as he spoke. He turned in his seat to face Braddock.

'You sure?'

'It's him.'

Cobb's tone left no room for doubt. Not for Braddock, anyway. They had worked together long enough that it was all the reassurance the lead agent needed.

'What's he driving?' Braddock asked as he turned the ignition on their Lincoln Continental, bringing the car to life and ready to move at Cobb's instruction.

'Gold and grey Triumph Daytona bike,' Cobb replied. 'About ten years old.'

'A bike?' Eden Grace sounded unimpressed. 'That means a helmet. How the hell can you be sure it's him?'

'Because he put the helmet on when he got to the bike, Princess. Before that he was on his cell. Satisfied?'

'Not in the least, no,' Grace replied. 'But looks like I'm outvoted, doesn't it?'

'Looks that way, yeah.'

Cobb turned his eyes back to the road. Seconds later they watched as traffic began to come to a halt on the United Nations Plaza, to allow for left turns from East 44th Street. Exactly where they had been parked for over an hour.

Braddock hesitated.

'Take the turn,' Cobb said, before Braddock could make up his own mind. 'Take the turn then kill your speed. He's on a bike and we know the direction he's going. He'll get to the front of that traffic and he'll pass us. Then we can stay on him.'

Braddock nodded. It was the decision he would have made, but Cobb's agreement was always welcome. Indicating his way into traffic, he made the left-hand turn just before the lights turned back to red.

Once on United Nations Plaza, Braddock lowered his speed down to thirty miles per hour. Any slower could be suspicious. Any faster and Dempsey might not pass them.

Seconds went by. The traffic from the United Nations Plaza lights began to move, all accelerating past their vehicle. Braddock kept his eyes on the rear-view mirror, looking for Dempsey or his bike.

But there was no sign of him.

'Where the hell is he?' Braddock demanded, turning at the wheel to face Cobb. 'Are you sure it was him? Are you sure he was going in this direction?'

'I'm sure,' Cobb replied, irritated. 'I saw his face, plain as I'm seeing yours now. And from the route he took, he's coming this way. Just wait and you'll see.'

'You better be right.'

'When am I not?'

'STOP!'

The shout came from Eden Grace in the back seat. Neither man had been watching the road as they argued, and so only Grace had seen the lights at East 49th Street turn red in front of them.

Braddock hit the brakes hard, bringing the Lincoln to a screeching halt with half the car's bonnet past the stop line.

'How about you two pay some goddamned attention to the road?' Grace demanded.

'Who the hell do you think you're speaking to, Grace?' Braddock replied, his anger caused more by embarrassment at what had happened than by genuine irritation. 'I'm the senior agent on this assignment. Watch your tone.'

'Or what? You'll note it on my record? And how are you going to explain the nature of the mission we were on when I was insubordinate, huh? Tell me that?'

'Both of you, shut the hell up.'

Cobb's intervention was low. Little more than a growl. That fact alone made both Grace and Braddock pay attention.

Cobb stayed stock still as he continued, his voice no higher.

'He's right next to us.'

Neither Braddock nor Grace showed any surprise. Both were far too well-trained for that. Instead they continued to face each other, as if still in conversation. As if Cobb had said nothing.

But however they might appear to the outside world, the attention of all three was now fixed on one man.

Dempsey had stopped his bike at the same red light, level and immediately next to the bonnet of their Lincoln. Far enough ahead that his bike's wing mirrors could give him a clear view into their car.

'Has he made us?' Braddock asked, careful to look as if he were still speaking to Grace.

'How would he?' Grace asked. 'He doesn't know we're coming.'

'Let's assume he's as paranoid as Knowles said. Has he made us?'

'Doesn't look like it,' Cobb replied. 'Doesn't look like he's paid us any attention at all.'

As Cobb spoke the lights turned green. Gunning his engine, Dempsey was gone in an instant. No hesitation.

Braddock did the same, keeping the bike within a visible distance.

If Dempsey had registered them then he would be waiting. Braddock knew that. And if he had not, well, they still had to stay on him. That was the job.

Either way, the sonofabitch has to die.

FORTY

Mansour wanted one thing and one thing only. Solitude.

David Carter had seemed friendly enough. Or at least as friendly as someone held in Belmarsh's High Security Unit could be. He had seemed keen to make friends.

That was not what Mansour wanted. Not with Carter. Not with anyone.

He took the staircase to the first floor, slowly, his eyes carefully fixed on each step. With the other inmates all accounted for, he knew that he could only meet guards between here and his cell. But he did not want to speak to them either.

He just wanted to be alone.

That desire was now a driving force, brought on by his discomfort with Carter's attention. And with the more indirect interest he had received from everyone else. Mansour had had no wish to be *anyone's* focus. An unrealistic ambition for a man in his position, he realised. But it had been his hope.

All of this was on Mansour's mind as he made his way back to his cell.

Had it not been, perhaps he might have taken a moment to look behind him as he finally reached Cell Twelve.

'Can I help you?'

Mansour was confused as he stepped into his cell and saw a large man in a prison guard's uniform standing at the end of his bed. A man he had not seen before.

Was this normal? Was it a search of his cell?

With nothing to compare it against, Mansour had no answer to his own questions.

'You need to search me?' he asked, still unsure of the protocol.

The guard said nothing, his expression unreadable. His unexpected presence had caught Mansour off guard. Had it been an inmate then Mansour would have been concerned. But a guard? That just made Mansour uncertain. Unaware of what new part of the prison routine he was about to experience.

What was it Michael Devlin had said? 'Keep your head down, Nizar. Do as you're told and stay out of trouble.' He intended to do exactly that.

'Sir, please, tell me what I must do. I do not know the rules. Please . . .'

The sound of heavy footfall on metal stopped Mansour as he spoke. More than one person. Moving fast, certainly faster than a walking pace.

And they were headed towards Cell Twelve. The very last cell on the upper floor. A place they had no need to be. And which they had no reason to reach in a hurry.

The sudden realisation struck hard. In barely a heartbeat, Mansour's confusion was replaced with absolute certainty.

The guard was not there to search Mansour or his cell.

The guard was there to kill him. With the help of whoever was rushing towards them.

The cell was six feet wide. Three of those were taken up by the bed. What little space was left was too narrow to accommodate more than one man. But the cell's depth of ten feet? That was more forgiving. It could easily fit the guard, then Mansour, then one other behind. Maybe even one more after that.

The calculation was not difficult. Far easier than those he had had to make in the war zone he had left behind. He made it in an instant.

He moved without warning. Fast and low. A desperate, one-time, all-out assault. Mansour had a single goal: to get to the other side of the guard and put the cell's wall behind his back. If successful, it would limit the potential attacks upon him to one at a time.

His only hope of survival, however slim.

The guard reacted to Mansour's movement quickly, but not quickly enough. With the full ten feet of the cell to build up momentum, Mansour was moving at maximum speed as he aimed his upper body low and slammed his right shoulder hard into the guard's lower gut.

He could feel the guard's breath being violently expelled with the impact on his unprotected abdomen. The guard hadn't expected Mansour to aim his attack there; he was used to inexperienced street fighters who invariably swung straight for the head, and so his massive arms had flailed pathetically towards his own face. Overconfidence and disrespect. A big disadvantage when facing someone who knows how to fight for their life.

In any other circumstances Mansour might have stopped there. To see if his opponent had suffered enough. Or, more likely, to take the opportunity to run.

Neither was an option here. He had just moments, and so he did the only thing he could.

Keeping his right shoulder low, he pulled it backwards, at the same time using every ounce of power he could summon to smash his left fist deep into the guard's exposed, vulnerable groin. Once. Twice. Three times in little more than a second.

Changing from left fist to right fist and back again, each blow struck deeper and deeper into the guard's testicles, until Mansour could feel the sensation of uncontrollable vomit hitting his own lower back.

It had been two, perhaps three seconds since Mansour had first moved, but already the guard was falling. Mansour could feel the weight bearing down. And so he did what he had set out to do. He pulled the man's lumbering form forward into the cell and let him collapse heavily to the floor, before stepping over him and placing his own spine against the cell's back wall.

He faced the door, unsure of who was about to come through it, or how many. Whoever it was, they no longer had the advantage. With just a three-foot width in which to fight and the obstacle of the decimated guard, Mansour had achieved his aim.

Because whoever came next, they could only come one at a time.

David Carter's face no longer displayed a friendly smile as he came through the doorway. His eyes flicked to the crumbled giant, prone on the cell floor, as he stepped inside. Then they returned to Mansour.

He took two short steps inside. Enough to make room between himself and the cell door, but still staying seven or eight feet from Mansour, who remained resolutely tight to the back wall.

Mansour found the movement telling. Carter had reached the door ready for carnage, and that was exactly what he had found. Only it was not the carnage he had been expecting. Mansour could see the uncertainty in his eyes. He was almost amused by the distance Carter was now keeping.

Less amused were Carter's companions, who seemed to have reached the cell with the same enthusiasm, but in whom it was not so easily defused. They forced their way into the cell behind him, struggling with the limited space.

Server One and Server Three.

The dirty man and the coward, Mansour thought to himself.

'How the fuck'd you do that?' Carter's first words confirmed the fear Mansour had suspected, as he indicated the guard. 'We was only ten seconds behind ya.'

'You were sent by Romeo?' Mansour had reached the obvious conclusion.

'You got some powerful enemies, Nizar.' He neither confirmed nor denied the name. 'Let's just say that.'

Carter looked down again as he spoke. At the state of the man on the floor between them. Then he looked back towards Mansour, and then around the cell.

He was assessing his next move, Mansour realised. How an attack would play out. An attack where Carter would be on his own, with his support literally trapped behind him.

'You're nervous?' Mansour asked. He already knew the answer. 'You should be.'

'Why? Because of what you did to him? You think that worries me?'

'I know that it does. Your eyes tell me.' Mansour smiled. 'You reach me first, you end up like him.'

'You think?'

'I don't think. I know.'

'We'll see about that, won't we.' Carter's voice was no longer as confident.

'When? You are talking much. But you are not moving.'

Carter said nothing. His eyes flicked nervously around the room. For a moment Mansour felt a surge of hope.

Would Carter baulk? Would he run?

That hope did not last.

'Are we doing this or what?' The question came from behind. Server Three. It was directed at Carter. 'Get the fuck on with it, would ya?'

'I'll do it when I'm ready.' Carter found some aggression to inject into his voice. It rang hollow.

'When you're ready? When you're fucking ready? This ain't a bungee jump. For fuck sake, get on with it.'

Carter half turned to face his companions, but as he did so Server Three pushed him hard in the back. It sent Carter stumbling forward towards Mansour. On a path that was blocked by the unmoving guard.

Carter's already unsteady feet collided with the guard's torso, causing his right leg to buckle as momentum carried him forward. He struggled to regain his footing, but could do nothing as he stumbled forward fast.

Seizing the opportunity, Mansour moved as quickly as he could. He forcefully grasped Carter's head and both accelerated and redirected its journey towards the cell's side wall.

Carter's skull impacted the brickwork with a sickening crack, sending him to the floor. The sound seemed to fill the room, and Mansour recognised the sensation of bone giving way.

He had experienced it before. Killing with his bare hands. It was the nature of a war against a better equipped enemy. And it was something he had hoped to never feel again.

That thought brought Mansour to a halt and, for just an instant, he forgot where he was. The danger he still faced.

It was the very worst thing he could have done.

The blow sent Mansour backwards, his world spinning inside his own head. A huge hit that somehow turned everything simultaneously black and orange. His senses recovered quickly, soon enough to realise that it was Server Three who had hit him. But his control over his own limbs did not. Before he could lift his hands he was punched again. Weaker this time. But with the effects of the first blow still reverberating, it was just as debilitating.

The third punch – another right – finished the job. Disorientated from the second blow, Mansour did not see it coming. So he was unprepared for the sheer devastation of Server Three's final overhand right. The world went completely black. And for a moment Mansour was confused by the feeling of the wall somehow sliding upwards against his back.

It took a moment for him to understand the reality. It was not the wall moving. It was Mansour. And that movement only stopped when he hit the floor.

He was done and he was helpless. Incapable of climbing back to his feet.

Not that he would have the chance. Server Three's right knee smashed into Mansour's nose just an instant later. The sound of cartilage caving under the strength of the blow was sickening. Worse was the explosion of agony as the back of his head made contact with the hard brickwork behind it.

The impact separated Mansour from his senses, and so he felt no further pain as he slumped against the wall and began to take kick after kick after kick. Aimed at his body and at his head. His face was quickly a mask of blood as the kicks became stamps.

There was no hope. There was no escape. These men

were there to kill him, and they would not stop until he was dead.

Or until someone stopped them.

At first Mansour thought that the final kick had killed him. That Server Three had succeeded where everyone since the Syrian Army had failed.

It took him several seconds to realise that he was wrong. That the room was now filled with screams and shouts that were not his own. With movements he could make out through the dripping blood that coated his eyes. And with the returning sensation of excruciating pain that came from his injuries, as full consciousness returned.

With his head feeling clearer, Mansour realised that his cell was now empty; that the sounds were coming from outside. He wiped the blood and the tears from his eyes and began to crawl forward. He needed to see what had happened. To see what had saved his life.

He moved slowly. Painfully. Pulling himself over the still unmoving guard. Past Carter, also lying where Mansour had left him and bleeding ominously from his ear.

He ignored the agony, the nausea and the disorientation that threatened collapse with every movement. Closer to the cell door. Closer. Closer.

Finally the blurry figures ahead of him began to take shape.

There were four of them. All black. All bearded. All Muslim.

Server One was nowhere to be seen, and so Server Three had their full attention. He was on the floor of the metal landing directly outside of Mansour's cell door, and by now he was as bloody a mess as Mansour had ever seen.

'You attack one of us, you attack us all.'

The voice was the same one Mansour had heard downstairs, in the meal line. Even now he could recognise it.

All four men had space to rain down blows. Not one of them was holding back.

'Your hands defile our brother.'

The same voice. Mansour's eyes felt ready to explode as he tried to focus on the speaker.

As he did so, he saw Server Three open his left eye. His stare seemed to be fixed on Mansour. It was a sight that would remain with him forever. The eye, white and milky, had the look of a slaughtered animal. A bull, its throat slit for its meat.

'You will die for your insult. All of you.'

He's going to die painfully, Mansour thought, shock bringing some clarity back to his disorientated mind. *And he knows it.*

Mansour opened his mouth to call out. To beg them to stop. To save the man's life.

No sound came out. He would later wonder why. Was he not capable after the beating he had taken? Or, deep down, did he not *want* the man saved?

He would never know, and nor did it matter. Whatever he might have said would have had no effect. He could do nothing but watch as the kicks finally stopped. For a moment he thought that the attack was over, until the four men, acting as one, picked Server Three from the metal floor, lifted him to their own heights and threw him from the first-floor landing, down to the floor below.

'The same fate for enemies of the Prophet.'

Mansour rolled backwards, horrified by what he'd witnessed. He closed his eyes in despair and felt them fill with tears as his consciousness began to slip again.

More death, he thought. He may have even said it. He no longer knew.

His world was slipping away. The darkness was returning.

Almazid min almawt.

More death.

FORTY-ONE

Joe Dempsey looked in his right-hand mirror as he passed East 59th Street. The road led to the foot of Central Park just a few blocks to his left, and it was this spot that provided the clearest view of First Avenue behind him. Long, flat and straight.

If he was going to spot anything, it was from here.

The Lincoln Continental back at the 49th Street lights had bothered him. He had been perhaps fifty yards behind it when the car had come to a sudden stop.

Bad driving, he had thought to himself. Nothing out of the ordinary for New York City.

It was only when he'd come to a stop next to the car that it had really caught his attention.

Dempsey thought of himself as an investigator. Others might describe him differently. Using words like 'killer' and 'assassin'. And ten years ago they would have been right. But not any more. He would kill if he must. But death was no longer Dempsey's purpose. It was an occupational hazard, and it only came to those who deserved it.

For all that, his life was no less dangerous now than it had ever been. And so spotting the unordinary was still an essential skill that helped keep him alive.

It was the passengers of the Lincoln that had caught his eye. Two men in the front, one woman in the back. All dressed professionally in black. Practical, unobtrusive hair styles.

Dempsey had seen Secret Service agents up close. Many

times. He had even worked alongside them. As an organisation, they had his respect; no one on the planet was better at what they did. And that was why it concerned him to see three agents – because they *were* agents; Dempsey was sure of that – almost crashing at a traffic light on United Nations Plaza.

Something distracted them, he thought. *Something distracted the guys who don't* get *distracted*.

It was the very basis of their training. Complete attention, twenty-four-seven. Always vigilant, never missing a movement. To protect their president, they needed to see every flicker, every hint of a threat, and then they had to assess it. To react, or to let it pass?

It required a skill level unmatched by anyone else.

A skill that does not miss traffic lights. Not without good reason. So what was the distraction?

That curiosity had led him to study them. And that's why he'd spotted it. The pretence of continued conversation. The rigid maintenance of position. The fixed stare and unmoving lips of the driver as he'd hissed his warning.

And the refusal to glance in Dempsey's direction, even when it was natural to do so.

That's when he'd known.

The distraction was him.

Ten blocks later and they were still behind him. A respectable distance. Changing lanes. Allowing other cars to occasionally come between them. Even an inconsistency in speed, to keep the distance varied.

Trained surveillance driving, Dempsey thought to himself as he passed East 63rd. *If it wasn't for their screw-up at the lights, I might not have seen them.*

He kept his eyes on their reflection in his mirrors as both his Triumph and their Lincoln moved further north. His trajectory was dead straight, the two vehicles now connected by an imaginary line of which only they were aware.

There was not far to go. Dempsey knew that, even if the guys in the car did not. It gave him little time to anticipate their plan. And so he gave up trying. They might not even *have* a plan, he realised. It could be as simple as a drive-by shooting.

With his stop coming up – and with it his moment of vulnerability – he would instead concentrate on staying alive.

Dempsey accelerated as he passed East 70th. Just to see what the Lincoln would do. The answer was nothing. Its driver allowed the distance to grow. As far as Dempsey could tell, they now seemed confident enough to lose sight.

Which means they know where I live, he realised. *They probably have someone up here already.*

Dempsey's eyes darted everywhere as he moved along the final four blocks. He slowed his speed again, to give him the best chance of spotting a second vehicle, but he saw nothing as he came to his right-hand turn onto East 74th.

He was about to find out why.

As fast as he had covered the distance between First Avenue and York on foot earlier, it was nothing compared to a bike. It took five, perhaps six seconds for him to reach the right-hand turn close to the very end of 74th Street, which led to the gated parking area of The Stratford building.

Bringing his Triumph Daytona to a halt in front of the gates, he searched his leathers for the remote control that opened the interlinking metal barrier. Tapping himself down, he had to open the zipper on his leather jacket to reach it. Once in hand, he clicked the single button and waited as the gate slowly rose.

To anyone passing, he looked like any other resident of any one of Manhattan's countless high-rise apartment buildings. Just a man, waiting patiently to access the parking facility he was lucky to enjoy. Nothing unusual. Nothing out of the ordinary.

In reality, he was no such thing. His eyes were once again fixed to his mirrors, intently watching the two black-suited men who were seated in the near-identical Lincoln Continental that was parked on the corner of 74th, almost directly across from the parking garage.

There was less than twenty yards between them.

Dempsey was waiting for them to make their move. To come and do what it was they were here for. Because when they came, he would be ready. His show at finding the remote had been exactly that: a distraction that had allowed him to open his tight jacket and provide free access to his concealed Glock 19 pistol.

He waited.

And he waited.

And they did not move.

The gate stopped, now fully opened. Dempsey pulled inside, just in time to glance to his right and observe the arrival of the other Lincoln Continental as it turned from First Avenue onto 74th.

They waited, Dempsey thought as he pulled into the parking garage and watched the gate closed behind him. *There were two of them right there, and they waited.*

They want this five on one.

They were not good odds, Dempsey realised. Not good at all. And then he thought back to what Tom Quilty had said only the night before, and it did something unexpected. It made Dempsey laugh.

He looked upwards as he spoke aloud. A message to a dead man.

'At least they're taking one of us seriously, Tom.'

FORTY-TWO

'I don't give a shit.' Eden Grace's voice was as raised as she could allow it to be. 'I've been sent here to make sure this mission isn't another damn screw-up. I can't do that if Cobb's inside and I'm out here. I have to be the one who goes in.'

Braddock had pulled up on the northwest corner of York and 74th. Well positioned to see both the main entrance to The Stratford and the gate to its underground car park. The other Lincoln containing Agents Swanson and Marks was not far away.

'And who the hell gave you the authority to decide how we act?' Cobb demanded.

'The president of the United States of America. When he sent me here to stop you assholes from causing another disaster.'

'And what the hell does he know?'

'What does he know? What does the guy who used to lead SEAL Team Six know? Have you idiots forgotten that? Have you forgotten what he did before he was president? That man has done more covert shit than each one of us put together. You think we should be ignoring his instincts?'

The answer seemed to hit home with most of the team. All of them but Cobb.

'Whole lot of difference fighting in a desert and killing a man in a city, sweetheart.'

'And you'd know, would you? You see much action in Afghanistan, Cobb? In Iraq?'

Cobb didn't answer.

'I didn't think so.' Grace turned to face Braddock. 'The president wanted this. There's no other reason for him to have sent me.'

Braddock nodded thoughtfully but Cobb still seemed unconvinced. A fact which posed little problem for Grace. Because as long as it was her against Cobb in the battle for Braddock's agreement, that meant a reasoned argument against macho belligerence.

Grace liked her odds.

'OK. Let's break this down. What do you think happens if Cobb goes in and this goes wrong?'

'That ain't gonna happen,' Cobb hissed. 'I could take this guy blindfold.'

'What then?' Grace ignored the interruption. 'We go back having failed. All because you ignored the precautions *against* failure that the president put in place.'

Braddock said nothing. Just nodded again.

'Now let's assume I go inside. The president's not stupid. He didn't pick me for my loyalty alone. He picked me because I'm a whole lot less of an instant confrontation than any of you.' She looked at Cobb. 'Especially you.' Back to Braddock. 'Best-case scenario, Dempsey's guard's down, he leaves with me, I bring him to you guys. Job done.'

Grace waited for an answer. None was given, but she could tell that common sense was winning.

'Let's aim for best-case scenario, shall we, boys? I'd like to walk away from this just as much as the rest of you.'

Braddock took a few moments more to consider what had been said. Not long. He had reached a decision.

'OK. You go in, Grace. Go in, identify yourself and tell him that you need to bring him downtown at the request of Assistant Director Meyer.'

'And if he asks why?'

'Plead ignorance. You don't know anything about anything. You're as junior as it gets and you're running an errand.'

'What if he refuses?'

'He won't refuse. He's an ISB Agent on US soil; you're Secret Service. He'll go with you.'

'Even if he suspects something?'

'If he suspects something he'll be on his guard. But he'll still come with you. He can't say no. We'll just have to be better than him.'

'He won't go easy. Not if he suspects.'

'Damn right he won't. But like I said before: this ain't our first time.'

'Where do I bring him, then?'

Braddock looked around, surveying the area. Assessing the location for likely witnesses and security cameras. His sweeping gaze stopped at the gated entrance to The Stratford's underground parking facility.

Grace followed Braddock's eyeline and spotted what he had just seen.

A camera, hidden in the dark on the inner side of the gate. From its angle of direction, its footage would be restricted to whatever was happening at the very front of the gate and nothing more.

'There,' Braddock said, indicating the parking entrance. We'll all gather there. Bring him to us, and, as soon as you hear us shout, you hit the floor.'

'Shout?'

'Play-acting for the camera. It'll look like we're demanding that Dempsey drops his weapon. A weapon you'll later confirm had been trained on you as you both left the building. We'll seem to be doing our damnedest to make him disarm and surrender, making it a justified kill when he doesn't.'

Grace nodded her head.

'Almost as good as an accident.'

'You've got to work with what you're given in this job,' Braddock replied. He gave her a final measured look. 'You ready for this?'

Grace took a deep breath and nodded again.

'Then let's get this done.'

FORTY-THREE

'It was expected. He's been unwell for some time. He wanted it kept . . . private.'

Nicolas Dupart sat across from Kelvin Cunningham in the deputy assistant's office. A place in which Cunningham was rarely to be found. Unusual as it was for him to take meetings in here instead of the Oval Office, Cunningham was glad for the privacy.

The news was more than unwelcome.

'Is there . . . is there anything I can do? Anything I can help with?'

'Everything was prepared for,' Dupart replied. 'The transition will be seamless.'

'Maybe professionally, Nick. But Theseus was your father. What about you? What about your family? Is there anything you need? Personally, I mean?'

Cunningham regretted the question as soon as he asked it. Dupart seemed no different now than from their meeting that morning. A time when, Cunningham now realised, Theseus Dupart would have been taking his last breath.

In other words, Nicolas Dupart did not 'do' personal.

'I know you were close to my father, Kelvin. But I assure you, everything that needed to be done has been done.'

'The trusts?'

'All in my name as of noon today.'

'And the companies?'

'Unaffected. All owned by blind trusts. No one has any idea that title has passed from him to me.'

From him to me.

Cunningham considered the words. Had he been as cold when his own parents had died? Maybe. Maybe not. But then *his* parents had birthed him dirt poor, they had raised him dirt poor and they had left him dirt poor. What the hell did he have to thank *them* for?

Theseus Dupart? He had left *his* son one of the richest men on the planet.

'And your mother?'

'I doubt she'll miss their arrangement,' Dupart replied.

Cunningham understood the answer. He had been close friends with Theseus Dupart for twenty years. And he had worked for him for much longer still. He regarded him as the father he *should* have had. The man his own father should have been.

It was a delusion. He knew that. Theseus Dupart had his son. His heir. He did not need another. But still, Cunningham had worked hard. He had used their connections to succeed. To put him in a place that would attract the attention of the organisation.

And look where I am now. Feet from the Oval Office. The power behind the throne.

'As I said, I know you were close to my father.' There was no break in Dupart's voice. 'Closer than *I* ever was. So do *you* need any help with this? Some time, perhaps?'

'No.' Cunningham's answer was firm. Perhaps too firm; it suggested he was concealing his emotion. His tone was softer when he spoke again. 'No. With everything that's happening, there's no time for that.'

'You're sure?'

'Yes. Yes, I'm sure.'

'Good.' Dupart rose to his feet. 'There's no use letting something like this distract us. Not now.'

'Agreed.'

It was all Cunningham could think to say. Theseus Dupart had been a cold man. A ruthless man. The man from whom Cunningham had learned his own skills. But his son?

From what Cunningham could now see, Nicolas Dupart was a robot.

What more is there to say?

The thought was in Cunningham's head, but somehow Dupart seemed to hear it. And with a final nod of the head and the smallest of false smiles, he turned and left Cunningham's office.

FORTY-FOUR

The call had come three minutes before. From The Stratford's head doorman, Freddie Garcia. Of the building's doormen, it was Garcia whom Dempsey had come to know well, and he had informed Dempsey that there was a woman in the lobby who wished to see him.

A woman from the US Government.

Has to be the one from the Lincoln, Dempsey deduced. *Unless there's even more of them I didn't spot. Maybe five on one wasn't good enough odds.*

He dismissed his own doubts. Five would be the number.

'Should I send her up, Mr Dempsey?' Garcia had asked.

'No. Tell her to wait where she is. I'll be right down.'

Dempsey found the whole approach confusing.

Why are they announcing themselves, he wondered. *They must know enough to realise it would put me on the defensive?*

Then again, how else would they flush me out of a secure apartment block? There's no way anyone is getting to the elevators without Freddie spotting them, and so no way they can get to me without me being ready for them. They must realise that.

So why not just wait? I have to leave sometime?

The reason came to him from nowhere. The only logical answer.

Because they can't *wait. They need this done quickly.*

There was no point wasting time trying to guess at the reason for their urgency. An investigator makes deductions, based upon evidence, logic and reason. Once they are exhausted, everything else is a shot in the dark. And Dempsey's previous life had taught him the value of those.

Instead he used the time productively. He stripped off the white shirt he was wearing beneath his suit jacket and biker's leathers, exposing his upper body. Next he opened the closet and pulled out the heavy metallic case that sat at the bottom.

Dempsey carried the case into his living area, placed it on the metal and glass table that stood against the side wall and opened it with a four-digit code.

Inside was an arsenal. Enough weaponry for a small war.

Six pistols; three more Glock 19s, three Glock 26s and enough fifteen-round and ten-round 9mm magazines to fill each ten times over. Four Heckler & Koch G36C close-quarters assault rifles, plus what looked like ammunition for a small regiment. And two solid steel pilot survival knives, each with a concealed forearm sheath.

Dempsey took the sheaths first, strapping one to each arm. The Velcro strap circled his forearm a few inches below the elbow, with the metal sheaths running towards his wrists. Satisfied, he carefully placed a razor-sharp knife in each.

Next he grabbed another white shirt. Short-sleeved this time to avoid the risk of the knives being slowed by a cufflink or bunched material.

Hanging next to the shirt was Dempsey's two-pistol holster, and so that came next. He selected an extra Glock 19 from the case. Adding a ten-round magazine, he chambered a round and placed the Glock into the left side. A quick check of the pistol he had been carrying all day and the right side was filled too.

Dempsey checked his watch. Two minutes since the call. He had to hurry.

Looking back into the case, he removed a single Glock 26

and slipped it into the holster that was already in place near his right ankle, under his loose bottomed suit trousers. Finally he picked up four spare magazines, secured them under his belt at the back of his pants, threw on his jacket, placed a leather envelope in its right-hand front pocket and headed to the elevator.

He locked the apartment door as he left. Whatever happened in the next few minutes, he knew that he would not be coming back any time soon.

FORTY-FIVE

Dempsey breathed deeply as the elevator doors closed and its mechanism came to life. Long, slow inhales. Exhales even longer. Flooding his system with the adrenaline he was sure he was about to need.

He was the elevator's only occupant, and the only floor illuminated on the console was the lobby. But that did not mean it wouldn't visit anywhere elsewhere en route, down from the thirty-fifth. It could stop at any floor without warning and the doors would open.

All it would take was for someone on that floor to press 'down'.

Someone. Anyone.

Including the men from the Lincolns.

Dempsey pushed his back tight against the left wall of the elevator. It provided little cover, but little was better than nothing. At least he would not be instantly visible if the doors opened. A sitting target.

He was sure that they would not attempt to ambush him at the lobby's elevator bank. Not where they could be overseen by not only The Stratford's staff and its residents, but also by one of its security cameras.

No. It would not happen there. But it *could* happen on any *other* floor.

The thought concerned Dempsey as the elevator continued down. It had been a mistake to step inside, he now realised. A rare error. And one on which they could capitalise. Because as good as he was, a shoot-out while he was trapped inside a box was only going to end one way.

The elevator began to slow. Dempsey focused on the information terminal above the doors.

Eight.

Seven.

Six.

The lift continued to decelerate.

Five.

Dempsey braced himself against the wall, doing his best to make his large, powerful physique inconspicuous. An impossible task.

Four.

He wracked his brain. Did the elevator usually slow here if it was heading for the lobby? He couldn't remember. It was one of the few details of his life to which he had paid little attention. Why would he?

Three.

Would they even risk an ambush this low? This close to the lobby?

Two.

The elevator came to a halt.

This is it.

Dempsey reached into his jacket and gripped his pistol, waiting for the doors to begin their slide open. Before they did, the display changed again. One last time.

Lobby.

Dempsey exhaled long and hard as a feeling of relief swept over him. He had made what could have been a fatal mistake and he had come through it.

He would not make another.

The elevator bank in The Stratford stood like a structural obstruction in the centre of the building's main reception area, with its doors facing the long, panoramic mirror that covered the lobby's back wall. Dempsey had often wondered about the design. Who wants to stare at themselves at the end of a long day, before they are slowly lifted up to bed?

He was grateful for it now. The mirror gave him a clear view of the lobby's backend, making an ambush here impossible. It allowed him to step out of the elevator with confidence, hiding the anxiety he had been feeling just moments before.

He turned right, walked to the end of the elevator bank and turned right again. It brought him to the side of the structure and revealed more of the main lobby with each step.

His first sight was Freddie Garcia, dressed in his brown uniform, wearing his peaked hat and standing at his wooden desk. He must have caught sight of Dempsey in his peripheral vision; he turned before Dempsey was even two steps into the lobby.

Dempsey had learned a lot about Garcia in his time in The Stratford. He had learned that Garcia was the eldest of six and, with his father's death and his mother's illness, the main provider for the whole family. He had learned that Garcia had ambition. An intention to put himself through college on a language course, hoping to offer translation services in New York's courts or even, he had once admitted to Dempsey, the United Nations. And he had learned that Garcia was friendly, loyal, honest and generous. All perfect attributes for the position he held.

But most importantly right now, he had learned that Garcia had the world's worst poker face. If a group of armed men were in the lobby, secreted behind the cover still provided by the elevator bank, Dempsey would have been able to read it in Garcia's eyes.

Eyes which were, as he stepped closer, as bright and as happy as ever.

Dempsey returned Garcia's smile. He knew he was safe. At least for the moment.

'Your visitor, Mr Dempsey,' Garcia said, indicating towards a spot Dempsey still could not see.

Two more steps and that was rectified.

It was the woman from the back seat of the Lincoln. Dempsey's view had been clear enough at the lights. He had no doubt.

'Thanks, Freddie.' Dempsey stepped towards the agent as he spoke.

He did not know what he had expected; his natural respect for US Secret Service personnel had taken a hit after their mistake at the lights. But whatever that expectation had been, the woman ahead of him surpassed it.

She was around five foot six, and clearly strong and athletic. That much was obvious even when disguised by the Service's near-uniform of black pants suit and white blouse. A suit that somehow looked *extra* black, now that Dempsey considered it. As if the light spectrum was being absorbed that little bit more. He quickly realised why. There was not so much as a single piece of lint or the tiniest speck of dust anywhere.

For a man with Dempsey's military background, such fastidiousness was immediately impressive.

His eyes scanned upwards, where he noted dark hair that was cut to be feminine, neat and entirely practical, and a pair of alert, intelligent brown eyes.

On the surface, everything about her was impressive. And

while that did not necessarily reflect her actual ability, it was still not the conclusion Dempsey had hoped to reach.

These guys might be the real deal after all.

He hid the thought and closed the remaining gap between them, holding out his hand in greeting.

'Joe Dempsey, International Security Bureau. And you are?'

The agent reached out, gripped Dempsey's hand and stepped close. When she spoke, her voice was low. So only Dempsey could hear.

'I'm Special Agent Eden Grace and I've been sent here to kill you.'

FORTY-SIX

Dempsey released his grip on Eden Grace's hand as his own right hand moved instinctively towards his holster. He took a step back in the same moment, and with just a brief glance he assessed the building's main entrance.

He saw nothing he had not seen a hundred times.

At the centre of The Stratford's double-height frontage was a metal and glass revolving door. It was flanked on either side by hinged glass doors, each seven feet tall. Next to them and running to either end of the lobby were two single sheets of slightly tinted glass.

Put together, it made for a single transparent wall. Stylish, but far from practical if someone decided to take a shot from the street outside.

Dempsey's eyes narrowed with that thought, taking in the details. Just beyond the glass was the building's drop-off point. A wide one-way lane that ran from the corner of 74th Street to the start of 73rd. Next to it was a low, decorative hedge, then a lawn, then the pavement of York Avenue.

Both the lane and the street looked empty. No threat that Dempsey could see. But that did not mean it was not there.

He turned back to face Eden Grace.

'They sent you alone, did they?'

'No. There are five of us.'

He took another step back. Towards the elevator bank. A small movement, but it removed any line of sight between Dempsey and the second floor windows on the buildings across the street.

The question had been a test. Dempsey knew he was facing a five-person team. At least that. Eden Grace had no need to confirm it. No need to tell the truth. But she had. And *that* suggested she could be trusted.

Still, Dempsey was taking no chances.

He took one more step backwards. It killed the line of sight from the first floor windows across the street too. The same movement brought Freddie Garcia back into his peripheral vision.

It reminded him that the doorman was there. The only other person in the lobby.

'Freddie, get in the back.' Dempsey's voice left no room for questions. 'Lock the door and keep anyone else in there with you. Understand?'

Garcia nodded his head furiously, but failed to move.

'NOW!'

It was a tone perfected in combat, when obedience is the difference between life and death. Dempsey had used it countless times, and he resorted to it now. It cut through Garcia's moment of paralysis. He moved away, a near run. It left only Dempsey and Grace in the lobby.

With no one else within sight, Dempsey drew his pistol from its holster and pointed it at the agent.

'So how do you see this playing out?' Dempsey asked, hiding his own hesitation. The Glock 19 was trained precisely on Grace's forehead.

'I was hoping you'd help with that part,' Grace replied. She eyed the pistol with concern and for the first time she seem less than certain. 'My plan ended with that warning.'

Dempsey took one final step back. Into the shadow thrown by the elevator bank, where he was no longer visible from anywhere outside the building.

He glanced at the corridor to his left. It led to the service entrance, just past the post room. A solid metal security door, it was the only other way into the building from the street.

It was closed. And therefore locked. One followed the other.

This meant that only one open access point was available to Grace's team. The main one.

That fact allowed him time to focus on Grace.

'And why the hell would you give me a warning?'

'Because I'm a Special Agent of the United States Secret Service. It's my job to protect this country and its president. But I draw the line at murder, Mr Dempsey. I'm not an assassin.'

She sounded sincere. There was nothing in her body language to say otherwise. But in these circumstances, that was not nearly enough.

'So what? You're walking away from your team on principle? To save some guy you don't even know.'

'They're not my team,' Grace replied. She sounded as if she found the suggestion distasteful. 'I live by a code. A code taught to me my whole life. I do my duty and I do what's right. Killing you? That's neither.'

In a career that spanned more than two decades, Dempsey had spent literally years undercover. He knew how to tell a lie. And he knew how to spot one. Skills that had kept him alive as often as his ability to kill.

Grace did not seem to be lying. Which made her either an ally or a better covert agent than him.

'Who sent you here?' he asked.

'Assistant Director Jack Meyer,' Grace replied. She spoke without hesitation 'Head of the Presidential Protective Division.'

'I know who he is. Why'd he send you?'

'Like I said. He sent me here to kill you.'

'I get that. *Why?*'

'I didn't get an explanation. Just an order.'

'Why you?'

For the first time, Grace hesitated. When she spoke again, it was with an answer that did not justify the stumble.

'I . . . I don't know that. Like I said, I didn't get an explanation.'

Dempsey did not like the answer. It was an obvious lie. But that, in turn, made everything else she had said truthful; Grace could not be such a poor liar on one subject while being an accomplished one on everything else.

It was a helpful discovery. Now that he could trust most of what she had said, Dempsey could see where Grace's story married up with what he already knew.

What Quilty told him was true, he realised. *And now they were getting rid of anyone that truth had touched.*

There was only one more piece of information he needed.

'The order to kill me. Did it originate with Meyer? Or was the president involved?'

Grace hesitated again. Dempsey guessed why. It was the same reason as before.

He glanced at his watch. This was dragging on for too long. He adjusted his grip on his pistol. A visible message.

'I need an answer.'

Grace's eyes moved back to the Glock. Maybe she would have answered without it. Maybe it made the difference. Either way, when she spoke again he was satisfied that she was telling the truth.

'The order initially came from Meyer.' She sounded dejected. 'But yes. The president is aware.'

Dempsey did not reply. It was the answer he had expected. But not the one he wanted.

There was a time when President John Knowles had enjoyed Dempsey's respect. One of the few politicians who genuinely impressed him. Dempsey had had high hopes for his presidency. Hopes which had only increased after the events in Trafalgar Square and Northern Ireland that had taken place two and a half years ago.

Back then Dempsey had brought down his own agency – the UK's Department of Domestic Security – and it had been Knowles who had taken the lead in the aftermath. Knowles who had instigated the expansion of the ISB. An intelligence agency built to serve the entire world rather than the interests of one nation, for years the ISB had been underfunded and essentially powerless. But with Knowles' support and the need for international cooperation clearer than ever after the fall of the DDS, the ISB was finally given the status and the remit for which it had been created. And a budget to headhunt the best operatives from around the world; it was Knowles who had supported Dempsey's recruitment as its principle agent.

Dempsey had been disappointed, then, by Knowles' performance in the years since. Yet another president who promised one thing and delivered something very different. Who focused on what was good for big business while much that needed to be done for the people was forgotten. Who used the US military as a political battering ram, risking the lives of young American soldiers in war zones that needed diplomacy instead of bullets.

In other words, just another damned politician.

Knowles had turned out like the rest of them. No better. No worse.

But now, with Grace's answer, Dempsey had to accept that his conclusion was wrong. Knowles had sent a Secret Service hit squad to kill a man who might expose him. On top of whatever else he might have done, including the murder of Tom Quilty and the bombing of Flight PA16.

Hundreds of deaths. All to cover up his war crimes.

Like the rest of them? No. Knowles was worse. Much, much worse.

'Look, I've answered your questions. Now if it's all the same to you, how the hell are we gonna deal with what's about to happen?'

Grace's words broke into Dempsey's thoughts.

'What do you think happens now?' Dempsey asked. He had not quite registered the question. 'You think I can just let you walk out of here?'

'Walk out? Are you serious? Have you not been listening? We're in this together, pal.'

'What?'

'They're coming, Dempsey. And they're coming now. Whether I like it or not, that puts me on your team.'

Dempsey was surprised by the suggestion. Grace was not only trying to warn him, she was volunteering to put herself in harm's way . . .

'So what's the damn plan?'

Dempsey hesitated. His every instinct told him that Grace was playing it straight. Instincts that were fighting to overcome his natural paranoia.

'Dempsey, for Christ's sake.'

It was time to make a choice.

He lowered his pistol.

'OK. Where was the ambush supposed to happen?'

'Seventy-Fourth Street,' Grace began. 'I was supposed to lead you out near to the parking—'

She did not get the chance to finish her sentence.

The side service entrance, at the end of the corridor to Dempsey's left, was designed to keep out the uninvited. It was an expensive security door. Probably more than was necessary for a residential apartment building in a good Manhattan neighbourhood.

But all barriers have their limits. And whoever designed this one had not expected to contend with the point-blank blast of a Remington 820 Tactical shotgun.

The sound was unmistakable. An explosion of metal upon metal as the upper hinge of the security door was reduced to shrapnel.

There was no danger from where Dempsey stood; there was a corridor length between him and the damage. But still he felt his adrenaline spike, and with it he felt as if time around him was beginning to slow.

This was happening. And it was happening now.

FORTY-SEVEN

Dempsey had turned at the first shot. By the time of the second – another Remington blast, this time to the door's lower hinge – he had stepped forward. Back towards the lobby and away from the corridor.

Grace had done the opposite. Her pistol was in her hand within an instant of the first shot. By the time of the second, she was at the corner of the corridor, her weapon ready to meet whoever came through the door at its end.

She assumed that Dempsey would have done the same. That he would have mirrored her positioning.

'Where the hell are you going?' she demanded.

'It's a diversion,' Dempsey replied. 'One man. The others are coming through the front.'

'What? How the hell can you know that?'

Dempsey removed the Glock 26 from his ankle holster and a magazine from under his belt. He threw both to Grace.

'Because the entrance to this building is a forty-foot glass shooting gallery. You have that, why come through a door that needs an artillery to open it and leads directly into a bottle neck?'

Grace nodded.

'They *want* our attention this way.'

'They do,' Dempsey answered. 'And they can have yours. Put covering fire down that corridor and I promise you he won't take a step inside.'

Grace nodded again. She placed the spare weapon and

magazine into her own belt and aimed her SIG Sauer P229 towards what had, just moments before, been The Stratford's secure service entrance.

'What about you? What are you doing?'

Grace glanced over her shoulder as she shouted the question. From there she could see Dempsey striding towards the front of the building, his pistol raised.

He glanced back.

'Me? I'm going to show your friends how this is *really* done.'

FORTY-EIGHT

Dempsey wasted no more time explaining. If the attack was properly coordinated – and he had to assume it was – then he would have only seconds to act. But each of those seconds were an advantage.

Grace's former team was expecting to blindside Dempsey while his attention focused on the corridor. They had no way to know that he had seen through their diversion. And so no reason to expect that he would be waiting.

They would learn that soon enough.

Dempsey kept his gun raised as he stepped further into the lobby. He moved fast, scanning the glass frontage as he closed the distance.

The first sweep revealed nothing.

They're waiting for my first pistol shot, he realised. *Confirmation that the ruse has worked.*

He heard Grace begin to unload covering fire into the corridor behind him. He kept moving forward, his eyes scanning left to right.

Dempsey had expected the reaction to be instant. That they would attack immediately after the very first shot. It's what *his* team would have done; if it had been *them* out there, he and Grace might have been dead already.

It was a relief, then, that there was a delay. Little more than a second, it was all he needed.

It was no more than a flicker of movement behind the

hedge. The first steps of a man who had taken position there for visual cover.

The first steps. And the last.

Dempsey's conclusion and his decision were simultaneous. A single 9mm round shattered the lobby's long pane of glass and ripped into the agent's skull before he was even fully on his feet.

Dempsey didn't wait to see him go down. His eyes were already focused through the other stretch of window, now just feet ahead of him. A second round and it, too, was brought crashing down.

Dempsey picked up his pace. The dead agent was *his* diversion. A shock to catch the attention of whoever else was out there.

A shock from which they would not be given the time to recover.

He was through the broken window in a heartbeat. Moving at a run, he spotted two more agents, both to his left. As intended, the death of their colleague had slowed them.

But it had not stopped them.

The men were ten, maybe fifteen yards apart. One was on the access lane, armed with an assault rifle. The other on the grass, carrying a SIG pistol.

Both men tore their eyes from their fallen teammate and raised their weapons as they registered Dempsey. They recovered from the shock and moved faster than he had hoped.

It left him with a choice.

As dangerous as the SIG was in trained hands, the potential spray of an assault rifle was far worse. Thinking quickly, Dempsey changed direction to give the SIG carrier a difficult moving target while fixing his own focus on the agent in the lane.

The agent with the military-grade hardware.

Dempsey fired two shots. A double-tap. So close in time to almost sound as one.

The first bullet hit its target, leaving a hole in the front of the agent's head. The second – unnecessary as it was – did the same.

As the agent fell lifeless to the ground, Dempsey moved on to the remaining threat.

The agent with the SIG.

In the instant he had available, Dempsey recognised the man. The front passenger from the Lincoln.

Still moving fast, Dempsey swept the barrel of his Glock 19 towards SIG. His intention was to fire first. To neutralise the threat before SIG could take a shot of his own.

The odds of achieving that goal were not in his favour.

His barrel swept towards its next target with inhuman speed. But before he was even halfway there, Dempsey knew that even this had been too slow.

Dempsey's arm was still moving as he saw the tell-tale tightening of the man's knuckles and the almost imperceptible upward movement of his forearms. Both natural precursors to a shot, designed to steady aim.

Dempsey knew in that instant that he could not beat the man to the pull. And so he did the only thing he could to survive.

He did not try.

Instead Dempsey threw himself into a dive, removing the target of his upper body as the other man pulled the trigger. Mid air the first shot passed harmlessly over his head. The second one did not.

The gunman had fired again immediately, just as Dempsey would have done, and this time he must have anticipated his target's trajectory. He felt the bullet bite deep into his left shoulder. Ignoring the pain, Dempsey contorted himself in the air, and landed heavily on his back. The impact sent a surge of pain through his wounded shoulder, but it did nothing to slow him down.

The man could not be allowed another shot.

Dempsey's gun had been aimed as he fell, and he opened fire the instant his movement stopped.

Six rounds. All found their target. First the chest, then the neck and finally the head of SIG. They sent him crashing to the floor while the arterial spray of his neck wound fired into the air.

There could be no doubt that the shots had been fatal.

Dempsey climbed to his feet. Slowly. The pain in his left shoulder was excruciating. The bullet had torn through essential muscle. He could feel that already.

Taking the leather envelope from his jacket pocket, he let his coat slip backwards to the floor and pushed the envelope into his belt, next to the spare magazines.

With the jacket off, he ripped his shirt open to expose the wound.

The bullet was gone. Dempsey's angle of descent had allowed for it to pass through his shoulder completely. It meant one less job for later, but it left two open wounds. One entry. One exit. The extra wound would not double the blood loss, but it was far from ideal.

And it doesn't leave me much time.

Dempsey was moving before the thought was even fully formed. Back to the lane and towards 74th Street.

The Stratford's service entrance.

FORTY-NINE

Eden Grace placed two more shots into the corridor, using her left hand so as to keep herself out of sight. The choice affected her aim, but her role here was not to kill. It was to keep whoever had the shotgun busy while Dempsey was out front.

So far, so good.

A pattern had quickly emerged. The first two shotgun blasts had taken out the door. A third blast had followed, sending the burning contents of a cartridge down the full length of the corridor. Grace felt the pellets pass her from behind the cover of the corridor's corner. Still capable of tearing apart flesh, but too far away to do anything other than superficial damage to the structure.

Which makes Dempsey right, she had thought. *This is a diversion.*

Grace had returned fire with three shots of her own. Inaccurate but effective. All that was needed.

The pattern had been repeated three times since. A shotgun blast and three bullets in return. Until the final exchange, as Grace's ammunition was exhausted. She managed two shots instead of three.

This time the shotgun was fired sooner. And twice.

Shooter's counting, Grace realised. *And he thinks I need to reload.*

She pulled Dempsey's Glock 26 from her waist, peered around the corner and fired a further three shots before the Remington could reload and shoot again. As she pulled the trigger she caught sight of the shooter retreating through the doorway, his attempt to enter the building aborted.

Braddock. The sonofabitch.

'What happened to me bringing Dempsey to the parking garage?' she shouted.

No answer.

'Braddock. You listening to me, you piece of shit?'

For a moment it seemed like she would be met by silence again. Until:

'Grace. That you?'

'Who the hell else?'

Both voices were loud. Shouting. The inevitable result of gunfire.

'So? What happened to the plan, huh, Braddock?'

'What happened to "I'll do my duty"?'

'Can't argue with that, I guess.'

'No, you can't. Now how about you come out and show yourself, sweetheart?'

'You think I'm that stupid?'

'I think you're that screwed. But you're better with me than with Cobb. He gets to you before I do, no chance you live.'

'And what makes you think Cobb is getting anywhere near me?'

'Because what's gonna stop him? Dempsey?'

'Already has,' Grace replied. 'And you're next.'

Grace did not know if she was right. She *hoped* she was. And she had good reason. There had been no further shots from outside as she exchanged words with Braddock. If that meant Dempsey was dead, why had Cobb and the others not come through the front?

And if she was wrong?

If I'm wrong, well, then I'm dead anyway.

Her thoughts were cut short as Braddock burst through what was left of the doorway. He was moving fast. As if he was running from something.

Or someone.

He headed for the post room, six or seven yards along the corridor and to the left. And he did so without a glance towards her. It was as if Grace offered no threat to him at all.

It would be his final mistake.

'Drop the gun, Braddock!'

Braddock was barely two yards from the post room. From cover. From where he could protect himself with potshots for as long as his ammunition lasted.

The decision Grace had to make in that moment was life-changing. She hesitated, and as she did she heard the voice again. The voice that had guided her for her entire life.

Do your duty. Do what's right.

She fired twice.

It would not take a third.

FIFTY

Eden Grace was standing over the fourth man's corpse as Dempsey stepped through the now devastated doorway. The sight came as no surprise. Dempsey had heard two shots as he approached, and they had not come from a shotgun.

As he came closer he could see that Grace looked shaken.

'You OK?' he asked.

Grace looked up, towards Dempsey. Her eyes were blank. Dempsey had seen the same reaction before; she was struggling with what she had just done.

'He was your first.' It was not a question.

Grace nodded her head, unwilling or unable to speak. Dempsey put his hand on her shoulder.

'It gets everyone, Agent Grace. Especially if it's someone you know. But we don't have time for this now. We have to get out of here.'

Grace did not react to Dempsey's words. Instead she looked down, back towards Braddock's corpse. Then a thought seemed to occur to her. She turned quickly back to Dempsey.

'The others?'

'All gone.' Dempsey did not elaborate. What he had done was necessary. It was not something to be celebrated. 'Now *we* have to go.'

Grace did not seem to hear his final words. Instead she gazed left and right. At the destruction all around them.

The shock was hitting. Dempsey recognised it well. Very few come through their first fatal encounter without it.

But right now they did not have the time.

'Listen . . .'

'You're hurt.' Grace had noticed his bloody shoulder. 'We need to get you to a hospital.'

'Dammit, you've got to listen to me!' Dempsey grabbed Grace by her shoulders, ignoring the agony the movement caused to his own. 'We can't go anywhere near a hospital. We've got to get ourselves out of here now.'

Grace looked at him, shocked.

'Get out of here? What the hell do you mean, "get out of here"? You're planning to run?'

'Damn right I'm planning to run. We just killed four US Secret Service agents. Members of *your* team. You think this ends well for us once the NYPD and the FBI get here?'

'It was self-defence. They were here to kill you.'

'In a hit sanctioned by the head of your department and by the president of the United States himself. You think *we're* the ones the Feds will be listening to?'

'President Knowles . . .'

Grace stopped herself before she could finish her sentence. Dempsey noticed, just as he had seen her hesitate the first time Knowles was mentioned. But there was no time to press her.

Right now, he had to keep them alive.

'Agent Grace, we don't have time for this discussion. This place will be crawling with cops in no time. I can't allow myself to be taken. So I'm leaving. You can come with me or you can stay. It's your choice.'

Grace said nothing.

'You've got about two minutes.'

Dempsey walked away, past the post room and back

towards the lobby. He was headed to the building's staff area. The place he had sent Freddie Garcia a few minutes earlier.

He reached the back room and banged on the door.

'Freddie. It's Joe Dempsey. You can open up now.'

The noise from inside the room was instant. And telling. Freddie Garcia was not alone. The mixed voices of at least six members of staff seemed to be discussing whether the door should be opened.

From the outside it sounded as if it was becoming an argument. An argument he couldn't wait around for. He took a single step back and launched a powerful kick, aimed just below the door-handle.

Dempsey stepped inside as the door crashed open, its upper hinge ripped from the frame. The faces that met him were all terrified. The last reaction Dempsey had wanted to cause. But there was no time for delays.

'Everyone, you're all safe.' Dempsey held up his hands as he spoke, his palms facing outwards. 'It's over. It's done.'

'What . . . what was it? What happened?'

Dempsey turned to Garcia.

'I can't answer that, Freddie. And I need to get out of here.'

'But—'

'No "buts",' Dempsey interrupted. 'Is there a medical kit in this place?'

'I . . . I . . . erm, what?' Garcia was still shaken.

'A medical kit. Bandages. Stitches. That sort of thing.'

Garcia gave a nervous shrug. Dempsey looked around the room but no one else looked up. This was already taking too long, but he couldn't afford to ignore his shoulder wound.

He turned back to Garcia.

'I need pliers. Do you have some?'

'In the maintenance box. Behind you.'

'Get them.'

Dempsey ripped off his shirt as he spoke, pulling it out from under his holster as Garcia returned with the tool.

'Thanks.'

He took a G19 magazine from his waist, took out a single 9mm cartridge and replaced the clip. He then took the pliers from Garcia, gripped the flat end of the cartridge and slowly pulled the primer from the rest of the metal, careful to avoid a spark.

With the primer separated, he placed it down – still in the grip of the pliers – and slowly poured a thin covering of the cartridge's now exposed gunpowder onto the two wounds, sitting one above the other on the front and the top of his shoulder.

'What are you doing?' Garcia seemed confused.

'Let me have your lighter,' Dempsey said, making no effort to explain.

'But—'

'Just pass me your lighter, Freddie.'

Garcia did as was asked, handing Dempsey a cheap, neon plastic lighter. Dempsey placed it close to the first of his two shoulder wounds, took a deep breath and flicked a flame into life.

The smell of burning flesh was almost instant, as the layer of gunpowder was set alight. Dempsey gritted down on his teeth at the pain. He had to suppress his natural instinct to beat at the flame.

'JESUS!!'

Garcia jumped backwards at the sight, horrified. A reaction that was only amplified as Dempsey set alight his second wound in the same way.

'ARE YOU CRAZY?'

Dempsey did not answer. The pain was too much; it was all he could do to stop himself from crying out. Instead he used his ruined shirt to tamp out the first wound's flame, then the second.

Each had been alight for around two seconds.

Long enough to cauterise, Dempsey told himself.

He took a deep breath and only then did he notice the room of shocked faces around him.

'I had to stop the bleeding,' he explained.

Dempsey pointed to a leather jacket hanging on one of the staff coat hooks. He recognised it as belonging to Marlon, the only doorman larger than Dempsey himself. Which would make it the perfect fit.

'Freddie, pass me Marlon's jacket,' he said.

Dempsey had no doubt now that he would be obeyed. Self-cauterisation was a sure way to raise a person's stock in the eyes of other men. And so he was unsurprised when Garcia did as asked without question.

He pulled the jacket over his now bare torso, wincing at the pain of both movement and contact. Once on, he zipped up the front, placed his leather envelope into the inside pocket and turned to Garcia one last time.

'Take care of yourself, Freddie. And when you're asked, it wouldn't hurt if you told them I headed uptown.'

FIFTY-ONE

'**S**o are you coming with me?'

Grace turned to see Dempsey walking towards her. He had changed clothes. A leather jacket in place of his bloodied white shirt.

He had been gone just minutes, but it had been long enough. She had shaken off the shock of Braddock's death. There was no time to process that she had taken his life. Not now. There was only staying alive.

'Where are we going?' she asked.

'Away from here for a start,' Dempsey replied. 'That's all that matters for now.'

It was not in Grace's nature to act without a plan in place. But now was not time to argue that point.

'Whatever. I'm with you.'

'Good.' Dempsey glanced at her hand. 'Holster the weapon.'

Grace looked down and noticed the pistol in her hand. She had forgotten she was even holding it.

Perhaps my head hasn't *cleared that much*.

She concealed the Glock and followed as Dempsey led the way out of the service entrance and into the street outside.

They turned right, towards the corner of 74th and York.

'Where's your cell phone?' Dempsey asked.

'In my pocket.'

'Anyone you'll need to call when we're away from here? Family? Husband?'

'I don't have any family,' she replied. 'Just my, erm, my partner. We're engaged.'

'You know his number? In your head, I mean?'

'No. It's stored in the phone.'

They began to cross York.

'Then you should note the number down.'

'Why?'

'Because you'll need to contact him once we get going, but you need to lose that cell first. Before we leave.'

'Lose my cell?' Grace's momentary surprise was immediately overtaken by understanding. 'Shit, yeah.'

'Exactly. It's a damn homing beacon. Mine too.'

They reached the front of the bodega on the opposite side of the street. The door was closed.

'Give me your wallet.'

Grace did as Dempsey asked and watched as he rifled through its contents. He pulled out the cash, handed it to Grace and threw what was left in the trash.

'They could have a tracer in your Secret Service ID,' he explained. 'Plus the chips in your credit cards are as easily located as your cell.'

'I know,' Grace replied. 'I'm not new to this, Dempsey.'

'I'm just trying to keep us alive, Agent Grace.'

It was all the explanation Dempsey offered as he reached out, took Grace's cell and dismantled it piece by piece. Done, he crushed each separate cell component against the trash can, throwing them inside as he was done.

Grace could already hear sirens in the distance. She had no doubt where they were headed.

'Do you hear that?' she asked. 'We don't have much time.'

'I know,' Dempsey replied. 'Let's get inside.'

He tried the bodega door. It was locked. A single bolt on a rickety frame. It stood no chance as Dempsey struck the frame hard with his open palm.

The door swung open and Dempsey stepped inside, closing the door once Grace was through.

The place was empty, which was hardly a surprise. With the street outside turned into a war zone, it was likely that every shop, bar, restaurant and apartment building on the block had barricaded their doors.

'What now?' she asked.

'Ali!' Dempsey shouted. 'It's Joe Dempsey. I need you to come out.'

For a moment there was no response. But then Grace could hear movement coming from the back of the shop. A few seconds later she saw a thick-set, dark-skinned Asian man move carefully into a far aisle.

'Mr Joseph?' He seemed surprisingly calm. 'You're OK?'

'You saw?'

'How could I not? But you're OK?'

'I've been better. And I'm in trouble, Ali.' He indicated to Grace. 'We both are.'

Ali nodded.

'Who were they?'

'They were government agents.'

'But you work for the government, Mr Joseph.'

'Not every government can be trusted. Turns out this government is one of them.'

Ali nodded again. His only reaction.

'We need to run, Ali. Can you help us?'

'Me? Why would you—'

'Cards on the table, Ali,' Dempsey interrupted. 'You know

what I am. And I can tell what you *were*. So I'm asking you, one soldier to another: will you help us?'

Ali said nothing. Just fixed his eyes on Dempsey. Dempsey returned the stare, neither man blinking.

In the silence, the sound of sirens was piercing. They were close.

'OK.' Ali broke the silence. His tone seemed more determined. More confident. 'I will help you. What do you need?'

Grace felt a flood of relief. It was interrupted almost immediately by a flashing red light in her peripheral vision. She turned and through the glass of the bodega she could see the arrival of the first two NYPD squad cars.

For Dempsey, it did not seem to be a distraction. He didn't turn.

'I need your cell phone and your car.'

'OK. Follow me.'

Ali turned without another word. Dempsey and Grace went after him, through the far aisle and into the back rooms of the bodega. Ali passed Dempsey his cell phone as they walked. A basic model. At least a decade out of date.

And probably perfect for what Dempsey has in mind, Grace thought.

They moved through four back rooms, one after the other, all packed with boxes of stock. Finally they reached a back door, which opened onto a mid-block alleyway designed for deliveries. Parked in the alley, close to the door, was a thirty-year-old black Audi 100 Sedan. It looked every day of its age, and in dire need of a wash.

'That's your car?' Dempsey asked.

'It is.' Ali held up the keys. 'You take it and you run.'

'I'll bring it all back, Ali. I promise you that.'

'Just be safe. Please, my friend.'

'We will. Thank you.'

Dempsey took the keys and climbed into the driver's seat, while Grace moved into the passenger's side. Without another word to Ali, Dempsey started the car and began to drive away.

As they reached the end of the alleyway, Dempsey indicated right, onto 74th and away from The Stratford. As he took the turn, he passed Ali's phone to Grace.

'I need you to dial a number for me.'

'Is it safe?'

'This one is,' Dempsey replied. 'The only one that no one would think to tap.'

FIFTY-TWO

Elizabeth Kirk did not notice her increased heart rate. Or the fact that she had neither breathed nor blinked for at least a minute. The images on her office television screen had her absolute attention.

She knew the location. The Stratford building. 1385 York Avenue. And she knew what that meant.

Joe Dempsey.

After a lifetime in covert and military intelligence, Kirk could spot a dead body when she saw one. Even when that body was covered and being filmed from a distance. And especially when there was more than one.

Whoever was behind the camera was doing their best; Kirk could see that. They were trying to capture a meaningful shot from behind a strict police cordon which, from what Kirk could see, covered at least the full width of York Avenue. From a street away, the footage could give only a hint of the carnage that had occurred.

To Kirk's experienced eye, that hint was more than enough. But for the voyeurs who would be watching for kicks? Probably not. And so for them, there was the Fox News commentary to provide context.

It was a man's voice, speaking over the live, ongoing footage that was playing out on screen.

'It's still unclear exactly what happened here, but in scenes unheard of in the surroundings of Manhattan's wealthy Upper East Side, reports suggest that a short gun battle took place in and around this prestigious residential apartment building. And that the terrible scenes being played out now are the result.

'At this time there is no information about the identity of the victims. Nor is there anything we can tell you about the gunman or gunmen who took their lives. We are awaiting an update from the New York Police Department but for now the incident seems to be over.'

Kirk silenced the volume but kept the screen on. She slowly rose from her seat and moved closer to the images. For a clearer view of the area outside of the building, and of the covered humps dotted around it.

Three, she counted. *Three bodies.*

Please don't be one of them.

It had been Kirk's first thought as the news report broke. Dempsey's own words, returning to her the moment she recognised The Stratford.

'They're cleaning house', Dempsey had said to her. And he had been right. Starting, as it turned out, with him.

He would have expected it, Kirk knew. But had that been enough? Had he managed to escape? To fight his way through? Or was he still at The Stratford, growing cold under one of those white sheets she could see on the screen?

There was no way for her to know. The three bodies could be anyone. And Dempsey was definitely capable of taking on three killers and walking away. That much Kirk *was* sure of.

But if he did, she thought, *then where the hell is he?*

The uncertainty clouded Kirk's thinking. Her concern was for Dempsey. She liked the man. She even considered him a friend. But Kirk was not employed for her humanity. She was the director of the ISB because she was the best at what she did. Because she was the consummate professional.

And she forced that professionalism to take over as she stared at the screen. It caused her focus to shift, allowing her to see what the attack on Dempsey *really* meant.

It was confirmation that they were right. Quilty's death might have been enough, but now – after this – there could be no doubt. What other reason could there be to try to murder one of her agents? To murder *this* agent?

The realisation hit hard, and Kirk responded in the only way she knew. She steeled herself and she prepared to fight back.

Dempsey was either alive or he was dead. She had no control over that now. If he was alive then all the better; he was her best agent and an invaluable asset in what might follow.

And if he was dead? Well, then Kirk would mourn him when the time was right.

But right now it was time to act. To fight fire with fire.

If it was a war Knowles wanted, then it was a war Knowles would get. But it would not be fought on the battlefield of his choosing.

It would be fought in Knowles' past. In Afghanistan.

If we're going to beat them, we're going to beat them there.

Kirk walked back to her desk as she thought through her next steps. Her mind was racing as she analysed scenarios and formed strategies. There were many ways forward. It was her job to pick the correct one.

Kirk picked up her desk phone and hit 'nine'. Her assistant – Henry – answered immediately.

'Ma'am.'

'Henry, find Shui Dai and then get me the rest of Joe Dempsey's Alpha Team. I want them in my office now.'

'Ma'am.'

'And Henry?'

'Ma'am?'

'I want you to arrange for a UN plane out of LaGuardia within two hours. Direct it to Montreal. Then I need an Airbus A330 waiting at Montreal, non-stop into Kabul.'

'Ma'am.'

'This is need to know, Henry. Understood?'

'Perfectly, ma'am.'

'Good. Make it all happen.'

'One thing before I do, ma'am.'

'What is it?'

'I have Father Sam Cooke here to see you.'

It took Kirk just an instant to place the name.

'The Catholic Chaplin? What the hell for?'

'He won't say, ma'am. But he says it's extremely important. That he's under the direct order of Agent Dempsey.'

Hope immediately stirred in Kirk's chest.

'Send him in.'

FIFTY-THREE

Kelvin Cunningham's grip tightened on his cell phone. Its hard, metal sides dug into his fingers, hurting him far more than it was damaging the handset.

It was better than feeling nothing.

It was also better than what he was hearing.

'And where is he now, exactly?'

The question was hissed. Cunningham was doing his best to keep his voice level. Not because of his surroundings; he had raised his voice in the Oval Office many times in the past.

No. It was embarrassment.

He glanced over at Special Agent Hodge, the only other man in the room. Hodge was Cunningham's personal protection officer. A man to whom he had no need to defer; the power balance was entirely in Cunningham's favour. But still, he was ashamed to show weakness. To show anything but complete control.

'He's in the prison infirmary.'

Romeo Meyer's voice was matter of fact. Even now, when reporting abject failure, he sounded arrogant. It irked Cunningham.

'So what are you saying?' he asked, his voice still low, turning his back to Hodge. 'Our friends can't get to him in a hospital bed?'

'Not when he's under police guard,' Romeo replied. 'Which he is now. They've stationed a cop right next to him. We can't just go through a British cop to get to Mansour. Not without blowing the whole thing up.'

Cunningham did not like the answer. Not because it was correct – which it was, to a degree – but because of who delivered it. The deputy assistant did not want Romeo Meyer to be right about *anything*. As far as he was concerned, Jack Meyer's idiot son was responsible for this entire mess.

He pushed aside his distaste and moved on.

'And why is he not dead already? How the *hell* did our friends fail to kill a baggage handler?'

'Turns out the baggage handler can fight,' Romeo replied, his tone as nonchalant as ever. 'He took out a couple of the people sent in to do the job.'

'A couple? You relied on just two men for something this important?'

'No, sir. I relied on four. And it almost worked.'

'ALMOST?' Cunningham's temper finally erupted, set off by Romeo's casual delivery. 'ALMOST? AND YOU SAY THAT LIKE IT'S FINE? LIKE YOU WANT CREDIT FOR FUCKING ALMOST?'

'Well, I—'

'SHUT YOUR FUCKING MOUTH, BOY! SHUT IT BEFORE I HAVE SOMEONE SEW IT SHUT.'

Cunningham did not even glance towards Hodge. Whatever emotional restraint the agent's presence had provided was long gone.

'I WANT THIS DEALT WITH AND I WANT IT DEALT WITH TONIGHT. FUCK THE COP WHO'S WITH HIM. HE CAN DIE TOO! I'LL DEAL WITH THE FALLOUT.'

'Sir, that is absolutely impossible. The cop isn't the only problem.'

Cunningham was taken aback by the answer. It was as if his verbal explosion had not affected Romeo Meyer at all. The momentary surprise allowed Cunningham to regain control. Though inwardly it only stoked the fire of his hatred.

When he spoke again he was no longer shouting, but his voice seethed with rage.

'Another problem? And what is that, exactly?'

'Our friends in Europe can't help us any further. At least not straightaway. Not after what happened to the prisoner who went after Mansour.'

'What do you mean "can't help us further"? Just when the hell did this become a partnership? We say jump, they jump. It's not a fucking discussion.'

'But they don't have anyone left with access to the Secure Unit at Belmarsh. They had to contract this one out. To an old associate. He won't help again. Not after his man was killed.'

'Are you seriously telling me there's no one else to do this?'

'That's right, sir. No one else is willing to cross the Muslims.'

'And what the hell does *that* mean?'

'It was a Muslim gang in the unit that saved Mansour. By the sound of it they beat one of the guys to death. They're not screwing around.'

'Shit.'

Cunningham took a few moments to consider what he had been told. He was beginning to calm, which was in turn allowing him to think more clearly. A few seconds more and he could see a way forward.

'OK. OK. He's due in court tomorrow, correct?'

'Yeah. But I can't see him making it. Not in his state.'

'Exactly what I was going to ask. And exactly what I wanted to hear.'

'Why, sir?'

'Because if we can't get to him in Belmarsh, and clearly we can't get to him in the court itself, then we have to get him on his journey *to* court.'

'OK, no problem, my team can do that.'

'Really? Because from the report I saw today, he was due to go to Woolwich Crown Court.'

'So what?'

'You haven't done your research at all, have you?'

'I . . .' Romeo trailed off, which confirmed Cunningham's suspicions.

'See, this is why you screw things up. Piss poor preparation. If you'd done your homework, you'd know that Woolwich is next door to Belmarsh, and that there's a tunnel that connects them. Which means no opportunity to get near Mansour as he travels between prison and court.'

'So how does that help us?' Romeo Meyer sounded genuinely confused.

'Clearly it doesn't. But if proceedings are being delayed because of the attack, that gives us time to get them to change the court. Do you follow that?'

'I . . .'

Romeo paused. Cunningham presumed the over-privileged lug had finally caught up.

'But how will you change the court? Away from Woolwich?'

'You don't think the president of the United States can get the Brits to move a man from one court to another?'

'Well . . .'

Cunningham stopped listening as the concealed door next to Hodge began to open. The door leading from the White House Office.

The lack of either a knock or an announcement told

Cunningham that President John Knowles was about to enter the Oval Office.

'I'll call you back once the arrangements are made.'

Cunningham disconnected the call as two Secret Service agents stepped into the room and stood aside, flanking the doorway. They were followed by Knowles and then Nicolas Dupart. The two men were in mid-conversation. Both looked as fresh as they had at the morning meeting.

It was the exact opposite of how Cunningham *felt*, but at least he could now see a way forward now. Knowles would have to be told about how things had played out, he realised. But not yet. Not until Cunningham had resolved the situation.

And certainly not with Dupart in the room.

Cunningham had no intention of telling *him* any of this.

'You're making yourself at home, Kelvin.' Knowles' tone was serious. As close to a reprimand as Cunningham ever received.

The deputy assistant chose to ignore it. He had too much on his mind to be concerned with a presidential tantrum.

'Nick.' Cunningham acted as if Knowles had not spoken. He focused his attention on Dupart. 'You're still here? I thought you had other business to attend to.'

'It can wait,' Dupart replied. He said no more.

Knowles looked quizzically at the two men. Clearly he was curious about whatever conversation he had missed, but Cunningham had no intention of bringing the president up to speed. He turned to the six Secret Service agents who had entered the Oval Office with Knowles.

'All out,' he ordered.

General Secret Service protocol does not allow for the president to be alone and without a protective detail. But there are exceptions, one of which was the Oval Office, on the proviso that there is an agent immediately beyond each of the room's four doors.

Cunningham turned towards Knowles as the detail vacated the room. He opened his mouth to begin, but he did not get the chance as he saw Knowles' eyes sweep past him.

Cunningham turned to see Jack Meyer had entered the room. His face was pale, he seemed out of breath and there was sweat on his brow. None of this was normal.

Meyer stepped forward towards Knowles and Cunningham, his stride long and brisk. He looked with concern at Nicolas Dupart.

An unfamiliar face, Cunningham realised.

'Mr President. Mr Cunningham. There's a security issue. One I can only discuss in the earshot of those with clearance.'

He indicated towards Dupart with a nod of his head.

Knowles nodded in understanding and turned to face Dupart.

'Nick, I think you need to leave us.'

'Mr President—' Dupart rose to his feet, 'I'll be available to continue this at your convenience.'

'Thank you, Nick.'

Dupart headed back out the door through which he had entered. Cunningham watched in silence as it was closed behind him. Once satisfied that they were alone, he turned to Meyer and braced himself for what could not be good news.

'What is it, Jack?' Knowles spoke first.

'It's the team we sent to New York, Mr President. To deal with the Joe Dempsey problem.'

'From the look of you, I'm assuming it didn't go as planned?'

'No, Mr President. It did *not* go as planned. My team is dead, sir. Every man I sent. Dead.'

'What! How?' Cunningham could feel a pain growing in the back of his head as he asked the question. As if physical pressure was mounting within it. Why was nothing going as planned?

'I have no idea, sir.' Meyer was visibly upset. 'The men on that team were the best we had at this and he massacred them. In literally seconds, according to witnesses. Who can do that, sir? Who the hell *is* this guy?'

'We did warn you not to underestimate him, Jack,' Knowles said coldly. 'Joe Dempsey is not just another agent.'

'Yeah? Well you didn't tell us we were dealing with fucking Superman, did you?'

'Let's not turn this into a conversation anyone will regret,' Cunningham interrupted, stepping closer to Meyer. He could see that the assistant director was near breaking point; the inappropriate language he had directed at the president proved that. Another outburst would not be helpful now. 'We can work out what went wrong later. First, we need to find the sonofabitch.'

He looked from Meyer to Knowles, then back again. Meyer still seemed close to the edge. The president, in contrast, was calm.

'What about Agent Grace?' Knowles asked.

'What about her?'

'Is she among the dead?'

'Christ knows.' Meyer's shoulders slumped as he continued, his tone dejected. 'We haven't found her.'

'You think she's dead?'

'No reason to think anything else. If he could take my guys, he could sure as hell take her.'

'But no body?'

'No. There was no sign of her at the scene. Most likely she's dead somewhere else in that building. It's a big place. I have a team scouring it as we speak.'

Knowles nodded. For a moment he was silent.

'Keep me updated on that,' he finally said, a small catch in his voice.

Cunningham noted it. Knowles was trying to hide it but the loss of Eden Grace had hit him. Before the assignment Cunningham hadn't been aware that the president knew the young Secret Service agent by name, let alone that he regarded her as 'one of his'. And so it had been a surprise when he'd insisted she join Meyer's team. Cunningham had been too focused to read too much into it. But now? With Knowles taking her death personally?

He made a mental note to find out what the link was between the two of them. But first he had to resolve this latest disaster.

'Forget Eden Grace,' he said. 'She'll turn up, one way or another. The priority is finding Dempsey. We need to put an end to this.'

Meyer and Knowles both turned to face him.

'How?' Meyer asked. 'If Dempsey's gone to ground – a man that good – how are we supposed to find him again?'

'We bring in his boss. She must know his habits. Some idea of where he's gone.'

'Elizabeth Kirk?' Knowles looked doubtful. 'Won't she want to know why we're interested in her agent?'

'I imagine she already does,' Cunningham replied. 'How do you think Dempsey came across Quilty in the first place?'

'But Elizabeth never believed any of that,' Knowles argued.

'Well, clearly that's changed,' Cunningham snapped. 'It can't be a coincidence. And even if she didn't put him up to all this, there's every chance he's reported back to her with whatever he's found out. I told you three years ago to keep her close, back when she wouldn't believe a bad word said about you. You threw away her loyalty.'

'I know what I did.' Knowles spoke slowly, irritation in his voice. 'And I'll own my own mistake. But what's done is done, Kelvin. And now she's a director of a UN agency. We can't make her disappear as easily as the others.'

'I don't see that we have much choice any more. We can't let this get any worse than it already is. Dempsey is going to need help. We have to make sure he doesn't receive it.'

Cunningham had no intention of explaining himself any further. He turned from Knowles to Meyer.

'Get yourself to New York, Jack. To the Manhattan office. Once you're there, get Elizabeth Kirk in and find out what she knows. It's time for that bitch to talk.'

FIFTY-FOUR

The Wyldecrest Inn looked like every airport motel in every movie Dempsey had ever seen. The two-storey complex stretched for perhaps one hundred yards from one end to the other, with fifteen basic rooms per floor. Each room faced outwards, with a door and a window that overlooked the motel parking lot, and beyond that the Borough of Queens.

Dempsey had waited in Ali's car while Grace had booked the room. A single night, paid in cash from the leather envelope Dempsey had taken from home.

To anyone paying attention, they were just two ordinary people taking a cheap room for a few hours with no questions asked. No ID required. Luggage free. The mainstay of the motel business model.

For Dempsey and Grace, it offered exactly what they required. Privacy. A place to hide while they awaited Elizabeth Kirk's call, away from prying eyes and possible identification.

Neither expected to be here for long.

Grace had been silent since they had stepped into the room almost twenty minutes earlier. Dempsey had made no effort to change that. After what they had just been through, he understood her need to regain her calm and to consider her next steps. Because now they were out of immediate danger, those steps would not necessarily mirror his own.

And so Dempsey had occupied himself in other ways, leaving Grace to her thoughts. To be ready to move as soon as the necessary arrangements were in place, there was work to be done.

The black leather jacket he had taken from The Stratford was dumped untidily on the room's only bed. Without it, Dempsey's torso was exposed, along with the burns that had sealed the two bullet wounds in his left shoulder.

The dank, mouldy motel bathroom had hardly been ideal sterile conditions for what had followed, but Dempsey had had no choice. They had stopped at a local pharmacy en route to Queens, where Grace had purchased toiletries, basic medical supplies, water, food and a few items of cheap clothing. Dempsey, the most likely of the pair to feature as 'wanted' on any televised news bulletin, had again remained in the car.

Once in the privacy of their room, and with Grace's attention elsewhere, Dempsey had used the medical supplies to do what he could to clean his wounds and to calm the burns that had cauterised them. It was almost certainly not enough, he realised. But it would have to do. With that decision made, he went on to then bandage his shoulder.

The injury was beginning to be a problem. The range of movement in Dempsey's left arm was severely impaired. He could lift it to a few inches below shoulder height through sheer force of will. But that movement was slow, his arm refused to go any further, and the pain involved in achieving even that made it next to useless.

To carry that injury with what was going to follow was far from ideal. But it was the reality Dempsey had to face, and it forced him to make a decision he did not like. He needed to fashion a sling.

First he pulled on the heavy, loose-fitting jeans and one of the cheap white T-shirts Grace had picked out. Then, using the remaining bandages from the medical kit, he made a field-style sling that freed his damaged left shoulder from the weight of its arm.

The whole exercise – cleaning and dressing his wounds, changing his clothes and finally bandaging his arm – took almost twenty minutes. Done, Dempsey was moving back from the bathroom and into the bedroom when Grace finally spoke.

'Can you believe anyone actually sleeps in this place?'

Her words were unexpected. They caused Dempsey to look around, to re-evaluate their surroundings.

'It's not The Ritz, is it?' he replied, noticing the visible stains on the bedclothes. 'You wouldn't want to use a blacklight in here.'

Grace nodded. She seemed to be only half listening, as if the answer didn't interest her. Dempsey understood why. She had been unable to think of what else to say, and so had filled the silence with an inane observation.

'How are you feeling?' Dempsey asked. 'Now you've had time for things to sink in?'

'What do you mean?'

'I mean you killed your friend, Agent Grace. That's going to be hard on anyone.'

'Braddock was no friend of mine,' Grace replied. 'That asshole deserved to die. They all did.'

The response was unexpected. Dempsey had assumed that it was the man's death – by her hand – that had thrown Grace.

'Then what's troubling you?' he asked.

'What's troubling me?' Grace sounded incredulous. 'What's *troubling* me? How about that we're on the run from the Secret Service. From *my* Service. And how about that I can't even contact anyone and hand myself in to smooth this whole thing out. After today, I don't know who I can trust.'

'You know who you *can't* trust,' Dempsey's answer was blunt. 'That's a start.'

'What kind of help is that?' Grace seemed irritated. 'What use is knowing for sure who's against us? When we can't be sure who isn't?'

'It's enough that we know how high the rot goes,' Dempsey replied. 'You can't trust Knowles and you can't trust Meyer. Which means you can't risk trusting anyone who works for either of them.'

'But what if you're wrong?' Grace sounded uncertain. 'What if this whole thing isn't what you think?'

'What do you mean?'

'What if the mission to kill you . . .' Grace hesitated. 'What if it wasn't exactly . . .'

Her voice trailed off. Dempsey looked at her, confused. The Secret Service had tried to kill him at the instruction of the president. She had told him that herself. He couldn't see what the confusion was.

'Agent Grace, if you know anything else you're not saying, I need to know—'

He was interrupted by the shrill pitch of Ali's antiquated phone.

Dempsey reached out for the handset and looked at the Caller ID. He recognised it instantly.

Father Sam Cooke.

He glanced at Grace. Moments before he would have taken the call in front of her. But now? She was hiding something and Dempsey had no way of knowing what that was. That alone did not make him doubt his instincts about her; she had saved his life and there was no way she would have turned on her own team – no way she would have played a part in their deaths – if she was loyal to whatever the hell was going on with Knowles and Meyer. But clearly there was something he didn't know about.

And as long as she was keeping secrets, Dempsey would do the same.

He climbed to his feet, holding the phone.

'I need to take this outside.'

FIFTY-FIVE

With Dempsey gone, Grace thought through her options. Options which, when analysed, were reduced to one.

Of the few people on the planet who had her absolute trust, none were here. And none were accessible without putting both her life and theirs in jeopardy.

Which just left Joe Dempsey. A man already in as much danger as Grace herself, and who had proved himself more than capable of dealing with it. Whatever this thing was, it had thrown them together. If she was going to get through it – if she was ever going to return to her life – Dempsey was her best chance.

What was the saying? My enemy's enemy is my friend.

We might not agree on exactly who our enemies are, Grace rationalised, *but we sure as hell have the same people trying to kill us.*

It made her decision a simple one. Grace would stay with Dempsey. She would go where he went, and she would help him to do what needed to be done. But she would not be anyone's subordinate. She was an equal and she would be treated as such.

And so before she would agree to anything, she wanted to be briefed.

She was on her feet as Dempsey re-entered the room and closed the door behind him.

'Was that Elizabeth Kirk?'

Grace had overheard Dempsey's earlier call to his friend,

Father Sam Cooke. It had been too risky to contact Kirk, whose phone records were no doubt already being scrutinised by the Secret Service. Father Cooke was based in the United Nations Secretariat Building, Dempsey had explained to her. He had access to Kirk, but would not appear anywhere on the White House's radar.

The message had been a simple one. Cooke was to speak to no one but Kirk, and when he did so he was to hand her his own cell phone and tell her to call Dempsey on Ali's number.

'It was,' Dempsey replied. 'She'd already seen the TV.'

'She knew you were alive?'

'Hoped, I think.'

'And me?'

'Seems there's been no mention of you yet, Agent Grace. Not officially.'

'That'll change soon.'

'It will.'

'And when it does? Where will we be?'

Dempsey hesitated. As if unsure whether he was going to share his plans with her. He moved in silence to the motel room's only armchair. A battered fabric lounger, the kind no one had dared to make since the 1970s. He lowered himself into the seat, wincing from the pain in his shoulder as he settled.

Grace took a seat of her own. The end of the unused, poorly made bed.

'I'm going to Afghanistan,' Dempsey finally said. 'That's where this all started.'

'How does this go back to Afghanistan?'

'OK. Look, you know the president's history. Probably better than I do. So you know he won his Medal of Honor.'

'I do.' Grace knew the story far better than Dempsey could

suspect. But she wasn't ready to show her hand just yet. 'What about it?'

'There's credible intelligence that the mission they were on was not as it's been reported. That it was a cover. And that the team committed war crimes, including murder and rape. Led by Knowles.'

'Bullshit.' Grace's voice was firm. She could not hide her anger. 'That's not true!'

Dempsey did not answer. Instead he studied Grace, who realised instantly that her reaction had been too forceful. When she spoke again she had driven the belligerence from her voice.

'What I mean is, we would have heard about that. There's no way it could have stayed secret.'

'It didn't stay secret, did it? *I* heard about it.' Dempsey's voice remained calm. 'That's why we're in this situation. The allegation was raised by a CIA analyst named Tom Quilty. He was killed this morning, along with what was almost certainly a Secret Service assassin.'

'What?' Grace's expression was a mix of shock and disbelief. 'How . . .'

'Think about it. Within days of Victor Dale talking about Knowles on British TV, hinting that he knew something about Knowles' war record, he's killed on Flight PA16. And within twenty-four hours of that explosion, Quilty – the source of the story – is dead. And now they're after me because I went to see him yesterday.'

Grace could not quite believe what she was hearing.

'Are you . . . are you suggesting that the president of the United States had that plane brought down? To kill *one* man?'

'Can you think of a better explanation?'

Grace did not reply. How could she? She had no better explanation. She searched for a flaw in Dempsey's logic. There was none. He was right, the series of events could not be coincidence. And yet this last allegation – the death of over five hundred civilians, to silence one man – was too much.

She would not accept it. She *could* not. Not of John Knowles.

But that certainty didn't help her. Because if Dempsey was wrong about Knowles – and she was sure he was – then just what the hell *was* going on?

Grace had no idea. Not yet. And she saw only one way to change that fact.

She would stick with Dempsey, and they would discover the truth together.

'So what *is* the plan?'

'I go to Tootkai, Agent Grace. I find Quilty's source and I prove what Knowles did there. I get whatever evidence there is. And once I have it, I bring this whole thing crashing down.'

Grace nodded her head. It was a good plan. Exactly what she would do, if she'd had the same aim as Dempsey. But it worked equally well for her own purposes, assuming that *she* was right about the president.

'I'm coming with you.'

'Are you sure Agent Grace? It will be dangerous. But I could use your help.'

'Then you've got it,' she replied. 'Not like I can leave a one-armed man to fend for himself, is it?'

She took a deep breath and held out her hand.

'But if we're doing this together, you've got to stop calling me Agent Grace. My friends call me Eden.'

Dempsey smiled and took Grace's hand in his only good one.

'Nice to meet you, Eden. People just call me Dempsey.'

Ten minutes later both Dempsey and Grace were set to leave.

The plan was to drive Ali's car the short distance to the private entrance at LaGuardia that was reserved for diplomats, politicians, United Nations personnel and other VIPs. Kirk had assured Dempsey that there would be no security stop and no search at the perimeter, and had arranged a private jet to fly them to Montreal. Once in Canada, they would change planes for the long flight to Kabul.

Dempsey had spent the time checking, reloading and re-securing his pistols, safe in the knowledge that he could take them on board the two private flights. Grace had done the same. She still had her SIG Sauer P229, plus the Glock 26 Dempsey had given her back at The Stratford. Now he gave her the other two spare magazines, and one of the two pilot's knives he had strapped to his forearms before he had left his apartment.

They would have access to guns and ammunition at the other end, Dempsey knew. But he felt safer knowing that they were both well-armed from the start. Caution and care. Two reasons he had lived this long.

Satisfied with the weaponry, he finally turned to his last resource. The leather envelope. It was his emergency preparedness kit, containing tens of thousands in cash in four major currencies; officially authorised passports from five different countries, none of which contained any mention of a 'Joe Dempsey'; driving licences corresponding to each passport; four sets of safety deposit keys, each with a home in one of four major world cities; and a single bank card that provided access to a single account, unconnected and unconnectable to either his real identity or to any of the five for which he carried a passport.

It was everything he could need to disappear. Plus one other item.

He pushed the passports aside as he looked for it. Using his fingertips, he felt to the bottom of the envelope. For an anxious moment he could not find it, until he felt the reassuring cold of a small gold medal. He moved it to the palm of his hand and removed it from the envelope.

St Christopher. Patron saint of travellers.

It was Dempsey's most cherished possession. Capable of reassuring him – of calming him – whenever he touched it. This moment was no different.

'Are you OK?'

He dropped the medal back into the envelope and turned to face Grace.

'Yes. Yeah. I'm fine.'

Grace looked at him with suspicion, but Dempsey was telling the truth. Satisfied that he had everything he could need – practically and emotionally – he was now thinking as clearly as he ever had.

'So are we ready to go?' Grace asked.

'Once I've dealt with Ali's phone,' Dempsey replied. 'They'll catch on to it eventually, so best we lose it now.'

He took the handset from his pocket and was about to take it apart. He stopped just as he began to remove the thick battery.

'Your fiancé.' The thought struck Dempsey out of nowhere. 'Don't you want to call him? To warn him?'

Grace looked taken aback by the change of subject.

'Warn him of what?'

'Eden, if they don't know you're with me already, they will soon. And once they know that, they'll go after anyone close to you. For leverage. So your fiancé, he needs to run. He needs to hide. Before they come for him.'

Grace hesitated for a moment.

'I don't need to call him.'

'You have to. You can't just leave him a target.'

'He won't *be* a target. It's fine. I keep my private life private. No one knows he exists, not in the Service or in the White House.'

Dempsey couldn't understand her reaction.

'How can you be so sure?' he asked. 'That there isn't anyone who knows about your relationship?'

'There's not, OK. Can we just leave it at that?'

'This is his life, Eden. It's a hell of a risk to take. Think about it. Is there anyone you could have mentioned him to? Anyone who might have seen you wearing an engagement ring? Even in a picture?'

'I've never worn an engagement ring,' she snapped. 'I'm not the one who *has* the damned thing.'

'What? What does that—'

'Jesus, you won't quit. Look, the reason I'm so sure that no one knows about the man I'm engaged to is that she's *not* a man. I'm gay, Dempsey. And since no one at work has any idea of that, there's no way any of them can connect me to Natasha.'

The revelation was unexpected, leaving Dempsey unsure of what to say. An uncertainty which caused an awkward silence to fall between them.

'Look, I know you didn't mean to force that.' Grace relented after a few moments. 'I just don't like discussing my personal life with anyone who isn't in it. But take it from me, as far as anyone who could come after us is concerned, Natasha doesn't exist. And I want to keep it that way, OK?'

'OK.' Dempsey nodded his head in understanding. If there was one desire he could appreciate, it was for privacy. 'And I'm sorry. I shouldn't have pushed.'

'It was just attention to detail,' Grace replied. 'And if that keeps us alive, you won't hear me complain.'

She smiled. A peace offering, Dempsey realised.

'Now don't we have a plane to catch?'

FIFTY-SIX

Elizabeth Kirk moved the phone from her ear as the line went dead.

The conversation had been brief and precise. In less than five minutes she had agreed the steps that could bring down a presidency.

If Dempsey's plan worked, he could have the evidence of Knowles' war crimes in little more than a day. Evidence that would bring down Knowles' administration more surely than any other scandal in the history of the White House.

The thought turned Kirk's stomach. A mixture of nerves at what was to come, and the knowledge that this could damage her country's reputation. But what was the alternative? To keep a corrupt killer in the Oval Office? Kirk had returned to that question repeatedly in the last few minutes. The answer was clear.

The long-term damage of *not* taking Knowles down was worse. Far worse.

Dempsey's plan was the best way to save America from the evil that had hijacked its highest office. Kirk was sure of that. And as a patriot, she had no choice but to play her part.

Kirk stood up and moved towards the chairs by the TV screen, her arm outstretched and Sam Cooke's phone in her hand.

'Thank you, Father.'

Cooke rose to his feet as Kirk approached.

'I appreciate your help with this. And your friendship to Agent Dempsey.'

Cooke took the offered handset from Kirk's hand.

'No need to thank me, Director,' Cooke replied. 'They came after Joe. As far as I'm concerned, whatever happens now they've brought on themselves. I just want to see my side safe.'

'That's good to know.' Kirk enjoyed the thought. 'And much appreciated. Can't hurt to have God in our corner on this.'

'Now I didn't promise that,' Cooke replied, his eyes betraying a smile. 'But I wouldn't worry about that. He's never been that hands on with the help, has he?'

'No, I guess he hasn't.' Kirk laughed, grateful for a moment of levity. 'But again, thank you for this.'

'You're welcome. Now I'll leave you to it. Sounds to me like you have some arrangements you need to make.'

'I do.' Kirk nodded her head. 'Bye, Father.'

Cooke responded with a wave of his hand, before turning and leaving the office. Kirk watched him go. She had appreciated the brief distraction, but the priest was right. She had work to do.

She returned to her desk and glanced at her wall clock.

5.24 p.m.

Dempsey and Eden Grace would be boarding the plane at LaGuardia in forty minutes. That would have them in Montreal by 7 p.m. EST. Assuming a one-hour change over to the Airbus and then fourteen hours to Kabul, they would land in Afghanistan around 10 a.m. tomorrow morning.

Which would make it 7.30 p.m. over there, Kirk calculated. *A night operation.*

Happy with the timings, she mentally ran through the phone conversation. Kirk remembered it exactly. Every detail. A talent necessary in a world where even a notebook scribble could undermine an entire nation's security.

The sound of her office telephone interrupted her thoughts. Kirk answered it on the second ring.

'Henry.'

'Ma'am. I have Assistant Director Jack Meyer of the United States Secret Service on the line.'

'Meyer?'

'Ma'am. He says it's essential he speaks to you now.'

Kirk hesitated. She had expected this. Maybe not so soon, but it had been coming.

'Put him through,' she instructed, a feeling of dread growing in her gut.

'Ma'am.'

There was a single second of delay, as the lines switched.

'Elizabeth.' It was Meyer's voice. Rough and deep. The stereotype of a tough guy.

'Jack.' Kirk noticed a slight break in her voice. A sign of weakness she could not allow. She corrected it with a cough. 'It's been a long time.'

'We both know this isn't a social call, Elizabeth.'

'Do we?' Kirk lied. A lifetime of professional dishonesty had prepared her for this moment. 'I have no idea what you're talking about.'

'I need to see you.' Meyer ignored Kirk's response. 'To put an end to this before it blows up and more people get hurt.'

'More people?' Kirk feigned confusion. 'What people?'

'Don't play games with me, Elizabeth. Believe me, this could just be the beginning. Whatever your boy managed to pull this afternoon, he won't get that chance again. He's going down. Don't be dragged down with him.'

'I genuinely have no idea what you mean.'

'THIS ISN'T A FUCKING GAME, ELIZABETH!'

Kirk pulled the phone away from her ear as Meyer's voice screamed out of the handset. The shout was a surprise. She had never liked Jack Meyer, but in all the years she had known him she had at least admired his professionalism.

It's not like him to lose it, she told herself. *Which means this is going badly.*

Dempsey is moving too fast for them. It's left them playing catch up.

Kirk had to make the most of their advantage. She had to buy Dempsey as much time as she could. Which meant dragging out the pretence. She injected some emotion into her voice as she spoke again.

'Look, Jack, whatever this is—'

'I'm on my way to New York now,' Meyer interrupted. 'Wheels down in an hour, I'll be in the Brooklyn Field Office by seven p.m. Meet me there then. Don't be late.'

The line went dead, but Kirk kept the phone in hand – still against her ear – and pressed 'nine'.

She had arrangements to make, and time had just become of the essence.

'Ma'am?'

'Henry. The flight arrangements to Montreal and Kabul. I want you to book another set.'

'When, ma'am?'

'Tonight. As soon as possible.'

'It will take a few hours, ma'am. We were lucky to get the last set up.'

'Do whatever it takes. But make sure that it's tonight.'

'Ma'am.'

'Now, where are we with locating Dempsey's team?'

FIFTY-SEVEN

Will Duffy awoke with a start.

The sound of his mobile's ringtone was muffled, while the buzzing of the handset's vibrating alert seemed weakened. Neither was enough to wake most people, but then Duffy had always been a light sleeper.

He climbed to his feet, his mind fully awake and entirely clear. He had fallen asleep on the reclining leather chair, in front of a television that was perpetually set to whichever channel was showing the latest boxing news.

He turned in a complete circle as he looked for the source of the ringtone, only to realise that the handset had slipped into the side folds of his chair. It explained the low volume and the suppression of the vibration, both of which increased as he retrieved it.

Duffy looked at the phone's screen. It told him two things. Bruce Bull was calling. And he was doing so after midnight.

Duffy connected the call, retook his seat and downed the last mouthful of now warm white wine that was sitting in a glass next to his chair.

Only then did he speak.

'Bruce. It's a bit late, big man.'

'I know, I know. But it's important.'

'I bloody hope it is. What's up?'

'It's Nizar Mansour. He's been attacked in prison.'

'What? Is he OK?'

'I wouldn't go as far as to say OK, no. He's hurt. Bad enough that he's in intensive care. But he'll live.'

'Shit. Who did it?'

'Inmates is the party line,' Bull replied, 'but I think there's more to it than that. There was a guard hurt in the incident. Officials are saying he went to Nizar's aid and got hurt then, but it doesn't ring true with the rest of it.'

'You think he was in on it, eh? The guard?'

'Yeah. It's got all the hallmarks of an attempted prison hit. I think someone organised this. To shut him up for good.'

'It's easy to "think", Bruce. Not much you can do when you have no evidence, though.'

'You're telling me. But still, it's enough for me to have put a guard on Nizar. I've got my best man with him. He won't leave him for a second.'

'So he's safe for now.'

'For now.'

'And how long can that last?'

'I can keep him protected for a few days at least,' Bull explained. 'After that? We'll see. But this has taken a real turn. I knew they'd want him out of the way, but I didn't think they'd act this fast.'

'Aye, it's quick. Especially to get at someone held in the unit. These guys have got some proper resources, Bruce. You still happy we're going up against them?'

'I never said I was happy about it.'

'Aye, well, I am. Even more now. Bring the bastards on, I say.'

'I really hope you don't regret those words, Will.'

'Time will tell, eh?'

'I guess so.'

'What about tomorrow?' Duffy asked, the thought just occurring to him. 'We're supposed to be in Woolwich for his first hearing.'

'Not a chance. He won't be fit. We haven't had the prognosis yet, but it'll be Monday at the very earliest.'

'My wedding anniversary. That'll please the wife.'

'It's just a morning. She'll let you off.'

'You've not met my wife,' Duffy laughed. 'Anyway, look, I'll let Michael Devlin know about tomorrow. And I guess I'll see you on Monday, eh?'

'There's one more thing,' Bull said, keeping Duffy on the line. 'I was going to tell you tomorrow but since I've got you.'

'What is it?'

'It's what we discussed earlier. About Nizar's sister.'

'Aye. You find something?'

'I'm afraid I did. We heard back from the Italian police pretty quickly on this. They found a body matching Yara Mansour four days ago. Washed up in the Bay of Naples.'

'Shit.' It was the very last thing Duffy wanted to be told. Not least because it would now be for him to inform Nizar Mansour. 'Are they sure of the ID?'

'No, not yet. They had no idea who it could be until we contacted them. But from everything you've told me, it sounds like it's her.'

'Bollocks.'

'It can't be a surprise, Will. They were never going to keep that poor girl alive. It's a miracle Nizar made it himself.'

'I know. I know. I just wanted some good luck for the poor man. That's all.'

'Careful, Will. You're in danger of becoming a nice guy.'

'Piss off, Chief Inspector.' Duffy was too disappointed to laugh. 'And thanks for telling me. I'll see you on Monday.'

He did not wait to hear Bull's reply. Instead he placed the phone down, refilled his wine glass, sat back into his chair and looked at the ceiling as a single thought dominated his mind.

What god has Nizar pissed off to bring all this on himself?

FIFTY-EIGHT

Elizabeth Kirk glanced at her watch as she reached the main door of the Secret Service New York Field Office, situated at 335 Adams Street, Brooklyn.

7.20 p.m. Twenty minutes later than Jack Meyer had demanded.

Enough of a difference to needle. Not enough to ignite fireworks.

She opened the dark glass door, stepped into the building's marbled reception area and headed straight for the manned front desk. The receptionist – a young black woman who sat behind a name plate that read 'Susan' – was the only other person in the room.

'You must be Director Kirk.' Susan beat Kirk to the introduction. Her tone was almost robotic. 'Assistant Director Meyer expected you twenty minutes ago.'

'Then Assistant Director Meyer doesn't know much about Manhattan and Brooklyn traffic, does he?' Kirk was ready for whatever Meyer intended to throw at her. Starting with Susan the receptionist. 'Is he coming down or am I going up?'

'My instructions are to bring you to him myself,' Susan replied. She pressed a button, which audibly locked the building's glass front doors, rose from her seat and indicated for Kirk to follow. 'This way, Director Kirk.'

Three minutes and seven floors later, Kirk was escorted into a large, imposing office. A room designed for intimidation, it maximised distance between the entrance at one end and an oversized mahogany desk at the other.

The idea was to make the walk between them – under the eye of the desk's occupant – an ordeal in itself.

Cod psychology, Kirk thought to herself. *Why am I not surprised?*

'Sir, I have Director Kirk of the International Security Bureau for you.'

Susan's deep, monotone voice filled the room more effectively than Kirk had expected.

'Elizabeth.' Jack Meyer stood up as he spoke. 'Please, come and take a seat.'

He turned his eyes on the receptionist.

'That'll be all for today, Susan.'

'Thank you, sir.'

Susan spoke as she backed out, closing the door behind her. It left Kirk and Meyer alone together.

'I won't bite, Elizabeth. Come on, take a seat.'

Kirk hesitated for a moment. She didn't know why. She had arrived full of confidence, but suddenly she felt nervous. Perhaps the intended intimidation had been effective after all. Whatever the cause, she was beginning to doubt how convincing her deception would be.

She would not let that doubt beat her. She strode forward without a word, took the seat and looked Meyer directly in the eye.

'You look well, Elizabeth.' It was Meyer who broke the silence. 'The UN suits you.'

'Just what the hell is this all about, Jack?' The role Kirk had chosen to play demanded immediate outrage. 'I'm not used to being screamed at down a telephone. Or ordered across town without warning.'

Meyer looked annoyed.

'Straight to the point, Elizabeth. Fine, I'll do the same. Where the fuck is Joe Dempsey, and what the fuck has he done with Eden Grace?'

The first question was expected. The second was not. Kirk kept her face impassive, giving nothing away, as she considered the meaning of what Meyer had just revealed.

They've no idea their own agent's turned on them.

'I haven't got the first clue where Joe Dempsey is,' Kirk lied, going for a combination of confusion and belligerence. 'And I've never even heard of an Eden Grace. Anyway, why? What's Dempsey done that's pissed you off so much?'

'We're dealing with a national security threat, here.'

'From Joe Dempsey? Are you serious? Look, Dempsey is many things, but he's no security threat. The man's an attack dog. Dangerous and loyal as hell. No one on our side has anything to fear from that man.'

'Yeah? What about the four Secret Service agents he killed in Manhattan this afternoon? What about the fifth agent who's unaccounted for? You wanna tell them that he's nothing to fear?'

Kirk allowed her jaw to drop.

'What ... what the hell are you ... are you saying the incident in Yorkville today, that ... that was Dempsey?'

For the first time Kirk saw doubt in Meyer's eyes. Her performance must have looked as good as it felt. He was buying this.

'You know exactly who it was,' Meyer replied, his tone far less certain than his words.

'I ... I don't ... what happened?' Kirk allowed her voice to rise as she spoke. 'What were your agents doing there?'

'You know what—'

'NO, JACK!' It was Kirk's turn to shout. To catch him off guard. 'NO, I DAMN WELL DON'T. NOW TELL ME WHAT HAPPENED.'

Meyer looked as uncertain as Kirk had ever seen him.

'Jack,' she implored, 'if my agent has killed your men, I need to know exactly what's happened. I need to act, dammit. Someone's gone rogue here and we have to figure out who.'

Meyer remained silent, studying her.

Kirk rose to her feet, feigning impatience.

'You know what? Screw this. If you won't tell me what the fuck is going on, Knowles sure as hell will.'

She reached across Meyer's desk, picked up the handset of his landline phone and spun the console to face herself. She had already dialled the DC area code – 202 – before Meyer slammed his huge hand down onto the phone's switch hook and cleared the line.

Kirk looked directly into Meyer's face, her own a mask of pretend anger. In return, she saw his rage disappear.

The act had worked.

'Are you gonna tell me, Jack?' she asked. 'What do I need to know?'

When Meyer replied, his voice was calmer.

'Sit down, Elizabeth.'

Kirk did as instructed, never taking her eyes off of Meyer.

'Look, I thought you must have known. I thought Dempsey must have been acting on orders.'

Kirk shook her head.

'What orders? Why the hell would I send him after your men? The president's men? I haven't even seen Dempsey in days.'

'It's not that,' he replied. 'It was . . .'

He trailed off. And Kirk knew why. There was nothing Meyer could say that did not risk putting Kirk on the path he had – until moments ago – thought she was already on.

'It was what? Come on, Jack. It's me. What the hell is this?'

'I . . . I can't tell you,' he finally answered. 'Like I said, it's a national security threat and you don't have that kind of clearance any more.'

Kirk suppressed a smile. She had this.

'Just know, if Dempsey contacts you in any way, directly, indirectly, you need to contact me immediately. He's a threat, Elizabeth. A massive threat. And there's only one way we can deal with him.'

Kirk felt her eyes widen. Almost like it was no longer an act.

'You mean there's a sanction on him?'

'He killed four, maybe five US Secret Service agents. What do you think?'

Kirk looked down. Allowing the right amount of time to pass, she put just the right amount of regret into her voice when she looked back up.

'I understand,' she said. 'If he contacts me or if I hear anything, I'll get in touch.'

'You have my cell?'

'Have you changed it lately?'

'Not in two decades.'

'Then I have it.'

Meyer paused before replying. As if he was running through his remaining thoughts.

'OK,' he finally said. 'In that case, I guess you should be going. What needs to happen now, you don't need to be here to see. Not when it's one of yours.'

Kirk rose to her feet.

'I appreciate that, Jack. I really do.'

'Don't. I'm just disappointed it has to happen at all. I'd rather I had my team back.'

Meyer seemed genuinely sad. If Kirk had been naive, she might have even felt sorry for him.

But naive was something she had never been.

She reached out her arm, palm open. Meyer took it and gently shook her hand.

'Good luck, Jack. I hope you find him.'

'Thanks. Me too.'

Kirk held Meyer's gaze for a moment more, allowed herself a sad smile and then opened her hand, releasing his grip. Then, without another word, she turned and walked to the door.

FIFTY-NINE

Dempsey reached up and pressed his hand softly against his left shoulder. He could feel the dressing beneath his T-shirt. The same one he had applied back in Queens. It had been a short-term, field-style fix. Designed to hold him over – to prevent infection – until he could see someone with medical training.

It was no longer looking so temporary.

The flight time from Montreal to Kabul was fourteen hours and they were not yet three hours in. It meant at least eleven more before someone properly qualified could look at his injuries. Maybe longer, depending on what they encountered at the other end.

Ordinarily Dempsey would have seen a nurse at Montreal, before he boarded the flight. Today he he'd been unable to take that risk. Knowles could not know they were heading for Tootkai, and so their tracks had to be covered.

Even a rumour of an ISB Agent with a bullet wound in the closest Canadian airport to New York could give them away.

Every interaction had to be minimised. Hence no medics on the plane either. The United Nations-owned Airbus A330 could hold 335 passengers plus crew. Tonight it carried Dempsey, Grace and two pilots.

The otherwise empty flight had initially provided a distraction. Dempsey had never had a $240 million aircraft all to himself. The effect was strange, even from the First Class cabin. A ghost flight.

'How's the shoulder?'

Eden Grace's voice unexpectedly interrupted Dempsey's thoughts. She had seemed asleep for the past two hours.

'It's fine,' Dempsey lied.

'Doesn't look it. You can hardly move the thing.'

'It'll hold. I can get it checked out at the other end.'

'That's half a day away. You could have an infection by then.'

'Nothing a little penicillin can't handle. Besides, what are we going to do? Turn back?'

'I could take a look for you.'

'You?'

'Yeah, me. I'm not completely useless. We do get a little training in this, Dempsey.'

'I didn't mean to sound rude. I'm sure you get training, but it'll be the same as mine. First responder stuff. Not the same as proper treatment.'

'Maybe not, but unlike you I can take a close up look. Plus I have two hands for the dressing, and I guarantee this plane has better equipment than a pharmacy first-aid kit.'

Dempsey thought for a moment. He needed treatment. He knew that. But for some reason he was hesitant to let Grace provide it. He did not know why. An unwillingness to show weakness, perhaps?

Whatever it was, he knew that he was getting in his own way.

He adjusted his sitting position, to get a clearer view of Grace's seat. The movement sent an eruption of pain shooting up his arm and into his shoulder. It caused him to wince, and in doing so it settled the debate.

'Enough's enough, Dempsey. You're in pain. If that gets any worse you'll be no use to anyone when we get to Afghanistan.

And I'll be damned if I'm getting killed for the sake of a changed bandage.'

Dempsey said nothing, just nodded. Grace was right.

She got to her feet.

'I'm going to get you some painkillers, and once they've kicked in I'm changing that dressing.'

Dempsey sat shirtless on the centre of the three stools at the Airbus A330's First Class Bar. His left arm was rested on the bar itself and he watched closely as Grace carefully cleaned the first hints of pus from his two shoulder wounds.

She had returned from the cockpit armed with Vicodin, antiseptic lotion, antibacterial gel and a medical kit stocked for every eventuality that could occur on a full flight.

Dempsey had been hesitant to risk the tablets. They were sure to dull his senses and ability. But with over eleven hours of flight time left, he had to concede that any such effects would pass long before they reached Kabul.

Anticipating the pain to come and conscious of the tolerance that came with his physical size, he had taken three. He was now glad of that decision.

With the opiates in full effect, Dempsey's previous pain was almost gone. The impact on his equilibrium and the temporary dulling of his mental faculties were as expected, but a small price to pay for that relief.

The sting of the antiseptic lotion on the gunpowder burns should have been agony. With the effects of the Vicodin, it was barely an irritation. Still, Dempsey shuddered as it was applied. An instinctive reaction.

Grace had clearly noticed. She began to speak, to provide a distraction.

'Did you not have anyone to call?' she asked, her eyes still fixed on her work.

'When?'

Dempsey's mind felt . . . foggy.

'When you were telling me to call Natasha. I noticed you didn't call anyone.'

'I called Father Sam,' Dempsey replied. 'And I spoke to Kirk.'

'That's work,' Grace replied. 'That's the mission. I mean personal. Don't you have anyone they could connect to you?'

'Not any more, no.'

Dempsey was surprised to hear himself answer. Grace was touching on a subject he never discussed. Not even with his closest friends.

It's the drugs. It has to be.

'Divorced?'

'Never married.'

Grace put the lotion aside and inspected the wound.

'What was her name?'

'Maria.'

He had not said Maria's name in eight years. He had thought it. He had thought of her. Every day. But the word itself had not passed his lips in all that time. It sounded strange to hear it out loud now.

'How long were you together?'

'Just a year,' Dempsey replied. 'A long time ago.'

'How long?'

'She . . . it was . . . eight years ago.'

Grace stopped what she was doing. She seemed surprised. And now genuinely interested.

'And there's been no one else since?'

'I never wanted anyone else.' Dempsey couldn't seem to stop himself from speaking. 'She was everything.'

'Oh.' Grace looked concerned suddenly. 'Is she . . . did she die?'

'No.' Dempsey shook his head. 'I broke it off. I left her.'

'You left her? Why?'

'I couldn't put her through the life,' Dempsey replied. He was speaking to himself as much as to Grace. It felt like a long-overdue confession. 'I couldn't let her suffer for the things I had to do.'

'What things? What did you have to do?'

'The fighting. The killing. I couldn't keep exposing her to it. Exposing her to what I was. It wasn't fair on her.'

'What you were? What does that mean? What the hell were you?'

'I was a killer. An assassin.' The Vicodin was like a truth drug. Dempsey was no longer even thinking about his answers. Just responding. 'They called it something else. Called me a specialist operative. But that's what we were, every one of us. I was trained by the British Army. Well trained. And once I was good enough, they sent me around the world to do their dirty work.'

'Like Braddock and Cobb?' Grace's question was blunt.

'I was a *lot* better than Braddock and Cobb,' Dempsey replied, his honesty in full flow. 'But overall, yeah. What those guys were sent to do today? That was my every day.'

Grace stepped back from her stool and away from Dempsey. As if she wanted a clearer, fuller view of the man.

'And now you regret that life?' she asked.

'Every day.' In his mind, Dempsey was back in the past.

Reliving the experiences that had made him. 'I was indoctrinated, Eden. And I didn't even know it. They recruited me when I was a kid and they filled my head with ideas of patriotism, with bullshit concepts of black and white. Right and wrong. Of friends and of enemies. If it happened in any other situation, we'd call it brainwashing. In the army they call it education.

'But either way, I believed them. I believed that they'd only send me to do what was right. That I was only sent when there was no other choice; when the killing was justified. I trusted my government and my superiors absolutely. And so I did whatever was asked.'

Grace nodded; she seemed to understand.

'Then how did you even meet Maria? If that was the life you were leading?'

'I met her in Colombia,' Dempsey replied. 'I was in hospital there, about nine years ago. After a mission had gone wrong. I'd had a run in with someone I knew and I ended up hurt. Maria was my doctor.'

'She was Colombian?'

'No. American. She was a specialist, seconded from the US embassy to help after I was brought in.'

Grace nodded again. Dempsey saw her eyes flit to his torso. Even through the fog, he was aware she was inspecting his visible scars. Each a small piece of evidence that supported his story.

'And what happened?'

'She changed my life.'

Dempsey noticed Grace hesitate. He supposed it didn't look like much had changed. But she didn't say anything.

Instead she turned her attention back to Dempsey's wounds, smoothing the antibacterial gel across the burns.

'So what did she do?'

'Who?' The pause had derailed Dempsey's thought process.

'Maria. You said she changed your life. How did she do that?'

Dempsey thought for a moment. He was back there again.

'She . . . she made me see the world for what it really was. She made me realise that I'd been lied to. Lied to and used. And she made me want to be a better man.'

'What happened?'

'I opened my eyes. I started to understand that not everything I was asked to do was justified. But that didn't mean that *everything* was wrong. A lot of what I did was still necessary. For the greater good. I just didn't take it as read any more. I needed to be shown before I'd act. Persuaded.'

'And your superiors were OK with that?'

'I was the best at what I did.' Dempsey could hardly believe his own words. Since Maria, the only person he'd shared any of this with was Sam Cooke. 'They had no choice.'

'And Maria?'

'She understood. She knew that I had to do what I had to do. For the greater good. Without me innocent people would have suffered and died. Maria understood that and she supported me.'

'But you still left her? After all of that?'

'I had to.'

'Why?'

'Because I hurt her. I saw it happen. And I could never allow that to happen to her again.'

Dempsey could feel the sting of tears in his eyes. A sensation he had not experienced in years. At least not without some physical cause. His emotions were getting to him.

He began to push back. To fight through the fog.

'You mean you hit her?'

'Hit her?' The question shocked him. 'No. No, never. I would never.'

'Then how did you hurt her?'

'It was a letter.' His head was clearing. But still he could not help but answer. 'When a special forces operative gets deployed they write a letter. To their wife or partner, but left with the unit. It's a goodbye, to be passed on if we don't make it back. You know the sort of thing I mean?'

'I can imagine.'

'After almost a year together we got engaged and Maria moved to the UK. To live with me. And then a month after that I was sent away. To Africa. A problem in the Congo. It didn't go well; I had to go to ground and I was reported Missing in Action.'

'And Maria was given the letter?' Grace guessed.

'She was devastated. Torn to pieces. And so was I, when I came back and saw what it had done to her. It broke me. I couldn't put her through that again. I . . .'

Dempsey broke off, reliving the memory.

Grace gave him a moment before pushing further.

'Then why not leave? If you didn't want to put her through that, why not resign your commission to be with her?'

'I fought with myself over exactly that question. And believe me, there was nothing I wanted to do more. But I'd done so many terrible things. I needed to make them right. I *still* need to make them right . . .'

Dempsey forced himself to stop. He had to get control over himself. He couldn't face his past right now.

'Look, I . . . I don't want to talk about this any more. I need to stop.'

Grace nodded.

'I'm sorry. I didn't mean to ask so many questions. It's your personal business.'

'I did the same to you earlier,' Dempsey replied. He noticed that Grace had finished with the antibacterial gel and so he handed her the clean bandages. 'Maybe that makes us even.'

'I guess it does,' Grace said, unrolling the material and preparing to dress the clean wounds. 'But for what it's worth, Dempsey, what you did – whatever it was, however bad it was – that's not the man you are now. You don't have to spend your whole life making amends.'

'I wish that were true,' Dempsey replied, 'but sometimes you get so far down one path, every other one closes behind you. She's married now. Two kids and happy. And I'm happy for her.'

'But maybe . . .'

'There's no maybe. The past is the past.' Dempsey could feel his head clearing. A loosening of the Vicodin's grip. 'Let's leave it where it is. We've got enough to deal with in the present.'

'Focus on tomorrow?'

'Focus on tomorrow.'

SIXTY

The room drifted in and out of focus as Michael opened his eyes. The sensation combined with a dull pain pressing against the inside of his skull. All in all, it was not a happy introduction to the morning.

He turned to his right, towards his bedside table. The jet-black cylinder that sat upon it was blasting the sound of early morning radio into the room.

'Alexa. Off.'

Michael's voice was croaky, his throat dry. But still, the words did as intended. The music and the chat stopped instantly.

He turned to his left. Towards Sarah. Or at least where he expected Sarah to be. Her side of the bed had been slept in, he could see that. But it was now empty. Michael reached out an arm and touched the sheets.

Still warm.

He turned back to the bedside table and reached for his mobile phone. It was not there. Confused, he sat up. He always brought his handset to bed, to plug into its charger. He looked for the white cable and found it in seconds. Plugged into the wall but unconnected to a phone.

Michael allowed his body to fall back onto the bed sheets as images from the previous evening forced their way into his mind. He scanned through the memories. Broken and incomplete though they were, they still painted a picture.

A picture that Michael could taste, and which he could feel in his head and in his stomach as he became increasingly awake.

Whisky, he thought to himself. *Lots of whisky.*

The thought – the memory – made him want to vomit. Not that he would allow himself that respite. A day that started *that* low was no day at all, Michael believed. And so he forced himself out of bed and towards the en suite bathroom.

He needed to shower. And he was halfway there when he heard her voice.

'How's the head this morning?'

The mere sound of her soft American accent improved Michael's mood. He felt a smile spread across his face as he turned towards the bedroom door. It only grew wider as he saw her standing there.

'Would you believe me if I said it had been better?' Michael replied. He noticed his own accent as he spoke. A sure sign of a hangover.

'I wouldn't believe anything else.' Sarah laughed. 'You were . . . not your best self last night. Is everything OK?'

Michael paused a moment before he answered. He was trying to recall what he might have said while drunk. Anything that could have led to Sarah's comment.

He remembered nothing.

'Everything's fine,' he lied. 'I just had a few too many, that's all.'

'And the Johnny Cash?'

'Ah, come on now, I had the house to myself. I deserved to have a bit of Johnny.'

Michael made his way towards Sarah. Only a few steps, but painful ones thanks to his thumping head.

He gave no hint of the discomfort and took Sarah by the waist, pulling her close.

'And you? How are you feeling this morning?'

'A lot better than the last few days,' Sarah replied. 'Otherwise your Lagavulin breath would be sending me straight to that bathroom.'

'Well, you look good.'

Sarah gave him what looked like a nervous smile, but she said nothing. For an instant it seemed strange to Michael's foggy mind. A moment later and that thought was gone.

The realisation that Sarah was fully dressed and ready to leave finally sank in.

'You off already?' he asked.

'Yes, in a minute. Just wanted to deliver your message before I left,' Sarah replied.

'What message?'

'I had a call from Will Duffy this morning.'

'Will called *you*?'

'Actually he called you, but your phone was off. Apparently you didn't charge it last night. It's still downstairs. I plugged it in for you.'

'Thanks. What did Will want?'

'It was about Nizar Mansour. He was attacked in prison last night.'

'Attacked?' Michael was shocked. 'Is he OK?'

'He's OK. But he won't be at court today. That's all Will told me. Well, he also said that I should get myself to New Scotland Yard to break the story while it's still an exclusive. But that part was for me, not for you.'

Michael nodded his head, now understanding.

'Hence the early start.'

'It's not that early, Boozehound.'

'What time is it?'

'Eight a.m.'

'What?' Michael stepped back, his heart suddenly racing. 'I'm on in Woolwich at nine forty-five!'

'But Mansour won't be there?'

'That doesn't matter. *I* still need to be there. To explain what's happened to the judge, and to fix the next date when Mansour *can* attend.'

'I'm sorry. I didn't realise that. I thought you wouldn't have to go, so I let you sleep in.'

'Don't say sorry. It's not your fault.' Michael looked around the room. His head was now clear. Panic was the great hangover cure. 'But I need to rush.'

'OK. I'll leave you to it. Have a great day.'

Michael stopped himself. No matter how late he might be, he would not let Sarah leave like that. He turned back, took her face in his hands and kissed her gently on the lips.

'You too, gorgeous.' He took a step backwards, one hand still on her cheek. 'Good luck with the story.'

'Good luck with the judge.'

'Trust me, mine's easier than yours today.'

SIXTY-ONE

Michael gripped the wrought-iron railings that led from his front door to the street, threw his red robe bag over his shoulder and trod carefully onto the first step down.

The snow from the previous night had settled on the paths and roads of Chelsea. It looked magical; as if the residential square on which their townhouse was set had been designed for a picture postcard. But magical was not the same as practical, and so Michael took care as he negotiated the ice-covered steps to the street.

Once on the pathway he turned right and headed towards the King's Road, checking his watch as he moved.

8.15 a.m.

It's gonna be tight.

The journey from Chelsea to Woolwich Crown Court was simple enough, but it was not quick. Sloane Square Station to Plumstead via tube and then an overland train. An hour and five minutes, not including waiting, delays, or the time it would take to be searched and then change once he reached the court.

And Michael was expected to be before the judge in an hour and thirty.

It's gonna be bloody tight.

He walked fast. Left onto the King's Road and then straight ahead, towards Sloane Square. Unusually he was carrying just one item of luggage, his red robe bag. It contained his wig, his silk robe and a single blue counsel's notebook. Far less than he would usually need for a day in court, but then this morning's hearing was going to be unusual. He was travelling all the way to Woolwich Crown Court to explain Nizar Mansour's medical unavailability. Nothing more.

The fact that the hearing had to go ahead at all was a scandalous waste of time, but it at least allowed him to travel light. And that in turn allowed him to travel quick. A silver lining of sorts.

Nizar Mansour's medical unavailability.

The thought popped back into Michael's head as he walked, reminding him that he did not know any of the details behind it. If he was going to explain what had happened, he needed to first find out for himself.

He reached into his overcoat pocket and pulled out his iPhone. He'd rushed out of the house too quickly to give it time to charge but Sarah had left her portable power pack for him to use. Michael turned the phone on, hoping it finally had enough juice to come alive. Within seconds he was rewarded with the welcome sight of the start-up logo.

The phone's alerts started to go off as the message notifications began to roll in. A backlog from the hours the handset had been ignored and then powered off.

Michael scrolled through them as quickly as he could. The earliest were from Sarah the previous evening. Before she had made it home, Michael realised. Most of the others were from Will Duffy. One at 7 p.m. A few later. And three early this morning.

But before he could return the calls, he noticed another. A missed call and voicemail from someone who *never* left a message. A man who rarely called at all, in fact. And had now done so twice in one day.

After the conversation they'd had yesterday afternoon,

Michael knew that Joe Dempsey could not have been calling with good news.

He felt his heart race as he put the phone to his ear and connected to Dempsey's voicemail. It only increased as he listened to the message.

He stopped walking as it ended, his blood as cold as the snow beneath his feet. He pulled the phone from his ear and checked the time of the call.

Last night. Jesus. Anything could have happened.

He put the phone to his ear again and replayed the voicemail as he began to walk.

. . . my source . . . killed this morning . . .

. . . you're on their radar . . .

. . . we can get you and Sarah somewhere safe . . .

Michael increased his pace, his eyes everywhere as he moved. Dempsey sounded worried. And Dempsey *never* sounded worried. Life and death was what he did.

If *he* was concerned, Michael had to follow suit.

Michael looked across the street as he passed the iconic Chelsea Registry Office. Towards a man in a tan overcoat. Something about him had caught Michael's attention. Was it paranoia? The effect of Dempsey's message?

Probably, Michael accepted. *But if that's what keeps me alive . . .*

The man was around Michael's size and build. Michael thought he could make out a black suit beneath the overcoat.

He was also looking the other way. Into a shop window.

Which is what's off, Michael suddenly realised. *Who the hell goes window shopping on the coldest morning of the year?*

Michael forced himself to look away. If he had called this right, he did not want the man to know. Instead Michael kept him in his peripheral vision and, where possible, in the reflection of glass shop fronts.

Michael increased his pace again as he drew level and carried on past him. A near power walk.

At first the other man did nothing. He just continued studying the window display. It made Michael doubt himself. To almost accept it as paranoia.

Almost.

He allowed himself a turn of the head as the distance grew between them. Just in time to see him cross the King's Road – to Michael's side of the street – and begin to walk fast in the same direction.

It could be nothing, Michael told himself. But he didn't really believe it.

He turned again. As he did, the man immediately stopped and began to inspect another shop window.

A women's shoe shop. Michael knew it well; it was Sarah's favourite. And so he knew that it was very different from the previous store, which sold Scandinavian toys. Either this man was buying some *very* varied gifts on a snowy January morning, or Michael's instincts were right.

Shit.

*

'Mitchell has eyes on Devlin. He's covering from the Town Hall.'

The voice in Romeo Meyer's ear came from the first member of the observation team. Special Agent Tad Brooke. Brooke had observed Devlin from his home until the Town Hall, where he had been relieved by Mitchell.

It was standard observation protocol. A succession of

agents, all following a target for a specified portion of that target's expected journey. Designed to ensure that no one agent was active long enough to be noticed. At least, that was the *usual* intention.

'Understood.'

Romeo was speaking from his own position, just outside of Sloane Square Underground Station. Still half a mile west.

He continued.

'Mitchell, you online?'

'Here.' Mitchell's voice was deeper than Brooke's. Distinctive.

'Did he make you?'

'One hundred per cent.'

'Good. Stay on him 'til Smith Street.'

'Understood.'

Romeo looked westwards from the station. Towards the King's Road and — unseen right now — Michael Devlin. He allowed himself a small smile as he considered what was about to happen.

The operation had been planned to the last detail. Two agents engaged so far, Brooke and Mitchell. Plus two more to come.

Robinson would pick up the observation at Smith Street and see it through to Duke of York Square and the Saatchi Gallery. The last leg would be covered by Clegg, from one Square to another. Duke of York to Sloane. Both would be more discreet than Mitchell. The plan required that *they* were not noticed.

And then it would be Romeo's turn. A short leg, compared to the others, but with a big responsibility. It was Romeo's job to be spotted as well. To confirm Devlin's suspicions and his fears, just as he descended to the station's platform.

The platform where Special Agent Frank Hart would be waiting.

There would be no mistakes this time. No near miss. Hart would do what Hart did best. He would remain unseen, letting Devlin's fears do the work for them. It would be Devlin's desperation to board the train – to reach the safety it provided – that would put him in position. That would make him force his way to the edge of the platform. It was just human nature, after all.

Only then, when the time was right would Hart approach. One firm push. And Devlin would find himself beneath the wheels of a thirty tonne District Line carriage.

An accidental victim of Sloane Square Station's rush-hour overcrowding. Unfortunate. Tragic. And just about the least suspicious way a man like Michael Devlin could die.

Exactly as Kelvin Cunningham had demanded.

The thought made Romeo's smile grow wider. This time he would get the credit he was due.

*

Michael scrolled through his recent calls and found Dempsey's number. With his hands shaking from a mixture of cold and adrenaline, he pressed the connect icon and lifted the handset to his ear.

'*The cell phone you are trying to reach is no longer in service.*'

'Shit.' Michael did not even intend to speak aloud, but still the words came out. 'Shit.'

He stuffed the phone into his pocket. As he did, he chanced a look behind.

There was no sign of the man in the overcoat.

Shit. Where the hell has he gone?

Michael almost stopped walking. Almost turned. He caught himself just in time. No matter how natural the reaction, he could not risk that. The man could be *anywhere*. He could be watching. Michael could not give him any cause to think he had been spotted.

He forced himself onwards. Towards the station. Whenever he could, he looked for the man who'd been following him, using the succession of shop windows he was passing.

He didn't spot him once.

Could I have been wrong? he began to ask himself. *Could it have been paranoia after all?*

He did not think it was. Not really. And yet there was no sign of the man. Of him or of anyone else who looked out of place. What did that mean? The further Michael walked the more he was forced to question his instincts.

Right up until those instincts were proved correct.

Michael spotted Romeo Meyer from forty yards. Perhaps more. It was impossible not to, even for Michael, who had never seen the Secret Service agent with his own eyes.

Bruce Bull had described Romeo to Will Duffy, and Will Duffy had passed that same description to Michael. At the time it sounded ridiculous. An exaggeration that no doubt grew more fantastical with each telling. But as Michael now approached a figure who could only be one man, he saw how accurate Bull had actually been.

At around six feet six inches, Romeo was almost a full half foot taller than Michael, his shoulders twice the width. He was, Michael could tell as he came closer, as powerful and athletic as any of the giants who now dominated heavyweight boxing, but with none of the flab that some carried in the midriff.

If anything, he made those guys look a little out of shape.

Michael had no doubt. This man could be no one else; he matched the unusual description too perfectly. And that, in turn, could mean only one thing.

Dempsey was right. I am on their radar.

And this is it.

SIXTY-TWO

Michael went through the station's ticket barriers, keeping his eyes resolutely forward. He was determined to give no indication that he knew something was wrong. Given even a moment to consider what he was doing, he would have realised that the ruse was pointless.

But he had no such moment. And right now he could think of nothing else.

It at least gave him the comfort of having some form of plan.

He joined the long stream of men and women who were making their way down to the Eastbound platform, towards Westminster and the City of London.

Even in the heavy January snow, Sloane Square Underground Station was busy.

More than enough witnesses to keep me alive, Michael hoped. *The safest place I can be.*

The crowd moved slowly down the stairs to the platform, their speed limited by sheer numbers. The pace gave Michael some fleeting confidence. Anyone trying to rush would cause a commotion, and a commotion was a warning.

It would give him time to act.

With every step down he looked behind. Scanning for Romeo Meyer. For the man in the tan overcoat. Or for anyone else who stood out, as difficult to spot as they would now be.

Michael's section of the crowd reached the bottom of the

stairway a few seconds later, and, as it did, the commuters began to spread out along the platform. Normally Michael would carry on straight ahead, walking towards the far end, where the front of the train would stop. But today the darker stretch at the back of the platform seemed to offer greater cover.

He hesitated at the foot of the stairs, unsure which way to go. He chose neither. Instead he pushed his way back into the descending crowd. He took another look upwards, to the top of the staircase. To spot anyone familiar coming down, hidden in the endless tide of commuters.

He saw no one who stood out.

The information screen listed the next eastbound train as one minute away.

A feeling of physical relief was beginning to stir in his gut. With the train almost here, it was unlikely that anyone not already on the staircase would reach the platform in time to board it. Michael could be safely on the nearest carriage and away in a matter of just seconds.

A final glance up the stairs. The crowd of people coming down the stairs had grown. With Michael standing at the bottom, the result was inevitable. A mass of bodies – scores of them, funnelled into a tight battering ram and determined to reach the platform in time – began to push him backwards.

He turned with the momentum as it carried him towards the platform's edge. Close enough that he was inches from where the carriage would soon be. He scanned the opposite westbound platform too. Not that they could get to him from there. Soon he would be on a train and be away from the danger behind him.

The danger behind me.

Staring down at the tracks from the edge of the platform, with the pressure of the crowd against his back, he felt a sudden moment of dread.

Why the hell was someone as distinctive as Romeo standing out front like that? Where he couldn't be missed?

A feeling of panic began to rise up from his gut.

And why was the first guy so easy to spot? They were acting like amateurs.

The realisation hit him hard.

They wanted me to see them. To make me panic. To make me flee.

Michael had not escaped the danger. No. He had walked right into it. Because if someone wanted him dead and wanted it to look like an accident, *this* was exactly where that someone would want him to be: inches from the platform edge, with a station full of impatient commuters pushing at his back.

'Shit.'

Michael's eyes scanned the platform as he tried to force his way back into the crowd. It moved, but not by much. Just a few inches further from the edge. Nowhere near enough to be safe. Not while the jostling crowd kept him off balance.

Not if some faceless bastard was to shove me from within the crowd.

He could hear the train approaching now. He pushed harder. Both into the crowd and along the platform, towards the front. He had no idea why he was heading in that direction. Perhaps the familiarity of his usual spot was offering an illusion of safety.

Whatever it was, as he surveyed the crowd again Michael realised that his unexplained instinct had kept him alive.

A face he thought he recognised.

A heartbeat later he placed it.

The agent from the magistrates' court.

Michael had been right. He'd been corralled onto the platform like a steer into a slaughterhouse. And now they were ready to strike the killing blow.

SIXTY-THREE

The agent moved towards Michael with more speed than should have been possible. He was pushing through the same crowd Michael had struggled through, yet the man's powerful body was hardly slowed by the resistance.

Commuter after commuter was physically thrust aside as he cut the distance between himself and his target.

Michael's first impression, picked up in their short interaction in Westminster Magistrates' Court, struck him again now. This was a dangerous man, intent on doing him harm. And for all Michael knew, he might not be alone.

He remembered Dempsey's words:

'None of your heroic shit this time, mate. These people, they're well out of your league.'

In a lifetime marked by threats and by danger, Michael Devlin had never been a coward. He had always stood his ground. But never before had he had so much to lose. And never before had he been so certain that he would lose it.

He had to find another way out.

They want this to look like an accident, he thought. *But what if it can't?*

The train's cab appeared in the distance, at the dark end of the platform. With the crowd still in their own commuter trance, it was unlikely that many – if any – had noticed the two men shoving their way along the platform. A fall now could still appear innocent. A tragic mistake.

Michael's best chance to save his life was to change that.

'HELP!'

Michael did not stop moving towards the end of the platform as he shouted.

'HELP! HE'S TRYING TO KILL ME!'

He didn't stop to point him out. His pursuer was too close to risk the delay. And he knew no one in this crowd would do anything, anyway. The result of confusion and the deep-seated reluctance to get involved in trouble.

But help was not the point. The point was attention. To ensure that whatever now happened, it could not be written off as an accident. It was, Michael had figured, his best chance – perhaps his only chance – of persuading the man in black to back off.

'HELP!' he shouted again. 'HELP ME! SOMEONE!'

*

A moment more and Frank Hart would have had him.

The entire set up had been almost perfect. Devlin had reached the platform in a panic, and in a few seconds he was exactly where Hart had wanted him to be; at the head of the crowd, just inches from the platform's edge.

In response, Hart had moved himself into position. Close. So close. Three, maybe four bodies away. Enough that one strong push might have been sufficient.

But 'might' was unacceptable. Romeo had made that much clear. They had to be certain of the man's death, which meant two things: Hart had to be sure that Devlin would fall; and Devlin had to fall just as the train arrived.

The second factor had forced Hart to wait for the train's arrival. It had added only a moment or two, but in that short time Devlin had clearly realised that something was wrong.

When Hart first saw Devlin step back he didn't think anything of it. But as Devlin squeezed further into the crowd, he knew the lawyer had sensed the danger. Hart started to make his way after him, and it must have been that movement that had caught Devlin's attention.

'HELP!'

The shout made Hart stop in his tracks. Just for a moment, but long enough to see those commuters closest to Devlin turn in response. In that instant, he understood what the lawyer was trying to do.

Clever mother—

A heartbeat later and he was moving again. Pushing forcefully through the crowd, to keep up with Devlin. Though what he would do then, he didn't know. What Devlin had done had already undermined their plan.

'The lawyer made me. He knows what's going down.'

Hart barked the words into his wrist mic as he followed Devlin towards the far end of the platform. Where, in just a few moments, the front of the train would stop.

'Keep on him.' It was Romeo's voice, beamed directly into Hart's earpiece. 'We can't fail this time.'

'We've already failed,' Hart replied. 'He's shouting his damn head off, drawing attention to himself. This can't look like an accident now. We need to abort.'

'We're aborting nothing!' Romeo's voice betrayed a hint of panic. 'That fucker is not to leave this station alive, understood?'

'Are you serious? With a platform full of witnesses?'

'Just do it. I'll deal with any fallout.'

Hart hesitated. They were coming to the end of the platform, Devlin only slightly ahead of him.

Both men stopped moving as Devlin turned to face him.

It was time to make a decision.

'OK.'

Hart had his orders.

It was time to act.

*

Michael stood with his back to the platform's end, facing the man in black. His shouts had caught the attention of the crowd. Everyone had backed away from them. Exactly as he had expected.

The train was pulling into the platform now, slowing down.

The two men stood motionless. Each one's eyes fixed upon the other. Michael had no idea if his plan had worked. With everyone's attention on them, was he safe?

He did not have to wait long for his answer. And as the man in black moved, Michael did the same.

Fear and desperation were all that drove him as he instinctively turned to his only escape route. Running ahead of the train as it slowly came to a halt, he leapt into the darkness at the mouth of the tunnel.

SIXTY-FOUR

Michael felt his left ankle give way as he hit the ground hard. It brought him stumbling down to his knees, with his hands hitting the small, sharp stones that filled the tunnel as they broke his fall.

He tried to ignore the pain. To concentrate only on the rails that were either side of him, illuminated by the train's headlights.

Two of the tracks were designed to carry the vehicle on its directed route. The third to power it. That one must be avoided at all costs.

As he clambered to his feet he couldn't ignore the damage his landing had done. He would be running no further.

The thought was immediately banished by the sound of footsteps on the loose stones. He looked up, in no doubt of what he was about to see.

The man in black had been careful. He had climbed down from the platform slowly. Deliberately. It had cost him a few seconds, but had spared him the kind of injury that now hampered his prey.

Michael noted this with dread in his gut. It hardly mattered. Not now. He had staked everything on the hope that the agent wouldn't follow him at all. That with all the attention and the commotion, he would take the easy way out.

His gamble had lost. And now, injured and alone in the dark, so would he.

A grim smile grew on the man in black's face. Half-hidden in shadow, it made him look all the more sinister.

'Got to tell you, counsellor. That leap of yours? I did not expect that.'

Michael raised his hands. A boxer's guard, for all the good it would do him. His injured ankle made any kind of footing impossible.

'Are you here to talk, or are we gonna do this?'

Michael heard the confidence in his own voice. It was a confidence he didn't have. In his mind he had just one thought.

I can't beat this man.

Michael was going to die. He had no doubt about that. The thought terrified him. But it also freed him. If the outcome was inevitable, there was no holding back. He would lose, but he would not lose easy. He would fight with everything he had.

With that realisation, Michael felt his rational mind begin to retreat. It left something else. Something primal. That thing – that other self – that he had called on so many times before.

He moved without warning. With no thought to the pain or to the damage it was causing. He launched himself off of his injured ankle and towards his opponent, now just feet away.

The sudden movement caught the man off guard, but he managed to avoid Michael's lunging right-hand punch by leaning out of range. The movement put him off balance, and he took the impact of Michael's follow-up body charge full-on. It staggered him backwards but it didn't knock him down; Michael was shocked to feel the sheer strength as he hit the resistance of the agent's body.

It took only three faltering steps for the man in black to regain both his footing and his composure. A recovery that was much too quick for Michael.

With momentum still carrying Michael forward, the agent planted his left foot down and allowed his right side to give way. The movement removed all resistance to Michael's charge, causing him to stumble forward with no control. As he did so, the man pushed Michael downwards.

Towards the tracks.

Michael could do nothing to stop his fall, but his instincts remained sharp. He had to avoid the power rail. *That* was instant death.

He threw both hands out ahead of him, to break his fall. As they hit, he felt his right arm give way, causing him to take the full force of the fall on his left.

The impact sent a searing jolt of pain through his body. He was too heavy to take his full weight one-handed; it broke his wrist and dislocated his left shoulder in a single blow.

It also saved his life, as his awkward one-sided landing rotated his body away from the lethal third rail.

It was the difference between life and death, but it was not perfect. The motion did not propel him far enough to miss both rails and so, as his left arm gave way, his head fell forward and hit the immovable steel of the second.

Everything went black.

Michael had no idea how long he was out. It could have been only an instant. Or it could have been longer. Whatever it was, he regained his senses to a roar of noise and vibrations. For a moment he was confused. Then, to his horror, he realised what it must be: the train, leaving the platform and heading towards him.

Fear forced Michael to his feet, intending to leap aside, but as he did so he saw that he was wrong. The eastbound train was still at the platform, stationary and with its driver looking on in shock at what was happening in front of him.

Michael had no time to consider his mistake. Back on his feet, he was aware of just how unsteady he was. The agony of his left ankle forced him to place all of his weight onto his right, while the pain in his left arm rendered it useless.

The man in black was standing in the weak beam of the train lights. The sneering smile was still there, only this time it was joined by something much worse. The glimmer of a long blade, held in his right hand.

Michael knew what that meant. The fighting was over. Now only the killing remained.

He placed his injured left foot in front of his right. An attempt to stabilise himself. But as much as he tried to focus, the impact with the rail had left him bloody and dazed. The world seemed to be spinning. Filled with the roar of a train that didn't appear to be moving.

'You're in bad shape, counsellor.'

'I've had worse.'

Michael's words were defiant, but his condition said otherwise. Sheer will to survive was all that was keeping him upright.

He threw a punch. It was slow. Clumsy. Weak. The man in black leaned backwards with a taunting grin, avoiding the blow as easily as if he were up against a child. As he did so he brought his blade upwards, under Michael's outstretched right arm, and cut deep into his triceps.

Michael pulled his hand against his chest and stumbled backwards. His left moved instinctively towards the cut, only for agony to fire again through his dislocated shoulder and broken wrist.

The sight made the agent laugh. A cruel, mocking sound.

'You're just delaying the inevitable.'

Michael didn't respond. The man was right but he could not let him see that. He forced his mind to focus through the pain. To look for a way out. For just a moment, he thought he might have it.

The agent had not noticed how close he was to the power rail. Two feet at most. Stumbling distance, if Michael could only push him in the direction.

It was a moment of hope. But only that. In his weakened state Michael was far from subtle, and the agent had followed his glance.

'You think you can force me onto that?' he asked, his voice as scornful as his expression. 'The condition you're in?'

Michael knew then it was hopeless. The noise and the pain in his head were deafening now. Disorientating him. Whatever strength remained, whatever he could put into one final, desperate blow, it was not going to be enough.

He tried anyway.

The punch was even weaker than before. And, inevitably, the agent saw it coming from Michael's first movement. As before, he leaned backwards to avoid the blow. An exaggerated distance. Much further than was necessary as the fist that sailed clumsily past. A cruel attempt to humiliate a beaten man.

That vicious smile never left his lips as he began to correct himself and raise the blade. This time it would not be Michael's arm that took the razor sharp cut. He was done playing with his prey.

Even through the disorientating roar of the tunnel, Michael could see the focus in the man's eyes. The murderous intent.

And then, for just an instant, Michael could see the horror.

With the eastbound train going nowhere and their attention on each other, neither had considered the westbound tracks right next to them. And so neither was aware of the risk the man in black had taken by leaning backwards.

Into the path of the oncoming train.

The screeching arrival of the train drowned out the sound of the front carriage's metal edge impacting the man's skull. Not that Michael would have heard it anyway. The shock of what he had seen combined with his injuries to overcome him.

He staggered backwards and fell hard to the ground, just as the agent's lifeless body slammed into the stones next to him.

SIXTY-FIVE

'What's our first move when we land?'

It was 3 p.m. in Kabul. Which made it 6.30 a.m. in New York.

Dempsey and Grace had been in the air for almost eleven hours. Seven of those they had been sleep. And apart from thirty minutes of Vicodin-induced small talk, the rest had been spent in silence.

Now Grace wanted to know what was coming.

Dempsey was seated with his feet up on the first-class chair-bed across from her own. He seemed to take a moment to think through his response.

Grace thought she knew why.

He's deciding what I need to know. And what I don't.

'We're meeting with Thomas Quilty's Afghan contact,' Dempsey finally offered. 'Jangi Shah Karzai. The man who first told him about Knowles and Tootkai.'

'How will we find him?'

'He'll find us,' Dempsey replied. 'Quilty never lost touch with the man. He gave me every different means of contacting him. I've asked Kirk to track him down. To have him meet us at the airbase in Kabul, then to travel with us to Tootkai.'

'What if he doesn't want to cooperate?'

'The people we're going up against, they're responsible for Quilty's death. Shah's not going to like that. He and Quilty go back decades. To when Afghanistan was a Russian war zone instead of a Western one. He'll cooperate.'

'And that's the whole plan, is it? We speak to this one guy. And then we fly to Tootkai. What then?'

'Then we track down Jangi's source and anyone else we can find who was there that night. We get the truth. And then we find the evidence.'

'And what if the truth isn't what you want to hear?' Grace was hesitant, still not quite ready to show her hand. 'What if Knowles did nothing wrong in Tootkai?'

Dempsey took a deep breath and stretched his injured arm outwards before he answered. He grimaced at the effort.

'Eden, if Knowles did nothing, then in just three days someone has killed a lot of people for no reason. Does that make any sense to you?'

Grace thought for a moment. It was a difficult question to answer.

'No,' she finally said. 'No, it doesn't. But a lot of other stuff doesn't make sense to me, either. So I'm asking you again, what if the stuff about Knowles and his unit *is* bullshit?'

'Then we still need to find out what's really going on. Why someone has committed mass murder to cover up something that wasn't even true.'

'And how will we manage that?'

'I have a few ideas. Look, cards on the table. I can tell you don't think Knowles is responsible.'

Grace was not prepared for the sudden disclosure.

'You . . . how?'

'It's my job to read people. To read their intentions. Just like it's yours. My instincts say that you want me to be wrong about Knowles. But those same instincts, they say you'll do your job anyway. However this plays out. I trust that you're going to help me because it's in your interests to find out the truth one way or the other. Just as much as it's in mine. Am I right?'

'Yes. Yes, you're right. About . . . about everything.'

'Good. Because believe me, I don't *want* to be right. I would much prefer we were up against a bunch of rogue agents than the president of the United States of America. Our odds are a lot shorter that way.'

Grace nodded. She appreciated his honesty.

And now it was her turn. She took a deep breath and looked Dempsey in the eye.

'What if I told you that I believe President Knowles added me to Braddock's team so that I could warn you?'

Dempsey lowered his feet and sat forward. Grace could tell that, for once, it was his turn to be surprised.

'What? Why would you think that?' Dempsey asked.

'Because of something he said. Because of something he always used to say.'

Dempsey rose to his feet, his eyes narrowed. When he spoke, it was not the question Grace was expecting.

'You've known him a lot longer than three years, haven't you?'

'What?' Grace's advantage had lasted just seconds. Now *she* was on the back foot. 'How can you know that?'

'He trusted you on this assignment, Eden. Now whether that was to kill me or to warn me, that's a hell of a lot of trust. A hell of a lot more trust than he would have in an agent so junior that she can't have spent more than a few hours in his direct company. Not even one second of which would have been alone.'

Grace said nothing.

'Then you mentioned "the thing he always used to say". Not "the thing he always says". Past tense. Which means he'd say it to you *before* your access to him was restricted by your official roles. So answer the question, Eden: how long have you known John Knowles?'

Grace stared at Dempsey. She hadn't intended to give quite so much away. But the man was sharp and it was too late for her to backtrack. She had no choice.

'I've . . . I've known him since I was a child.'

Grace could hear how vulnerable she sounded as she spoke, her voice stripped of her usual confidence. What she was about to tell Dempsey, only two other people on the planet knew. One was her fiancée, Natasha. And the other was the president of the United States of America.

'How?'

'He . . . he knew my dad. My dad *and* my mom. And after my dad died, he kind of . . . stepped in.'

'With your mother?'

'No. Not that at all. With me. He became, well, he became like a father to me. He guided me. Helped me. He made me what I am. Then my mom died when I was eighteen and I have no other family. Until Natasha, John was all I had.'

'How did he know your parents?'

'My father was under his command in SEAL Team Six,' Grace explained. 'His name was Pablo Lopez.'

Dempsey seemed to think for a moment.

'The SEAL who helped Knowles with the Black Hawk? Who won the posthumous Medal of Honor?'

'Yes. The president and my dad, they pulled those guys from the burning helicopter together. They carried them back through enemy fire. The president made it out of there alive. My dad didn't.'

'Eden, that happened on the way back from Tootkai. If what Jangi Shah says about what took place there is true . . .'

'Then my dad was guilty of war crimes as well.'

Grace fixed her stare on Dempsey, her confidence returning.

'That's why I don't believe it, Dempsey. It didn't happen.'

'How can you be so sure? You must have been what, fourteen years old? How would you even know.'

'I was thirteen, but that doesn't change anything. I'm telling you what I know. My dad couldn't do those things. And neither could John Knowles.'

'But what if they *could*? What if they *did*? Sometimes things happen in wartime. Sometimes you don't know people as well as you think.'

'If they did it then I want to know. Because if they did, then I've been lied to my whole life. If they did, then I've been wrong about everything.'

Dempsey stayed silent. He didn't seem to know what to say.

Unlike Grace.

'But I'm not wrong,' she continued, her voice firmer. 'And you're going to see that when we get to Tootkai. John didn't do this. And neither did my dad.'

Again, Dempsey said nothing.

'Think about it. If John is guilty of any of this, why would he send me to warn you, Dempsey? Why would he do that?'

'What makes you think he was sending you to warn me?' he asked. 'Did he order you to do that?'

'No, not explicitly. But I don't think he could,' Grace explained. 'There were five other people in that room with me. And who knows how many in his room with him.'

'So what? He's the president. What does it matter who else is there or who else hears him?'

'I don't know the answer to that, Dempsey. If I did I'd be at the goddamned White House, helping him, instead of here helping you. All I know is this: he told me to "do my duty, do what's right". And he said it twice.'

Dempsey didn't seem to be convinced.

'And that's something he used to say? When you were growing up?'

'Always. Every lesson I ever learned. Every decision I ever made. If I asked him, it's what he would tell me. You always do your duty and you always do what's right. It was a message. I am one hundred per cent sure of that. A message meant only for me.'

'And if those two things conflict? How do you know he didn't say it to convince you to carry out his actual order?'

'You don't understand. That *was* the lesson. Your duty *is* to do what's right. Whatever the order might be. It's what's *right* that matters. He was telling me to ignore the orders. He was telling me to save you.'

Dempsey didn't answer. Instead he took a long step back and, using his one good arm, he lowered himself into his seat. He seemed shell-shocked by what he'd just been told. Grace could understand why; after being so certain of the president's guilt, he could not understand why the man would apparently save his life.

It only made sense if Grace was right. If somehow John Knowles was *not* behind the deaths and the attacks that had occurred. But if he was not, then who *was*? And why? And what sort of hold did they have over the president?

Questions Grace had asked herself. So far she had no answer.

'I don't understand this, Eden.' Dempsey spoke after less than a minute of silence. 'Knowles has been in your life ever since your father died?'

'Since before, even. When he was Dad's SO.'

'Then how did no one know about this? How did the Secret Service not know? They would never have let you become part of the White House detail if they'd known about your prior relationship.'

'I know that. That's why I kept it quiet. That's why I kept *everything* quiet. Shit, Dempsey, my kind-of-adopted dad was one of the most famous politicians in the country. And then he became president. I could have walked into any boardroom or university or whatever the hell I wanted to, but I wasn't raised that way. Not by my parents and not by John Knowles. I didn't want to get anywhere on nepotism or tokenism. I wanted my achievements to be *my* achievements.

'But when I set my sights on presidential protection, it was more important to hide that connection. I wanted to succeed on my own terms. Same reason I didn't want them knowing my father was a war hero, and since I'd always had my mom's surname I didn't have to. I got here all on my own, Dempsey. And thank God I did, or neither of us would be sitting here now, would we?'

'What about your birth certificate?' he asked. 'The Service would have seen your father's name on there.'

'They would have, if it was there. But my dad was a paranoid man. Thought his time in the SEALs was going to come back and bite him at some point. That someone might come looking. That's why him and Mom never married. And it's why he kept himself off of my birth certificate. To keep us both safe.'

Grace watched Dempsey's reaction as he processed everything she'd told him. When he spoke again, he focused on the one question Grace couldn't yet answer.

'OK. OK. Let's say for a minute that you're right. That Knowles is the great man you say. That he did nothing wrong in Tootkai. That he even sent you to warn me. If that's true – if you're right – then why is any of this happening?'

'What do you mean?'

'I mean, why has everyone who has even mentioned his war record been attacked?'

'I don't know.'

'And if the president is aware that death sentences are being handed down by the Secret Service, why is he doing nothing about it? Why did he have to speak to you in code?'

'I don't know, Dempsey!' Grace's voice was raised and emotional. 'I haven't had a personal conversation with John Knowles in three years. Ever since he went into that office. He is never alone. Ever.'

'Never?'

'No. And it's changed him. He isn't himself. He had all these dreams. Things he was going to do to make the country and the world better. He's done *none* of them. And the things he *has* done? Backtracking on environmental protections? Arms sales to Saudi? The medical insurance stuff? Damn it, *everything* he's done in the last three years . . . *none* of that is the John Knowles I know. *None* of it. He's not himself, Dempsey. And he's not the president he was supposed to be.

'I want to know why that is, just as much as you do. And I'm willing to do whatever it takes to get to the bottom of this. Even if it means proving you right on Tootkai. Even if it means discovering that Knowles and my dad were *never* the men I knew.'

She took a deep breath.

'Whatever it takes. I just want the truth.'

SIXTY-SIX

In the three years since his appointment as deputy assistant to the president, Kelvin Cunningham had not missed a single day of work. In fact, he had not missed even five minutes of a meeting.

His schedule was strict. He awoke each morning at 4 a.m. He would exercise, shower and dress, all in time to leave by 5.30 a.m. so he would be in the White House Office no later than 6 a.m.

The routine had become infamous. The source of endless conversations that included the question 'how does he do it?'

A question which, to Cunningham's mind, was the wrong way around. He could not understand why others did *not* live that way. He thrived on it. On the workload. On the schedule. He could hardly imagine another way of living.

And that, he always told himself, was why *he* was Kelvin Cunningham. Why he'd succeeded over those around him.

It was this obsessive routine that made today such an anomaly. It was 6.20 a.m. and Cunningham was not even up yet. He was still in his dressing gown, seated upright against the velvet head of his king-sized bed.

The contents of four manila files were strewn around him.

Four files. Four individuals. One mother-fucking nightmare.

File One. The largest by far. Information on Dale Victor.

Whatever Cunningham had been willing to admit, Victor *had* posed a problem to his organisation. The man was a populist. Just as John Knowles had been before the last election. Sure, Victor had none of Knowles' brilliance. And certainly none of his beliefs. But still, the man *was* electable. He *could* have beaten Knowles.

And if he had, he would have been that rare thing. An uncontrollable politician.

It was an unacceptable scenario for the organisation. A president they could not buy or blackmail. Dale Victor was too rich for the former, and too shameless for the latter. No scandal ever seemed to touch the man. He cared about nothing but his own rise to power, and it damn well looked like he might pull it off. And so when it seemed he might have something damaging on Knowles – something that could at the very least cost Knowles re-election and see him replaced with the uncontrollable Dale Victor – Cunningham had acted without hesitation.

After all the efforts the organisation had made to take control of the presidency? Cunningham couldn't lose it.

No. Victor had had to go. And so Cunningham had seen to it. He had done the right thing, he remained sure of that.

Even if it had triggered the shitstorm that had followed.

File Two. Much smaller. Nizar Mansour.

Where things had started to go wrong.

Mansour had seemed the perfect patsy for the bombing of Flight PA16. A few camera movements here and there, to dispel any doubt as to who had placed the bomb in the hold. A little planted evidence, to firm up the perceived motive. All designed to point to one man, a refugee from an Islamic war zone. And all ready to be found once Romeo Meyer's team had silenced him.

Except Mansour had *not* been silenced. Not yet, anyway. And as long as he was alive, he remained a ticking bomb. A problem that needed to be addressed. And in that respect he was far from alone.

File Three. Thicker again. ISB agent Joe Dempsey.

This one was a complication of a different kind. Another mistake. But this time his. The file told Cunningham of a long list of exploits and assignments. Information Cunningham *should* have accessed before authorising Braddock's team.

If I'd read this first . . . if I'd known what this sonofabitch was capable of . . . I'd have sent a whole fucking regiment.

But the mistake had been made. That couldn't be changed now. And because of it Dempsey was still alive and had gone to ground. And from what the file said about him, Cunningham doubted he would be found any time soon. Certainly not until he had achieved his objective.

And Cunningham thought he knew what that objective must be.

He wants to bring all this to Knowles' door. Afghanistan. Quilty. Victor. The plane. Everything.

It was a complication, yes. But as Cunningham thought more carefully, he began to realise that it was a complication that could work to his advantage.

Perhaps Knowles has served his purpose. Perhaps it's time for him to face the consequences of Tootkai . . .

His eyes settled on the final folder as he ruminated on the idea.

File Four. The slimmest of the bundles. Just a few pages. It was also the most recently complied.

Michael Devlin.

Cunningham shook his head as he picked up the paperwork

for the second time that morning. Another of Romeo Meyer's failures.

How the hell is this guy still alive?

Cunningham's stress had been building since he had taken the call two hours earlier. A call to tell him that the mission had failed. That instead of Michael Devlin, it was Romeo Meyer's best man now lying dead on a London railway track. Which meant that not only was the lawyer still alive – leaving a direct line open for Dempsey to find out what Mansour knew – there was now the body of a US agent to deal with.

Somehow Cunningham had suppressed his anger. He had not even raised his voice. What would have been the point? Romeo Meyer seemed oblivious to even the harshest criticism.

But now? As he looked at his best-laid plans strewn across his bed, a physical representation of the mess in which he now found himself, he could feel his blood pumping through the carotid artery that passed his right ear.

It had gone as far as he could allow, and so he knew what he had to do next. The thought made his heart beat even harder.

It was time to call the boss.

He reached out for the telephone next to his bed. One of two encrypted satellite phones on the property. Only a single person ever called it. And it, in turn, only ever called one person.

It was answered on the first ring.

'Kelvin.' The voice gave no hint of mood. It never did. 'You haven't used this line for a while.'

'I haven't needed to,' Cunningham replied. 'Not until now.'

'Are you calling about the mess in Manhattan or the mess in London?'

Cunningham had no answer. It was not how he had hoped to begin this conversation.

'Did you think I didn't know?'

'No. No. Of course … I …' Cunningham could hear himself flounder. He forced himself to calm down. 'No. I just thought I should bring you up to speed.'

'Seems a bit late for that. Since you've been trying to keep me in the dark about all this.'

'I haven't. I assure you. I just … you had other concerns. I didn't want to trouble you until everything was resolved.'

'Resolved? How, Kelvin? Resolved by way of four dead agents in New York? A dead agent in London? A professional killer now out there somewhere, gunning for Knowles? None of that sounds very resolved.'

Cunningham hesitated.

A dead agent in London? How the hell did he know that already?

'You're wondering how I know about Agent Hart.' It was not a question. 'The organisation has a lot more reach than you seem to think. If you had just come to me earlier, this could have been fixed immediately. It isn't like you haven't had the opportunity.'

'But—'

'Instead you have taken the chance of a lifetime and converted it into a noose around your own neck.'

Cunningham felt a chill at Dupart's choice of words. The organisation did not make idle threats.

'This has all gone too far, Kelvin. It needs to be over.'

'It will be. It—'

'I don't need blind reassurance. I need results. Clean up your mess. And if you don't, it will be cleaned for you. A process which you will *not* enjoy. Understood?'

Cunningham said nothing. For the first time in as long as he could remember, he was literally speechless.

` 'I'll take that as a yes.'

The phone went dead.

SIXTY-SEVEN

The roar of Will Duffy's car engine was deafening as he took the left-hand turn from Old Church Street to the Fulham Road and accelerated west.

Sarah Truman barely heard a thing.

She had been in a state of shock for almost an hour, the time it had taken Duffy to cover the distance from Belmarsh to Chelsea. Fifty-six minutes, to be exact. During which Sarah had just one thought in her mind and one aching fear in her gut.

Michael.

It had been Duffy who had taken the call, and so it had been Duffy who had broken the news to Sarah.

He'd been at Woolwich Crown Court waiting for Michael. They were due to conduct the short hearing where Michael would explain Nizar Mansour's condition to the judge. An essential stage of case management, where future dates would be set when Mansour would be well enough to attend court and enter his plea.

The case was listed for 9.45 a.m., but the time came and went with no sign of Michael. Duffy made call after call, all unanswered. Eventually – and unusually – the judge allowed the hearing to go ahead in Michael's absence, with the prosecutor explaining the facts of Mansour's assault and Duffy present to answer any questions the judge might have for the defence.

Even with the delay, the hearing was done by 10.30 a.m.

It left Duffy to spend the next two hours trying to find his barrister.

He called Michael again. No answer.

He called Sarah. No answer.

He called Michael's chambers. An answer, but no clue.

And so he finally called Bruce Bull. In the hope that the Detective Chief Inspector could make enquiries no one else could. By now Duffy was worried. A concern fuelled by the attack on Mansour. Danger and violence seemed to surround this case.

Bull, as always, had taken the request seriously. He promised to make all possible enquiries and come back with any news.

That would not be for several more hours, Duffy had anticipated. And so in the meantime he made the short, cold walk from Woolwich Crown Court to Belmarsh Prison, to visit the injured Nizar Mansour on the prison's hospital wing. It was a journey he made with both hope and dread.

Hope that Mansour would finally be awake, for the reassurance that he had suffered no lasting physical damage.

And dread for the news of Mansour's sister that Duffy would have to pass on if he *was* awake.

It was a dilemma Duffy did not ultimately face; the call came much sooner than expected. He'd not yet reached the hospital wing when he was intercepted by a prison guard and informed that he had a call waiting from New Scotland Yard.

The news from Bull made Duffy leave the prison immediately. He called Sarah as he did so but she remained unavailable. It was only as he passed through the prison's outer reception that he realised why.

Sarah was there, alongside her cameraman, demanding

access to an official and to be told what had happened to Nizar Mansour. The story Duffy had given her that morning.

And the story she abandoned as soon as he told her the news about Michael.

The next fifty-six minutes had passed in silence, save for the sound of Duffy's engine as he ferried Sarah through the London snow-bound traffic, determined to get her to Michael's side.

They reached the main reception of the Chelsea and Westminster Hospital within a minute of joining the Fulham Road. Sarah's passenger door was already opening as Duffy screeched the car to a stop.

'Don't wait for me,' he said as Sarah climbed out. 'I'll park and I'll be in right after. Get yourself moving, lass.'

Sarah didn't reply. For a moment, she didn't do *anything*. She seemed to freeze. All she could do was stare at the building's entrance, as the thoughts hit her like waves.

Michael ... Michael's hurt ... What if ... And ... And the baby ... he doesn't even know ...

She felt herself grow dizzy. A return of the nausea that had plagued her for days. Only this time it was not just her stomach. It was ... everywhere, making her head spin.

She stepped forward. A forced movement, and a weak one. It caused her to stumble. Only the thin signpost she grasped for stability kept her upright.

For a moment Sarah was unsure if she could take another step. If she could deal with what she might find inside. What if Michael never woke up? What if she never got to tell him. What if ...

Every possible negative thought crossed her mind at once. Exaggerated by the hormones flowing through her system. She felt her legs begin to buckle under their weight, as the world began to rotate around her.

She felt a strong arm under her own. It halted her fall, and then it lifted her back upright.

'C'mon now. We can't have both of you in hospital beds.'

Sarah looked into Duffy's smiling, reassuring face.

'Now let's get you inside.'

It took almost ten minutes for Duffy and Sarah to reach the ICU. Ten minutes of searching. Of redirection. Of broken lifts and confusing stairwells.

When they finally reached the ICU's main reception desk, Sarah had to reach out and grip the wooden surface to steady herself. She took a few long, deep breaths to regain her composure. They did nothing to clear the fog from her mind, but they seemed to catch the attention of the ICU nurse.

The nurse climbed to her feet and moved around the desk, towards Sarah.

'Miss, are you OK?'

'I'm . . . I'm fine . . .' Sarah replied shakily. 'My fiancé is here. Michael . . . Michael Devlin.'

'Miss, you don't look OK.' The nurse looked concerned.

'I said I'm fine, I just need to find Michael.'

'Miss, I think—'

'No!' Sarah's adrenaline sent a surge of defiant strength through her body. The flood focused her mind, if only for a moment. 'I want to see Michael. Where is he?'

The nurse stepped back. For a moment she seemed unsure what to do. Then she moved back around the desk and accessed the computer.

'What was the name again?'

'Michael Devlin,' Duffy replied. Sarah flashed him a grateful look as he took over. 'He was involved in some sort of fight on the Underground.'

'Oh.' Duffy's description had worked better than a name. 'Yes, sorry. He is here.'

'Where?' Sarah demanded. 'I want to see him?'

'I'm sorry, you can't. Not yet. He's undergoing tests.'

Sarah felt her legs give way. Only Duffy was keeping her upright.

'I want to see him.'

'I'm afraid you can't.' The nurse's response was firm. 'But please, listen. Michael is OK. He was hurt, yes. He's broken his wrist and his ankle, he's damaged his shoulder and he has some blood loss from a head injury. But he's awake now and he seems OK. Alright? He seems OK.'

'He's . . .' Sarah could not finish her sentence as she began to cry.

Duffy pulled her into himself, holding her close. Then he turned to the nurse.

'What tests is he having?' he asked.

'He had a head injury and he was unconscious. It's standard procedure that he has to have a CT after that. But still, he seemed fully with it when he woke up.'

'You're sure?'

'I'm as sure as I'm allowed to be. Your fiancé is in good hands. You'll be able to see him soon.' She indicated to Sarah. 'Now, if you don't mind me saying, you look like you need to sit down.'

SIXTY-EIGHT

T he secure compound for the United Nations Assistance Mission in Afghanistan was located fifteen miles south-west of Kabul.

First built on a much smaller scale during the time of Soviet occupation in the 1980s, it had been all but abandoned during the 1990s and the rule of the Taliban. A period when outside interference of any sort was unwanted there.

The invasion of the Western coalition following 9/11 had changed that. It quickly broke the Taliban's grip on Afghanistan, but at the same time it had caused a humanitarian crisis of a different kind. A crisis that once again called for the attention of the international community.

The United Nations had answered the call, and with its near-unlimited funding it had gradually turned its previous Afghan outpost into virtually a city. The compound had every convenience and amenity its predominantly Western inhabitants were used to. Including, crucially, one of the few runways in this part of the country that could accommodate an Airbus A330.

Eden Grace shook her head as she descended the long staircase from the plane to the tarmac.

'This is Afghanistan?' she asked, looking back towards Dempsey. He was several steps behind her.

'This doesn't exist,' Dempsey replied. 'At least not officially. The actual headquarters is in the city itself.'

'I was talking about the weather. I thought it was hot out here?'

'In the summer it is,' Dempsey replied. 'But it's winter now.'

'So what the hell is *this* place?' she asked, returning to his first answer. 'If it doesn't exist?'

'This is where things actually get done. When the UN moves into a country, they get gifted a base. Usually too small, usually impractical. And always bugged from top to bottom. They always take it. Diplomacy and all that. But then they find somewhere of their own. Somewhere secure and off the radar.'

'This is off the radar?'

'What that means differs from country to country. If this were Europe then they'd make do with a few farms, maybe, all next to each other, disguised so as not to be too much of a public insult. But here? It helps to be a little more . . . overt. Sends a message of their capability.'

'So the Afghans know about this?'

'Of course they do. Every country knows about every private compound. They just pretend not to. And the UN pretends the same.'

'Really?'

'It's a fiction, Eden. A smokescreen. It always has been.'

Grace shook her head again as she reached the bottom of the staircase.

'Is anything I've ever been told true?' she asked as she stepped onto the crisp snow that was settling on the tarmac.

'I'm sure there must be *something*,' Dempsey replied with a smile.

He joined her on the ground just as two UN representatives approached. A man and a woman. Both in their thirties, a few years older than Grace. And both dressed for the cold.

The woman spoke first. Her accent was Texan, for which Dempsey had a soft spot.

'Agent Dempsey. Special Agent Grace. Welcome to Kabul.'

'Thank you,' Dempsey said, shaking her hand. 'And you are?'

'Olivia Henson.' She indicated to the man beside her. 'And this is Bill Walker.'

'Pleasure to meet you.'

Walker's accent was as American as Henson's, but from a very different part of that massive country. Midwestern, to Dempsey's ear.

'You too,' Dempsey replied. He turned back to Henson. She had taken the lead from the start and was clearly Walker's superior. 'Is everything arranged?'

'It is. Though Jangi Shah Karzai still won't be here for a few hours yet. He was . . . difficult to control.'

'What does that mean?'

'It means that once we told him of Thomas Quilty's death, he said he needed to deal with a few things. And he refused to come with us until he had done so. But he assured our team that he'll be here to meet with you as soon as he can.'

'And what exactly are the "things" he was dealing with?'

'He wouldn't tell us any more than that. But I get the impression he'll have something useful for you once he arrives.'

Dempsey was less than impressed. He had expected Shah to be here, ready to move without delay. From the moment he and Grace had entered the compound, there was no way to keep their presence a secret. UN employees or not, the odds were on someone here being loyal to whoever was pulling Jack Meyer's strings. Dempsey had to assume that. And so time was now of the essence.

But still, he could do nothing without Jangi Shah.

He turned to what he could control.

'Do we have the transport set up? To take us into Goshta once we're ready to move?'

'We have an MH-X Stealth Black Hawk, fully fuelled and waiting to deploy. Just like you asked.'

'And weapons?'

'Anything you need, sir,' Walker replied, which suggested that the armoury was his department. 'We're fully stocked and waiting.'

'You're the quartermaster?'

'Sir.'

'OK. Agent Grace and I will come over and take a look shortly.'

Dempsey turned back to Henson.

'And the medical team I asked for? To check out my shoulder?'

'Primed to go. And as requested, it's a tight team. Full clearance only. No one else will know you've seen them.'

'Good. We need to keep the procedure locked down. Because I need them to do something a little extra for me while they're there.'

'Sir?'

'I'll tell them what it is when they're ready. It won't cause a problem.'

'Sir.'

Dempsey turned to Grace.

'Eden, I'm going to the medics alone. If Jangi Shah is still hours away, that gives you a chance for a few more hours' rest. I suggest you take it.'

'You sure you don't want me with you?'

'No, I'm fine. It won't take them long to patch me up properly. After that I'll be getting some sleep too. It might be a while until we get another chance.'

'And once Jangi Shah is here? You'll come for me, right?'

'There's no way I'll do this without you, Agent Grace. I promise.'

'You're sure?'

'I'm sure. Now go get some shut eye while I let these guys sew me up.'

SIXTY-NINE

Knowles tried to focus on what he was being told. With everything else that had been happening, environmental policy wasn't his priority.

'He's willing to start a trial run on the clickbait algorithm immediately, Mr President,' Nicolas Dupart was saying. 'Even before the funding is in place. In my opinion it's the sensible course to take. And I've taken the liberty to speak to Kelvin on the topic in advance of this meeting and he agrees with that assessment. Don't you, Kelvin?'

Nicolas Dupart paused, clearly awaiting a contribution from Cunningham.

Knowles' eyes followed in the same direction.

Cunningham was in his usual seat. His mind, though, seemed somewhere else entirely.

'Kelvin?'

There was a tone of irritation in Dupart's voice that surprised Knowles. He usually found the senior advisor to be quite emotionless. And it was rare for anyone to direct any form of displeasure at the intimidating deputy assistant. It seemed to break through whatever had been preoccupying Cunningham.

'Yes?' He turned to face Dupart.

'Are you OK, Kelvin?' Knowles had never seen Cunningham so distracted either. But then his mood was understandable.

Cunningham's eyes flicked towards him.

'Yes. Yes, I'm fine. Why?'

'Because you don't seem to have heard a word Nick's been saying. Is something wrong?'

Cunningham glared at Knowles. And the president knew why. Yes, there was something wrong. But it was not something Cunningham would want to discuss in the presence of Nicolas Dupart.

'I'm sorry.' Cunningham smiled. A false one, Knowles could tell. For the benefit of their guest. 'I . . . I didn't get much sleep last night. It must be catching up with me.'

'You're sure that's all it is, Kelvin?' Dupart asked, though without a hint of concern. 'It's not something we can help with?'

'No. No, Nick. It's nothing. I just . . .' Cunningham seemed to be thinking fast '. . . maybe I should have listened to your advice yesterday, after you told me about your father. I think it hit me harder than I realised.'

Dupart nodded his head.

'I thought that might be it. Remember what I said to you yesterday. If you need time, time to . . . whatever, I'm sure President Knowles will give you it.'

'I hadn't realised anyone had died.' Knowles was confused by the exchange. 'Your father, Nick?'

'Yes, Mr President. Yesterday. After a long illness.'

'I'm sorry to hear that. And Kelvin knew him?'

'For a very long time, Mr President, yes. He was kind of a mentor to Kelvin. Wasn't he?'

'Then why are you both still here?' Knowles did not wait for Cunningham to answer Dupart's question. 'For Christ's sake, this stuff can wait, surely?'

'My father would have wanted me to keep working, sir,' Dupart explained. 'It was very much the family ethos. I would be dishonouring him if I did not follow it now.'

'But—'

Knowles did not finish his sentence. He was interrupted by a knock on the one of the Oval Office doors. Knowles looked towards it, just as Assistant Director Jack Meyer stepped through the doorway.

Once again, Meyer looked red with stress.

Dupart rose to his feet immediately.

'Mr President, I think I know this drill. I'll be in my office when you're ready to continue.'

'Thanks, Nick.'

'Of course.'

Dupart turned and left without another word, passing Meyer as he went. For his part, Meyer hardly seemed to notice him at all.

With Dupart gone, Meyer silently indicated for Special Agents Hodge and Reynolds to follow suit.

The agents did as they were instructed, with Reynolds closing the office door behind them. Meyer checked that it was fully closed before he stepped forward.

'Sir, we've located Joe Dempsey.'

'Where?'

It was Cunningham who spoke. He was on his feet and inches from Meyer by the time he did so, having almost leapt from his chair at the news.

'Afghanistan, sir. In the United Nations compound southwest of Kabul.'

Cunningham shot a glance towards Knowles. This was unexpected, and it could only have one meaning: Dempsey was going after the truth about Tootkai. And he was moving much more quickly than anyone had anticipated.

He turned back to Meyer.

'How good is your intelligence?'

'Solid, sir. We have people in that compound. They report that an Agent Joe Dempsey arrived there by Airbus A330 within the last hour. He was carrying an injury to his shoulder that needed emergency medical care.'

'Shit.'

'And he was not alone, sir.'

Bitterness had crept into Meyer's voice. Knowles could not miss it. Nor could he mistake the hatred that now filled the man's eyes.

Knowles knew the answer to his next question before he even asked it.

'Who was he with?'

'According to my sources, he was travelling with Special Agent Eden Grace of the United States Secret Service.'

Cunningham's eyes shot back to Knowles. This time there was no look of shared concern. This time, the glance was an accusation.

'Eden Grace is with Dempsey?' His eyes remained fixed on Knowles as he questioned Meyer. 'You're sure?'

'Not a doubt in my mind,' Meyer replied.

Cunningham nodded, his eyes still fixed on the president.

Knowles knew what they were thinking. After everything he had told them – after his assurances of Grace's loyalty – it made no sense that she would have betrayed them. There could be only one explanation . . .

'Why did you insist that Grace went after Dempsey?' Cunningham's voice was low. Dangerous.

'What are you suggesting, Kelvin?'

'I'm not suggesting anything, *John*.' The use of Knowles' first name was a message. The daily pretence of who was in charge had been suspended. 'I'm just asking you a question. Why did you put her on Jack's team?'

'I put her on there because I thought I could trust her.' Knowles spoke slowly, as if educating a child. 'I sent her to avoid the screw-ups you've made throughout this whole thing.'

'BULLSHIT!' Cunningham's self-control seemed to snap. 'DID YOU SEND HER TO HELP HIM? DID YOU FUCKING *PLAN* THIS?'

The president rose to his feet, standing tall at his full six feet three inches. He towered over Cunningham. A size difference that did nothing to intimidate the smaller man.

Still, Knowles pressed what was – for now – his only advantage.

'You need to remember who you're speaking to, Kelvin.'

'Who I'm speaking to?' Cunningham's volume had lowered again. His disrespect had not. 'I'll tell you who I'm speaking to. A fucking puppet. A pretend fucking president who's here to do whatever the fuck I tell him. That's who *I'm* speaking to. And *you* better not forget *that*.'

If Cunningham could see the hate in Knowles' eyes . . .

If he had noticed the president's large, powerful fists, driven into the leather top of the Resolute desk . . .

If he had observed either, they did not seem to concern him.

Cunningham believed that he held the power. Knowles knew that. And he believed there was nothing that Knowles could do to change that. Cunningham was about to discover he was wrong.

'Did you send her to help Dempsey?'

Knowles said nothing.

'DID YOU SEND HER TO HELP DEMPSEY?'

Cunningham screamed the question into Knowles' face. It left spittle running down the president's cheek. And it was more than Knowles could tolerate. With a speed unexpected for a man of his size, he swept his right hand up from the table and struck Cunningham full in the face with an open hand.

The sheer power of the blow sent Cunningham to the floor, stunned.

An instant later and Knowles was moving. Around the desk. Towards the prone Cunningham.

And directly into the sights of Jack Meyer's drawn pistol.

'You need to calm down, Mr President.'

Knowles stepped back, his eyes never leaving Cunningham as the deputy assistant climbed to his feet.

'Get back behind that desk and take your seat,' Cunningham ordered. He brushed down his now dishevelled suit and straightened his tie.

At first Knowles didn't move. Not until Meyer reiterated the instruction by gesturing with his pistol. Even then Knowles thought twice, but he knew enough to recognise his own limitations.

And so he did as Cunningham had instructed.

'I think it's time you told me some truths,' Cunningham said coldly. 'Why would you want to save Dempsey? You understand what you have to lose if this all unravels?'

'You know I do,' Knowles replied. 'If I didn't, I'd have done much worse already.'

'One call, John. One call to the Blackspear compound

outside of Tootkai and the threat becomes real. Is that what you want?'

'Go fuck yourself, Kelvin.'

'Go fuck myself? Go fuck myself? Jesus, John. When did you grow these balls? Twelve years you've been quaking about Tootkai. Enough to do whatever you're told, just to keep it quiet. And now I can go fuck myself?'

'Nothing happened in Tootkai. And you know it.'

'If I say it happened, it fucking happened . . .'

Cunningham trailed off. It seemed that all was becoming ever clearer to him as he spoke. He took a few seconds to gather his thoughts.

'That's what this is all about, isn't it? You think Dempsey can find out the truth. You knew you couldn't send anyone directly, not without us finding out. So you somehow orchestrated this whole thing. All to prompt Dempsey to go to Afghanistan. So he can exonerate you.'

'I couldn't give a shit about being exonerated.' Knowles was angry. He was through playing games. 'I'm finished, whatever happens, Kelvin. I've let you own me. You and the sonsofbitches you answer to. I let you control this office. I let you control my presidency. I'll pay the price for that. But I didn't do it for me. And you know that.'

'I know who it was for, you pathetic fucking martyr. That's why this is so sad. Because everything you've done for them – everything you've let happen, just to protect them – well now it's been for nothing.'

Knowles had known the risks. The consequences should Dempsey and Grace fail. How could he not? This was the very threat that had been hanging over him for his entire political career. But knowledge did not make it any easier to accept.

He stared at Cunningham in furious silence.

'Did you think we wouldn't do it?' Cunningham demanded. 'That after everything, it was just an empty threat? Well think again, Mr President. Because within the hour we'll have twenty, thirty different victims and witnesses, all in place in Tootkai, all ready to testify to what you and your unit did in there. Once the world has heard from them and once it's seen the video of your good friend Chief Lopez in action, you'll be lucky if all you get is life imprisonment.'

'You piece of shit. You know that video isn't what it looks like. You know why he killed those men.'

'What I know, Mr President, is that my organisation has a video of your chief petty officer killing two US citizens in Tootkai. The same man you put up for a Medal of Honor with no mention of what he'd done, making yourself a liar in the process. Now it's time to pay for that, John. And thanks to you, every one of your unit is going down with you.'

Knowles was silent. What was there to say? For now, Cunningham held the cards.

For now.

'Oh, and in case you think I forgot your little friend from the Secret Service. Well, I haven't. We're going to send Romeo's whole unit to Tootkai to link up with the Blackspear team. And together, they're going to find Joe Dempsey. Even *he* can't take *that* many.

'And once they've found out from him just how much your little masterplan has compromised us with the ISB? He'll die, John. Which will leave your little friend Eden with no one to protect her from Romeo, from every one of his men and from whatever Afghan goat-herders might be passing by. All because of you and your big fucking ideas.'

Knowles' fists tightened at the reference. He was ready to leap from his chair. Only Meyer's pistol kept him in place.

'You thought you were smart, John,' Cunningham continued. 'And you were. But I'm smarter. And now everyone you tried to protect? They're all going to be dead or in jail. Every one of them. And it was you who did it to them all.'

SEVENTY

Will Duffy opened the door to the Intensive Care Unit and stepped back to let Sarah go through first.

It had been an hour since they had arrived at Chelsea and Westminster Hospital. An hour since they had been reassured that Michael would live. An hour since Sarah had finally allowed herself to breathe.

Unable to see Michael while he underwent routine tests, Duffy had given his number to a nurse who had promised to call them as soon as Michael was allowed visitors. Sarah had still been reluctant to leave the reception desk. But she finally allowed Duffy to persuade her to join him in the Starbucks by the building's main entrance.

And as they were sat there, Duffy had guessed her secret.

'How far gone are you?' he'd asked.

The question had hit Sarah like a bolt of lightning. She'd sat upright, too flustered to even meet his eyes at first.

But once she'd admitted he was right, she'd felt a surge of relief. She'd thought about little else for days, but had had no one to talk to. In a way, it had helped that she didn't know Duffy well. And she'd been grateful to finally have a release for her pent-up thoughts and questions. And so for the next half hour they had distracted themselves from Michael's condition, and from the threat that still hung over them.

A distraction that had ended when Duffy had received the call.

Sarah felt increasingly nervous as they moved towards

Michael's room. The anticipation of seeing him – of finding out exactly how bad his injuries were – was bad enough. But with what she had to tell him as well? Perhaps it wasn't the right time. But she wasn't sure how much longer she could keep the news to herself.

Taking a steadying breath, Sarah stepped into the room. The first thing she noticed was that they were not alone. Bruce Bull. Sarah recognised him from her coverage of the case.

'Bruce,' she heard Duffy say as he came in behind her. 'What's going on?'

'Just following up with Michael after the attack on him this morning,' Bull replied. 'Given his involvement in the Mansour case and the . . . complications.'

Sarah paid no attention to their conversation as she stepped hesitantly towards Michael's bed. Her first view of him gave her a jolt of energy. He was not only awake but smiling. Rushing to his bedside, she threw her arms around his neck.

'You're OK,' she said. She could hear the tremor of emotion in her own voice. 'You're OK.'

With two visibly damaged arms, Michael could not hug back. Sarah, though, didn't notice. She just gripped him tight.

'I'm OK,' he said, as she finally let go and stepped back to look at him. As she did she saw Duffy and Bull approaching the bed.

'How are you feeling, big man?' Duffy asked.

Sarah could see a haziness in Michael's eyes as he looked up in response. Painkillers, perhaps. Or the head injury.

'Lucky,' Michael replied. His accent was almost indiscernible through his low, scratchy voice. 'I should have died.'

'Should have nothing,' Duffy replied. 'You're here and that's all that matters.'

'You know what happened?' Michael asked.

'I know what Bruce told me,' Duffy replied, indicating towards Bull as he spoke. 'And the rest of the story tells itself, doesn't it? The station cameras show a guy pushing his way after you, to the end of the platform, then climbing down after you.'

'It was him. The Secret Service agent from the court yesterday.'

'Hang on,' Sarah interrupted, confused. 'You were attacked by someone from the Secret Service? The US Secret Service?'

'Yes,' Michael said. He turned to look at Bull. 'It was definitely him.'

'I don't doubt you,' Bull said. 'Not that anyone's gonna be able to prove it.'

'What?' Michael replied. 'Why not?'

'The man on the tracks couldn't be identified,' Bull confirmed. 'No ID, no identifying marks or tattoos, no fingerprints on record, no dental records known. All of which makes sense if what you've just said is right. If he's a spook, we'll never pin him down.'

'And this is all because of the Mansour case?' Sarah asked, hardly able to believe what she was hearing.

'Undoubtedly,' Duffy replied.

'Then . . . then what the hell happens next?'

'You're all getting protection,' Bull replied. 'It's already arranged. There'll be an officer on the door to this room for the duration of Michael's stay. In the meantime, I'm putting you into protective custody, Miss Truman. To be joined by Michael when he's released from the hospital.'

'Protection? From the Secret Service? You're not serious?'

'I'm afraid so,' Bull replied. 'It's the only way we can guarantee your safety.'

'But . . . but for how long?'

'No way of knowing. Until this all settles, certainly.'

'But that . . . that could be months. Years.'

'I doubt that,' Bull replied. 'But honestly, it will take as long as it takes.'

Sarah shook her head, feeling slightly dazed as she looked from face to face. Finally, her eyes settled on Michael.

'I can't believe this is happening again,' she said.

'I'm so sorry,' Michael replied. 'I was . . . look . . . the last thing I wanted to do was put you in danger.'

'This isn't your fault, Michael. You couldn't have known when you took the case.' She glanced towards Duffy. 'Neither of you could have known.'

'But still. I can't keep doing this to you. Police protection. For Christ's sake, Sarah. Who else has to do that twice in a year?'

Sarah took a deep breath. This was not an ideal situation. But it was what it was. They would get through it. Just like they'd got through everything else.

'Listen to me, Michael Devlin,' she started. 'I thought maybe I'd lost you today. I haven't and that's all that matters, really. And if keeping you means I have to do this again? Then I have to do this again. Because I'm not losing you, Michael. And I'm not losing our family.'

'You'll never lose me. I'm still here after today, aren't I? And you won't lose Anne, either,' Michael said firmly. He turned to Duffy. 'Is Anne here, too? Is she coming with us?'

Sarah felt a flicker of nerves. Michael had misunderstood her reference to family.

'Who's Anne?' Duffy looked confused.

'She's Michael's sister-in-law,' Sarah answered. 'She lives with us, although she's back in Ireland at the moment. But she's not who I meant when I said family.'

Sarah placed her hands on her abdomen as she spoke and looked at her fiancé with a smile.

Michael's brow furrowed for a moment.

And he finally understood.

'You're bloody joking?'

Sarah could hear the emotion that filled his voice. He forced his body upwards, his face a mix of disbelief and happiness.

Sarah met Michael halfway, her arms once again around his neck.

'It's true,' she whispered. 'It's true.'

Michael took the embrace and all the pain and the tears that came with it. And when it was done, he held Sarah close and looked to Bull.

'OK, whatever you need us to do. Wherever you need us to go. We'll do it.'

SEVENTY-ONE

Dempsey opened his eyes at the sound of approaching footsteps, bringing himself from sleep to full consciousness in a heartbeat. An instant later and he was on his feet, his pistol gripped in his good right hand.

The sound of a light tap on the door made him lower the weapon. The UN Assistance Mission compound was secure enough. And assassins rarely knocked.

'Who is it?'

'It's Eden.'

'OK. Wait a sec.'

Dempsey grabbed a black undershirt from the fully stocked cupboard Olivia Henson had arranged. He pulled it on slowly, careful to preserve the surgical-standard dressing that was finally protecting his left shoulder. Then he turned to his new, fibre-optic framed sling.

The specialists had taken their time with this one. They had ensured that it supported Dempsey in all the ways he wanted, allowing him to continue with his mission despite his injury. But for it to remain effective required care, and so Dempsey had paid close attention to exactly how the sling was to be worn.

Grace had a quizzical look on her face when he opened the door. She seemed to find the sight of a now fully dressed, mission-ready Joe Dempsey amusing.

'You always take that long to get dressed?' she asked, her tone mocking.

'You'd rather I was still in my underwear?'

'Like I'd even notice.'

'I guess that's a fair point,' Dempsey replied. 'So what's up?'

'Jangi Shah.' The change in subject removed all humour from Grace's voice. Back to business. 'He's on site.'

'About time.' Dempsey looked at his watch. 'He was only supposed to be a few hours. It's been almost ten. Has he given anyone an explanation for the delay?'

'Henson says he's been in Tootkai,' Grace explained. 'And she says he has big news.'

The answer was not unexpected. They had been told on arrival that Shah had taken the news of Quilty's death badly; that it had compelled him to carry out his own investigation. It made sense that it would end where it had begun.

What Dempsey had not expected was that Shah's investigation would go anywhere. After all, Quilty had discovered nothing himself when he had investigated the Tootkai incident. So to now hear that Shah had 'big news'?

If he's been making progress this whole time, all the better.

Dempsey slipped his pistol into the belt-mounted holster that had replaced the previous shoulder harness and indicated to the door.

'Let's go hear his news.'

The small meeting room was well-furnished. A sixty-inch flat-screen television was mounted on the wall. Positioned for the clearest view from any of the five mesh-backed office chairs that surrounded three sides of the room's square, wooden-topped table.

A table which, when Dempsey and Grace entered the room, was already occupied by Jangi Shah. A tall, slim man with a gentle voice and delicate, manicured hands, he was dressed in a perfectly fitted tweed suit. No doubt expensive when first purchased, it had seen better days. Still, Shah wore it with a dignity that was at odds with the hell through which he had lived.

Everything about the man was unobtrusive and respectable.

The perfect spy, Dempsey thought.

'You knew Thomas Quilty?'

Shah's English was perfect. His mind sharp.

Dempsey spotted the test.

'Well enough to know that only two people ever called him Thomas,' Dempsey replied. 'And that neither of them was you.'

Shah smiled sadly. It told Dempsey that he had given the right answer.

'Sometimes the simplest questions reveal the most important truths,' Shah said.

'In what way?'

'You are not the first man to come to me who claimed to know Quilty.' Shah stopped for just a moment. 'But you are the first who truly did.'

Dempsey saw the underlying message for what it was.

'When was this? Do you know who they worked for? Did you tell them anything?'

'The men came a month ago. I did not know who they worked for.'

'Then that would have been Victor's people. But what did you tell them?'

'They did not know Quilty. That much was clear from their first words. And so I told them nothing.'

'You didn't tell them anything about Tootkai?'

'Like I said. I told them nothing.'

'Then . . .' Dempsey hesitated. 'Then Dale Victor really did know nothing. You didn't tell them, and Quilty sure as hell didn't. Which leaves no one else.'

'I think that you are correct,' Shah replied.

Dempsey thought back to the footage of Dale Victor.

What was it he'd said?

Dempsey closed his eyes, replaying the recording in his mind.

Things happen in war. Bad things. We'll see what the president has to say about those things when the time comes.

'He never mentioned anything specific,' he confirmed. He opened his eyes as he spoke.

'And he was not a man to hold on to a secret?'

'He was not,' Dempsey replied. 'If Victor had known something, he'd have said it. No matter the consequences. He was just that way.'

'So what was he doing?' Grace asked. 'If he didn't know anything . . .'

'He was testing the waters.' Dempsey's mind was racing. 'He'd got wind of *something*. Enough for his men to ask Quilty for the specifics. There must have been some mention of Shah in Quilty's file that led them here when Quilty wouldn't say anything, to see what *he* could tell them. But that was all. He . . . he didn't have any facts.'

'You mean he got himself killed for nothing?'

'It looks that way. Him and all those other poor people on the plane with him.' Dempsey turned from Grace to Shah. 'OK, you didn't tell Victor's men. Have you ever told anyone else?'

'This information? I only ever passed it to one man, Mr Dempsey. To the one man I could trust. And to no one else.'

'You mean Quilty.'

'I do.'

'And you know he died for what you told him, don't you?'

'I am aware.' Shah looked to the floor as he acknowledged Quilty's passing.

'Then you also need to know this: I intend to find the men who caused Quilty's death. The men behind this entire thing. I don't care who they are. I don't care if it's the president of the United States himself. I am going to find them, and I am going to bring them to justice for what they've done. To do that, I could use your help. Will you help me? For Quilty?'

Shah did not blink as he looked up from the floor and met Dempsey's gaze.

'Then you have the same intention as me, Mr Dempsey. Quilty, he was my brother. As true as my own blood. But for him, but for what he did for me, I would have died many times. Just as he would have without me. A man does not forget that, Mr Dempsey. And a man does not forgive. So yes, I will help you. I will help you to avenge my brother.'

Dempsey said nothing in response. Just nodded his head. He could see that Shah had more to say.

'And I will start that help by telling you this . . . The devil who did this? Who is behind *all* of this? It is *not* your president.'

SEVENTY-TWO

From the beginning of the meeting Grace had deferred to Dempsey. He'd proved himself effective and honest. She trusted him. And besides, of the two of them, this was his world, not hers.

But after Shah's statement that President John Knowles was *not* behind Victor or Quilty's deaths?

'How do you know that?'

Grace asked the question instinctively, before Dempsey had the chance. It brought Shah's full focus onto her for the first time since they'd entered the room.

'You are Secret Service?' Shah asked. A deduction from their earlier introduction.

'I am. I work at the White House. And I've been telling Dempsey all along that the president didn't do these things. Are you saying that I'm right?'

Shah looked from Dempsey to Grace, then back to Dempsey. He seemed unsure whether to respond to her interjection.

'She can be trusted,' Dempsey offered, for what his word was worth to a man he had just met. 'I wouldn't be with her if she couldn't.'

Shah nodded and turned to Grace. When he spoke again he sounded weary.

'What I am saying is that your president did not do the things he has been accused of in Tootkai. He has nothing to cover up. And so it seems unlikely that he had anything to do with these deaths.'

'I don't understand,' Grace was genuinely confused. It was what she wanted to hear, and yet it made little sense. 'It was *you* who originally told Quilty that the president and his SEAL team committed war crimes. Why did you tell him that if it's not true?'

'Because I only know *now* that it is wrong,' Shah replied. 'Three years ago I was told very specific details, by a resident of Tootkai, of what had happened. A man I had every reason to trust. So I passed that intelligence on to Quilty.'

'And who had told you this?'

'My contact was Aryo Bahnam Karzai. One of my own tribe. A brother since the hills. He told me he was present when the attack occurred. That he had been hidden but had witnessed it. I believed him then. He was a loyal brother.

'No others in Tootkai spoke. They were too afraid. But something *had* happened. Knowles' team *had* been there. People *had* been hurt and killed. I saw the graves. I believed then that was enough to confirm the story.'

'How did he know it was President Knowles?' Grace asked.

'Because in the years since the attack, they had seen Knowles on television. They had watched as his power grew. *This* was why the villagers would not speak, I was told. They feared the Americans. They feared that if they named the man who was now the president, the Americans would come back.'

Grace glanced back to Dempsey again. The explanation made some sense, she had to admit. But still, it did not fit with what Shah had already said.

'So what makes you think the story isn't true now?'

'Quilty always doubted what Aryo had told me. And he told me his superiors felt the same. The last time we spoke, he said he was no longer sure any more. He said he was going to ask around again. I did not hear anything more from him.

'Then your people found me, told me of Quilty's death. That changed everything. They had murdered my brother. They had killed him to hide what I had discovered. I could not forgive that. I could not dishonour myself by doing nothing. I vowed to avenge Quilty. To do that, I needed Aryo.'

Shah paused to take a sip of water.

'Did you find him?'

'Yes. I went to Tootkai. I found Aryo.'

'And what did he tell you?'

'At first nothing. He refused to speak. He refused to help me at all. As if I were a stranger. It was unexpected.'

'So?'

'So I forced him to speak. To tell me the truth.'

'You forced him?' Dempsey interrupted. 'How?'

'This is not a question to which you want an answer,' Shah replied.

Dempsey opened his mouth to respond, but Grace spoke first.

'What did Aryo tell you?'

Shah took his eyes away from Dempsey and focused again on Grace.

'He told me that everything he had told me before was a lie. President Knowles and his team, they *were* there. They *did* go to Tootkai. But their reason was truthful. American citizens had been taken hostage by a Taliban group in the village. They went there to rescue them. They did that and they left. Nothing more.'

'But the graves. You said you saw—'

'Yes, the graves. I saw them and they were why Aryo lied to me. The story that he told me, it was not ready to be revealed. It was for later. But I found the mass grave and I demanded an explanation. And so Aryo told me the lie, because he knew he could not tell me the truth behind it. And he did not think that his lie would reach the Americans.'

'The truth?' Grace ignored the final sentence.

'The truth that the graves came from a second incursion in Tootkai. One which occurred much later. A year, perhaps.'

'By who?'

'There is a private defence contractor – mercenaries, we can call them – based near to Tootkai. They call themselves Blackspear. It was the executives of the company that owns this base who had been taken hostage. Who Knowles' team had been sent to free. And during Knowles' mission, the mercenaries from the base were already in Tootkai. Looking for the same hostages.'

'You mean the missions crossed over?' Dempsey asked.

'Yes, at first. But Knowles ordered them to leave when he and his team arrived.'

'And what does that have to do with the second incursion? What happened?'

'Aryo told me that it was Blackspear again. They drove into Tootkai and just attacked. They killed men, women and children. They raped. They tortured. And then they told the villagers that were left alive that worse would come to them if they did not cooperate.'

'Cooperate how?'

'They said that a time might come when new villagers would arrive. Brought in by Blackspear. These new villagers would tell a story. A story that blamed American forces for what Blackspear had done. They were told to support that story, whatever it might be.'

'New villagers? What . . .'

'Professional witnesses,' Shah explained. 'Taught to lie. And taught the details needed to support those lies. They would be brought to Tootkai as if they had lived there their whole lives. Imported victims, trained to bring down your president.'

Grace could not believe what she was hearing. It was . . . incredible.

'I don't understand,' she said. 'Why . . . why would they set all of this up to incriminate President Knowles and then . . . well . . . *not* incriminate him.'

'What do you mean?'

'I mean that Aryo told you these lies three years ago. So this whole thing – this whole set-up – it's been ready to go for that long. So why hasn't anyone come after Knowles? Why has the story never come out?'

'Because it's a threat, that's why.'

Grace looked at Dempsey, puzzled.

'What?'

'This wasn't done in order to get rid of Knowles. This was done to *control* him.'

'Blackmail . . .'

'Exactly.' Dempsey nodded. 'Using a story that isn't true. And one which will never do him any harm provided he does as he's told. But one that can be brought to life with a single phone call to Blackspear.'

'Jesus Christ.'

'You said it,' Dempsey agreed. 'This lot weren't interested in bringing down a president; they did this to *own* a president. The question is, if it isn't even true, how've they got him to go along with it? They must have something more compelling than some fake witnesses.'

Dempsey turned to Shah.

'When you left Tootkai did you notice anything? Any unusual activity?'

'No. What are you thinking may have happened?'

'I'm thinking that our arrival in Afghanistan will have reached the White House by now. It was always going to; I knew it put us against the clock. But if a single phone call can put this whole thing in motion . . .'

'Then they could already have pressed "go" on the set-up,' Grace concluded.

'Exactly. For all we know, Blackspear could already be moving the fake victims and witnesses into place.'

'So what do we do?'

'We get to Tootkai as soon as we can. And we find Aryo.'

'Aryo?' Shah asked.

'You said he was your tribesman. A brother. I know what that means, Jangi. It means he was a fighter, just like you. Not a man to be intimidated by anyone.'

'That would be a fair description.'

'A man like that, he didn't lie to you because someone threatened him. There had to have been something else. He must have been paid to tell you this story.'

Shah nodded.

'I reached the same conclusion.'

'Which means he'll have details on who paid him. Information we can use that proves this is a set-up.' Dempsey looked at Shah for confirmation. 'He might even have some sort of solid evidence.'

'He knows enough that he can help,' Shah agreed. 'Real

evidence? I do not know. But it is possible. Aryo has never been a fool.'

'Either way, he's the only witness we've got. And we can't use what he said to Jangi under coercion. Only his direct evidence will do.'

'And you think he'll talk?' Grace asked. 'Without being, you know . . .'

'I haven't got a clue what he'll do. But what else do we have?'

Dempsey was right, Grace realised. If what Shah had told them was true, the presidency of the United States had been hijacked.

And their only chance of proving it was in Tootkai.

SEVENTY-THREE

John Knowles' gaze remained fixed on Jack Meyer as a door to the Oval Office opened for the first time in almost five hours.

It could only be one person. Only Kelvin Cunningham was able to come and go as he pleased. But Knowles did not even look up. Right now, Cunningham was not his immediate obstacle. That was Jack Meyer.

And so Meyer had his president's full attention.

It was far from unusual that a president and his closest advisors should hole up in the Oval Office for hours at a time. Maybe not for *this* long, Knowles thought. Nine hours so far. But still, the isolation itself was common enough.

Certainly no reason to suspect that the president's a prisoner at his own damn desk.

A prisoner of Jack Meyer. Assistant director of the Secret Service, both chief and a thirty-year veteran of the Service's Presidential Protection Division, and an agent known in Washington for his unimpeachable loyalty to the Oval Office.

Meyer turned his head stiffly as Cunningham entered the room, stifling a yawn as he did so. The first indication he had given that the wait was getting to him.

'Any update?' Meyer asked.

Cunningham smiled, directing his answer at Knowles, who remained seated behind the presidential desk.

'It's underway,' Cunningham replied. His voice carried a sense of victory. 'Blackspear have started to deliver our "witnesses" to Tootkai. And Dempsey and Grace haven't left the UN compound outside of Kabul yet. By the time they get to the village, all they'll find are victims who blame you and your SEAL team, John, for the terrible crimes you committed there.'

Knowles shook his head at the satisfaction in Cunningham's tone. It was a stark contrast to the depression that was now threatening his own mood.

It can't end like this, he thought. *After everything I've done. The years of planning. All to bring down Cunningham and the bastards he works for. They can't win this way. They can't win this easily.*

The negativity threatened to overtake him, but Knowles fought it. He was stronger than that. This was not over yet.

'You think they'll just accept that, do you?' he asked. His voice sounded confident. No hint of his inner despair. 'Dempsey and Grace. After everything that's happened, you think they'll just buy the set-up?'

'I couldn't give a shit what they buy,' Cunningham replied. 'They're as good as dead the moment they step foot in that village? You think we'd let them live?'

'Then why the rush to get your bullshit witnesses in place?'

'Because once my Secret Service team kills the agent you sent as part of your "cover-up", well, that team will then discover what it is you were covering up. They're gonna have to meet the witnesses who can finger your unit for what you did there all those years ago. And then they're gonna have to bring those witnesses into the public eye.'

Cunningham had been as good as his word. The threat his organisation had held over Knowles for all these years – the threat that had handed them control of his presidency – had always been a live one.

Today, its fuse had been lit.

'You don't have to do this, Kelvin.' Knowles knew as he spoke that his entreaties would go nowhere. But what else did he have? 'You don't have to put the blame on my team. It was *me* who tried to undermine you. Not them. Put the blame on me and, if you keep my team out of it, I'll go along with whatever you accuse me of. I'll confess to whatever you need.'

'A noble offer,' Cunningham replied. 'Exactly what I'd expect from you. But you can keep your nobility. You see, I don't *need* your confession. Remember the video, John. Remember the footage of your man killing two American citizens. Murders you didn't report, committed by the man you put forward for a Medal of Honor. With that video? And with the extra evidence that's winging its way to Tootkai right now? This whole thing's a slam-dunk.

'You're going down, and your team's going with you. That's the price you pay for trying to undermine me.'

The response was not unexpected, but still Knowles took it hard.

Twelve years it had been. Twelve years in which he had allowed Cunningham and his organisation to permeate every aspect of his political – and, later, his entire – life.

It had begun so gently. Just an approach from a well-known lobbyist.

Knowles had been at the start of his political career back then. Just months out of the Marine Corp and fresh off of his very public receipt of the Medal of Honor. He was the hero of the hour, a guaranteed seat in Congress ahead of him.

And then came Kelvin Cunningham. The man with the body cam.

The content of the footage came as no surprise to Knowles when Cunningham first approached him. He knew what Lopez had done in Tootkai. His chief petty officer had stumbled upon three private defence contractors – mercenaries – as they'd lined up to rape a village girl no older than sixteen. And he knew that Lopez, the loving father of a daughter just a few years younger, had executed two of the three before being dragged from the house.

What Knowles had *not* known was that the third man – the man left alive – was wearing a body camera and had filmed the murders. If Knowles had known that, he would not have left the incident out of his mission report. And he would not have nominated Lopez for a Medal of Honor, in recognition of the firefight in which Lopez had lost his life less than an hour later.

But Knowles had not known. And so he had filed his incomplete report and he had made his nomination and he had commenced his political career on the back of them both. And now here was Kelvin Cunningham, with footage that could bring everything Knowles had built upon that mission, and upon that medal, crashing down.

Which was not, Cunningham had explained, what he wanted. What *he* wanted was to see Knowles soar. What *he* wanted was to see Knowles win. Sure, his employers had the damaging video, but all they wanted to do was suppress it. They supported Knowles. They agreed with his politics. And they would back him financially, for as long as he agreed with theirs.

Looking back, Knowles had been naive to think it would stop there. Perhaps deep down he had always known what he was really agreeing to. But he had done it anyway. He could not allow the footage to be released. And nor could he really afford the life of a politician. Through Cunningham, he solved both of these problems. And so Knowles had thrown his lot in with him, and with his unseen, unknown employers. And all it had cost him in those first years? A few abstentions and a few votes which, he told himself, he might have taken and made anyway.

It was, then, a symbiotic relationship. A simple quid pro quo. Everyone got what they wanted from it. Until that balance of interests came to an end.

It was during the 2016 presidential campaign that everything changed. A race to the White House that was not worthy of the description; never had there been a candidate so plainly guaranteed to win as John Knowles. He had almost forgotten how to doubt in himself, and so it was that – when asked by Cunningham to take a policy stance with which he disagreed – Knowles stood his ground. He said 'no', with little thought to the consequences.

And he lived to regret it.

What Knowles discovered that day was that, inevitable as his presidency was, he would never truly control the White House. The threat of the footage was bad enough. It would undoubtedly end his career at a stroke. His whole persona – his myth – was based on that mission. A mission about which he had now lied repeatedly, by always omitting the actions of Lopez.

But the footage was not the worst of it. It was not even close . . .

Because it was then that Knowles learned of the set-up that Cunningham and his organisation had put in place years before. Of the trained witnesses. Of the faked assault. Of the terrified, cooperative villagers. All of it designed to frame Knowles for an atrocity he did not commit. All of it supported by the video evidence to prove his own lies.

And all designed to take down not just him but his entire team. Eighteen men. All patriots who had endured hell for their country. Who had risked their lives again and again. And who now faced an inevitable life sentence for crimes they did not commit.

It was his weak spot, and the organisation knew it. As Cunningham had explained, they expected that he would be willing to sacrifice himself. But he would not so willingly condemn his men.

And so the choice had been simple: 'You run. You win. You do as we say. And none of this will ever happen.'

He remembered it as the day that everything had changed. That any pretence of it being an equal partnership had disappeared. He *had* run. He *had* won. And for the next three years he had done whatever was asked of him. Cunningham had called the shots on issue after issue. He set the agenda where he wanted. From tax to defence. From foreign policy to their current focus, environmental protection. As was the arrangement, Knowles had deferred to his deputy assistant and to the organisation on every subject that touched on their interests. He had compliantly handed his office to Kelvin Cunningham.

But compliance was not the same as acceptance.

Whatever impression he had given, Knowles had had no intention of giving up without a fight. He'd had no intention of betraying the country he had served his whole life.

It would require a different approach to the one he was used to – a chess match instead of a special forces assault – but the endgame remained the same: the destruction of Kelvin Cunningham, his organisation and their influence on the office of the president of the United States.

And so the fight had begun.

The first shot fired had been Elizabeth Kirk, and the allegation she had brought to him from Tom Quilty. A close confidant and supporter, Kirk had not believed it. She had made that clear. But Knowles did not want that. He did not want Kirk to accept the easy explanation. And so he ended her tenure with the CIA and had her appointed to the directorship of the new United Nations' International Security Bureau.

It was a 'promotion' which, Knowles knew, would both frustrate Kirk and feed any suspicions she might have had. Cunningham had been against it, at first. He saw Kirk as no threat; she clearly did not buy the Tootkai report, so sending her away was needless. But Knowles had insisted, and he had persuaded Cunningham that the directorship of the ISB would keep her focus elsewhere.

That much was true. Kirk knew only one way to do her job, and that was with absolute focus.

But Knowles knew that it would also eat away at her. She would see it as banishment, and she would always wonder why. And that, in turn, would keep the Tootkai allegations at the back of her mind. Ready to be deployed if the opportunity arose.

An opportunity which had taken the dangerous form of Joe Dempsey.

Knowles had first encountered Dempsey in Trafalgar Square in London, during the assassination of British politician Neil Matthewson. That had been a little over two years ago.

Knowles had followed Dempsey's investigation into that shooting, during which the Brit had proved himself effective, ruthless and – above all else – utterly incorruptible. Hell, the man had killed his closest friend and brought down both his own agency *and* the man tipped to be Britain's next prime minister.

All because it was what his duty demanded.

Knowles had identified then that Dempsey was the weapon Kirk would need to unravel the fiction of Tootkai. And so he had manipulated the fallout from the Matthewson shooting, to bring Dempsey to New York as primary agent of the ISB.

To place him under Kirk's direct command.

It had been Knowles' masterstroke. Kirk and Dempsey were the ideal team to investigate his presidency. All that was needed was the right prompt to get them started. And then Knowles was sure that they would discover what really happened.

But then his plan had stalled. He needed Cunningham to make a mistake. To draw attention to Knowles. Enough to make someone start looking for answers. But for the next two years there was nothing. The man was faultless.

Until this week.

It would be to Knowles' eternal despair that the mistake had finally come in the form of Flight PA16. Over five hundred lives lost.

It was not the trigger Knowles would have wanted. Innocent people should not have had to die to set Kirk and Dempsey on their course. But Cunningham had acted without consulting him and so Knowles had had no chance to stop it. And now that it was done, there was nothing he could do to change it.

But what he *could* do was to make sure that those deaths counted for something. That the organisation could claim no more lives. It was time to act. That was why he had finally risked exposure to keep Dempsey alive, by sending Eden Grace to warn him.

Grace had saved Dempsey's life, exactly as Knowles had intended. And together they had traced this thing back to where it had started.

To Afghanistan. To Tootkai.

Only now, as Knowles eyed Jack Meyer's pistol and Kelvin Cunningham gloated over his imminent victory, it seemed that they might already be too late.

SEVENTY-FOUR

The V8 engine of the 1979 Jeep CJ-5 Renegade roared as it pushed the heavy utility vehicle through the January snow.

It was impossible to tell if they were on- or off-road. For Dempsey, at least. With snow settled in every direction, the jeep was the only feature – other than the distant hills and mountains – that stood out in the white expanse spreading all around them.

Everything else was a blanket of soft, iced powder.

The pilot of their MH-X Stealth Black Hawk had landed on Jangi Shah's instruction, around five miles outside of Tootkai. The appearance of a Western helicopter, Shah had explained, would both alert the Blackspear compound nearby, and potentially spook the locals.

It was a valid concern, Dempsey had accepted. And so they had taken Shah's lead, landing where he'd advised and transferring to the jeep, which Shah had left waiting for them at his preferred landing spot.

The journey from there to Tootkai was only five miles, but it was slow, painful progress. Especially for Dempsey, whose shoulder wound was feeling every bump.

Few vehicles were made for this terrain or for these weather conditions. Fewer still were made for both.

The Renegade could just about handle the ground, but it offered no protection from the cold. It was lucky, then, that Bill Walker had provided suitable clothing for an operation in the freezing Afghan winter when he had stocked Dempsey, Grace and Shah with their weaponry.

'How much further?' Dempsey asked.

He grimaced in pain as another obstacle in the 'road' sent the jeep's left-side two feet into the air. Once back on four wheels he adjusted his sling, checking it had not been loosened by the sudden, violent motions of the jeep.

'Almost there,' Shah replied. 'When we are four hundred yards out we will park. The rest of the journey we take on foot.'

'Got that,' Dempsey replied. He turned towards the back seat. To Grace. 'You doing OK?'

'Other than hypothermia?'

'Other than that,' Dempsey confirmed, feeling himself smile at the answer.

'Other than that I'm good,' Grace replied. 'Just want to get this done now, you know?'

'We will. In and out. We collect Aryo and we're gone.'

'You seem certain.'

'Trust me, Eden. One way or the other, we're leaving Tootkai with the evidence we need.'

'I've trusted you so far, haven't I?'

'You have.'

'Then just don't let me down at the final jump, OK, and we can end this thing happy.'

Dempsey smiled again, before turning back to face the windscreen and what was left of their hard, featureless journey.

SEVENTY-FIVE

Grace had never been to Afghanistan before, or anywhere like it. So she had no idea what to expect from Tootkai. As they entered the village, she looked around her with interest.

Tootkai was basically a collection of small, irregularly placed living spaces. Mostly just single storey, barely wide enough for two rooms at best. A very few only slightly bigger than that.

Covered in snow, the buildings' usual uniform brown colour was still visible here and there. Evidence of the mud and mortar bricks with which each was roughly constructed. The location of the buildings, too, followed no set pattern that Grace could see. They seemed to have been built where best suited their first owner, which left them dotted around the village as if they'd been randomly dropped into place.

However many had been here at first, the number of buildings must have grown over the years, gradually building up around the single dirt road that ran through the centre of Tootkai. Eventually, there were enough, Grace guessed, to justify the construction of the low, impractical wall that now provided the village boundary.

The only openings in the wall were at the village's two 'gates'; there to allow for the central dirt road to pass. Even so, these were hardly a barrier to entry. As well-maintained as the wall was around the outlying parts of the village, it was far too low to provide any real obstacle. Grace estimated that she and her companions could have climbed over it in seconds, with little to no difficulty.

Not that they had needed to. The road that ran through its only opening was deserted. And so, it seemed, was the village itself.

At least so far.

Shah led the way. His bespoke tweed suit was gone, replaced by a thick, white bodysuit made entirely of man-made fibres. A Western answer to the extremes of temperatures within Afghanistan, the bodysuit was joined by a white utility jacket, designed to carry everything an operative would need in the field. In Shah's case, this meant four knives, a SIG Sauer P229 pistol and a collection of magazines containing ammunition for both the handgun and the Heckler & Koch G36C close-quarters assault rifle he was openly carrying.

Grace was behind him, similarly dressed and identically armed. She had questioned the fact that none of them were making any attempt to disguise themselves or their hardware, to which Shah had provided a compelling answer: the average Afghan male stood five foot five in his bare feet and, in shape, weighed around one hundred and forty pounds. With Dempsey standing six two and weighing around two twenty-five, it would not take visible weapons for anyone to notice that a stranger had come to town.

It was Dempsey who covered the rear of their three-man procession. Still injured, he carried just his Glock 19 in his good right hand, with another secreted inside his utility jacket alongside six full magazines of ammunition and the two pilot knives he had brought with him from Manhattan.

They moved further into the village, away from the road

and up a shallow incline that led to the second, third and finally the fourth rows of houses that made up this side of the village.

Shah strode forward with confidence. He knew where he was going, and he seemed unconcerned who might see them as they made his way.

It was a lack of concern which was *not* shared by Dempsey and Grace.

Shah took a left turn as he reached the mid-point in the row of buildings. A change in direction that would take them to a fifth row of homes. Larger than the ones they had passed before, although still small by American standards.

Grace had already lost her bearings as Shah hurried them through the maze of streets.

'Is there a town square in this place?' Dempsey asked. His voice was whispered, yet it somehow carried in the cold wind. A skill that could only be learned in deployments like this, Grace guessed. 'Anywhere a little more open?'

'No town centre in a village of this kind,' Shah answered. 'But there is an area where trade takes place. That is as large and open as you will find here.'

'And where is that, exactly?'

'It is five hundred yards southeast of here,' Shah pointed as he spoke, not breaking his stride for a moment. 'You cannot see due to the other buildings.'

Dempsey followed Shah's direction and nodded.

Grace threw Dempsey a quizzical look. Why would he need to know that? He offered her no explanation. His attention remained on Shah.

'Are the streets always this empty?'

'No, sir,' Shah replied. 'Tootkai is not busy like your towns.

But it is still alive. Today? Today there is no one. They know danger is coming.'

'Do you think Blackspear got here before us?'

'I don't know. I hope not, but we must hurry.' The concern on Shah's face was clear to see. 'If they are here, we have to reach Aryo Bahnam before them. Before they can silence him forever.'

SEVENTY-SIX

The sight of the makeshift wooden door that marked the entrance of Aryo Bahnam Karzai's single-storey residence made Dempsey's heart race.

It was barely a minute since Jangi Shah had revealed his concern about the arrival of Blackspear. A minute which Dempsey, Grace and Shah had spent at full-sprint through the final snow-covered alleyways of Tootkai. Each determined to reach Aryo before anyone else could do so.

The sight of the door – ripped from its rope hinges and trampled underfoot by whoever had reached the house before them – told Dempsey that they were too late.

He raised his pistol and indicated for Grace and Shah to line up behind him, against the front wall of the house. Shah first, Grace last. It was where Dempsey wanted them, ensuring that the woman he *knew* he could trust had constant sight of the man he *hoped* he could trust.

Dempsey almost raised his left hand. To indicate a countdown. He caught himself just in time. Shaking his head at the impracticality of his injury, he instead communicated wordlessly with his companions.

A nod to the right told Shah where he wanted him to go when they entered the first room. A nudge to the left did the same for Grace. Both nodded their understanding.

Dempsey returned their confirmation, tightened his grip on his Glock and – for the first time in his career – he mouthed the countdown.

Three.

Two.

One.

Dempsey was gone instantly. Through the open door of the building, he scanned the central room in an instant. Shah and Grace did the same, to the right and left rooms respectively.

Both of which were empty.

The central room was *not*.

Dempsey waited for Grace and Shah to return from their own inspections before he approached Aryo's body. What they needed to know – if anything – they would find out together.

'He is dead.' Shah's statement was unnecessary. The sight of Aryo's throat and the resulting pool of blood in which his chair now sat ruled out any other conclusion. 'We're too late.'

'Any idea how long he's been dead?' Grace asked.

'Doesn't matter,' Dempsey answered. He took a single step back as he spoke. 'The Blackspear unit won't be far. They must have known we were coming. We need to move carefully.'

The words were barely out of his mouth when Dempsey spotted a small red spot on Shah's chest. A spot which, he realised, must have been on his own back just an instant before.

'JANGI! DOWN!!'

The shouted words came out as quickly as Dempsey's brain could make the connection, but still they were too late. A single round ripped into Shah's chest. He was falling before Dempsey had even shouted his name.

The sound of the gunshot told Dempsey the calibre, while

the placement of the round told him the damage. From the combination of the two, Shah would not be getting back up.

Dempsey knew that immediately and so he made no move to check for a pulse. Instead his eyes scanned the room for Grace.

He found her in an instant, exactly where she should be. Grace was well trained for action under fire – it was the very purpose of her role in the Presidential Protective Division – and she had reacted as she should at the sound of the first round.

She had dived for cover.

Dempsey had done the same, and so both were already on the ground when the full assault of gunfire started. In just seconds the air in the room was filled with the acrid smell of red-hot metal and burning gunpowder, as bullets were fired at every possible angle through the windows of Aryo's home.

'What do we do?' Grace called out as she crawled towards Dempsey.

'Stay down,' Dempsey replied. 'And stay exactly where you are!'

Grace did as instructed, while Dempsey pulled himself close to the front wall of the building. Once there, he placed his back firmly against it. Then he closed his eyes.

And he listened.

The bullets continued to fly. A near constant stream, interrupted in intensity only by reloads. That fact alone pointed towards multiple shooters – some were still shooting while others reloaded – but Dempsey knew that already, from the angles of entry.

At least three.

He continued to listen. Counting the reload times.

Four.

A little longer. More reloads.

He opened his eyes and crawled towards Grace.

'There's five out front,' he said. His tone left no room for doubt. 'Which means two out back at least. Probably three. They're waiting out there without firing a shot, to lure us in. To make us run out there into a crossfire.'

'So what *do* we do?'

'We run out there into a crossfire,' Dempsey said. 'Or at least that's what they'll think we're doing.'

He moved without another word, keeping himself tight to the floor as he approached Shah's body. Seconds later and he had stripped Shah of his utility jacket and his assault rifle. That done, he crawled to the insecure back door to the residence.

He signalled for Grace to join him, and to stay low as she moved.

'What now?' she asked as she came level.

'We're going to have a second. Maybe a second and a half.'

'For what?'

The fire from the front of the house was less deafening at its rear. Still, it remained impossible to ignore as brickwork and pieces of structural support dropped all around them.

'To spot the numbers and the locations of whoever they have out back,' Dempsey explained, flicking stray mortar from the front of Grace's hair, where it could obscure her vision. 'There won't be more than three of them, not when they've got five out front. They'll be left and right. And maybe straight ahead, if there *is* a third.'

'How do you know that?'

'Perfect crossfire,' Dempsey explained. He found himself

ducking further as the angle of incoming firing seemed to change. 'This is an ambush, so they've had time to do it right.'

'What are you going to do?'

'I'm going to wrap Shah's rifle in his coat, and I'm going to jam the trigger with his knife. Then I'll to throw it out there. They'll think they're seeing someone in a white coat, running out and firing. So they'll fire back.'

'For a moment,' Grace added.

Dempsey moved his head aside as a bullet hit the wall behind him, sending brick fragments into the back of his neck.

'It's the best we can do,' he said, feeling his neck for injury. 'When I call three, you scan to the left. OK? Leave the front and the right to me. You just scan left.'

Grace nodded her head in confirmation.

She was nervous. Dempsey could see that. And she doubted her ability to do what he was asking. But she was still here, and she was willing to try.

And that was as much as Dempsey could ask.

He smiled once. And then he went to work.

Using his one good hand, he carefully placed the G36C assault rifle inside Shah's bloody jacket. Satisfied, he removed next one of Shah's secreted knives and moved his own body as close as he could to the back door while still remaining hidden.

Once in place, he turned to Grace.

She was no more than a step behind him.

'You ready for this?'

'As I'll ever be.'

'OK. On three.'

'One.'

The bullets behind them were getting lower. Closer to the

floor. It could only mean one thing: at least some of the five gunmen were moving towards to the building, which gave them a better downward trajectory. It also meant that they would soon have access to the front windows.

And once *that* happened, neither Dempsey nor Grace would have cover.

'Two.'

Dempsey exposed the trigger on the G36C and placed the blade of Shah's knife alongside it. The trick was to stab the blade across the trigger and through to the other side of the jacket. The resistance from the other side would set the blade in place and provide the necessary downward pressure needed on the weapon's automatic setting.

'One.'

In one smooth, swift motion, Dempsey rose to his feet, stabbed the end of the knife through the jacket and, as the rifle began to fire, he threw the full, white bundle into the rocky clearing that sat at the rear of Aryo's home.

The jacket had been in the air much less than a second when the sound of one automatic weapon firing became the sound of four. Dempsey knew what that meant: three hidden gunmen – Blackspear operatives, he assumed – opening fire as one upon Shah's fast-moving jacket.

An instant later and only one was still shooting; the other two had already deduced that their fire had been drawn.

The realisation would have hit them hard, Dempsey knew. As would the moment of confusion that must have followed. But neither would hit so hard as a nine-millimetre bullet.

Dempsey had seen the central shooter first. Inevitable, really, as the man was straight ahead. He was also the only one of the three whose sightline was obscured by the still airborne jacket, which had been thrown directly between him and the building's rear door.

It meant that the central shooter would realise the truth of the situation later than his teammates. By less than a second, probably. But in a combat situation, even the smaller unit of time can make all the difference.

With that single second advantage, Dempsey ignored the central shooter and instead turned right, just in time to catch sight of the last muzzle-fire from the gun of the right-hand shooter.

And so it was the right-hand shooter who died first, with two pistol slugs bursting into and then out of his skull in quick succession.

A heartbeat later and Dempsey was back with the central shooter, ready to unload two more shots before the man had even registered the ruse with Shah's jacket.

The sound of four rounds being fired to Dempsey's left delayed him for just a breath, but still not long enough to give the central shooter a chance.

Two more bullets and the man was as dead as his teammates.

Dempsey turned to Grace. Her weapon was still raised, the heat visible on its barrel.

'Good job, Eden.' Dempsey grabbed her arm as he spoke and pulled her into a run. 'Now come on. We've got to get down to the market area Jangi mentioned. And we've got to take the long way.'

Grace matched Dempsey for pace, but she looked confused. 'Why?' she asked.

'Because there's five killers with automatic weapons out front and they're blocking the direct route.'

'What? No, I mean why the market square?'

'There are other ways to get the evidence we need,' Dempsey said.

'But . . .' Grace began to slow slightly.

'Either you trust me or you don't, OK?' Dempsey slowed too. For an instant. Long enough to look Grace in the eyes. 'But if you *do* trust me then trust me: we have to go now.'

Grace increased her pace.

'I trust you.'

SEVENTY-SEVEN

It took ten minutes for Dempsey and Grace to find their way to Tootkai's marketplace.

Ten minutes of moving in a full semicircle around the outskirts of the village. Of creeping carefully between darkened houses. And of avoiding the five gunmen who had already tried to kill them. Plus however many others they might have in support.

Grace had been content to follow Dempsey's lead. To let him find the safe way to their destination. His instincts and their combined skills had kept them alive when anyone else would have died. Not once but twice, in less than twenty-four hours.

With that track record, he had earned her cooperation.

But now, as they came to a halt against a building wall that provided cover from the south end of the market area, it was time she knew more.

'So are you gonna include me in this plan?' she asked.

'Plan? The plan is to get the evidence we need. Always has been.'

'And where the hell are we going to get that?' Grace was irritated by the response. 'Aryo's dead. Shah's dead. You think anyone else is going to step up? After what's happened to everyone so far?'

'We don't need a *willing* witness, Eden.'

The answer only confused Grace further.

'What the hell does *that* mean? You said yourself, we can't go torturing people.'

'I'm talking about an information exchange. Whoever's behind this, *they'll* want to know how much *we* know. They'll want to know how compromised they are. We can use that.'

Grace looked around, her heart rate rising. She suddenly understood why Dempsey had brought them to the clearing, instead of out of Tootkai.

He has no intention of leaving, she realised. *He's offering himself as a deal. He's offering us both.*

'You can't be serious. How will you even find—'

'They're already here.'

Grace was silenced. Her eyes wide in disbelief. She couldn't quite understand what she was being told.

'But . . . that . . . I thought that was Blackspear.'

'Back at Aryo's? It *was* Blackspear. I didn't mean them.'

'Then who?'

'I mean the Secret Service team, Eden. Jack Meyer has sent his team. Or what's left of it.'

'But . . . here? How?'

'They would've been sent after us the moment we landed. We couldn't just waltz into a UN compound and keep that a secret. No chance. They would have had eyes there.'

'You didn't say—'

'We needed to flush them out. This was the best way. To let them know we were in Afghanistan and heading to Tootkai. Once they knew that, they'd panic. And after everything that's gone wrong so far, in that panic they'll have sent everyone.'

'I don't . . . I don't believe you planned all that. You could have told me, Dempsey. You could have trusted me.'

'I do trust you, Eden. As much as I trust anyone, after all this. But this is a live operation. The fewer people in the know, the less chance something slips.'

'But you're telling me now.'

Dempsey smiled.

'Whatever goes right or wrong, it happens in the next few minutes. I think we're safe from any accidental disclosures.'

Grace opened her mouth to argue, only for a new question to force its way to the front of her brain.

'Aryo. That was what? A distraction? A decoy?'

'No,' Dempsey replied, before exhaling deeply. 'That was a Hail Mary. If he'd had any evidence we could have used, well, then I wouldn't have had to take the risk I'm about to. But that clearly didn't work out. So we're back to Plan A.'

'And what the hell *is* Plan A?'

'Like I said. Information exchange. You're gonna stay here, while I go tell them what we know.'

'You're serious? You're giving yourself up? Dempsey, they'll kill you where you stand.'

'Not straightaway.'

'What? Dempsey, they just tried to kill us back in Aryo's. No warning. No questions. What makes this different?'

'That was the Blackspear idiots. Typical mercenaries, they don't know any other way. Out there? That's gonna be the Secret Service, Eden. Corrupt or not, they're still professionals. And they've been compromised. They'll want to know by how much.'

'But—'

'And more than that, they'll want to know where *you* are. I can't tell them that dead, can I?'

'Dempsey, please. This is all . . . all so . . . You can't be sure of any of this. Please. Don't gamble with your life. What if you're wrong?'

Dempsey smiled one more time. A knowing, cryptic smile.

'What if I'm wrong? You just wait and see.'

He climbed to his feet and, without another word, he strode into the clearing of the marketplace, leaving Grace hidden in the shadow of the building.

SEVENTY-EIGHT

'OK, MEYER. ENOUGH OF THIS. YOU WANT TO KNOW WHAT I KNOW, I'M HERE.'

Dempsey had walked into the centre of the market square, removed his utility jacket and slowly thrown all of his weapons and equipment clear of his body.

'I'M HERE AND I'M DAMN COLD. YOU WANT ME, GET A BLOODY MOVE ON.'

His shouted words echoed around the buildings that surrounded the clearing. The effect was ghostly. As if he was standing in the heart of an empty village, in an empty district, in an empty country.

Only it was *not* an empty village. Far from it.

Dempsey knew that the Secret Service team had arrived. And he knew how to draw them out. How to make them face him, rather than just kill him from a distance.

At least he hoped he did.

Their organisation had been compromised. They knew that much. It was why they were here. What they did not know was how compromised. How much did Dempsey know? How much did Grace? How much had they passed on, and to whom? Jack Meyer would want to know all of that. He needed to know. And until he did, Dempsey would be kept alive.

He hoped.

'ARE YOU COMING, JACK?' he shouted. 'I HAVEN'T GOT ALL DAY.'

'No. No, you sure as hell don't.'

461

The answer was spoken in an American accent. A voice that dripped with confidence.

Or, to be more accurate, over-confidence.

He turned in its direction. The sight that greeted him was not exactly as he had expected. He had expected Jack Meyer would deal with this personally. The man he saw now was younger. But otherwise? It looked like Dempsey's gamble might have paid off.

The man was walking towards the centre of the market clearing. From the cover of a building much closer than where Dempsey had left Grace.

Had he been alone, perspective would have hidden the speaker's unusual size. But he was not. He was flanked by two men on either side. All walking in time, in a near line.

The additional four men were Secret Service agents. Dempsey had no doubt of that. The way they looked. The way they held themselves. The way they moved. He could have picked them out of any crowd.

Their chief, though? He was something else.

Six-foot-six and massive with it, Dempsey thought. *Handsome bastard, too.*

The last thought almost made Dempsey laugh. It was a strange thing to notice in the circumstances, but it was just too hard to miss. The speaker's movie star features were flawless.

'You five always creep around like that?' Dempsey asked. He kept his tone determinedly nonchalant. 'You could've saved me the shouting if you just made some noise.'

'Maybe I wanted to hear what you had to say,' the giant replied. Dempsey had been right. He was clearly in charge. 'Not that it turned out interesting.'

'I'm sure I know some things that'll interest you,' Dempsey answered. 'I didn't catch your name.'

'I didn't give it, Agent Dempsey.'

The giant made a point of carefully enunciating the last two words. If they were intended to unnerve Dempsey, they failed.

'What's that make it?' Dempsey asked with a smile. 'Advantage you?'

The giant hesitated for a second.

Looking for a smart answer, Dempsey realised.

'I don't play ball games, agent,' he finally offered. 'Combat sports only.'

Dempsey failed to suppress a laugh at the answer.

'Is that supposed to intimidate me, son?' he asked, a smile growing across his face.

For a moment the giant seemed flustered. An instant more and it was gone, but Dempsey had noticed the reaction. It added to the picture already forming in his mind.

'It's not supposed to do anything. And trust me, if I wanted you intimidated, you would be.'

'Sure I would.'

'Enough small talk.' The giant's patience had not lasted long.

'Fine by me,' Dempsey replied. 'You want to know what I know.'

'Soon enough,' the giant replied.

His confidence was back. No doubt renewed by the sight of five more armed men approaching the marketplace.

The Blackspear team, Dempsey surmised. *Minus the three we killed*.

The giant did not acknowledge their arrival as he continued.

'But first you're going to tell us where we can find Eden Grace?'

'Grace is dead. She was killed escaping from the house your friend's here shot up.' Dempsey indicated the newly arrived Blackspear five. 'She bled out halfway down the hill.'

'Bullshit. They'd have found her body. She's here somewhere. Call her out.'

'I told you. She's dead.'

'OK. Then *I'll* call her out.'

The giant placed a hand to his mouth and shouted at full volume.

'GRACE, YOU'VE GOT TEN SECONDS. IF YOU'RE NOT OUT HERE BY THEN, THIS LIMEY SONOFABITCH DIES.'

'Kill me?' Dempsey kept his tone certain. No hint of concern. 'You can't kill me. You need to know what *I* know about your employers. You need to know how far this investigation has gone.'

The giant turned to face Dempsey, his expression as arrogant as his voice.

'You really think that, do you? You really think I give a shit about your investigation? I hate to disappoint you, pal, but I ain't got no orders to find out what you know. You're alive so I can flush out that bitch Eden Grace. She's who we want. Not you.'

He looked at his watch, turned his head back towards the clearing and re-raised his catcher's mitt of a hand to his mouth.

'YOU HEAR THAT, GRACE? I DON'T NEED THIS MOTHERFUCKER. SEVEN SECONDS GONE. SO IF YOU'RE NOT OUT HERE ON A COUNT OF THREE . . .'

It took less than one.

Dempsey watched as Grace walked out from the cover behind which he had left her. The building was behind Dempsey, and so she was walking towards the ten armed men.

'Romeo Meyer.' Grace's voice was strong. She sounded fearless as she strode forward. 'I should have known you'd follow in your father's footsteps.'

'Funny you should mention my dad,' Romeo shouted back, raising his pistol. 'He asked me to make sure I gave you this.'

Dempsey knew what was about to happen. Determined to place his body between Grace and Romeo – to protect her in any way he could – he had already started to run towards her. But even as he moved he knew that he was attempting the impossible.

Grace was just too far.

And so he could nothing as Romeo fired twice, sending one bullet high towards Grace's neck and the second deep into her gut.

SEVENTY-NINE

G race fell hard, scattering the fine snow in every direction with the impact.

Dempsey reached her in seconds and dropped to his knees beside her. Without hesitation he ripped open her bodysuit to expose the two wounds he had seen her take.

The second bullet had hit her in the centre of her stomach. Dempsey had watched the impact. Without attention such wounds were fatal, but they were also slow. And so his priority was her neck.

Moving his fingers up towards Grace's throat, he examined it as carefully as the situation allowed. Blood was already flowing from the wound, but not as freely as he had feared. Had the bullet hit an artery then Grace would have been beyond help.

'Leave her,' Romeo said. 'We're gonna have that talk after all.'

Dempsey ignored him, instead switching his attention to Grace's stomach wound. He ripped open the bloody undershirt that hid it, and focused on the deep, clean wound to her stomach.

'I said leave her where she is.'

Dempsey's eyes met Grace's.

'You're gonna be OK, Eden. You're gonna be OK.'

Grace opened her mouth to speak, but no sound came out. Only blood. It was not a good sign.

'I WON'T TELL YOU AGAIN!'

Romeo's shouted threat made no difference. Dempsey

continued to ignore him. Three warnings and no bullet? It proved his instinct right. Romeo *had* been ordered to question him.

'You're gonna be OK, Eden. You just have to get through the next few minutes, you understand?'

Grace nodded.

'You need to press down on your wounds, OK? Press down hard. Do that for me. Do it now.'

Dempsey placed one of Grace's hands on her own neck and one on her stomach, applying pressure to both. He could only hope that, in the time she had, Grace would stay focused and keep that same pressure up.

'You'll be OK,' he said, one final time. 'I promise. Just trust me.'

With ten gunmen only a few yards away and with a mission to complete, it was all the help Dempsey could provide. He turned and rose to his feet.

'She needs a medical intervention right away,' he said, looking directly at Romeo.

'What?' Romeo's brow furrowed as he spoke. 'Are you insane? You think we're going to get her a medic?'

'All I'm saying is that she needs a medical team.' Dempsey spoke slowly and clearly. 'And she needs it now.'

'And all I'm saying is that you're some sort of fucking idiot if you think we're getting a medic for a bitch I just shot. Now, what have you got to tell me, Limey? Or should I just put a bullet in your head now?'

Dempsey didn't answer the question. He had done all he could for Eden.

'Is that how the Secret Service does things now, Romeo?' he asked. 'You shoot your own agents?'

'Fuck the Secret Service,' Romeo replied. 'What she got, she got for betraying my dad in New York yesterday. Shit like that, it doesn't stand. Not in my family.'

'Jack Meyer *is* the Secret Service, you idiot.'

Dempsey took a step towards Romeo as he spoke. It was all he could do to not rush the man. Not to rip out his throat before his men could intervene.

Romeo took a step back in turn. Dempsey found the reaction instructive. Still, when Romeo spoke he remained belligerent.

'Who the hell are you calling an idiot?'

'I'm calling *you* an idiot. The idiot son of the assistant director of the Secret Service. A man who just admitted that his father sent a death squad to come and kill me in New York yesterday. A death squad thwarted by Agent Grace here. Not to mention, the same idiot who just tried to kill Agent Grace in full view of a witness.'

'You're only a witness if you live.' Romeo seemed less sure of himself. Confused by Dempsey's confidence. 'And we both know you won't.'

'You're not even going to deny it, then? Any of what I just said?'

'Why the hell would I deny it? I've been sent to this country to put you in the ground. So what the fuck do I care what you hear?'

Dempsey sensed the uncertainty in Romeo's voice. It was time to end this.

'So why am I not in the ground already?'

'What?'

'You heard me, Romeo. Why am I not dead already, if that's all you're here for? We've been speaking for five minutes.

You have me outnumbered ten to one and I don't even have a weapon. So why the hell am I still breathing?'

'Dempsey, go—'

'I'll tell you why. It's because your father needs to know what *I* know. His little organisation, they need to know how compromised they really are.'

Romeo looked around him. Towards his own four men, and to what was left of Cunningham's Blackspear team. Dempsey could tell what was on his mind.

He knows I'm right, but he doesn't want to admit that and lose face.

Dempsey looked back to Grace. She did not have the time for him to drag this out. He had to cut through Romeo's conflicted machismo.

'So, you want me to tell you what I know?'

'I couldn't give a shit what—'

'Yes you could, Romeo. Whether you want to admit it or not. So let's go, shall we? Your father, Jack Meyer of the US Secret Service, works for an organisation that has infiltrated the White House, and which is currently blackmailing President John Knowles. It's also infiltrated the Secret Service. Probably via your father. And probably not too deep beyond that. In fact, I'm willing to bet it goes no further than you five arseholes here.'

'You think?' Romeo did exactly what Dempsey had expected of him. Eager to regain the upper hand – to save face in front of his team – he jumped on the first mistake. 'Oh, there's more than just us five, buddy.'

'There *were* more,' Dempsey corrected. 'Four more, right? Yeah, that's right. The same four I killed yesterday in New York.'

Romeo's eyes widened and he said nothing. A reaction which told Dempsey two things: he had been right that the New York four were the rest of the number, and Jack Meyer had not risked telling his son about their loss.

In case it spooked him, Dempsey surmised.

'But forget them,' Dempsey continued. 'Let's get back to this. The blackmail of Knowles – your father's organisation did that. They faked an attack on Tootkai, terrified the locals into cooperating and now they've brought in trained witnesses. All primed to name Knowles and his unit, if Knowles ever stepped out of line. Am I right? A pre-packaged false flag operation, with your Blackspear back-up based right here next to Tootkai. Ready to put the wheels in motion with just a word. Am I getting close, Romeo?'

Romeo said nothing. He didn't need to. His nervous smirk spoke volumes.

'All of which kept Knowles in line for three years. Right up until Dale Victor got wind of the false allegations. A man who could ruin everything. And so you guys arranged for the bombing of Flight PA16. You killed hundreds of people. Just to keep your patsy in the White House.'

'That's what you think, is it?'

Romeo suddenly seemed excited. And Dempsey knew why.

'You think we bombed the plane to keep Knowles in office? If you think *that* then you don't know shit. We couldn't care less whether it's Knowles or some other fucking puppet in that place. All that matters is that *we* can control them. And we *couldn't* control Dale Victor. No one could. So we killed him. It had nothing to do with protecting Knowles.'

Dempsey said nothing. Still excited, Romeo continued.

'And what, Agent Dempsey? Is that all you've got? Is that all you know? Christ, it was hardly worth the trip to find out.'

Dempsey slowly turned his head. Back towards Grace. She was still conscious. Still pressing onto her wounds.

She still has time.

A grim smile spread across his face as he lifted his right cuff to his lips.

'Is that enough, Elizabeth?'

Romeo looked confused at Dempsey's words. Not that Dempsey noticed. He was waiting for a response, and when it came it could not have been clearer.

Elizabeth Kirk's perfect diction, transmitted into the almost invisible device in Dempsey's right ear, left no room for doubt.

'More than enough.'

'My team's in place?'

'Ready and waiting.'

'Good. Take all but the big one.'

The smile remained fixed on Dempsey's face as confusion spread among Romeo and the nine men standing with him. A confusion which, for all but Romeo, would end as quickly as their lives.

Dempsey stayed perfectly still at the sound of the first 'pop', and watched as one of the five Blackspear operatives suddenly dropped to the floor, only a fine red mist hinting at what had just occurred.

The same 'pop' was repeated almost immediately. This time taking out one of the four Secret Service agents.

And then again. And again. Nine times in all, in less than two seconds. Long enough for those who were last to have realised what was about to happen. But much too quick for them to escape it.

Unlike Grace, not one of them survived the drop. A bullet to the gut *might* cause a long, painful death. A bullet to the head guarantees that last part.

Only Romeo was still standing, his pistol thrown to the floor as he realised what was happening to the men around him.

As soon as the final shot was fired – as soon as it was safe to move – Dempsey was back at Grace's side, ripping off the top half of his body suit and using it to press down on her wounds.

'What the hell . . . who the hell . . .'

Romeo seemed to be trying to rationalise what had happened around him. Not that Dempsey cared. His full focus was on Grace. He raised his cuff to his lips again.

'How long for the medic, Elizabeth?'

'Dai has just reached the clearing,' Kirk answered. 'Southwest.'

Dempsey looked up and saw exactly what Kirk had promised. Shui Dai was racing towards him with what he assumed was a medical kit on her back.

I knew it'd be Dai who got the message.

He watched as Dai passed Romeo. The size difference between the two was so great that they could have been a different species to one another, and yet it was Romeo who seemed nervous at the arrival of the much smaller ISB agent.

If Dempsey had had any residual doubts about the man's character, that reaction would have dispelled them.

Dai reached Grace a moment later, and within seconds she was working on the agent's wounds.

'What do you think?' Dempsey asked, stepping back to give Dai room.

Dai didn't immediately answer. Methodical as always,

she first examined both injuries. Only then did she look up to Dempsey.

'She will live,' she answered. 'It will be a long recovery, but she will live.'

Dempsey stepped back. It was all he needed to hear. Grace would not die there in the dirt and the snow. Not now that she had Shui Dai beside her. There was nothing more that Dempsey could do for her.

Which meant he could now turn his attention elsewhere . . .

Romeo was still in the same spot. He had made no effort to move away, or even to edge towards the weapon he had dropped as his teammates fell.

Even now, as Dempsey began to walk towards him, he seemed frozen in time.

Dempsey indicated to the fallen men around him.

'You want to know why you got to live?'

Romeo didn't seem to understand. Dempsey was not even sure the man had heard him. He seemed to be in shock.

'Did you hear me, Meyer?' He spoke more loudly. This time, it at least made Romeo look towards him. 'Why are you alive?'

Romeo took a moment to look around. At the nine bodies now bleeding into the snow. He seemed unable to answer; if anything, his shock was increasing.

'Focus, Meyer. You chose this life. Time to face the consequences.'

Romeo looked around one last time. Then he raised his eyes to meet Dempsey's.

'You need a witness,' he said. 'Same as they needed you. You need someone to tell you everything. To bring down my father and Cunningham.'

'And you'd do that.' It was not a question. Dempsey had doubted he could dislike Romeo more, but now, as he realised how willingly the coward would turn? It *was* possible, after all. 'But you're wrong. I don't need a witness. I already have everything I need.'

Romeo didn't answer. He seemed unsure of Dempsey's meaning.

'Why do you think I needed you to talk, you idiot?' Dempsey asked.

Romeo's eyes fell onto Dempsey's sling.

'You recorded me,' he said, his voice flat.

'Every damned word,' Dempsey confirmed. He indicated to his incapacitated left arm. 'Amazing how small they can make cameras these days, eh? A few bandages and they're invisible.'

'Then . . . then why . . .'

'Why are you alive? Because you don't get off that easy. Not after what you just did to Eden. You're gonna find out what they do to pretty lads in prison.'

Romeo took a step back for the first time.

'You can't,' he said, his voice dripping with fear. 'I'm not . . .'

Romeo looked around him as Dempsey spoke. At the men and women now entering the clearing, coming from every direction. Salvatore Gallo. Dylan Wrixon. Kate Silver. Adama Jabari. And Elizabeth Kirk.

Five of them. Seven with Dempsey and Dai.

Dempsey could see the man's mind working. Doing the maths. Romeo had no time to consider how he would flee Tootkai. Or how he would find his way out of Afghanistan. For now, his focus was on escaping the clearing.

Four directions. Four routes out.

Three of them towards armed ISB agents. The fourth towards Dempsey. A weaponless man with a useless arm.

There's only one decision . . .

Romeo rushed forward. A slow, clumsy charge. The violence of a man who had hidden behind his size and his family name for his entire life. Dempsey remembered again his first impression:

Handsome. Flawless features. The face of a man who'd never had to fight.

Dempsey was no bully. Most of the time he detested violence, even when it was necessary. And against an amateur like Romeo? He would usually hold back. He might even have pitied him.

Not today. Today, Dempsey's pity was with the young woman now bleeding into the Afghan snow.

He moved smoothly and with control, as if the oncoming size of Romeo meant nothing. Which, to Dempsey, it didn't. He shifted his left leg backwards. The movement put his body at an angle, protecting his left shoulder and so his sling from any impact that might follow.

Romeo was feet away in barely a second and closing fast. To Dempsey, he might as well have been wading through treacle. Using his good right arm, he struck out a single blow to Romeo's throat. Perfectly placed and powerful enough to smash Romeo's carotid artery into his windpipe, Dempsey could feel the devastating effect of the blow as Romeo's legs buckled.

Stepping to one side to avoid the weight of Romeo's impending fall, Dempsey moved his right hand away from the agent's throat and up towards his left ear, gripping it firmly before bringing his own right leg high and driving it down, into and through Romeo's left knee.

The impact halted Romeo's stumble forward, while the pain caused him to scream out in agony.

But neither caused Dempsey to stop. With the thought of all Romeo Meyer had done still at the forefront of his mind, his right foot had barely reached the floor before his left knee drove upwards and into Romeo's now low, prone face with every ounce of force that Dempsey could muster.

With Romeo's ear still gripped in his hand, there was no way for the agent to avoid Dempsey's strike; Dempsey felt his own kneecap slam into Romeo's face, destroying bone and cartilage in one blow.

It was more than Romeo could take. He was unconscious before Dempsey had regained his footing, with only Dempsey's grip on his left ear holding him up from the ground.

'That's enough, boss. He's done.'

Dempsey turned towards the voice. It was Kate Silver. Then he looked back at Romeo. For a moment, he envisaged striking him again. A killing blow.

For a moment. A moment more and he was back in control.

Dempsey opened his hand, released Romeo's now torn ear and turned his back, not bothering to watch as Romeo slumped face first and unconscious into the snow.

EIGHTY

John Knowles watched with interest as Kelvin Cunningham checked his watch. The deputy assistant had done the same thing fourteen times in the last twenty minutes. On each occasion he had looked increasingly worried.

There could be only one reason for the concern. Whatever was supposed to happen in Afghanistan it was due to happen now.

Knowles had been in enough time-sensitive operations to spot the signs.

He could also spot growing nerves, which was exactly what he saw on Cunningham now. His deputy assistant had been confident when gloating of his success earlier. But his body language undermined him. It suggested that his happy ending was far from a foregone conclusion.

It was the most that Knowles could expect. The odds were not as he had planned. But if anyone could overturn them, it was Joe Dempsey.

His eyes shifted to Jack Meyer, whose earlier signs of tiredness had only increased. Knowles understood why. Meyer was getting old. Already past mandatory retirement age for an active agent, he had always lacked the nervous energy that still drove Cunningham. And, unlike Cunningham, Meyer had been stationary in the same location for half a day.

He's beginning to flag, Knowles thought.

It was not by much. But it might be enough to make a split second's difference. To someone with Knowles' training and experience, that split second could be all that mattered.

Or so Knowles hoped.

His eyes moved back to Cunningham, in time to notice him glance at his phone and disconnect whoever had been calling.

Third time in an hour, Knowles noted. *He's keeping the line clear. He's waiting for news.*

'You need to take that call, Kelvin?' Knowles tone was light. Mocking. He was determined to appear confident. 'Don't let me stop you.'

Cunningham looked up sharply. He seemed surprised by the comment. The reaction of a man who had been deep in thought.

'You didn't,' Cunningham replied, his voice bitter. 'You need to stop thinking of yourself as relevant.'

Knowles smiled. It was a petty answer, designed to sting. The kind of barb usually beneath Cunningham. It confirmed Knowles' suspicions.

He's nervous. He's very nervous.

The president rose to his feet.

'Where are you going?' Cunningham demanded.

'I've been sitting for seven hours straight,' Knowles replied. 'I need to stretch my legs.'

'I'd get used to that if I were you. No room for walks in a prison cell.'

'Maybe. But I'm not there yet, am I?'

Cunningham looked to Meyer, who replied with a shrug of his shoulders.

'OK. Keep it brief.'

Knowles smiled to himself at the instruction. He was far beyond taking orders from Kelvin Cunningham. The hold over him was gone. Tootkai had been activated. One way or another Knowles' presidency would soon be at an end.

Other than the gun in Jack Meyer's hand, Knowles had no reason to ever obey Cunningham again.

Knowles moved slowly around his desk. He made a show of stretching his limbs and his lower back. They *were* sore, he had to admit. For a man who had once remained motionless in a Borneo jungle for four days, the realisation was a little disappointing.

He came closer to Jack Meyer and noticed the dark rings under the man's eyes. A reminder of the tiredness Knowles had already seen. But was it enough? Before the president was within six feet, Meyer had straightened up and redoubled his grip on his pistol.

Tired or not, he was still alert.

Knowles noted the reaction before turning his attention back to Cunningham.

Another glance at his watch.

'What's the matter, Kelvin?' Knowles forced himself to sound amused. An intentional effort to irritate Cunningham. To force a mistake. 'Things not going to plan?'

Cunningham glanced upwards. If he was nervous, he didn't show it. His reply came in an instant.

'Don't get your hopes up. You'll still be in a cell by the morning. If you're lucky.'

Knowles smiled. The first direct threat of his death. Cunningham *was* worried.

And Knowles was about to find out why.

One of the two hidden doors that led to the White House Office opened without a knock. All three men turned at the familiar sound as the bottom of the door breezed against the thick carpet.

Nicolas Dupart said nothing as he closed the door behind him.

For a moment, Knowles didn't know what to think. The wordless, confident arrival of the senior advisor was unexpected. He immediately shifted his attention to Cunningham. The deputy assistant did not seem surprised to see Dupart.

No. He seemed horrified.

'Nick. What—'

'Don't even speak,' Dupart interrupted. 'Not until you're spoken to.'

Cunningham said nothing. Knowles watched with shocked fascination as he slumped down into one of the two office sofas.

'You can't be in here.' In his surprise, Knowles had almost forgotten Meyer. He remembered him now, as the assistant director rose to his feet. 'You don't have the clearance to be in here.'

'Engage your brain before speaking, Mr Meyer.' Dupart's gaze was piercing, but his voice remained emotion-free. 'And then don't speak again.'

Dupart turned back towards Cunningham. Knowles followed his gaze. Cunningham's entire demeanour had changed. He looked completely defeated.

'You know why I'm in here, Kelvin?' Dupart asked. 'You know why I've been calling you?'

Cunningham said nothing.

Meyer looked furious. 'Just who the hell do you think—'

Dupart held up a hand. It stopped Meyer mid-sentence.

'Read the room, Mr Meyer. And then realise who it is you work for. Who it is that Kelvin works for.'

Knowles watched Meyer's expression change. *Now* he understood.

Dupart turned back to Cunningham.

'You've been ignoring my calls, Kelvin.'

Again, Cunningham said nothing.

'You remember what I said, don't you? You clean up this mess, or I'll have it cleaned up for you.'

Cunningham looked up, his expression desperate.

'I am cleaning it. I'm waiting for the call. As soon as I got it I was—'

'I've already had the call, Kelvin.' Dupart's voice remained as flat as always. 'Your operation in Tootkai has failed. Everyone you sent? Dead. Agent Dempsey and Agent Grace? Alive. And now protected by Dempsey's team. You've been outmanoeuvred at every turn. You're done.'

'Dead?' The question came from Meyer. His voice was breaking. 'All of them? Even . . .'

'No. Your idiot son's alive. For now.'

Meyer paused to take in the answer. At first he heard only Romeo's safety. A second later and he noted the threat.

'What . . . what do you mean, "for now"?'

'I mean that whether he lives or dies depends on you, Mr Meyer. At the moment, Dempsey and his team have evidence implicating Kelvin Cunningham, you and a faction of the US Secret Service in the bombing of Flight PA16, in the blackmail of a US president and in a succession of murders and attempted murders over the course of the last week. Right now any prosecution will be limited to those facts. And while that's a setback, it isn't fatal.'

'What does that have to do with Romeo?'

'As much as it has to do with you,' Dupart explained. 'You see, Kelvin here knows the true scale of this operation. His arrest and his prosecution is guaranteed. And I can't risk him disclosing what he knows.'

'Nick, I would never—'

Dupart held up the same hand that had silenced Meyer. It had an identical effect on Cunningham.

'I told you what would happen, Kelvin. I don't make empty threats,' Dupart continued without even turning his head. 'Now, Mr Meyer. Were Mr Cunningham and the president to die in this room, murdered by the president's implicated head of protection, that would leave only you. And you, I know, will disclose nothing. Because that way your son gets to live. Do we have an understanding?'

Cunningham rose from his seat. He was shaking.

'Nick, you don't need to do this. Have I not been loyal? My whole life, Nick. Please.'

'You were loyal to my father,' Dupart replied, his focus shifted to Cunningham. 'All you've done to me is lie. Keep things from me. And fail. Why do you think I insisted on being appointed as senior advisor here? When has anyone from my family felt the need to be so close?'

Cunningham opened his mouth to respond, but Knowles beat him to it. The last few minutes had been a series of shocks. But they were starting to fill in some gaps he had not even noticed.

'Your family? Your family runs this . . . this organisation?'

Dupart's gaze moved to Knowles. When he answered, there was still no hint of emotion. Just cold fact.

'This isn't a democracy, Mr Knowles. *I* run this organisation. I own it, in fact. Just as I own this office.'

'You own this office? You arrogant little shit. No one "owns" this office. You might have compromised me. You might have blackmailed your way to control *my* administration. But you own nothing. My time here's done. And so is yours.'

Dupart smiled. The first hint of humanity, however dark.

'Is that what you think?' Finally some emotion, even a touch of humour. 'You think this is just about you? You think you're the only one?'

Knowles felt a shiver move up his spine.

Dupart continued.

'Mr Knowles, do you really think this begins and ends with your administration? You're a speck, John. You're nothing. My family have owned this office for sixty years. We have owned every president who has sat behind that desk since the time of my grandfather. Every. Last. One of them. And we'll still own it, long after your death.'

Knowles could not quite believe what he was hearing. And yet he had no doubt that it was true. He glanced away. Towards Meyer. Then towards Cunningham. Nether showed any sign of doubt.

'But how?' Knowles heard himself ask. 'How is that even possible?'

'Open your eyes,' Dupart said. 'Absolute power is possible if you're willing to do what you must to take it. And what you must to keep it. My family? We were willing. We backed the Kennedys. That was our first try at this. And when Jack and Bobby fought against the deal their daddy had made, look what happened. And once we were there? Once we were in? We were too powerful to stop. It's like my grandfather always said, John. If you take the White House, you take the world.'

Knowles shook his head. The thoughts. The questions. They were coming too fast. This could not be right. This could not be the world? Surely . . . surely someone would have stopped them?

'But the presidents? They haven't all had the same agenda. They—'

'We allow them to do their job when it doesn't affect us,' Dupart replied. 'Just as we have with you. But when it's *our* interests? Then *we're* in charge. And it works, John. You've seen it. It works.'

'Not always.' Knowles held out his hands, indicating their current predicament. 'Not always.'

Dupart smiled again.

'Ah. You think you're the first. You're not. Kennedy, he was a problem. You know how we dealt with him. Nixon? A drunk and an addict. We handled him more delicately. Reagan? He was warned and then he was sidelined. And those are the just ones who made it this far. Others? The ones we knew we couldn't control? The likes of JFK Jr and Dale Victor? We stopped them before they ever got close.'

Knowles felt sick. A horrible, gut-wrenching emptiness in the pit of his stomach. What he was being told was turning everything he knew upside down. Complete control, going back to a time before his birth? That might continue far beyond his death?

It was more than he could accept. More than he could allow.

He glanced down at his desk, trying to shake off the effects of Dupart's words. As he did, his eyes fell onto the small, brass plate that had sat there for three years. It carried an individual presidential motto. Every president had one, ever since Harry Truman and his reminder that 'the buck stops here'.

Knowles had chosen *Memento Mori*.

Remember you are mortal.

Words that had been whispered in the ear of every Caesar by his most trusted slave, reminding him that for all the power he held, he was just a man.

A reminder to himself. To a man with, he had once thought, near absolute power. Now, as he read the words again, every drop of confusion – of hesitation – left his body. Replaced by focused determination.

He looked at Dupart.

Remember you are mortal.

Knowles covered the few feet between himself and Meyer in two steps. He moved fast and with the advantage of surprise, but still Meyer reacted. Age. Exhaustion. Distraction. None of it stopped the veteran agent from raising his pistol and firing a round.

Luckily for Knowles, what it *did* affect was Meyer's aim.

The bullet ripped into Knowles' left bicep. He hardly seemed to notice; his perfectly aimed right hook was already inches from the sight of the vagus nerve exposed at the point where Meyer's jaw met his throat. Their height difference gave Knowles a clear shot with the power advantage of an upward trajectory. He felt his fist connect, hard.

As he knew it would, the blunt trauma to the essential parasympathetic nerve was all it took to render Meyer unconscious.

Knowles had already taken a knee as Meyer fell, ready to collect the beaten man's pistol. It gave Dupart and Cunningham no time to react. No time to rush forward. No time to retreat.

Knowles rose back to his feet. Slowly. His pistol trained on Dupart.

As he stood up, all four doors to the Oval Office burst open. Secret Service agents streamed in. Reacting to the gunshot they had heard moments before.

Knowles eyed the group as they entered, and stopped them with the same raised hand motion Dupart had used. He felt every set of eyes burning into him. Men and women sworn to protect him; this was not the scenario they had expected.

The president with a gun, Knowles thought. *Now who do they protect?*

He turned his attention back to Dupart.

'Am I the first one to do *this*, Nick?'

Dupart's eyes were fixed on the gun.

'Still think you own this office?'

'Killing me changes nothing.' Dupart stumbled over the words. His demeanour had changed in an instant. He was desperate. 'Someone will take my place.'

'You know, I don't think that's true,' Knowles replied. 'Not with everything you just said. And if it *is*, well, I think I'll cross that bridge when I come to it.'

He had made up his mind and he did not hesitate, leaving less than a heartbeat between his final word and his first bullet.

Three more and he was done.

Every Secret Service agent in the room stood rooted to the spot, unsure how to react, as Knowles stepped forward and looked down. At Dupart. At Cunningham. Both lifeless at his feet.

'Because no one owns the White House.'

EIGHTY-ONE

Nizar Mansour looked up from his bed as two men entered the Belmarsh intensive care suite. It was one of the few private spaces in the prison's hospital wing, designed for only one patient at a time. For the past five days, that patient had been Mansour.

He recognised the men on sight. Detective Chief Inspector Bruce Bull and Will Duffy.

For almost all of his five days in the suite, Mansour had been in an induced coma; the preferred treatment for the swelling his brain had suffered after his attack. The first two of those had included around-the-clock police protection. In case he was targeted again.

That threat had subsided three days ago following events in the United States and in Afghanistan, the details of which Mansour would never know. And so for those three further days he had been in here alone.

He had finally been brought out of unconsciousness that morning. Four hours later, Bull and Duffy were his first visitors.

Duffy approached the right-hand side of the bed, while Bull took the left.

'How you feeling, lad?'

'I am much better, I think,' Mansour replied. 'I . . . I . . .'

Bull stepped in.

'You don't need to speak, Nizar. You're still recovering.'

Mansour smiled a thank you. His head was a strange mixture of pain and fog, and finding the correct words was difficult.

Bull continued.

'We're just here to tell you that – when you're ready and feeling able to move – you'll be free to go. All the charges against you, they've been dropped.'

Mansour squinted his eyes at Bull's words. He was unsure if he had misheard. He slowly turned his head towards Duffy.

'It's true, son. It's over. You're a free man. An innocent one, too, eh?'

'But . . . why? I . . . I placed the bomb . . .'

'You didn't know you were doing that,' Bull replied. 'And if it hadn't been you, it would have been someone else.'

'But still. What I did, I know it was a crime.'

'Listen, son, stop asking questions,' Duffy said. 'This decision has nothing to do with what's a crime and what's not. It's much bigger than that. And it comes from a much higher place than any of us. OK? Just accept it and get back on with your life.'

Mansour looked between the two men's faces. He was conflicted. He wanted to ask more questions, but he realised instinctively that Duffy was right.

And so he took the advice.

'Mr Duffy, thank you. For all you have done.'

He turned to Bull.

'And to you, Mr Bull. For helping me. May I ask, sir. Am I now safe? From Romeo and from others?'

'From what I've been told, Nizar, those men will never be bothering you again. Or anyone else.'

Mansour understood Bull's not so subtle meaning.

'Thank you, sir.'

'You're welcome, Nizar. Now listen, I have to go but Will

here is going to stay. There's something he needs to discuss with you. So you take care now, OK? Be safe.'

'I will, Mr Bull.'

Bull reached out a hand and Mansour took it gently, his grip still weak. The two men shock.

'Goodbye.'

'Goodbye.'

Mansour turned to Duffy as Bull left.

'What is it, Mr Duffy? What must we discuss?'

Duffy took a seat near to Mansour's head, took a deep breath and began.

'Son, it's about your sister . . .'

EIGHTY-TWO

Michael Devlin pressed the disconnect icon on his mobile phone and placed it on the kitchen island ahead of him. He took a few moments to register what he had just been told, before looking up to face Sarah.

'You want another exclusive, sweetheart?'

'Who was that?' she asked, indicating towards the handset.

Sarah was sitting on a tall stool directly across from Michael.

'It was Will Duffy,' Michael replied. 'Seems they're dropping all charges against Nizar Mansour.'

'You're kidding me?'

'Nope. All true.'

'On what grounds?'

'Officially? Or actually?'

'Let's try both.'

'Officially, no evidence of his involvement. No confession. No CCTV. Nothing. They got the wrong man.'

'So what's the real reason?'

'Off the record?'

'I wouldn't be asking *you* if I was planning to report it.'

'Political. Seems with everything that happened with America and with the White House, they didn't want Mansour standing trial. Too much risk of the truth coming out.'

'What truth?'

'Who the hell knows. But it must mean that there was more to this than just some rogue Secret Service agents being involved.'

'You think it's got anything to do with Knowles' injury?'

'It has to, doesn't it? It's too much of a coincidence otherwise.'

'What's Dempsey said?'

'Joe? That's like speaking to a brick wall on stuff like this. All he said was that we shouldn't mention anything about the Secret Service to anyone. When I pressed him on it, nothing else.'

'He'll tell you one day.'

'I wouldn't bet on it. Anyway, are you sure you don't want to run with the Mansour story? The official one, I mean? It's not out there yet. Not until the morning.'

Sarah lowered her chin into her right hand and stared at Michael from under her eyes. She placed her left on her stomach.

'You know, after everything that's happened? I think I need a rest.'

Michael stepped down from his seat, moved around the island unit and wrapped his arms around Sarah's shoulders.

'I think we both do,' he said. 'Let someone else break the news for a change.'

EIGHTY-THREE

Dempsey stepped onto the balcony of Apartment 35D of The Stratford. He was carrying three mugs of tea, steaming in the late-February air.

One for him. One for Father Sam Cooke. And one for Eden Grace.

The view was as incredible as ever. As it had done so many times before, it brought Dempsey peace.

He handed the first mug to Cooke and the second to Grace. With both seats taken, he sipped his own and leaned against the frosted glass and metal balcony frame.

All three drank in silence for a moment.

'I was sure Knowles would go,' Cooke offered, his mug already half empty. 'When you told me everything that happened. I'm glad he didn't. He's a good man, I think.'

'He's definitely that,' Dempsey replied. He glanced towards Grace. 'And a smart one too. Talk about playing a long game.'

'And Jack Meyer?' Cooke asked. 'Any more news on what's gonna happen to him?'

'He'll spend the rest of his life in federal prison,' Dempsey replied.

'What if he fights a trial? The stuff that'll come out of that.'

'Already been thought of. There's no trial. Meyer is going to plead to killing Cunningham in exchange for a promise that his son gets a shorter sentence. Twenty years served, instead of life. That way at least one of them'll see the sun again one day.'

'Jesus, man.' Cooke whistled out an exhale. 'The secrets you lot keep. If it wasn't you telling me, I'd never believe it.'

Dempsey responded with a nod, bringing the conversation to a temporary halt. Another comfortable quiet. Nothing but the sound of wind and the occasional distant siren.

It lasted for minutes, until broken by Eden Grace.

'You really think they're gone?' Her voice was harsh. A residual reminder of Romeo Meyer's bullet. 'The organisation, I mean.'

'They're more gone than if it had been left to us,' Dempsey replied. 'After Tootkai, we'd have taken down Meyer. Which would have freed the president up to take down Cunningham. But the rest? The Dupart family? None of that was on anyone's radar.'

'You think they'd have carried on?'

'Not with Knowles as president, no. They'd have made sure he went. And probably not with whoever followed him either. But after that? Sixty years of absolute power, Eden. No one's going to let that go lightly. And the Duparts, they were far from being no one. If Nicolas Dupart hadn't put himself in the middle of this, then yeah, I think they would have carried on. Four years away from power. It would have been a blip.'

'Jesus, man,' Cooke said again. The blasphemy came easy to the only Catholic priest among them. 'Can you believe this shit really happened?'

'It's a new one on me,' Grace said.

'Sort of thing happens to me most days,' Dempsey said, a smile spreading across his face as he downed what was left of his tea.

'Speaking of which, when are you back to work?' Grace asked, indicating towards Dempsey's shoulder.

'They insisted on six weeks away from active duty,' Dempsey replied. He stretched out his left arm as he spoke. Unconsciously proving a point, even if only to himself. 'Which I didn't need. My shoulder was fine after half that. And I'm bored as hell.'

Grace and Cooke both smiled. Neither seemed surprised by the answer.

'What about you? When are you going back?'

'I . . . I don't know.' Grace's hand instinctively stroked her gut as she spoke, her tone even more uncertain than her words. 'I'm not sure . . . I'm not sure I'm going back.'

'What?'

'It's just, you know, I spent my life striving to do the right thing. To serve my country, like my dad did. And then this happened and I find out it's all been bullshit. For decades, it's all been for the same bunch of corrupt rich scumbags, making themselves richer while everyone else suffers. While everyone else is ignored. I . . . I don't think I want to be a part of that any more.'

'But that's over,' Cooke said, his voice gentle. 'The Duparts, they're gone.'

'And what about everyone in their organisation?' Grace replied. 'We still don't know exactly who they had on their payroll. We've stopped it for now, but how long until someone takes their place?'

'You can't think like that, Grace,' Dempsey said. 'We stopped them, and Knowles is still there, doing the good he should have been doing since the beginning. The White House is the cleanest it's been in sixty years. You can't assume it'll go bad again.'

'I can. Or at least I can assume that someone will try. It's like Dupart said to Knowles: when you take the White House, you take the world. Who isn't gonna want that?'

'But there'll be more protections in place now, surely?' Cooke offered. 'To stop it ever happening again?'

'How can we say that for sure? John Knowles killed two men in full view of half the Secret Service agents in the White House. They covered it up. Sure, I want what's best for John. And I want him to still be there, doing it right this time. But seriously? If they can cover *that* up?'

Cooke said nothing. Dempsey knew why. It was a difficult point to dispute. And if he was honest, he was unsure if *he* agreed with Knowles remaining in office, after everything that had happened. Still, he'd have to prove himself in the election soon if he wanted to stay another term.

'So what are you saying?' He decided to avoid the point. 'You're just gonna walk away. If you think there's a future risk, surely you need to be there? Protecting the office from anyone who tries to take the Duparts' place?'

'Being there is too close,' Grace replied. 'That's what I've been trying to say. It's like, you know, you can't really see the Grand Canyon when you're in it. Not really. You have to be outside to see the full picture.'

Dempsey finally understood.

'Are you saying what I think you're saying?'

'The ISB does seem to provide a good view,' Grace answered with a smile. She gestured from the balcony as she spoke. 'So what do you think?'

Dempsey looked towards Cooke and smiled, before turning back to Grace.

'I think you're gonna need a reference.'

Acknowledgements

Most books come with a single name on the cover, but no book is a one-person job. And proud as I am that it's *my* name on the cover of *Power Play*, I am very aware that it would not exist without the help of many people along the way. And so . . .

To my Cheerleaders:

Victoria. Still my most enthusiastic supporter and the world-class procrastination-buster I so badly need. Without you I could do none of this. You keep our life moving around us as I sit motionless for hours on end, thinking up ever increasing dangers for Joe Dempsey and Michael Devlin to face. You stay patient and engaged as my head dives ever deeper into whatever carnage is happening on the page, ready to pull me out when it's time to come back to reality. You stay enthusiastic and supportive as I read you page after page of disjointed action and dialogue, never complaining as I stop to correct and reword as I go. And somehow you manage to make all of this seem effortless! I couldn't ask for more – although I probably will – and I can never thank you enough.

Mum. Once again you've listened endlessly in one-sided conversations, this time about the White House and the Oval Office and the Secret Service and everything else that became *Power Play*. I have no better sounding board, no clearer voice of reason, no more realistic an arbiter of 'yes' and 'no'; in fact, I'm starting to think I should be paying you for all this! But none of this is new, is it? Because you have listened to all my jumbled ideas since I was a little boy obsessed with superheroes and Greek mythology. And now, looking back, I'm fairly sure that those hours of patience and indulgence are why you still have to listen to it now.

To my Whip-Crackers:

My sister, Kate. I sent you the first half of *Power Play*, back when I was in need of some independent assurance that it was on track. I got that assurance. And then, almost immediately after that, I started to get daily texts saying simply 'Any more book?' In the middle of an Old Bailey murder trial I found myself having to explain why I had not yet had time to finish Chapter 22! For someone who is not in the publishing world, you can push a deadline with the best of them, and boy did I need it this time. So thank you, little sister.

My friend – and the man in need of more books for more plane rides than anyone else I know – Grant Benjamin. Naturally hyper-critical and having read pretty much everything in the genre, the lack of negative feedback as you worked through irregularly delivered tranches of *Power Play* told me that it must be going okay. Mate, you are a true friend, an amazing support and – like Kate – a very useful and persistent resource when it came to getting the book finished!

To my Book Family:

My amazing editor Pippa and her team, Donna and Genevieve. Three books now, Pippa. Three! How are you still speaking to me? I don't think I'll ever get over how much an author owes to his (or her) editor, and I will certainly never underestimate how much this book – and this entire series – owes to you. It's a full-on tightrope walk, isn't it? But we've walked it okay so far.

The rest of the brilliant team at Elliott and Thompson: Jennie, Sarah, Marianne and, of course, Lorne. As ever, the fact there is a book at all – any of them – is entirely thanks to you guys. I landed on my feet when I met you, I struck gold when Lorne agreed to take me on as a totally untested author, and I won the lottery when you managed to get my first book – *Killer Intent* – into the Zoe Ball Book Club, and then somehow my second – *Marked For Death* – into the Richard and Judy Book Club. I don't and won't forget how lucky I have been.

Angela, my remarkable publicist, my introduction to the other inhabitants of the crime-writing world, and my trusty guide and tutor as I make my way through the still early stages of a new career. Along with Anthony's help from behind the scenes, you have been there every step of the way. I'm fairly sure I'd have been lost without you.

And Gill, Sarah and the sales team. It would be a foolish author who underestimates the importance of those who actually get their books into the shops. I cannot thank you enough for ensuring that as many potential readers as possible have the opportunity to pick up and read all three of the Dempsey/Devlin series. And hopefully many more to come.

To my Experts:

Lady Kay Ord. You are the only person I know who possesses detailed, in-depth, real-life experience of what it's like to work inside the White House and to be close to the US President himself. I count myself incredibly lucky that you were willing to share it. Your help has been both generous and invaluable. Thank you.

Dr Dave, the Renaissance man. I'm sorry that my need for *your* expertise revolved around aircraft and flying, rather than medicine or the violin. And I remain more than a little jealous that any one man could be qualified to advise me on *all three* of those things. But envy aside, thank you for your advice so early on in this process; it gave me much needed guidance in how to take the plot forward, and it was genuinely appreciated. I hope the little homage you'll find inside demonstrates that.

'Bear'. For reasons you'll understand, I won't use your real name. Suffice it to say, I would be a lot more worried about the accuracy of Joe Dempsey's action scenes if I had not had your expert advice on how these things play out. Growing up where I did, I'm qualified to write a raw, Michael Devlin-esque brawling scene. But Dempsey's highly trained actions needed the input of a real-life special forces operative (retired). I hope I got it right.

To my Enablers:
Scott Ewing and Nicola Mitchell. I am consistently asked, 'How do you write these books when you're working full-time as a lawyer?' The answer is the two of you. But for your understanding and your unending support, there is simply no way I could mix the day job with the 'one book a year' demands of being a thriller writer. Without you, I would still be a barrister who wants to write, rather than the 'writer/barrister' I can now claim to be. You guys are the difference and I cannot thank you enough. (But I hope, Scott, that the character of Will Duffy is at least a step in the right direction.)

To my 'Borrowed' Names:
The majority of the names in *Power Play* come from my imagination. A few, though, are stolen wholesale from people I have known throughout my life, or from their relatives. And so Tom, Dylan, Charlie, Heather, Paul, Scott – and anyone I may have missed out – I hope very much that you're happy to see those names in print.

Monsignor John Kennedy. The name that somehow triggered the whole plot! Yet another thing for which we have to thank you, this time for being the inspiration to write this book in the first place.

And then the most important name. The name I cannot give here without spoiling the plot. Suffice it to say, that name's inclusion in *Power Play* is the result of a very generous donation to an amazing charity (Caudwell Children) by the wife of the character's inspiration. Thank you, Rebekah, and thank you, Mystery Man. You did an incredible thing for an incredible cause, and I hope I have done your namesake justice in return.

And finally, to my Readers:

This one is self-explanatory, but still completely necessary. I know that I would not be doing this but for the wonderful people who buy and read my books. Both of which have achieved success beyond my wildest expectations, thanks to you. I hope that *Power Play* will continue the trend and, if it does, I will know exactly where to direct my appreciation. Your engagement in terms of buying, reading, recommending and reviewing – as well as at festivals and events and on social media – all mean the world to me. No one truly writes just for themselves. We want to be read. We want to be enjoyed. And I could not be happier that, so far, that is exactly what I have experienced. Thank you, and long may it continue!

P.S. And to Joseph. You pretty much got in the way of this whole book, son. Because all I have wanted to do for the last eighteen months is play games with you, read to you and watch you grow. You have been nothing but a massive hindrance to this whole process, and yet you're also the greatest motivation behind it. Your Mum and Dad could not love you more.

ALSO BY TONY KENT

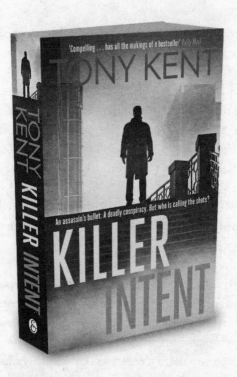

When an attempted assassination sparks a chain reaction
of explosive events across London, Britain's elite security
forces seem powerless to stop the chaos threatening
to overwhelm the government.

As the dark and deadly conspiracy unfolds, three strangers
find their fates entwined: Joe Dempsey, a deadly military
intelligence officer; Sarah Truman, a CNN reporter
determined to get her headline; and Michael Devlin,
a Belfast-born criminal barrister with a secret past.

As the circle of those they can trust grows ever smaller,
Dempsey, Devlin and Truman are forced to work in the
shadows, caught in a life-or-death race against the clock,
before the terrible plot can consume them all.

RRP: £7.99 • ISBN: 978-1-78396-382-9

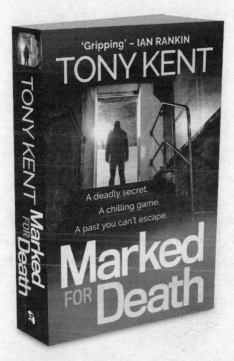

'Gripping' – IAN RANKIN

TONY KENT

A deadly secret.
A chilling game.
A past you can't escape.

Marked
FOR
Death

TONY KENT
Marked
FOR
Death

When London's legal establishment is shaken to its foundation by the grisly crucifixion of a retired Lord Chief Justice, Detective Chief Inspector Joelle Levy is tasked with finding his killer. With fifty years of potential enemies to choose from, only the identical murder of former solicitor Adam Blunt offers a ray of hope: what is it that connects these victims who met such a gruesome end?

Assigned to the story from the start, news reporter Sarah Truman sets out to investigate, not suspecting that the trail will lead straight back to her own front door and her fiancé Michael Devlin. A criminal barrister determined to prove the innocence of his own client, Michael is at first oblivious to the return of the murderous figure from his past – until tragedy strikes closer to home.

Struggling with his grief and guilt, and now caught up in a madman's terrible quest for revenge, Michael must race to bring the killer to justice – before it's too late.

RRP: £7.99 • ISBN: 978-1-78396-449-9

To hear all the latest news about Tony, his writing and his events, visit **www.tonykent.net** or follow him on Twitter: **@TonyKent_Writes**, Instagram: **tonykent_writes**, and Facebook: **Tony Kent – Author**